Real Men Do It Better

Don't miss these other sexy anthologies from St. Martin's Press

Burning Up

An All Night Man

Honk If You Love Real Men

Mr. Satisfaction

Real Men Do It Better

SUSAN DONOVAN

LORA LEIGH

CARRIE ALEXANDER

LORI WILDE

St. Martin's Griffin New York

 For information, address St. Martin's Press, 175 Fifth Avenue, New York, N.Y. 10010.

www.stmartins.com

Library of Congress Cataloging-in-Publication Data

Real men do it better / Susan Donovan . . . [et al.].—1st ed.
p. cm
Contents: His body electric / Carrie Alexander—Bed and breakfast / Susan Donovan—For Maggie's sake / Lora Leigh—Siren's call / Lori Wilde.
ISBN-13: 978-0-312-35979-9
ISBN-10: 0-312-35979-9
1. Erotic stories, American. I. Donovan, Susan.

PS648.E7R43 2007
813'.0108353—dc22

2006050800

First Edition: February 2007

10 9 8 7 6 5 4 3 2 1

Contents

His Body Electric

by

Carrie Alexander

1

"Cock-a-Doodle-do. May I help you?"

Thick wet breaths filled Karen Jaffe's ears.

Great. Another mouth-breather. "Sir?"

She heard movement. Far too familiar movement, accompanied by short grunts.

She adjusted her headset. "You've reached Cock-a-Doodle. How may I help you?"

The caller panted up against his mouthpiece. "Help me."

"Yes, sir." Karen looked at the computer screen, even though she'd memorized the company's spiel. "Would you like the Cock-a-Doodle special, three month's supply of pills billed at the amazing low price of eighty-nine ninety-five, plus shipping and handling? Or we have the Rooster Booster package, which is—"

"What'll the pills . . ." more wet breaths and slippery sounds ". . . do?"

Karen looked at the ceiling. He knew what the product did, or at least what the company claimed. But the callers always wanted to hear her say it. She closed her eyes and took a breath. "Rooster Booster is our trademarked powdered supplement, which may increase your potency and vitality in the bedroom. Our Cock-a-Doodle pills may increase the length and/or girth of your penis." She sped up because this was where the mouth-breathers always interrupted. "We're running a special this month for the—"

"It's getting bigger!" The caller's voice was harsh and excited. As if he'd climbed Everest. "*Damn almighty.* Lookee that. My dick grew just from talking to you."

Karen raised her brows at Kong, the overweight brindle cat sleeping in her lap. His whiskers twitched. She made kissy lips for him. "Would you like to place an order?"

"No—I mean, yeah." The squidging, fleshy sounds sped up. "Yeh. *Yeh, yeh, yeh*—"

Beep. Karen disconnected the call.

She sank her fingers into the cat's silken fur and returned to studying the water-spotted ceiling. She loved her big, old, rambling farmhouse, but it had come with a list of to-dos as long as Santa's naughty roster. For the past ten months, she'd been working her way through the house, painting, patching, stripping, and refinishing. Yet the space she used most often, the back room that had become her office and studio because of the tall north-facing windows, remained last on the list. Why was that, when, after nine years of marriage and one year spent discovering that she wasn't cut out for the Manhattan singles scene, she finally had no one to please but herself?

Another call came in. The computer software brought up the corresponding spiel and order forms as she checked the screen. She took 1-800 calls for products from a company that sold everything from foam mattresses to Miximakers, the ten-in-one kitchen appliance that looked a lot like a food processor to Karen.

Just her luck. Cock-a-Doodle again. It was almost seven-thirty in Iowa, so the PST-zoners must be getting home from work. She glanced at the sky, which had darkened to a steely blue within the past few minutes. The roots of her hair tingled at the electricity in the air.

She beeped in. "Cock-a-doodle-do. May I help you?"

A silence stretched before snapping with a short, sharp cough. "*Cack.* Uh. Sorry. Is this the, uh, place that sells, uh, those grow-your-penis pills, because, uh, like, my dick's only, uh, one inch long. Uh. One and a quarter."

"One and three-eighths," said a muffled second voice, followed by giggles.

"That's right." Karen answered with her sternest manner. She must have tensed up, because Kong jumped down from her lap with a heavy thud and an insulted *miaow.* "If you're over eighteen years of age, sir, you may place an order."

She heard more laughter, followed by urgent whispers. *Ten . . . nine . . . eight . . .*

The caller came back. "Uh, wait a minute. We're measuring for the record."

Seven . . . six . . . five . . .

"Because, uh, if my teeny weenie doesn't grow, I'm gonna sue."

Beep. Sometimes she didn't have to wait for *one.* The company wasn't a stickler about the age thing, as long as the credit card number was good. Crank calls could be suspended at her choice. Even though she was paid per minute of talk time, the sooner she hung up the phone the better, in her opinion. She didn't earn enough to listen to jokers and jerk-offs.

She was a VSR—virtual service representative. The job enabled her to work odd hours at home, making ends meet while she tried to spark gallery interest in her welded metal sculptures. She could set her own schedule, then, in between calls, sketch or work on twisted wire maquettes, small-scale replicas of her large pieces. Tools and bits of wire littered the desktop she'd made by resting an antique oak door on sawhorses rescued from the barn loft. For a make-do type of person, the old barn that had come with the house was a treasure trove.

She stared broodingly at one of the unfinished miniatures, abstract figures engaged in a twisted dance that looked a lot like sex.

Karen groaned. She had sex on the brain these days, and all because of her job. Not Cock-a-Doodle, which was as sexy as dirty socks and nose hair. But before Cock-a-Doodle there'd been a short-term experiment with phone sex, which she'd tried for the better pay, continued because she was good at it, then quit because it hadn't been good for her.

Two more calls came in. Karen kept them waiting while she got up and closed the casement windows around the room. She paused at the third to inhale. The sense of space and the clean country air had been what she'd missed most during her time in the city. Here in Iowa, her home state, she had room to think and to create. While the art scene in New York had been inspiring in an electric, intense way, she wanted her work to come from within. It was there, waiting to be released, if she could just find the key.

Thunder rumbled in the distance. Next came the soft patter of raindrops in the upper branches of the tall trees that surrounded the farmhouse, sparse enough that few reached ground.

The phone rang again. She shoved down on the warped window frame and took the calls, completing a couple of orders, including one for the Miximaker from a little old lady with a Texas twang who actually wanted to chat about her grandson's trouble with the police. While trying not to think about her own loneliness—*loneliness* being less accurate but more polite than *horniness*—Karen told the lady about the approaching thunderstorm and gently sent her off to make a solitary dinner.

Karen cleared the screen, shut down the computer, and crawled under the desk to unplug the phone line. It was too quiet outside. The air was dank and heavy with the threat of a bad storm. Power could be tricky in the countryside, going in and out at any provocation.

The rain increased, splattering against the windowpanes. Her skinny black cat, Shadow, appeared in the doorway with a tiny *mew.* Time to round up the animals for the night.

The house looked gloomy in the early darkness. Karen yawned and lifted her hair off her neck, where prickles sprang up as distant lightning briefly brightened the windows. The cats threaded around her legs on their invisible Hot Wheels track, racing through the front hallway and into the back parlor, with Shadow leading on the back-of-the-sofa homestretch. Shadow sprang, but the ponderous Kong didn't attempt the leap-to-the-mantel finish line.

Karen went to the mudroom and selected rubber boots from the utilitarian footwear that had replaced her small stash of designer shoes. She stomped into the boots, grabbed a windbreaker off the hook, then checked the wood box. A little low. It was mid-May, warm during the day, but she'd be wanting a fire if the electricity went out for long.

"You guys stay in," she told the cats, who were crowding the door. She nudged them aside with a boot toe, and slipped outside.

The leaves of the oaks and elms had ruffled in the rain. They lifted like the skirts of cancan dancers as a gust of wind rolled in off the open fields. Karen zipped up. She'd bought five acres, a house, a barn, and assorted outbuildings for less than what a rat-hole studio would cost in New York City. The adjoining land had been sold to a farming corporation, so she was surrounded by fertile fields. Kidder, the closest town, was seven miles away. POP. 1,259, the welcome sign read.

Karen's horses stood in the muddy corral with their heads down and tails clamped to their hindquarters. She'd read that turkeys could drown in the rain because they were too brainless to put their heads down. Sometimes she thought that horses were as dumb. They stayed outside in the worst weather.

At a glance, she saw that the chickens had more sense. They were tucked away in the henhouse, the rain playing their water dish like a tin drum.

She climbed the corral fence and shooed both horses inside, promising an extra ration of oats as she closed the stall doors behind them. Spindrift swung around to nose Karen's pockets for carrots.

She'd fallen in love with the dainty, dappled gray mare at a country auction. Buying a horse instead of a set of chintz china seemed the perfect way to celebrate her return to Iowa. A few months later, she'd come home with Tinker, an aged, chestnut gelding who'd been destined for the butcher's. She'd been compelled to save him, even though he was rarely ridden and about as useful to her as a crooked wheelbarrow.

The gelding whickered and stomped when she lifted the lid of the feed bin. "Greedy guts." To tease him just a little, she tipped the scoop into Spindrift's bowl first.

Doing without—even for five seconds—was good for the soul. So Karen had been telling herself since the bout with phone sex had revved her up with nowhere to go but dates with courting farmers and the appellate bankers and John Deere salesmen who believed the Olive Garden was the height of gustatory excellence. And romance. She'd never stayed to discover what was the height of sex. Most likely a workmanlike groping between flannel sheets.

Tinker had his nose in the feed bowl before she'd tossed in the extra scoop of oats. He whuffed and inhaled the meager ration in twenty seconds flat, chomping so hard a sweet froth foamed at his lips.

She stroked the gelding's velvet nose. While she might not be sexually fulfilled, outside of an ongoing experimentation with the alienlike attachments that had come with The Probe, the vibrator her old girlfriends had given her as a returning-to-the-hinterlands gift, she was content.

Contentment ought to be enough. She had raindrops beating on the roof. Warm horse breath on her hand. The rich smells of the barn. Her works in progress lurking in the shadows, potential caught up in every rusted bolt and twisted ribbon of steel.

A loud crack of thunder jolted her into action. She went to shut the back door. The horses would steam dry tucked safely indoors, dozing through the storm, dreaming of green grass and sunshine on their flanks.

"Sounds good to me." Karen shoved her hands into her jacket pockets and crossed to the front door. Thunder rumbled and the rain gusted, speckling her artwork with glistening silver droplets.

Lightning splintered the leaden sky. The blackened and rainbowed steel of the sculpture flashed blue and white. Karen turned all to goose bumps and prickly short hairs. The horses moved restlessly in their stalls. One of the barn cats looked down from the edge of the loft, a narrow silhouette with its tail standing straight in the air.

More thunder rumbled in Karen's ears like a train in a tunnel. She quickly secured a tarp over the art piece, double-checked that her equipment was unplugged, and stepped out of the barn, pulling the big rolling door shut behind her. Rain sheeted the concrete she had poured inside and out for safety reasons, the sparks from her welding iron an obvious safety hazard near an old wooden hay barn. Beyond, the dirt area below the grassy slope up to her house had become a mud slick.

She pulled on her hood and huddled for a moment beside the building, waiting for the next crack of lightning. They were coming so frequently now, with the thunder a constant rumbling refrain, that there was no need for counting one-banana, two-banana in between to pinpoint the location of the storm. Her property was right at the center of it.

Through the gray curtain of rain, the farmhouse's light-filled windows were a homely beacon of comfort. Sheltering in the barn for the duration didn't appeal to her. Karen made up her mind to risk the dash to the house.

Her hands clenched. She was jittery. Unusual for her, even in a thunderstorm as bad as this one. She was normally an even-keeled type of person, at least before divorce and moving and phone sex had rocked her safe little boat.

Lightning struck near the main road, where pavement made a thin line of wet silver among the trees. For one instant the world became a brilliantly hot white, as bright as day, and she thought she saw a man on the gravel driveway that curved between barn and house.

Couldn't be.

She squinted, half-blinded, as she ran for home before the next bolt was flung. The smell of ozone hung in the air from the last strike.

Thunder crashed. Karen slammed into a solid body.

She screamed, and fell onto her backside with a splat, her rubber boots slipping out from beneath her in the mud.

The man bent down, she thought at first to scoop her up, but he was shouting something that sounded like, "Stay away from me," over the crescendo of thunder and rain. A bold fork of lightning brightened the sky beyond his head and she got a glimpse of his face.

His expression. Jagged. Stripped. Terrified.

His eyes. A brilliant burning blue.

She put up her hands, but didn't know why. She was frozen to the ground.

He said, "Fuck it," and wound his arms around her, dragging her to her feet.

A sharp burst of electricity zinged through her veins. She yelped. The air was thick with the staticky charges.

"Go to the house." The stranger almost yanked her arm out of its socket to get her moving. "Run!"

They ran, slipping and sliding up the wet slope. Karen dropped once to her knees, but he got her up again almost without breaking stride, his hands on her ass as he propelled her up the stairs to safety beneath the porch roof.

Directly behind them, lightning tore from the sky. Flames leaped high at the point of the strike, splitting open one of the elm trees. Karen jumped. The crash of an ancient branch dropping to the ground was so loud and jarring it reverberated in her bones.

The stranger took hold of and folded her against his chest. She started to pull away, but he held her with a possessive security that was so comforting she was suddenly willing to stay, waiting for the sounds of the storm to stop ringing in her ears.

She saw the white flash of the next lightning bolt, even with her face buried against his chest. It seemed to be *inside* of her, sparking and sizzling, as if she'd stuck a finger in a socket, jumping from her body to the stranger's, then back again before she could draw breath. The electric charge became one continuous current, heating her blood, melting her resistance.

She felt shattered inside—pliant and weak. Dimly, the thought occurred that she was in a dangerous position. The man could be anyone . . . do anything. And part of her was already welcoming that idea.

"Inside," he said, pushing her away from himself.

Karen nodded numbly. Recognition returned as soon as he

released her. The sensation of electric shock lessened, too, although she could still feel it running through her, draining from her body like a fever that had broken.

What the hell? She swiped rain from her eyes, opened the front door, and stepped inside. The man was no longer beside her.

She turned, pushing aside in her mind the warnings about letting strangers into the house. Of course, she would invite him in. He'd practically saved her life.

He stood on the porch, hunched and shivering, dripping wet. He was breathing hard, eyes downcast. Despite his state, she remained aware of an intrinsic power and confidence. So very male. The cut of his body was harsh but beautiful. He had a solid build, all hard muscle beneath the jeans and shirt glued to his skin.

The exterior lights had gone out. It was difficult to discern his features except for the general impression that in better circumstances he'd be a good-looking man. She hesitated, thinking of his wild expression earlier, but something in the way he'd rescued her—and held her—said that she could trust him.

Rough as he'd been.

Electric as she'd felt.

"Come in," she said, barely audible above the storm. "Come in," she repeated in a louder voice, although she knew he'd heard her the first time.

He didn't move, except to shudder in reflex at the endless rolling boom of the thunder.

"The storm's not moving on." Her trembling hand reached for him. She was wary, and turned on, and mystified all at once. "It's too dangerous to stay out here."

He gave a quick nod. "Thanks." He stepped through the doorway, ducking sideways to avoid her hand when it hovered between them. She looked curiously at her numb fingers before giving them a shake as she bumped shut the door.

The past few minutes had happened so fast. Her mind was whirling with questions. Who was he? How had he appeared so suddenly? Normal sensations were slowly returning to her body, yet she continued to feel strange. Twitchy and uncertain. Her senses were heightened, but she'd also been numbed, as if her body chemistry had spun off-kilter and she hadn't adjusted to the new reality.

Merely the storm, she told herself. *You had the shit scared out of you.*

They stood in the front hall, a fancy term for the narrow passageway beside the stairs. Karen's stomach went hollow as she felt for the light switch. Futile. No wonder her reactions were off. The entire house had gone as dark and silent as the grave.

The man, too, but she was certain he'd react in an instant if he had to. Kind of eerie, that, especially when lightning flashed and she saw he'd been watching her all along. As if he could see in the dark.

She wet her lips. "Power's gone out."

He made a sound of agreement.

Her eyes were adjusting. "Stay there. I'll get flashlights and candles."

He took a big step out of her way when she moved off toward the backside of the house where the kitchen opened off the mudroom. Didn't trust her not to bump into him in the dark?

"I'm Karen Jaffe." She rummaged in a drawer, adding, "New in town," in case he was a local who hadn't heard of her. Which was pretty unlikely, since Kidder's grapevine yielded gossip like the Loire produced *vin*. In her first month of residence, whether she'd gone to set up bank accounts or purchase a sack of oats at the feed store, she'd been greeted with, "Yep, I've heard about you. Bought the Hanson place, didja."

"Tomzak," her mystery guest said from the doorway right behind her. His deep voice went up her spine like a chill.

Karen swallowed. "You scared me. I didn't hear you come in." The wide, plank floors she'd adored at first sight creaked badly, but between the thunder and rain—never mind her racing pulse—she wasn't hearing much else.

"Sorry. I'm Gabe Tomzak."

Her fingers closed around the slender Maglite she kept in the kitchen junk drawer. She flicked it on, just able to resist an intense desire to shine it full in her guest's face to get a good look at him. Instead, she followed the path of light to the mud room, where she kept a big, heavy-duty flashlight. Her mouth was as dry as mothballs.

She swallowed again. The sense of onrushing desire rose back up. "You from around here, Gabe?"

"Nope. St. Louis. I'm on . . . vacation. Staying at a friend's cabin on Torch Lake."

A few miles northeast of Karen's property. She switched on the big flashlight and set it on the counter to illuminate the kitchen. "What were you doing out in the storm?"

Gabe stayed out of the wide arc of light. "It came up fast."

"Yes." Her fingers tightened as she swung the weaker beam toward him. "But that doesn't answer my question."

He didn't try to avoid her inspection as she played the light across his face. Strong bones, even features. Younger than she'd thought, maybe late twenties.

"I was caught out," he said, looking at her with a blank expression. "Biking to town for groceries."

While he seemed trustworthy, she was torn. Her intuition was sending up alarms. The man had a secret. Not a serial killer, turn-her-internal-organs-into-canapés kind of secret, but . . .

She needed to see more. When the beam of light lowered toward his chest, still heaving despite his otherwise calm, she thought that his eyes flickered. A trick of the light, she told herself, before she caught the fleeting smile.

Aha. He was brash.

Well, so was she. Instead of glancing the light across his body, she let it linger. A vintage Barking Irons tee stretched across his broad chest, topping a white thermal shirt with ragged sleeves. Faded blue jeans sculpted his thighs and a nicely full package. She stared for a couple of seconds, her body turning warm and liquid, before she dropped her eyes. He wore big, heavy work boots with thick rubber soles.

"Biking, huh," she said. In those boots?

His hands flexed, hanging at his sides.

"I didn't see a bike," she added with a level calm to match his own, even though her libido was spiking off the charts.

"I left it behind when the lightning started. Metal."

"The tires are rubber." She moved the light across his boots.

He didn't reply. Didn't move. Except for a tightening in his abdomen, plainly evident under the thin skin of the wet shirts. And, again, the flicker of something secretive in his eyes.

She mused over the swell of his chest for another few seconds before a cold rivulet trickled down her nape and brought her back to the present. "We need to warm up." Ignoring that she was already warm enough, she grabbed candles off the top of the refrigerator and set them near the flashlight. "I'll go get towels. You'll find matches in the—"

A bolt of lightning cracked nearby. They both flinched. "Damn," Karen said. "The storm's still so close."

She leaned over the sink to see out the window. The flames were out. The rended tree smoked in the rain, raw and blackened where the branch had split away. The barn was barely visible through the downpour.

She snatched up the big flashlight and thrust it at Gabe. He fumbled, resisting. She pushed it on him. "Here, take this and go into the living room. There's a fireplace. We can—"

The flashlight crackled, then sputtered out.

"Shoot," she said. "I don't know if I have more batteries."

"It's not—" He stopped.

She aimed the Maglite at him. "What?"

"Nothing." He hit the back of the plastic flashlight casing against his palm, jiggling the batteries inside. "Nope. It's dead." He set the light on the counter. "Sorry."

"Take this one." She pressed the other flashlight on him.

"No, you keep it," he said, thrusting it away as the beam blinked out. A spark shot between their hands.

Karen let out a squeak and jumped away. The flashlight hit the floor with a *crack*.

For a moment, beneath the drumming rain, they stood unmoving in a black and total silence. Then thunder rumbled and lightning crashed, still dangerously close. Every hair on Karen's body rose in tingling warning. She'd seen in the flash of light that Gabe was shivering with tension, his eyes squeezed shut. Almost as if in pain.

Curious and curiouser.

He sucked in a breath and swayed away when she bent to retrieve the light. She straightened, tempted to touch a fingertip to his arm to see if another spark would fly.

But she didn't have to. The air around him crackled with energy.

She felt her eyes growing wide. "What are you, some kind of lightning rod?"

2

The question hung between them, zinging like electricity coursing through a high tension wire.

"Not—that is, *no.*" Gabe paused. "It's just the storm."

Karen squinted at him. Her hands were shaking. She shoved them into the pockets of her windbreaker and swallowed until she was able to laugh. "I was only kidding." She felt along the countertop for the candles. There were matches somewhere in the junk drawer, if she could find them in the dark. "What do you mean, 'just the storm'?"

"The electricity in the air."

"Right. Maybe we should rub against each other to light some sparks so I can see what I'm doing."

"That might be more of a distraction than a help." She couldn't see his face, but there was a smile in his voice.

"I could use a distraction." *Especially that kind.*

Even with all the weirdness going down, the chemical attraction between them was palpable. But when he didn't take her up on the hint, she made herself focus on the task at hand. Her fingers skimmed over a cat leash, foil yogurt tops, a gazillion garbage-bag ties, and an unused hole punch before she found the box of kitchen matches.

"Here we go." She struck a match, grateful for its meager illumination. If they weren't going to grope in the dark, she'd rather be able to see.

Farmhouse kitchens were supposed to be roomy, but hers had bad space planning and too many doors. Gabe had drifted toward the round drop-leaf table butted up against the wall between the fridge and the wide opening that led to what the real-estate lady had called the back parlor. Karen had furnished the small space with a big comfy armchair, a secondhand couch, and bookshelves, making it the coziest room in the house.

"Take a candle," she prompted. "You're not combustible, are you?"

His features knotted into a grin that was half grimace. "Not so far."

Not so far . . . ? She tilted her candle and peered at him. "What is it you do in St. Louis?"

"I was a linesman for a utility company."

"Hmm." She laughed a little. "Makes sense. That's why electricity likes you so much."

"I guess you could say that." He turned suddenly. "I heard something moving in the other room."

"My roommates." She lit another candle, sticking it in a water glass because she was out of candleholders. "Two cats," she explained at his questioning sound. "Shadow is shy. She probably ran from your voice. Or if you heard scurrying, it might've been the mice."

He looked back over his shoulder. "If you have mice, what good are the cats?"

"Bed warmers."

"I'm a dog man. Bigger bed warmers."

"But cats vibrate." *So do other things,* she thought, thinking of The Probe. In Gabe's hands, it would either short out or rev so fast she'd come like a burst dam. She felt herself blushing and was grateful that he probably couldn't tell. "Anyway, you haven't met Kong yet. He's the king of the house, a twenty-pound fur ball."

Gabe extended his arm toward the back parlor, trying to light the black hole. He seemed nervous about the cats.

She crept up behind him. "Looking for ghosts?"

At once, he moved off—practically bolted—into the darkness. He *really* didn't want her near him. "I see the fireplace. Have you got wood?"

"There's some stacked on the hearth and more in the mudroom off the kitchen. Here, catch." She tossed him the box of matches. "Don't forget to open the flue. I'm going upstairs to change. I'll bring you back a towel."

"Thanks."

"For matches?"

"And for giving me shelter."

She paused, resting a hand on the doorway molding. "You're welcome. I suppose I could have sent you to the barn to bed down in the manger, but that's far too Old Testament for me."

There was a beat of awkward silence. He slicked back his hair. "I don't plan on bedding down. The storm's sure to subside."

"Doesn't sound like it." She cocked her head to listen. Rain drummed the roof and pelted the windows. The violence of the lightning strikes—talk about biblical—had finally lessened, but the rolling thunder continued unabated.

"There are more candles on the mantel," she said, before

returning to the hall. A twisty shadow with reflective eyes shot up the staircase as she climbed. At the top, Shadow twined herself around Karen's legs. She scooped up the cat one-handed, burbling soothing nonsense about the storm passing soon, as she went into the bedroom.

Shadow leaped away, disappearing under the bed. Karen lit a couple of votives on the dresser and plopped down with a jounce of the bedsprings.

Holy crap.

She had a capital *M-A-N* in the house. Who'd appeared out of nowhere. Gorgeous and vulnerable, veritably begging to be seduced out of his wet jeans.

She exhaled a shaky breath. Chafed her hands. Anticipation had made her giddy. This was Christmas morning and she was getting her reward for being very, very good the past months.

All right, there was one problem. She'd dropped a pretty broad hint about being open to a move, but he'd remained standoffish. And maybe, just maybe, he was a bit too freaked out by the storm.

No *maybe* about it, considering the way sparks flew from his fingertips. That was some weird juju.

Never mind. Karen sprang up, dismayed to see she'd left a damp, muddy patch on the quilt. Gabe's arrival had made her forget that she was wet and dirty to the bone.

She stripped off the jacket, then stopped with her shirt raised mid-bra. *Wet and dirty to the bone.* Why had everything suddenly taken on a new meaning?

"Because you're way too sexed up," she whispered, ripping off the rest of her clothing. Granted, this was the perfect setup for a one-night stand. A rural farmhouse, a lonely divorcée, a sex-charged vacationer dropped from the sky. Cue the porn music!

She grabbed a candle and headed to the bathroom for a quick shower while the tank still held hot water. The lack of local prospects, combined with the strangeness of her secret life as a phone sex operator, had resulted in a fallow period in her love life. Even before that, she hadn't been fully satisfied. Her ex-husband had declined from an attentive young groom to a La-Z-Boy potato who thought that five minutes of perfunctory foreplay was enough to get her in the mood. She'd muddled along, living a half life in the Jersey suburbs, until the day that Chad had come home to say that he'd fallen in love with a pharmaceutical sales rep named Jenna Christine. She was wannabe actress/model, of course, who thought that Chad was connected because he owned a Manhattan limo company and had the cell numbers of celebrities. What a ditz.

"Thank God for the ditz." Karen stuck her head under the spray. Without Jenna Christine, she might never have had the nerve to change her life from top to bottom.

The doubter inside her spoke up. *Like living with two cats in a dumpy farmhouse, being little more than a wannabe artist, is so much to brag about?*

But I'm happy. That makes all the difference.

Happy except for . . .

Karen swiped a sudsy hand across her breasts. Her nipples sprang to diamond tips. The splash of hot water was luxurious and arousing, inspiring a liquid warmth inside of her.

She'd been celibate too long. Two, three, no—almost four months. In fact, she'd been laid only once since she'd moved to Kidder almost a year ago, and that had been a big mistake with the town cop.

A moan escaped her lips. Her palms slid over wet skin, cupping her breasts to lift them to the drumming water. Not enough. She ached for a man's touch. A man who would lock his mouth around her nipples and draw pleasure through her body. Sensuous pleasure. Hot, irresistible, completely shocking pleasure.

Gabe, of the electric touch.

Who'd avoided her.

She would have to seduce him. Lure and provoke him with her feminine wiles.

"I can do that," she whispered, ignoring the fact that she was a thirty-five-year-old with a "cute" face and childbearing hips that had never borne fruit, even when she'd suggested inventive food play to her ex. Ever dense, Chad had eaten the banana from the peel rather than out of her.

She stuck out her tongue and licked at the warm droplets that rained down. Would Gabe like it if she peeled off his wet clothes and slathered her tongue over his bare chest? She'd be mortified if he rejected her, but there *had* been that naughty gleam in his eyes.

He'd like it. And her hands would lower to his jeans. His cock would jump at her touch.

Yes. It could be so good.

Her fingers had dipped between her thighs. She parted herself, tilted her hips toward the shower spray to cool the hot flesh. No use. She was wet, hungry, aching.

Bracing one arm against the wall, one foot up on the tub surround, she angled to stroke two fingers back and forth over her clit. Her inner muscles tightened spasmodically, searching, grasping. She extended a finger and slid it past the soft folds, into inflamed flesh. Pushing, pressing, rocking her hips, her upturned face running with water. Harder, faster.

She whimpered. *Harder. Faster.*

Her sharp cry of release bounced off the tile walls. She smothered it, gritting her teeth as a sweet warmth spread through her belly. Mmm. Nice enough to take the edge off, but not what she really needed.

Quickly, self-consciously, she rinsed and shut off the shower. Wrapped in a towel, she listened for Gabe from the top of the steps. The scent and crackle of a wood fire drifted through the darkness.

She bit her lip. Bringing herself off like that, with a stranger downstairs? Either she was a daring woman, boldly taking control of her own sexuality, or she was just plain crazy and more than a little desperate.

Back in the bedroom, she stepped into a pair of bikini panties and a thick flannel nightshirt that hung to her knees. White wooly socks to keep her feet warm. She hesitated over a pair of pajama pants. Bottoms or no bottoms? The latter might give him ideas.

She grinned. Definitely no bottoms.

Next was the top drawer for one final detail. She mused. A condom tucked in her shirt pocket? Now *that* was blatant.

She took the condom.

A woman in control.

"Here's your towel—oh."

Gabe had stripped. His clothing was spread out on the fieldstone hearth and draped from the mantel. He stood beside the fire, toga-wrapped in the throw from the couch.

Karen clutched the towel to her ribs.

He looked at her, utterly composed, his eyes the bright, hot blue of a summer sky. "I hope you don't mind. I was really wet."

"Me too." *And I still am.*

"You've warmed up."

She mumbled something unimportant, too dazzled to listen to herself. Additional candles had been placed all around, giving the room a glow straight out of a romantic movie. Gabe was certainly worthy of being the star of the show. All buff and manly, rippling with golden tan muscles sprinkled with brown fuzz. Only a confident guy could pull off a yellow toile toga with tassels.

And untied work boots. She looked down and honked like a

goose at the sight of his hairy bare legs in clumpy boots with tongues splayed and laces dragging. "You can take those off if you want," she said between snorts. "I can give you a pair of socks."

His lips twitched. "I didn't want to strip completely. That would be presumptuous."

"Heavens, yes." Karen's breath was back. She tossed the towel on the chair. "The bathroom's upstairs, if you need to clean up. I'll go make us something to eat. Sandwiches okay with you?"

"I can help."

"Thanks, no." There were bananas in the fruit bowl. She couldn't be held accountable. "Tend the fire. I'll be back in a few minutes."

By the time she returned from the kitchen, he was back in the rearranged toga. A damp towel had been added to the hearth. His hair stood up in tufts, making him look like a hip-hopping skateboarder. "How old are you?" she blurted, setting a tray on the coffee table.

"Twenty-nine."

"I'm thirty-five." Might as well be upfront. "Divorced."

He seemed unbothered. And why not? He was hoping to get lucky, too.

Ugh. Her arousal cooled a few degrees. This *was* sleazy.

So she'd better get to know him first. Turn the one-night stand into a brief encounter of meaningful, heart-rending proportions, that must tragically come to an abrupt end. Heh.

"You said you're new in town?" He took the plate she offered. "Whew. Those are some sandwiches." Between hefty slices of pumpernickel, she'd layered horseradish, Italian beef, tomato, and red onion. Turkey breast, barbecue sauce, hot-and-sweet peppers, and Swiss cheese had gone into an onion roll.

"I've been here since last summer. I'm a sandwich aficionado." She gestured for him to sit down and dig in. "See, I used to live in

New York, then the Jersey suburbs. I was the takeout queen. Never learned how to cook. Now I'm here in the boondocks and there's no takeout to speak of, so I became a sandwich guru to survive."

Gabe was sprawled in the armchair, wolfing the food. "I'd marry you for a sandwich like this."

"Damn, and there I go, giving my talents away for free." Blushing, she busied herself with the pot of soup she'd prepared. "I could have done more with a working toaster oven. Toasted bread, melted cheese, grilled sausage, and peppers." She opened the fire screen and scraped together a small pile of embers, then set the pot nearby. "We'll see if that works. It's only canned soup, but I thought we could use something warm in our bel—uh, you know."

Gabe looked broodingly at the bowls and spoons stacked on the tray. "The storm's giving up."

The rain still came down, but the thunder and lightning had abated. "Yes, the power might come on before too long." She pointed to the telephone on the side table near Gabe's chair. "Try the phone."

Slow to react, he gingerly picked up the receiver of the retro phone she'd bought because it suited the old-timey feel of the farmhouse. She heard the crackling static on the line before he said, "It's out," and dropped the receiver into the cradle with a clatter.

"That's odd. We usually don't lose phone service in a storm."

"Lightning must have taken it out. Or struck a tree that fell into a line. It happens."

She sat on the couch with her legs tucked under her, the hem of the nightshirt pulled down over her thighs. "If you weren't on vacation, you'd be out working in a storm like this, hmm?"

"Depends." He swallowed. "Actually, I'm not on vacation. I'm on leave. Might be permanent." He stuffed in the last big bite of his sandwich.

"How come?" Karen tilted forward to slide half of her onion roll onto Gabe's plate. She'd forgotten how much men eat.

"I had an accident." He chomped on a pickle. "How about you? What makes a city girl move all the way out here to Iowa?"

"Divorce," she said blackly, even though she'd worked through her gnarled emotions about that situation, for the most part. "I'm not actually a city girl. I was from Iowa originally—Cedar Rapids. I still have family there."

He nodded. "You don't look like a city girl."

Girl. Bless his twenty-nine-year-old heart. "Was it the rubber boots that gave me away?"

She glanced down and blinked, seeing that he still hadn't taken off his own boots. They were planted far apart on her braided rag rug, his knees akimbo with the toile throw drooping between them. Her tongue moved in her mouth. She wondered if he'd removed his shorts.

A glance at the hearth told her no. Too bad.

"You don't seem like the city type," he said. Then he squinted. "Except when you were standing out in the middle of a raging thunderstorm, about to get your sweet ass zapped from here to China."

"Hey, there, Captain Howdy. *You're* the one who was wandering around in the storm, flirting with electrocution."

"I told you. I had to ditch my bike and look for shelter. That's why I came up your drive. What were you doing?"

"I'd gone out to the barn to shut the horses in their stalls. I thought I could make it back to the house. And I would have, until you showed up." She raised her brows. "The lightning came with you. For a few seconds there, I thought you were Zeus in disguise, throwing thunderbolts at me."

He shifted. "No harm done."

"Except to my tree." She handed him a beer, then went to check the vegetable soup. "It's kinda hot. Want some?"

He made a noncommittal sound. She filled his bowl anyway, laying a spoon on the folded paper napkin, then catching her tongue when she started to urge him to eat. Enough with the nurturing, or he'd start thinking of her as a mother. She might be six years older, but she wasn't a mother. Especially *his* mother.

Now that the worst of the storm had passed, the sound of the rain and the coziness of the candlelit room were a comfort. She curled up in a corner of the couch and relaxed, eating, drinking, and chatting with Gabe, keeping the sexual possibilities on slow burn. She couldn't quite push them to the back of her mind, though. They remained at the forefront, underlining every word she said, giving her a pleasant buzz that one beer couldn't touch.

Gabe was funny and interesting. Interested, too. He asked as much as he answered. When she couldn't help herself and prodded him about the soup, he ignored the spoon to pick up the bowl and slurp it straight down. She teased him about being a savage. He thumped his chest and made a rough, grunting sound that was so viscerally male she felt it pulse in her womb.

They talked about growing up in the Midwest. He was from a blue-collar family with three rowdy, outdoorsy brothers. He'd tried college and a desk job before realizing that what he preferred was work that didn't take over his off-hours. He was a hiker, a biker, and a kayaker. An athlete. That led to the typical comparison of sports rivalries. He was Cardinals and Mizzou Tigers, she was Cubs and Hawkeyes, or had been, before she'd moved away and forgotten that loyalty meant something to her, even if it didn't to dickhead ex-husbands.

She told him about getting married too fast, and how eventually the ambition to be an artist had seeped out of her, especially after she'd given up her best contact with the art world—working in a gallery, where she'd once met Richard Serra—to take an office job that paid better, so they could handle a mortgage and children. "I thought I'd get back to art in a few years," she said, "but that was naive. If we'd had that baby—" Her throat clenched hard because no matter what, she'd wanted the baby she'd lost. "—I'd have been in an even deeper hole."

"What happened?"

That was when she looked up at Gabe and felt her mind click into the same place her body had gone, as smooth as a bolt sliding into place. Somehow, he'd understood. There was more awareness in his gentle question than Chad had ever offered. Which was sad, really. She hadn't known it at the time of her miscarriage, but her husband had already been gone.

Karen stretched out her legs. "We had a divorce instead of a baby. I tried the city for a while longer, before I figured out that what mattered to me was having the proverbial 'room of her own.' So I put all my savings and the money from the settlement into buying this place."

"You're an artist then?"

"Trying to be." She toyed with her hair, which had dried into the bouncy waves and ringlets she usually tamed with a blow dryer. "I do other work to make ends meet."

She looked up and Gabe was staring at her legs. She pointed her toes, tightened her calves. "I'm a smooth operator."

He lifted his head off the back of the chair. "What?"

She smiled. "I'm a VSR, virtual service rep, which is basically a telephone operator. I answer one-eight-hundred calls and take down orders for merchandise. You know, the stuff you see in late-night infomercials."

"Oh. Like Ginsu knives and food dehydrators."

"Right." She studied him for a minute. His eyes were soft and lazy. There was stubble on his jaw. The upper half of the toga had slipped, displaying more of his sculpted chest. In a pumped-up state, his muscles would be rock hard. Right now, they were relaxed, still firm, of course, but rounder, softer, warmer . . . or so she imagined when she pictured herself cuddled in his lap like a purring cat, her cheek pressed close against his chest.

Yellow flames flickered. The air had become thick and hot.

So had Karen's blood. Her skin was flushed, her armpits were damp.

Her panties, too. She should have gone truly bottomless.

She itched with wanting him. That restlessness made her wiggle and flex, until finally she sat up and tucked her knees beneath her chin, wrapping her arms around her legs to keep the rampaging desire inside.

She cleared her throat. "I tried phone sex, too, but . . ."

Gabe jackknifed forward from his lolling position. His hands dangled between his knees. "Phone sex."

"Uh-huh. And even though I got to hate it, I was very good at it."

Idly, she stroked her bare leg, letting more and more thigh show while poor Gabe struggled to find his voice.

A naughty little smile crept across her face. "Want me to show you?"

3

"Please." Gabe dropped to one knee. He leaned across the coffee table, scrabbling desperate hands in parody of a parched castaway who'd been offered a drink of water. "Yes, please. I'll do anything you want, if you'll please show me your phone-sex secrets."

She poked at him with her foot. "Stop it."

He settled back in the chair, the blanket clutched at one hip. "You're teasing me, right?"

"Nope." He might have thought he'd disguised it, but he hadn't. A hard-on had sprung up in his lap. "I was a phone sex operator for a very long three months." She eyed him. "Have you ever tried it?"

"Yeah, sure." The smile that testified to his cocky confidence reappeared. "When I was young and plagued by a perpetual erection."

"You're still young." She left the rest unsaid.

He laced his fingers over the bump in his lap. "Phone sex operators aren't supposed to look like you."

She blinked. "Sorry to disappoint. Naturally, I always put on fishnets and a bustier to get in the mood."

He shook his head. "I meant legend has it that they're all hags in reality. Toothless, or overweight, or cross-eyed, or eighty. You're . . . not."

"Oh." She flicked her chin. "I may not be a fat, toothless, cockeyed senior citizen, but I *am* thirty-five."

"You told me that already. Was I supposed to be put off?"

"I wasn't sure if you were on."

His hands came up. His hips rocked in the depths of the armchair. He wasn't trying to hide anything any longer. "My switch has been flipped since the first time I touched you."

Then why the hesitation? she wondered.

Let it go. Tonight's about fantasy.

Gabe was studying her. "You said you hated it, the phone sex."

There had been several variables to her feelings about the work. She'd been a woman alone in the countryside, talking to strangers on the phone, treating sex like a business except for every now and then, when there was a tentative human connection, even a genuine spark of arousal, only to be killed by the guttural cry of a climax—followed by the click of an abrupt hang-up.

"It got to be weird," she said. "I began to feel so cold and distant about sex, but I was also . . ."

"Turned on?"

She shrugged. "What can I say? There was no one in my life at the time, and, frankly, with all that sex talk in the air, I needed to get laid."

"I'm sure you could have been, easily enough."

She thought regretfully of the fling with Officer Dan O'Shanahan, which never should have been flung, unless it was into the trash. Not that he wasn't a nice guy. He was—too nice, too concerned, too claustrophobic.

"I don't 'do' just anyone," she said, with a lofty air that didn't suit her at all. "I have standards."

"Lucky for me I'm a prime specimen," Gabe said. There was the cocky smile again. "So you quit the job? Did that help?"

She laughed. "A little. I don't have sex on my brain *all* the time."

"Until tonight."

"That's presumptuous." *But correct.*

"I can be presumptuous. You're not wearing a bra."

"Is that the signal?"

"It's a pretty good indicator, especially with a woman like you."

"This is fascinating." She curled onto her side so she could face him. Kong rose from the hearth and bounded up beside her, kneading the cushions before he settled into the nook at the back of her knees. "Tell me. What kind of woman am I?"

"Sharp. Wise. Direct. Friendly. Skeptical." Gabe lifted his arm to rub a hand over his scalp. The sinew and muscle in his arm pulled taut in an intriguing way. "And sexy as all get out."

"I thought men like you only look for big boobs and blonde hair."

"Like me?"

"Young. Fit. Vigorous. Outdoorsy."

"Maybe when I was twenty and calling phone sex operators. Now I know better."

"Stop there before you say something about desperate divorced housewives who are grateful for the attention." She smiled with wry self-awareness. "Even if that's kinda sorta true."

His brow furrowed. "I don't believe you fit that mold. But you are . . . waiting."

"Waiting, huh? Waiting for what?" Her stomach flip-flopped. She managed to keep her voice light and breezy. "I can hear the beginning of the story now: *It was a dark and stormy night when the thunder god arrived to pleasure the lady in waiting.*" Her mouth puckered. "This may turn into an X-rated fantasy yet."

Gabe proffered a lazy smile. "I'm hoping."

Karen looked into the fire, which had died down to hissing flames that licked across charred black hunks of logs. Several of the candles had guttered out. At most, it had been two hours since he'd picked her out of the mud. She checked her watch, then held it to her ear. No ticking. The time read 7:48 P.M., which was just about the time she'd gone out to the barn.

She snapped the metal band open and tossed the watch onto the table. "My watch stopped. Do you have the time?"

"I don't wear a watch."

She realized that the mantel clock had also stopped. Odd. No power, no phone, no working batteries. They were in a *Twilight Zone* episode where time had stopped and the outside world had ceased to exist.

When better to indulge in a one-night stand? She wouldn't even have to feel guilty, because when the real world started up again, all this would be like a dream. A beautiful, steamy, sexy dream.

Karen closed one eye, squinted through the other, and said, "*Brring, brring.*"

Gabe's face sparked. He sat up a little straighter.

"*Brring, brring.*"

He snatched up the phone, but held it loosely against his palm. "I'm supposed to call you."

"This is a special case."

He put the receiver to his ear. "Hello."

She made a phone shape with her hand and spoke into it, using the throaty voice she'd adopted back in the day. "Well, hello there, honey. This is Miss Velveteen of Talk Dirty. What should I call you?"

He smirked. "Thor, the thunder god."

"Not Zeus?"

"He only has lightning bolts. I'm the one with the hammer. The really big hammer."

"My goodness. You must be very well endowed to sound so confident."

"Endowed, sure. Or suffering from delusions of grandeur."

"Oh, there's no need to be embarrassed. I specialize in delusions of grandeur." She draped her left arm over the sofa and leaned her head against it. Twirled a corkscrew of hair. One knee bent, caressing her thighs together. "Why don't you tell me what you like, Thor?"

Gabe had pulled the phone away from his mouth, but he put it back to speak in a deep, thickened, growly voice. "I like women with short, curly, brown hair and mischievous mouths. I like curvy bare legs in white socks and long nightshirts that cling to naked thighs. I like full tits that sway back and forth without a bra. And I especially like women who talk dirty to me."

He stopped, breathing hard. During his speech, the room had become tight, black, dense—coal bursting into diamond.

Karen squinted against the blinding brilliance of their daring. She felt her heartbeat in her ears. In her fingers and toes. Her pussy. "That's very specific."

"Yeah. I know what I like." He let out a soft *grrr.* "What I want."

"I can give it to you."

"How?" His voice was so low he was almost whispering. "I can't touch you."

"You can touch yourself while you listen to me."

"Not good enough."

"It will be, I promise. I'll make you think it's me . . . me touching you." She abandoned the pretense with the phone and sat up straighter, running her hands over her thighs, over her breasts, into her hair. Her lips felt swollen twice their normal size and she pouted them like some kind of 1950s sex kitten. "Me with my mouth on your body. Kissing and licking and sucking."

He dropped the phone. Shoved his hand beneath the toile throw.

"Show it to me. Let me see that big hammer, Thor."

Gabe let out a short, hard laugh through clenched teeth. "This is too—"

"Play along and I'll take off my clothes, too."

"All right. But no more Thor."

She hid her momentary alarm. No fantasy—he wanted this to be *real.*

"And I can't touch you," he added.

She was surprised again. "We'll see about that."

"I'm serious."

"But I can touch you?" she guessed.

His hips tilted. He winced. "Nope. No touching."

"Whatever you say." She shrugged and undid several buttons so she could pull her shirt off one shoulder. Before she was finished with him, he'd be begging to make contact.

His gaze went to the hollow between her breasts, full and swaying the way he liked it, as she leaned toward him with her hands placed flat on the coffee table. "I'm not wearing a bra, Gabe. My nipples are hard from the sound of your voice. They're brushing against my shirt. They're tingling. I wish you could suck them for me."

He groaned.

"I'll have to play with them myself."

She rocked on the edge of the couch, feeling somewhat absurd about the cheesy lines she was spouting. But he was a man. They worked. Even on her. She was wet and wanting. Hurting so bad it was good.

"Go ahead," he said.

"You first."

With a kick of his foot, he knocked aside the blanket. He wore clingy, gray, boxer briefs. Very clingy. He'd slid a flat hand down the front of them, stretching the waistband to allow the engorged head of his cock to poke out the top.

Oh. Ohhh. Wow. He was so red and swollen he was almost purple. Painful-looking. She angled closer, hardly noticing when her shirt slipped all the way off her shoulders, baring her breasts to their hard, pink nipples.

"You're sure I can't touch you?" she asked hoarsely.

His eyes blazed. "This is phone sex."

Stubborn. Or was it . . . ?

She thought of their meeting beneath the raging sky. She'd heard him say, "Stay away from me." And then when they *had* touched—

She'd blamed the electricity on the storm.

What if it was Gabe?

The sparks. The batteries that went dead, the phone that didn't work. Her stopped watch.

Karen was transfixed by the question.

What would happen if they touched?

Lucky. God, he was one lucky sonovabitch.

Gabe Tomzak had started out with good intentions, but now he felt like a dog. His thought processes had degenerated to the most rudimentary one-thought, even one-word reactions, his bodily functions focused on the most basic needs. He was operating on animal instinct.

When Karen spoke, he barely comprehended. He knew only that he was one lucky, lucky guy. She was working her body, describing every move, but all that he really understood was the promise of full red lips, the pleasure of ripe melon breasts, the alluring female scent wafting from between her rounded thighs.

She'd made him very happy.

She asked him something about taking off her panties and he must have said yes—for sure, his body was screaming it—because she was suddenly standing bent over the couch with her backside pointing at him, sliding off her underwear. Her plump ass was succulent like a peach, and there, peeking from the sweet spot where round thighs met ripe cheeks, was the moist, pink heart of her, and just like that he was lost in the rush of heat and blood and driving need, thinking only of one thing, wanting one thing . . .

Pussy.

And he couldn't have it.

4

Gabe was panting. Karen gripped the backrest of the couch, glad that her face was hidden so he couldn't see her blushing and quivering and know that the sex phone temptress act was only that—an act.

But when did it become real? She had to admit that her panties were down around her ankles, her female parts were, without a doubt, on display, and Gabe was certainly exhibiting the responses of a man fully aroused.

Except that he still hadn't moved from the chair.

Feeling wicked and maybe a little ridiculous, she shook her rump the way she'd seen the hoochies do it in *Girls Gone Wild* commercials, then swiveled around and stepped out of her panties. She swooped down and tossed them to Gabe, who caught them lightning fast, and after a moment's hesitation slowly drew the undergarment across his face. He inhaled her scent.

She tried to swallow, but there was no spit left in her mouth. All her juices had been drawn south, where they were leaking out over her slippery thighs.

"I'm all wet and naked underneath my nightshirt," she said. "And I'm thinking about you, how you're so hard from wanting me. Can you see me when you close your eyes—my round tits and my hot pink pussy? Did I describe myself well enough?"

No response from Gabe. He'd thrown back his head and closed his eyes. His face was concentrated, his Adam's apple prominent, and the cords in his neck stretched taut.

She licked a trickle of perspiration from her top lip. "Hey. You still with me?"

"Yeah." He stretched out in the armchair. His chest expanded with every breath, hollowing the flat expanse of stomach beneath his ribs. One hand was wrapped around his cock, and he slid the pad of his thumb over the tight flange of foreskin, his fist squeezing and releasing, squeezing and releasing.

She watched, feeling the matching throb of need inside herself. "Can I touch you now?"

His lids flew open. "No."

"Please let me." Holding her open shirt against her breasts, she stepped around the table and knelt on the rug before him. "Why won't you let me?"

He seemed tortured. "I'll hurt you."

"How?"

"I'm—" He shook his head.

"You touched me before, out in the storm, and I survived."

"But you felt it, didn't you?"

"Yes. I felt the electricity."

His eyes became razors of blue steel.

She whispered, "I want to feel it again."

"That was only . . . like a hug. Sex is different. Wetter and deeper. I could hurt you."

"Then we'll stop if that happens."

He grunted. "Might be too late."

"Just let me try, okay?" Tentatively, being careful not to touch his hot skin yet, she plucked at his briefs until she was able to work them past his knees. "I can't get them over the boots."

"Leave them."

"All right. I'm going to touch you now. I'll lay one hand on your thigh, okay?"

He inhaled through his teeth. "Careful."

She lifted a trembling hand. Although she was mostly convinced that his conductivity was in his head, he gave off too much prickly tension for her not to be wary. And there were the household malfunctions to consider. *Something* had caused the batteries to short out.

As soon as her palm was within a few inches of his skin, she felt it. *Electricity.* Hot and tingling, forming a sort of force field around his body. She took in a breath and extended a fingertip.

A spark flew between them. She squeaked and pulled her hand back.

"See," Gabe said.

"That was nothing. Static electricity. I've caused more sparks when I pull my bedsheets back." She sucked in a quick breath and dropped her hand onto his thigh, determined to leave it there no matter what. A jolt of energy traveled up her arm, but it wasn't painful or unpleasant. It was stimulating.

"Wow," she said, and placed her other hand on his opposite thigh. More of the pulsing energy coursed through her, making the looping current she remembered from their embrace on the porch. "Freaky."

Gabe pushed her away. "I know. I'm a freak."

"That's not—I didn't mean to—"

He cut her off. "I was struck by lightning."

"Tonight?"

"No. Last summer. I was on the job. I almost died. And ever since . . ."

"What you're saying is that you *are* a lightning rod."

"Seems that way."

She looked at his erection, rising thick and hard against his stomach. The veins pulsed with vitality. She imagined him sliding it between her thighs, thrusting deep inside her. High-voltage fucking unlike anything she'd ever experienced.

His eyes had widened in recognition of her lust. "You're not afraid of me."

She slipped in between his knees, flinching a little as the electricity leaped into her body, but refusing to quit. The nightshirt had drooped to her elbows again. She cupped her breasts in the unbuttoned gap, moving sinuously against his thighs so her nipples grazed the surface of his hot skin, showering both of them with sparks of magnetic sensation.

Gabe jerked. Air hissed between his teeth. "Stop. Oh shit, you have to stop."

She wouldn't. Couldn't. "Put your hands on me."

"That's too much."

"No. I want to feel it." She caught his wrists and pulled him toward her.

Tiny sparks flew from his fingertips as he touched her breasts. Her mind whirled. White hot sparks and burning blue eyes brightening the darkened room. The energy inside her flickered. Burned higher. Perspiration beaded. Her hair lifted at the roots.

"Your mouth," she whispered, shivering with the strange and wonderful sensations. "Use your mouth."

He angled forward, scooping his hands around her butt so she was lifted higher. Her body bowed into a tight arc that presented her breasts to his mouth. "Aghhh," she said, as his lips locked on a nipple and sucked it against the velvet blade of his tongue, drawing it into the heat and voltage. Shocks detonated across her nerve endings in short, sharp bursts. *Pop. Pop. Pow.*

They slid to the floor. He knelt above her, hands hovering.

She was on her backside, legs loosely looped around his thighs. "Go ahead. Touch me there."

"Can you take it?"

"Y-yes. I think so."

He lifted the hem of the nightshirt. He was so intent, she could have sworn she saw the reflection of her wet, open sex in the sheen of his eyes. She'd never been so aware of herself, so plugged in to the effect her flagrantly naked body had on a man.

As he bent closer, one shaking hand descending between her thighs, she pressed her legs more firmly against him to maintain the electric loop, instinctively protecting herself from a sudden shock.

Still, she jolted with alarm when he stroked a finger between her swollen lips. A sizzling hot lightning strike ripped from her clenched pussy straight up through the center of her body. A squeal—almost a scream—flew from her mouth, but her thighs clamped convulsively, holding Gabe between them when he might have retreated.

"Don't stop," she pleaded. "Keep your fingers in me. It's better if we don't lose contact."

"Karen. Damn." He leaned over her, braced on one arm while the other reached between her legs. "I couldn't stop if I wanted to." His palm cupped her mound. He squeezed, then let his fingers play across the sensitive flesh, dipping shallowly inside her, sliding through the dewy effluence, flicking and rubbing at the pearl of her clit until she did scream, and scream again, with her body flung open beneath him as the electric current flowed through her in an unending stream of biting pleasure.

She floated in the tingling heat, drawn back toward full consciousness by the tug of his mouth on her breast. He had a finger inside her, an electric probe sending pulses to her womb, to her marrow, to her heart. The connection was grown so strong between them that she believed it would hurt worse to break away than to continue with the shocking coupling.

She licked her lips. "There's a condom in my pocket."

"Are you sure?" His face in the firelight was ax-hewn, all sharp angles and fierce need. The hot staff of his cock had melded to her thighs. She was quaking, anticipation and trepidation mixed as one, but she knew for certain that she wanted to feel the full extent of his power thrusting inside her. She needed it, to burn away the remnants of the woman she used to be.

They worked together to sheathe him. When her fingers closed around his jerking cock for the first time, she laughed. "Latex." Her fingers traced the ridges and contours thinly covered by the condom. "That's synthetic rubber, right? Like the soles of your boots. We're cool then."

"Saved by safe sex." He sank his hands in her hair and kissed her fully and voraciously on the lips.

The shock this time was that it was their first kiss. She flung her arms around his neck, consumed by the hot, peppery taste of his mouth and the bold thrust of his tongue. Everything about their encounter was turned inside out—why not this?

She was sitting in his lap now, his erection prominent between them, enticing her clit with every sizzling rub and roll. "Sweet mercy," she said. "I can't stand this. Take that lightning rod and fuck me with it."

He held her face at a slight distance, his expression serious. "I can't do that. You have to. And you have to stop if it's too much." His fingertips pressed into her cheeks and jaw. "Promise me you'll stop."

She nodded, doubting that she had the control any more than he did. But she loved that he was so concerned.

She rose up on her knees, staying close enough to slide her cleft along his cock so the current's hot spot wasn't broken. "Have you tried before, with anyone else?"

"Not like this." He kissed her. "You're my first, in a way."

"Keep kissing me."

Their mouths met. The intimacy escalated. It was even more erotic—and moving—having his tongue slide between her lips the same moment as she lowered herself onto the slickened head of his cock. She sank lower, gasping as her tight passage opened to accept him. He was all aggressive, invading male. All cock—thick and blunt and overwhelming.

A bolt of electricity lit her up inside. For an instant, she was at the center of a blazing sun. Then she lifted an inch higher on her knees and felt the relief of slippery warm liquid, before hard lust drove her down and the fireball ripped through her again. She tore her mouth from his and would have screamed, if every drop of oxygen hadn't been jarred from her lungs.

Gabe leaned away. His hands tightened on her waist.

No. Air scraped her throat when she inhaled. "Stay inside me."

"Fuck, yes." He'd only deepened the angle.

Her hips ground in small circles. He held her ass, trying to fix her in place to pump into her, but she was too lost in the roaring sexual delirium to have her movements contained. Each thrust was another shock, exploding with sharp pleasure and sweet pain. She couldn't stop. But after only a minute she felt herself collapsing, her bones melting in the bubbling cauldron at their point of joining.

He took care of that. With one great heave, he lifted her off the floor and dropped her on the couch. From the verge of withdrawal, he drove solidly into her again. Even deeper. Right to the hilt, catching her by the back of her knees and levering her legs up and open, open so wide there was a piercing pressure right where she'd been needing it.

Zzzap. A bolt of sensation struck her clit and zigzagged upward.

He caught her cry on his tongue. They kissed hungrily. Soon their lips and tongues were part of the motion, their fingers and nipples and navels. Every part of them, gliding thrusts and dissolving restraints, creating a synchronicity of wet friction and tight, spiraling pleasure.

Gabe let out a shout and accelerated to short, hard strokes as he came. An endless string of pulsing electric charges detonated inside Karen. Her climax was an inferno, burning hot, burning hard, until her mind was scorched bare and there was nothing left—not inhibition or reason or regret.

Gabe moved first, minutes later, when he dropped an open-mouthed kiss below her navel. "Are you okay?"

She wasn't ready to answer. Her body was still vibrating.

He licked, shooting a weakly quivering arrow into her.

"Huh." She put her tongue back in and closed her mouth. Tried to remember how to form words.

He reached up. A hand squeezed her breast. Another small dart of pleasure.

"I think . . ." Her neurons were firing up. "I drained you."

"That's right."

"I mean, when you touch me now, it's not quite so electric."

He chuckled against her lower belly. "You're saying the magic is gone?"

"Don't be a tease." She jogged his shoulders. "I'm serious. Maybe you're cured."

After a minute, he said, "Maybe," but she could tell he wasn't convinced.

The Thor thing wasn't entirely a joke. She had a thousand questions about his—what was it, a medical condition? Except she imagined that he'd been treated often enough as an extraordinary spectacle, practically a circus sideshow. The questions could wait.

He was drawing small circles over her stomach. Small tingling sparks followed his fingertips like comet tails. "You're sure you're all right?"

"As far as I can tell." She wiggled into the couch cushions. "I do feel rather, uh, incandescent. As if you stuck a light bar up me and flicked the switch." She patted his shoulder to let him know she was fine. "All I can say is—" She laughed. "Thank heaven for the rubber."

His gaze traveled up her lax body to her face. "You're not freaked out?"

"Do I look freaked out?"

"You look too stunned to react."

"Maybe. But my brain is starting to function."

"What about here?" He stroked between her legs, where she was damp and sore.

She couldn't hold back a wince.

"Poor pussy," he said, lowering his head. "I'll make it feel better." Gently, he parted the inflamed lips with his tongue. His hands petted and comforted.

The warmth of his mouth felt wonderful. She sighed and spread her thighs, shivering a little at the erotic fever of his tongue spearing through her slick flesh. He hummed sweet praise and hot breath against her blossoming folds. She thought of florists, gently blowing into roses to open the petals.

She drew up her knees. Reached down to stroke his hair.

And there was a loud knock at the front door.

"Oh, God, not now." She shoved Gabe away, when what she wanted was more of the healing power of his talented tongue.

The knocking had become pounding. A male voice shouted for her. "Karen? Are you home?"

"Damn it." She scrambled to her feet, gathering Gabe's clothes off the hearth in one fell swoop, and thrusting them into his arms. "It's Officer Dan. Go upstairs."

"What's an Officer Dan?"

"The town cop. We—we're friendly." She yanked at the nightshirt that had become a wrinkled flannel obi around her waist. "I'm sure he's here to check on me. I'll get rid of him as fast as I can, but he can't see you here."

Gabe's shoulders broadened. "Why not?"

"Don't get territorial on me." She whipped the toile throw off the floor. "This is a small town. I'd rather keep my private life private." She turned toward the front hall and hollered, "Coming!"

Gabe licked her ear. "Is that what you say to all the guys?"

Ticklish. She batted at him before the shiver became reckless desire. "Please, go upstairs. And for Pete's sake, pull up your shorts."

Even though Officer Dan continued knocking, she paused, falling into a brief reverie as she watched Gabe climb the steps with his pale moon showing, as he fumbled with the tangle of clothing and the briefs down around his knees. He had a fine, firm ass. A delectable ass. What a shame that they had so little time to become acquainted.

"Hello, hello? Karen?"

"Right," she said. "The door." Still, she hovered at the bottom of the steps, calling sotto voce, "My room is the one on the left. Make yourself at home."

The image of Gabe waiting for her naked in bed was so strong she had to blink several times to bring herself down to the reality of Officer Dan O'Shanahan standing on her porch, turned out for emergency duty in his blue uniform with visor cap. He really liked that uniform, with its badges and equipment and accompanying air of authority.

She said hello. "Sorry I took so long. I was—" *Indisposed* was not the word, when she'd been very disposed to appreciate every flick and swirl of Gabe's tongue.

The police officer looked at her tousled hair, bare legs, and the crumpled nightshirt. "In bed, were you?"

Suddenly she became all too aware of the slick juices leaking out of her. She squeezed her thighs together, forgetting to answer when a telltale trickle still managed to work its way south.

"I heard the storm was real wicked out this way." Officer Dan surveyed her yard. "Looks like the lightning hit you good. You've got a big branch down. The power's out, heh?"

"So's the phone." She stopped, nervously smoothing the shirt. "Isn't everyone's?"

"Must be only along this stretch of road." Officer Dan stepped past her to go inside, craning and swiveling as he checked out the house. He saw the candle stubs. "Haven't you got flashlights?"

"Actually, yes, but the batteries went out." Karen was remembering all over again why her fling with the officer had been such a mistake. He'd assumed their one foray into sex was permission to take over her life. And since he was one of those guys who is happiest when he's busy being useful, what had seemed sweet and thoughtful at the start quickly became bossy and intrusive. Extrication had been complicated. She hadn't wanted to hurt him, since his intentions were good; but she'd also been too embarrassed to admit that she'd gone to bed with him only because phone sex had given her an itch that he'd been handy to scratch.

Officer Dan marched into the kitchen and picked up the large flashlight. He turned it on and the beam cut through the darkness. "Huh, it's working now."

He walked to the doorway, holding the light up by his shoulder to illuminate the cozy parlor and dying fire. "How are you fixed for wood? I can carry some in for you, in case the electric stays out."

Karen cringed. The room reeked of sex, even with the masking scent of wood smoke in the air. The number of dishes on the coffee table were another dead giveaway. "Thank you, but I'm fine." Firmly, she took the flashlight from his hand.

He nudged too close, examining her face in his forthright way. Probably hoping for signs she'd become a damsel in distress. She prayed he wouldn't pick up on the braless signal instead.

"I don't like you being out here all alone."

Her smile was a reflex. "A little thunder and lightning can't hurt me."

Officer Dan frowned. He was suspicious. "I found a bike on the side of the road, not too far away. Didn't appear to have been struck or in an accident, so that means there's a stranger wandering out there somewhere. He didn't show up here, did he? I should go and check out your barn."

Karen shrugged. "If someone was there, he'd be welcome to the shelter."

"But you're an attractive woman, all alone . . ."

She quelled him with a look. They'd been over this.

Officer Dan clamped his jaw. His nostrils flared.

"Thank you for the concern," she said carefully, "but there's nothing to—" A soft thud from upstairs interrupted her dismissal.

"The cats," she said, not very subtly urging him to the door. "I'd better go see what they're up to."

"You're sure there's nothing you need?"

Need? That answer would be an emphatic *no.* She was finally completely satisfied.

"Don't worry about me. Go take care of the little old ladies and maybe a few of the younger ones, too."

Determinedly, she waved him off. Officer Dan was considered a catch around town. He was decent, ultra-competent, even handsome in a fortyish, thickening-around-the-waist way. He also had an ex-wife, two kids, an on-call work schedule, and an embattled township board to pacify. Too many complications for Karen, when she was looking for—for—

Peace and quiet, the freedom to work without being hassled. Or so she'd been saying.

Surely one rousing electric fuck hadn't changed that, no matter how eager she was to get upstairs to Gabe.

5

Gabe had become accustomed to not feeling like himself. After the lightning strike, when he'd first discovered his freak-show abilities and the doctors were equally baffled and skeptical about his apparent electromagnetic sensitivity, his family had reassured him that he wasn't changed in any way that was important. They said his affliction would pass with time, and meanwhile he was handy to keep around as a night light and fire starter.

But as the days and weeks went by, the burn marks faded, and still he remained a veritable lightning rod, he'd begun to fear that he might never be normal again. Of course, his family was accepting. They loved him.

The rest of the world was different. There, he was a medical oddity. A nuisance. Even a danger.

The getaway at a friend's hunting cabin was supposed to clear his head. He'd intended to come to grips with the facts, strange as they were, and make a decision about how to proceed. What to do with the rest of his life.

Now, he also had to figure out what to do with Karen Jaffe.

Other than *that* . . .

She trotted up the stairs with a beam of light bouncing before her, and entered the bedroom. “The flashlight’s working again.”

Gabe put out his hand. He might as well show her what it was like, being him.

She turned over the flashlight, watching curiously as the beam flickered, then died. “Wow.”

“Something in my body chemistry reacts with batteries and electrical systems. Which is why your watch and clock stopped. I can’t even use a remote control.”

“That’s got to be a pain in the ass.”

“Yeah.” The darkness felt safe to him. He’d become used to that, too. “I can’t drive either. Or even ride in a car for very long.”

“For real?”

“Not reliably. The systems don’t conk out as quickly as flashlight batteries do, but sooner or later they’ll malfunction. Makes it almost impossible to get around.”

Her eyes were wide, all iris black in the unlit room. “What about airplanes?”

“I haven’t dared try.”

“Then how did you get to Iowa?”

“Bus. I found out that if I sit in the back, buses are good, even for a long trip. Otherwise, I bike or walk everywhere I want to go.”

She seemed fascinated by his quirks, as most were, but not to the point that he felt like she’d paid her buck to examine a sideshow exhibit. “A bike’s got metal parts,” she pointed out. “But I did notice how you wouldn’t pick up that soup spoon.”

“I’m not always this sensitive,” he explained. “Sparks don’t shoot from my fingers on a daily basis. Lightning storms bring it out in me—all that electricity in the air. That's when I really have to watch myself."

She stood unmoving beside the bed. He wanted to reach for her, but he couldn't, even now. Especially now. The current was still running inside him. He could feel the higher voltage in his prickling hair, his sensitive skin, the way his balls had drawn tight into his body at the thought of laying his hands on her luscious body once more.

"Oh. Okay." She put the flashlight on the bedside table, then she lifted the covers and slid inside.

He balanced on the far edge.

After a moment's hesitation, she rolled toward him, splaying a hand over his ribs. A small shock passed between them, subsiding to a staticky warmth, as her palm coasted upward across his chest. "So when you said I was your first . . . ?"

"My first during a storm." He'd had a girlfriend at the time of the accident. She'd been great during his recovery, but the lingering aftereffects had alarmed her. When he'd seen how skittish she'd become around him, he'd done what she was too nice to do and ended the relationship.

Since then, with the few women he'd approached—or had been approached by—he was a curiosity. The worst was the woman who'd boasted in his favorite local bar about fucking the neighborhood freak.

Karen wasn't like that, but Gabe told himself to expect nothing from her beyond tonight. For all he knew, she'd had sex with him only to satisfy a kink in herself.

"Does that give me a special status?" Humming with pleasure, she stretched out alongside him. Her pinkie ticked his nipple. "I must at least qualify as legend, since I took a blow from Thor's hammer and lived to tell. I'm sort of the Energizer Bunny of sexual relations."

"Shut up." They laughed while they kissed. He found great delight in the simple gestures of being able to run a hand along her arm, sink it into her thick, brown hair. He kissed her chin, her nose. *Maybe . . .*

No. He would just enjoy her while he could.

Her fingers had found the scar on his shoulder from the accident, but she asked no questions. Just as well. He remembered little of the incident, except the sudden shock and a momentary sense of being lit up and torched from the inside out, then waking a day later in the hospital. The lightning had come out his feet. His soles had been burned so badly he hadn't walked for weeks.

Karen sat up and slipped off her nightshirt, then snuggled in again. "Umm," she said, nosing against his shoulder, smiling with her eyes closed.

He kissed them. Her lashes fluttered. "Who was at the door?"

"Office Dan, checking up on me. He's so predictable. Not," she added, "that I didn't appreciate it, except for the bad timing." Even in the dark, he could see the glow her face took on, thinking about what the cop had interrupted.

"He's got a thing for you?"

"How'd you guess?" She thumped him in the chest with a fist. "We heard you up here, you know. Did you purposely make noise?"

"That was Kong, I swear. He jumped off the bed when I got on." Gabe reflected. "Why? Did Officer Dan figure out that you had a man in your bed?"

"He's suspicious. But that doesn't matter."

"Oh, yeah? You seemed pretty set on hiding me."

"Like I said, I'm not fond of being an object of curiosity for the tongue waggers. But I'm sorry that I hurt your feelings. If it bothers you, next time you can wave your naked wing-wang out the window and—" She stopped abruptly and bit at her lower lip.

"I don't mean to assume that there will be a next time. Probably not." She worried the lip some more. The bridge of her nose creased as she squinted at him. "Right?"

"Right." He hadn't realized how badly he wanted the other option until right then. Karen was quirky, unpretentious, independent, and damned cute. Aside from the mind-blowing sex, he hadn't enjoyed a woman's company this much in months. Best of all, she'd accepted him, not without question, but certainly without making him feel like a Ripley's Believe It or Not exhibit. Even in the most incredible of circumstances.

She was a rare find. He could easily come to treasure her.

But he'd withdrawn into himself since the accident. It wasn't easy to put an offer out there.

"Unless . . . ," he said.

Karen looked up. Her body, so warm and pliable, stiffened.

"Unless we—you know. See more of each other." When she hesitated, still brittle, he backpedaled, saying *fuck fuck fuck* in his mind. "While I'm here, anyhow. A temporary arrangement."

"Temporary." The way she mulled the word, with her lashes lowered, he couldn't tell whether she loved or hated the idea.

But what woman wanted a clock-stopping, battery-frying, jobless bum around on a permanent basis?

"I can do temporary," she said, and reached between his legs.

Despite the sense of disappointment—of loss—his body sprang to life. He throbbed, the electric pulses gathering in the tip of his cock as she rubbed and squeezed through his briefs. In no time, without the extra charge of the lightning storm to blame, he felt as if he could shoot a thousand volts into her when he came. Her already tender pussy couldn't take that—not a second time.

"Let me." He removed her hands from his dick and levered them up above her head while nudging her onto her back. The prickly heat of his body blanketed hers. She arched against his weight. Her soft groan welcomed his mouth to her breasts as he nipped and tugged, rolling his face between the full orbs, going from one pebbled nipple to the other.

She tugged against his restraint, but he wouldn't let go. With his mouth and delving tongue, he hushed her complaints. She responded by wrapping her legs around him, thighs spread wide apart as she squirmed into fiery contact with the ridge of his erection. Making small whimpering sounds, she rubbed against him. Tempting him to take her. Teasing him when he refused.

He ran his tongue over her lips. "Minx."

"I don't like being held down in place. I need freedom to move."

"No? I bet I can make you like it so much you'll stay exactly where I put you."

She huffed. "Yeah?"

"Easy," he boasted.

Her eyes gleamed. "Put your money where your mouth is."

"Not a good idea, unless you want to be squeezing coins into your panties for the next week."

She laughed, flashing teeth. "At least I'd always be able to make change." Her thighs squeezed his hips. "You're something else, Gabe Tomzak. Who knew Thor would be such a wise-ass?"

He began kissing a path to her navel. She quivered when he tongued it, then sucked love bites into the soft skin of her belly. "Who knew a mere mortal woman could hurl thunderbolts with the best of them?"

She purred, coiling against him. "I don't know about hurling them. But I am a pretty good catcher."

Raindrops pattered the roof. He used a light touch to part her swollen labia, easing his way with the liquid that had collected there like morning dew. "You sting, don't you?" He traced the small wet opening. "Right here." Inserted a finger with a ticklish delicacy. The slick walls tightened. "And inside."

She nodded, tilting her head back as a tremor emanated outward from her core. He'd released her hands, but all she'd done was grab fistfuls of her pillow while sensations rippled through her, making her body twist and turn and arch, every movement a plea for more.

"I can help you." He slid lower, between her thighs, put his hands under her bottom, lifted her to his mouth, and puffed a warm breath against her reddened sex. "I'll make you feel better."

She gritted her teeth. "Then your tongue isn't a conductor? Sure felt like it when we were kissing."

He licked her. "How was that?"

Her body softened. "That was wonderful."

"And this?" He licked again, letting his tongue slowly unfurl inside her.

"Mmm."

"How about . . ." The tip of his tongue teased at her clit before he enfolded the nub in a gentle, sucking kiss.

Her ass had flinched in his hands. "That," she said, rising up a little as her muscles clenched. "Umm, m'God. I really felt *that*. But how am I supposed to know what's electricity and what's natural chemistry? Is there any difference?"

A warm pleasure opened in Gabe's heart, putting out searching tendrils of wonder and gratitude. He kissed the inside of Karen's thigh, where her skin was satiny smooth. *This woman is something special.* She'd known him for mere hours and already she'd made him believe that maybe he didn't have to be defined by his condition, that what they were experiencing might be a true attraction. Even something a little like love.

"With us, there may not be a difference." He put his mouth on her, wanting to bestow all the bliss she deserved, but the low-level current had seemingly gained energy from his emotion. He could do nothing to stop it as the charge passed through his tongue into her open, defenseless body. She yipped and slammed her fists down on the bed.

So much for the cure.

The rain drummed. Thunder gathered in a low rumbling chorus.

Quickly. He used his thumbs to spread her, his kiss to incite her, his tongue to invade her, and an instinctive singsong from the back of his throat to quiet her bucking hips. She thrashed, then went still, holding herself as tensely as a jumper on the ledge. The suctioning pleasure increased. Her legs tried to close around his head. He gripped the back of her thighs, keeping her open to every intense sensation.

The darkness had enveloped them. He was back to a one-track mind, bent on making her lose it as fully as he'd lost himself, in a luxury of female flesh and aroma and the thrill of feeling her body tighten to his command. He strummed her tiny clit like a virtuoso until she was gasping and pushing herself against his mouth, coming in a sweet flow that filled him with satisfaction so strong he was able to tell her searching hands and willing mouth no, and no again, while lightning slashed the night sky.

She'd given him a gift beyond sex. He needed no more.

6

"Cock-a-Doodle? You answer calls for Cock-a-Doodle?" Gabe laughed uproariously.

More than the occasion warranted, though Karen was wryly tolerant. On this clean, fresh morning, everything was brighter and better than before. The earthy scent of grass and mud and straw. Her fingers, caressing the supple, oiled leather of Spindrift's English saddle. Sunshine glanced off the puddles and rebounded on the metal sculpture in the barnyard doorway. She found herself laughing, too.

"Cock-a-Doodle-do," she said. "A hundred times a day."

"Sheez. A hundred times a day? I've got to get me some of those pills."

"Hah. I'd be a charcoal briquette before noon." She nipped her assumption in the tongue. "That is, if it was me you were . . ." She trailed off, reminding herself not to move so fast. *Casual. Be casual.*

Gabe wasn't put off. He smiled at her from across the barn,

teeth gleaming against the healthy red of his lips and the brown stubble of his morning beard. "Oh, it'd definitely be you I was fucking. No other woman can take me."

The brashness was back. But for once, she'd found a man who could back up his egotistic statements.

She giggled. "I've been wondering where my talents lie."

"What about this?" His hand traced the air near her abstract sculpture, following the curves as if they were a woman's.

"That's, eh, not quite right." But she was seeing the piece with clearer vision, she realized. She knew exactly where she'd gone wrong. If she hadn't wanted to waste a minute of her time with Gabe—*cool, stay cool*—she'd be working on the sculpture right now, blowtorch in hand.

"I'm no judge." He scratched his head, studying the configuration of steel and rust. "But it looks like a woman to me. Maybe even a self-portrait."

Karen stared. "You think?"

The sculpture *was* feminine. She'd never considered it to be autobiographical, except now that he'd said so, she realized there might be a measure of truth in the observation.

She cinched the saddle girth. "How come you said that?"

His shrug was self-effacing. "I don't know."

"Something made you say it." The knot of worry that she'd only produce what she saw in her head and not what she felt in her gut had loosened. Maybe she was going in the right direction after all. Gabe had recognized the sculpture's essential meaning, if only on an instinctive level.

"The way the metal twists, right there." He waved at a bend in the figure. "How it flares out here. That makes me think of you." He cocked his head at her, the blue of his eyes sparkling with wicked intent, his smile slow and predatory. "I think of you, in bed, going wild with my tongue stuck up your juicy little cunt."

Air sliced her throat when she inhaled. The hell with *brash*. He was brazenly confident. And there *she* was, stumbling over her tongue and worrying she'd say the wrong thing, while his boldness had her insides running with sticky sap.

Two could play that game. Mostly because it was more fun that way.

She unsnapped Tinker's lead and walked the horse toward Gabe. "Want to be there again tonight?"

He waited a beat too long. "Tonight?"

"Or tomorrow. Tomorrow's better. Dinner tomorrow night." Oh, she was cool, all right.

He dropped a possessive hand over her butt. "I'll be there." One hard knuckle raked the seam of her jeans, sending a mini shock wave through her private parts. "And here, too."

She whirled away. "I'll be expecting you." *Armed with condoms.*

They led the horses out of the barn. Spindrift curvetted with excitement as Karen mounted, but Tinker remained placid as Gabe set his foot in the stirrup. Even though he'd explained that he usually didn't give off as many shocks as he had the past night, she'd still noticed how he was careful with what he touched and how he moved. She'd given him a Western saddle—no irons, all good, thick leather, except for a few buckles and rings. If there were residual sparks lurking in Gabe, Tinker was so lackadaisical he could use the spur of a good shock.

They rode across the pasture, toward the fringe of trees beyond, where they could pick up a dirt road that would take them to Torch Lake, three miles away. Since Officer Dan had most likely appropriated the bike for the Lost and Found, Gabe had announced a plan to walk back to his cabin. Over breakfast—cold cereal because the power was still out—Karen had come up with the idea of a horseback ride. *Not* because she hated to see him go. Turning the one-night stand to a one-week stand was good enough for her.

She'd have her fill by then. Absolutely.

The setting was tranquil, rife with the pale golds and greens of spring. Birds twittered and pecked, flying up from the grass as the horses approached. They rode without speaking. The nod and swish of the horses' heads and tails became a rhythm inside Karen, fitted to the steady beat of her heart, the memory of rocking toward rapture in Gabe's lap.

She glanced at him, riding beside her. He was watching her, looking buff and gorgeous in his wrinkled thermal shirt and jeans. She smiled, feeling like a cheeseball, but drinking him in. Last night had been all about a dark, erotic, extraordinary journey. By daylight, she was growing captivated with the real man. The almost-but-not-quite ordinary man.

Thereafter, whenever she looked at him, he was looking at her. Which was flattering, and electric in its own way, until she realized that every time he looked at her, *she* was looking at *him*. Thoroughly besotted. She had to laugh. With so much checking out going on, they were lucky the horses hadn't wandered off into the gullies.

"What's funny?" Gabe asked.

"Me. I'm enjoying myself."

"I'm enjoying you, too."

The saddles creaked. Gabe maintained a steady hand on the reins, keeping Tinker from snatching at mouthfuls of spring grass. Karen admired his competence. "You've ridden before?"

"Now and then."

"I could leave Tinker at your place so you have transportation. If you've got a patch of grass, we could stake him out. I can drive over with—"

"No. But thanks."

"Oh. Okay."

"It's just that I don't want to be responsible."

She understood. But something made her push him. "You two seem to be getting along fine." She'd even caught him stroking the gelding's neck. "What do you think will happen?"

Shadows dappled Gabe's face as they entered the grove of willows and ferns. Peepers sang from a grassy stream bank. "Anything. Another thunderstorm."

Of course. Karen nodded. "I've been wondering how you ended up in one last night. I know what you told me, but—"

"But it wasn't the entire truth."

She waited. With a jingle of the bit, Spindrift shook her head, chasing away the black fly that circled her ears. Low-hanging branches drooped in their path and Karen snapped one off to use as a whisk.

"You're right." Gabe leaned forward in the saddle, looking ahead to the lichen-covered pile of rocks where they'd connect with the road. "I left the cabin intending to bike into town. But I was—I needed an escape. From myself. So I rode, for I don't know how long. I wasn't paying attention, only thinking of burning off my energy, and when I looked up the sky was getting dark."

"Why didn't you stop and find shelter with someone before the storm got so bad?"

He gave her a look. "You saw what happened."

"The clocks? The power? That's not such a terrible inconvenience that you should have risked your life to avoid it."

His expression remained grim. "I was hoping to find an empty house or a barn."

"I see." Karen whisked the flies off her mare. She could sympathize, but she couldn't ever understand how it was, living with so many constrictions. "How long has it been?"

"Since last August."

"There's nothing to be done to help you?"

"The doctors are mystified. There have been cases of people whose chemistry conflicts with watches and small electrical systems, but I'm off the charts." His look darkened even more, giving her a hint of what he'd been through. "They checked me into a research hospital so they could study me. There was even talk of electric shock therapy."

She swallowed a gasp of horror, aware that her first reaction was to imagine something out of Dr. Frankenstein. Gabe didn't need to see that. "No wonder you escaped."

"I didn't have to steal the keys or break windows. I walked out. Months ago. My life has been fairly uneventful since then, give or take a few inconveniences." He shrugged. "Apart from last night. But you were a nice antidote."

The way he looked at her made her throat thicken with emotion, but she swallowed again and croaked, "Yeah, sometimes you just have to get laid."

Gabe ran a hand along Tinker's satin neck. The horse's ears flicked forward and back. "And sometimes you just have to be loved."

Sparks showered the cement. Karen squinted behind the face shield of her helmet, concentrating on the white-hot spot of molten metal while sweat trickled down her temple and nape. Over her jeans and T-shirt, she wore a leather bib apron and thick cuffed gloves with Kevlar stitching. Her muscles were rubbery with exhaustion, but she couldn't stop. Inspiration burned as hot as the torch in her hand.

She'd been at it for hours, cutting, brazing, and welding the sculpture into its purest form. Every choice had felt right, every weld smooth and strong,

A cramp bit into her left shoulder. With a groan, she straightened and reluctantly set aside the electrode, the rod of filler material that melted in the arc of electricity to fill the joints of the sculpture. She tipped up the shield and rolled her head, then her shoulders, working out the aches and pains.

The blue sky was now gunmetal, tinged with purple and pink where the sun had sunk toward the horizon. Karen put down the welding torch, realizing that she'd even managed to tune out the constant annoying sound of the buzz box, the red metal welding machine that ran off an AC current.

She stretched. Ouch. New pangs had joined the more pleasant twinges from last night's exertions.

She eyed the sky. Almost dark. Damn, how late was it?

Well past quitting time. The horses hung their heads over the rails of the corral, demanding their supper with squeals and hoof stomps. Her own stomach was hollow. She stripped off her gloves and grabbed the water bottle to quench her thirst.

Her eyes wouldn't stay away from the sculpture. She'd cut away a few extraneous pieces, then added several lengths of rusted iron rebar she'd foraged at the dump, each piece arrow straight, male to the sleek female curves of the steel, except at the peak, where she'd been working at configuring a zigzag that reached to the sky.

The fatigue dropped away. She lowered her visor and pulled on the gloves.

She was at the top of the stepladder, beading the very tip of the sculpture amid the bursting fireworks, when she caught a movement out of the corner of her eye. Her head swiveled. It was too dark. She couldn't see much past the visor.

Ever mindful of safety around the hot metal and sparks, she climbed down slowly and set aside her gear. Scattershot pings of nervous excitement flew through the air. She dragged off the helmet and shook out her matted hair. Peeled away the gloves. The apron. Cool air washed her body.

And then she turned.

He leaned against the doorway, where the dark barn interior was cut by a slanted ray of sunset.

Her tongue moved in her mouth long before words emerged. "I knew it would be you."

7

"Officer Dan?"

"Not him." She pulled the T-shirt off over her head, stretching her rib cage taut. The evening air was caressing. Goose bumps popped up on her heated skin. The contrast in sensation was provocative. "He doesn't make me feel the way you do."

Gabe's gaze flicked between her and the sculpture. "You've been working."

"All day. I was inspired."

He looked at the cooling red tip where moments before sparks had flown. "So I see."

She walked toward him with a seductive smile. "I thought we had a date for tomorrow."

He put his hands in his jeans pockets and crossed one leg, setting his foot on the tip of the rubber-soled boots. "I couldn't stay away."

Emotion had roughened his voice. She felt the uneven texture against her skin.

His brows inched upward. "You're shivering."

She dropped the shirt, stopping in front of him with her breasts pushed together in a sturdy cotton sports bra. Not sturdy enough to disguise the tightened points of her nipples. She wasn't surprised by his arrival or hesitant about what to do next. Like her work on the sculpture, offering herself to Gabe this way felt right.

He still hadn't moved, except for the hot flames of his eyes, flickering across her as she peeled up the sports bra. Her breasts lifted, then dropped with a bounce. A soft hiss slid from between his teeth. "Sexy."

"I'm on fire."

"You're electric. Do you know how hot you looked with that welding torch, making sparks fly?" He frowned a little, taking in the buzzing welding machine. "Huh. Looks like the power's back on."

"The phone, too." She listened. The machine continued to hum. "And staying on."

"I'll keep my distance."

She pressed crisscrossed hands over her breasts, a futile attempt to ease the ache of wanting to feel them in his mouth. "I'd rather lose power."

He barked a deep laugh and suddenly came forward to swing her off her feet. She felt herself flying high through the air before coming around to be brought up snug against his chest. Her legs clasped his hips and their mouths came together like magnets locking in place. They were wild, with dueling tongues, clutching hands, needy noises.

Gabe staggered into the depths of the barn, where shadows gave them privacy. He set Karen on a stack of alfalfa hay bales, the small stock remaining from the winter's store, never removing his mouth, his supple, scouring tongue. She was dizzy from desire and exhaustion and heat and happiness, and she laced her fingers at the small of his back, holding him tight, pressing him closer, trying to rub against him with her legs spread wide, the seam of her jeans grinding into her hot crotch.

"Make love to me," she said. "Make love to me, Gabe."

His kiss was deep and moving. Swearing a promise that reached her heart. She whispered against his lips, returning the emotion, freeing herself from old disappointments and loss.

Sometimes you just have to be loved.

He set her back on the bale, bending to kiss the tip of one breast, then the other. She sighed, melting. He laid a palm against the twitching skin of her midriff and she felt the hot connection that had already become an addiction. Then his hands were at her zipper and he was skinning off her jeans, yanking one shoe off her foot, but leaving the jeans puddled around her other ankle when he couldn't tug them loose and was too impatient to try again.

The flat of his hand slid inside the front of her panties, through the patch of curls into the wet heat. She jolted. The lopsided hay bales swayed beneath them as he bent her back, yanking away her bikinis with a quick tug and snap, pushing down his jeans and underwear so his erection reared up, hot and red like a fire-breathing dragon, a mythical beast who spat sparks and flame. For a crazed moment she wanted to ask him to put it in her like that, naked and burning, but he had pulled out a condom, sheathed himself, and pressed the head against her slit, all in one motion, so smooth and swift she could only give herself, open herself completely, surrender to the consuming fire devouring her whole, as he thrust all the way home.

Pleasure and shock and need ripped through her. He put his arms around her and soothed the ragged edges, lipping sweet kisses across her collarbone, finding the pulse in her throat, grazing his teeth up her neck until he'd reached her mouth again—her mouth and his mouth, drowning in a rain of fire.

She rocked on the bales, squeezing and sliding over the shaft of his cock. Their perch shifted and loosened. She pushed up with her hips, but the stack was too unstable and she cried in frustration, wanting the deep thrust so badly she clawed at him when he pulled away.

"Like this." He lifted and turned her, saying "Bend for me" so sweetly in her ear that she sprawled across the messy bales, not caring about the stalks that poked and scratched, as she clutched handfuls of loose hay, bracing herself for the invasion of hard cock.

Distantly, she heard the whickering horses, the uninterrupted motor of the welding machine. Maybe she was right. Maybe she'd absorbed some of his—his—

Or not. Her ass flinched as he took hold with two hands, caressing for a moment before he parted them. Cool air touched her most intimate area. Except for harsh breathing, he was silent. She shuddered, knowing he was watching, seeing all of her, especially as he began to press for entrance. Her lids clamped shut, but the image was burned in her mind—the swollen head of his cock parting her pussy lips, stretching her folds until they'd made a tight rim around his thick shaft as it slowly, inexorably disappeared inside her.

He let out a grunt of satisfaction when he bottomed out. "That's my girl." He stroked a finger between her buttocks, around their melded flesh, to the inflamed button of her clit. She jerked at the touch. Her body clutched, from hands to stomach to sex. A low moan rolled off her tongue. He began thrusting.

Experiencing all that motion and emotion and pleasure at one time was too much. For a little while she lost touch with reality. She came back with a shock as he clamped down and hammered his cock in and out of her until she'd bounced off her toes like a rag doll. The tension coiled tight, then burst free, everything inside her rising so swift and strong the climax broke like a flood, all rushing sensation and tumultuous release.

Gabe bent over her prone body, cradling her breasts as he slammed into her with the quick hard strokes of his orgasm. Each thrust tugged at her clit. Small, gasping cries popped from her open mouth.

"Who's in there? What's going on?" Footsteps thudded at the entrance to the barn. "This is the police. I want to see your hands in the air."

Gabe and Karen had slumped into a heap atop the bales. The harsh command, coming from nowhere, seemed almost impossible. His arms went around her.

"Don't you touch her!"

"What?" Gabe said, but he slid away, flailing a bit to gain his feet among the slippery hay.

"I am an officer of the law. Do. Not. Move."

"The hell with that." Gabe yanked up his jeans and stepped in front of Karen as she scrambled through the hay for any piece of clothing at all. She found her jeans and tried to use them to cover herself, at least, but they were still caught around one ankle.

She huddled behind Gabe. His hands were in the air. "Don't shoot," he said with a dry, dead calm.

"Is that you, Karen?" Officer Dan queried uncertainly. "Are you all right? Was he hurting you?"

"Oh my God." She peered past Gabe, so numbed by the situation she was slow to react. Officer Dan was silhouetted in the doorway, both arms raised as he leveled a gun at them. She bit back a groan at the absurdity of it all. "Would you please put the gun away before you shoot somebody?"

The cop lowered his weapon. "Karen? It sounded like you were in pain."

Because you never heard me climax before.

"I'm fine." Her face was flaming, not unlike other parts of her body. "He wasn't doing anything to me I didn't want him to."

Officer Dan muttered, clearly embarrassed. But he held his spot. His head snaked forward as he peered into the barn, trying to get a good look at her companion.

Karen blessed the darkness that had saved them from complete exposure. "Um, Dan, could you give us some privacy?"

Gabe laughed shortly. "And can I put my hands down?"

"You think this is funny?" the officer blustered. "For all I know, you were forcing her."

"Then you didn't listen very well to the sounds she was making."

The cop advanced, the gun at his side, but unholstered. He grunted. "I heard enough."

"Stop it," Karen snapped. "I don't need you two cock-a-doodling at each other right now." She gave Gabe a shove forward. "Turn your back, please. Both of you." She stepped into her jeans, saw an old work sweatshirt on a hook nearby and grabbed that, even though it smelled like manure from mucking out stalls. She yanked it past her breasts. "All right. You can look now."

She was *not* going to say "I'm decent" when she felt so fabulously and indecently fucked. Despite Officer Dan's interruption.

Gabe was shooting black glares at the cop while he straightened his clothing. "Next time, knock."

"The door was open," he said defensively, "but don't worry, there won't be a next time."

Coming closer, Karen saw that Officer Dan's face was as red with embarrassment as hers must be. He couldn't look at her. Stiffly, he added, "I apologize for barging in. I had it figured that there was something fishy going on last night, and what with not knowing who was out in the storm, and what they—*he*—" Dan's lip curled in

Gabe's direction "—might do to you, I felt it was my duty to drop by to see that you were safe for the night."

"I appreciate the concern," she said.

Gabe snorted rudely from behind her.

Officer Dan was regaining his bluster. He stalked toward Gabe, demanding, "Who are you?"

Gabe's eyes were flinty. "Tomzak. Gabriel."

"Step into the light where I can get a look at you." When Gabe didn't immediately obey, Officer Dan took hold of his shoulder. A spark zinged and the cop let go, then quickly gave Gabe a shove to urge him forward.

"Am I under arrest?" Gabe asked.

Karen rolled her eyes.

Officer Dan used short punching stabs of a fist to push Gabe toward the doorway. Karen gasped. Directly in their path was the welding machine. And she'd been so carried away—literally—that she'd left it running.

"Careful," she warned, darting forward. "Let me shut down the buzz box."

The motor gave a couple of coughs as Gabe stepped around the machine. Officer Dan wasn't as watchful, or maybe too flustered to care. He stumbled, catching the toe of his boot on the cord. It yanked free of the outlet.

Karen was only able to cry out, seeing the impending disaster but helpless to stop it.

Dan went down, grabbing at Gabe as he fell. Reaching instinctively for something to keep him on his feet, Gabe's hand wrapped around the base of the sculpture.

The welding machine cut out with a loud *bzzzt* and a burst of sparks that showered down upon the men like fireworks. Gabe yanked his hand back. Too late. An arc of electricity streaked from the metal sculpture and into him.

Karen was too stunned to scream.

Gabe snapped upright. A wisp of smoke rose from his palm. She smelled scorched flesh. For an instant, he seemed to be looking at her, but his eyes were blank, frozen.

She opened her arms.

He collapsed in a heap on the cement.

Gabe swam in a darkness punctuated by arcs of colored lightning that streaked by at the corners of his vision. There was no direction, no sensation, no reason.

Except for one small pinpoint of hope.

An insistent pressure at the side of his neck.

He focused on it, his determination growing stronger. The pressure became a connection, drawing him toward consciousness. He swam the current of heat. Hearing his name. Seeing a blur of light.

"Gabe." Karen, sobbing. "Please, Gabe. Be all right."

His mouth tasted like old pennies. He opened it to speak, but nothing came. His tongue was too thick. Oxygen knifed his lungs. He sucked it in, ribs heaving in pain and relief.

"Gabe." She was kissing his face, washing him with tears. "Can you hear me?"

He nodded.

She gripped his hand. "Help is coming."

Her face filled his field of vision. Big brown eyes, quivering mouth, her complexion bleached with worry.

"I'm okay." He lifted his head, moved his arms and legs. "Shit. That hurt." He let go, smelling leather and realizing that her work apron was wadded beneath his head. "What happened?"

"Well, I guess you were electrocuted." Her voice caught. "My fault."

Gabe was remembering. Falling. The bite of metal against his hand. The sudden jolt of heat and pain.

"Accident," he whispered through dry lips. The corners hitched. "Those tend to happen around me."

Karen's laugh became a snuffle. She rubbed her hand beneath her nose. "Dan's up at the house, calling nine-one-one. His police radio wasn't working. Imagine that." She lifted Gabe's shoulders into her lap, hugging him and rocking and panting. "I thought you were a goner, but your pulse was strong."

"I felt that." He turned his face against her thigh. "Your fingers on my neck." A horrible thought slammed into his brain and he struggled against her. "You shouldn't be touching me." He pushed up to a sitting position. "Let me go."

She wouldn't. Her hands remained steady and warm, her arms encircling him. She kissed him over and over, on his shoulder, his neck, saying, "I won't let go, I won't let go."

"But—" He moved his fingers and heels against the cold concrete. "What if I'm worse?"

"What if you're cured?" She gave another shaky laugh. "That's the way it's supposed to happen. You know. The amnesiac gets a knock in the head and can suddenly remember everything he forgot. So maybe you're . . ."

"Normal?" He had no hope of that. Everywhere she touched him, he felt the charge of electric attraction.

"Let me try." She pushed up his shirt and drew a fingertip along the line bisecting his abs. No sparks flew, but there was the same magnetic, sizzling chemistry. Not any kind of normal chemistry. Way too hot for that.

Karen hugged him. "Not bad."

"You're crazy."

"I am." She brushed her lips over his ear. "I don't know how this happened or where we're going with it, but I'm not letting go of you, Gabe." Her tongue licked his lobe. *Sizzle.* "Remember, I'm the only woman who can take you and like it." She caught her breath in the hesitant, nearly shy way she usually tried to disguise with teasing smiles and distracting talk. He thought she was done until she added, her voice soft and throaty in his ear, "Take you and love it."

He closed his eyes. He'd come to this place full of questions, and although most of them remained unanswered, he knew that he'd found what he needed. Because in the end, after the lightning bolts and flames and hot electric sex had died out, there remained the simple need to be loved.

Epilogue

Two Months Later

Soft jazz played inside the house, the sweet strains floating out the open windows on the warm night breeze. Gabe and Karen had wandered into the grass barefooted, dressed in the skimpiest of clothing after a long evening of lovemaking. He took her into his arms, cupped her bottom, swayed her to the music. The sky above was vast and silent, its infinite reaches dotted with faceted stars.

After a while, Karen opened her eyes. "Look. The fireflies are out."

"You sure that's not me? I'm still feeling kind of sparky."

She rubbed against him. "You are not."

"I always am when you're around. Even if it's only inside."

The lightning bugs floated above them, blinking on and off. Karen sighed. Pure joy.

"Did I say that I loved meeting your family? And they seemed so glad to see you happy and settled."

"Oh, yeah, my brothers got a lot of enjoyment from calling me a househusband."

"A houselover. Every woman should have one." She gave him a squeeze. "Don't worry. You'll decide on a plan."

"I almost had them believing the one about buying a rubber factory."

"Thor Condoms. It's a possibility."

"In the meantime . . ."

"You do enough. Gardening."

"Kissing."

"Painting."

"Sucking."

"Sawing."

"Screwing."

She laughed. "I thought that was my job—to keep you screwed like a light bulb."

"M-hmm. You do it well. I haven't shorted out the electricity since the last storm."

He put a hand on the small of her back. The familiar pulse of attraction throbbed between them.

"My dad was impressed with your welding skills."

"Your brothers said I should try you as the torch."

"Figures."

"I didn't tell them that I already sort of had."

"No more guilt. I survived with no ill effects, except for the usual."

"Well, your mom thought the sculptures were too erotic, even in the abstract."

"Tell her your new gallery guy says sex sells."

"And it's better than phone sex."

"Or Cock-a-Doodle."

"Maybe we should get more chickens."

"Are you trying to turn me into a farmer?"

"God, no. Unless you want—"

"I want to do something I really like."

"Biking?"

"Licking."

"Hiking?"

"Hugging."

"Fishing?"

He chuckled. "Fucking."

"Two months, and you still have sex on the brain."

He nipped her. " 'Cause what I really like doing is you."

Bed and Breakfast

by

Susan Donovan

1

The high desert air snapped at Kate's cheeks. She inhaled the sharp fragrance of wood smoke and glanced overhead at the ink-black sky alive with swirls of stars.

She listened to the Santa Fe shuttle van bumping its way down the dirt road behind her and, with a sigh, grabbed the handle of her suitcase and dragged its wheels through the hard-packed soil. She lugged the case up the wide wooden steps of what she could only assume was the Windwalker Lodge. But hey—the shuttle driver could have dumped her at a psycho killer's lair for all she knew. It was utterly dark up here. Not even a porch light to welcome her. Some hospitality.

Kate pushed against the heavy, carved front door. The door didn't budge, but her bladder did, reminding her that she hadn't used the rest room since her connecting flight in Denver more than four hours before.

She put a hand on her hip and decided to recap, because recapping always made things look rosier. Just a month ago, her boyfriend disappeared, only to turn up in Vegas married to his nineteen-year-old receptionist. Because the emotional blow left Kate a bedridden mess for three days, she missed a meeting in San Diego and lost her company's most lucrative client. At her father's birthday party soon after, Kate's brother chose to announce to the extended family that he was a woman trapped in a man's body at the exact moment their father began to blow out the sixty-seven candles on his cake, which sent Dad into cardiac arrest. And a week after that, Kate was driving down Wilshire Boulevard, reached for her ringing cell phone, drove her brand-new Land Rover LR3 into a palm tree, and broke her nose.

And that was why she was standing there in the cold and the dark, her bladder ready to explode, her nose pounding, her head throbbing, exhausted and pissed off because she'd been forced to come to some God-forsaken spiritual retreat in the northern New Mexico mountains.

"Open the damn door!"

This was Monica's fault. Her boss and occasional best friend had pointed out that the universe was telling Kate it was time for her to change direction, and Monica insisted that she start the change here. Apparently, Monica experienced her own life-altering awakening up here a couple years back by hugging trees and smoking cactus or some such garbage, and insisted Kate go have the same alteration. How had Monica put it? *"This will be your first vacation in seven years. Use it to get yourself centered or don't bother coming back."*

Kate fumbled around in the dark until she found the doorbell. She pushed it six thousand times. She began to shiver. She heard a low moan from somewhere in the dark that could have been a cow. Or the psycho killer. A dog barked. Her patience snapped. And Kate managed to center herself well enough to kick the big wooden door with her pointy-toed Jimmy Choo ankle boot and flip her middle finger into the face of the night, yelling, *"Open this butt-ugly door right now!"*

The door opened. Kate gasped. A yellow sliver of light appeared, then a dark eye, which gazed out at her from a thickly fringed, heavy eyelid.

"What's up?" asked a deep male voice.

Kate's mouth fell open. She was left speechless by the man's rudeness.

He yawned. "Sorry. Can I help you?"

"For God's sake." Kate rolled her eyes. "I'm here for my freakin' spiritual awakening, so let's get this party started."

She watched a corner of the doorman's mouth tighten and twitch, and it was then she noticed his scruffy five-o'clock shadow speckled with gray. However, being the uncouth man he apparently was, he said nothing.

"My name is Kate Dreyfuss."

"That's cool." The man yawned again. Kate watched one of his hands travel up to his chin and rub his scratchy beard. Then he ran his fingers through his dark hair. And he just stared.

"Excuse me," Kate said, with all the sickening-sweet politeness she could muster while squeezing her thighs together. "I can't help but notice that you haven't yet opened the door. Is there a reason for that oversight?"

"You could say that." The guy opened the door just a bit more and, unbelievably, he let his dark, lazy gaze roam down the full length of her body, doing nothing to hide his audacity.

Kate was going to strangle Monica. Truly. Her first hour back in Los Angeles, Kate would hunt her down, choke the life out of her skinny little neck, and be glad about it. Spending the rest of her natural life in a women's prison would be a small price to pay for the privilege.

"You said you're here for the retreat?"

She gawked at him. "Do I look like I'm selling Avon?"

He glanced at her rolling suitcase and was about to speak, but she held up her hand and cut him off. "Would you mind very much if we just skip the clever banter? I'm cold and tired and I want to check in and go to bed."

The door opened a bit more. The man blinked at her, and then Kate watched an odd smile spread over his face, which she could see almost in its entirety at this point. He had beautiful, straight, white teeth and piercing dark eyes. His face was chiseled but boyish at the same time. "Well," he said with a sigh. "This might prove to be a tad bit inconvenient."

That was it—she was done being nice. Kate nodded slowly. "Look dude, if I'm not mistaken, my so-called best friend spent close to two grand to send me up here to get in touch with the life force and sniff the dirt and some other ridiculous New Age bullshit, and I'll tell you what's inconvenient—me standing out here on this porch freezing my ass off at one in the morning, all the while trying to deny the fact that I have to piss like a racehorse." She yanked up on the handle of her roller suitcase and a loud *clack* cut through the still night air. The dog barked again. "How about you let me in now? Will that work for you?"

The door opened further still. She saw a long leg clad in a baggy, forest-green pajama bottom. "Did you take the shuttle up from Santa Fe?" he asked, peering over her shoulder.

"Of course, I did!" Kate didn't know how many more seconds of patience and continence she had left in her. "You don't see any rental car out here, do you? What's with the interrogation? Just let me in, *please*!"

The rough pine door creaked as it opened wide. *All rightee, then,* Kate thought to herself. The narrow opening hadn't revealed the overall hottie index of the man with the unshaven face and substandard manners. He was gorgeous, in a rumpled, naked-from-the-waist-up kind of way. His hair was a messy mop of nearly black curls, pressed flat on one side. His feet were pale, long, and narrow, peeking out from under the lounge pants. His chest was covered in dark curls, his build lean and hard but not bulky. His waist was tapered and his abs were ripped. His upper arms were defined.

"Oh, well. Follow me, I guess." He let her in, shut the door behind her, and turned. Kate noticed immediately that he was just as fine going as he was coming. He had a tightly sculpted behind, and she might have been cold, tired, and in desperate need of indoor plumbing, but she was still able to appreciate the view revealed by the loose drape of his drawstring pants.

The wheels of her suitcase clacked along the tiled floor as she followed him. He led her across a large, cold lobby that offered no welcome. He walked right through a rounded archway to a dim hall littered with chairs, desks, and ladders. Kate followed the man into an alcove, starting to sense that there was something very wrong with this picture.

She could hardly believe it when the hottie paused to scratch the seat of his pajamas before he flipped on a light.

"Sleep tight, Miss Dreyfuss."

Kate stared, incredulous, first at the room and then at the man. He'd just gestured toward an unmade, plainly carved four-poster bed, burgundy cotton sheets rumpled, and pillows newly indented. The room smelled of wood smoke, night air, and maleness. It was chilly. A book entitled *Earth Voices* was opened face down on the bed. The hottie grabbed it and tossed it onto the nightstand.

"See you in the morning," he said, heading back out into the hallway.

Kate whipped around. "Stop right there!"

He did stop, then turned and stared at her, blinking again. He yawned. "Yeah?"

"Is this some kind of joke?" She spread her arms out to her sides and laughed nervously. "Did Monica put you up to this?"

He frowned at her, then his face relaxed into a smile. "Monica Taraborelli?" He laughed. "Oh, right. You're the high-strung chick she was telling me about."

Kate brightened sarcastically. "And thank heavens she did, otherwise you might not have been expecting me!"

He nodded, squinting at her. "Cool. Well, I'll make breakfast for you in the morning before you head back." He turned again.

"Just a minute!" This was horrible. She had to pee so bad her brain was short-circuiting. And she realized her voice was coming out in a very unflattering screech, but she couldn't help herself. "You expect me to stay in here? This is *your* room! What kind of woo-woo operation is this? What about that brochure I received going on about how to 'unwind your spirit and take a pilgrimage into your own landscape'? I reserved a private room with a queen-size bed! I paid for a group tour! I opted to experience the deep relaxation of the optional hot-freakin'-stone massage! You can't just dump me in what is obviously your own bed! And *go back* where? Is this an episode of *The Twilight Zone*?"

The man had leaned against the doorjamb while she'd had her temper tantrum, and Kate couldn't help but notice how the muscles in his abdomen rippled with the slight movement. He crossed one foot lazily over the other. "Well, first of all—"

"Who are you? What is your name?"

He sighed deeply and folded his arms over his chest. In the light, his biceps looked even more impressive. "My name is Rod Serl—"

"Not funny."

He chuckled, then cleared his throat when he realized she wasn't going to join in. "Yeah. Okay. My name is Jorey Matheny and you were correct—that's my bed right there. In fact, Miss Dreyfuss, that's the very bed I was sleeping in when you began pounding on my door, cussing loud enough to wake the ancestors. And this is my lodge. And I wrote every crappy word in that brochure you liked so much."

Kate felt slightly ashamed for her attitude. But just slightly. "And?"

"And what?"

"What's your point? Where's my room? Where are the eight other quote-unquote 'pilgrims' in this group tour?"

Jorey turned away, grabbed the doorknob, and began to pull it closed. "Good night, Kate. We'll deal with the details in the morning. Let's hope you'll be less cranky by then."

"Hold it!" She launched for him, clamping her hand down on his. "Tell me right now what's going on. I demand an answer!"

Jorey extricated his fingers from her grip and sighed. "The thing is, Kate . . ." He paused to stretch and yawn yet again, causing the drawstring waist to fall even lower on his hips. She thought she'd faint. "The pilgrimage you signed up for was last month. I wondered why you were a no-show."

"What?"

"You got the dates mixed up. Windwalker Lodge is in the process of a complete renovation. We're in the off-season. There are no rooms available because they've all been gutted for new plumbing, heating, cooling, and wiring." He nodded toward the rumpled comforter. "That right there is the only bed in the place. The furnace is not working at the moment, but I do have electricity and running water. And extra blankets. Sweet dreams."

With that, he was gone.

When she shuffled into the lobby at about nine the next morning, it appeared her sleep had been anything but sweet. Kate Dreyfuss was wearing a pair of tight, black yoga pants that hugged her slim hips and flared below her knee, topped with a lime green scoop-neck T-shirt that cast an unflattering glow on her pale skin. She had dark circles under her eyes and, in the morning light, he could tell that the bridge of her nose was swollen. She looked like a size-six prizefighter. And a braless one at that. Maybe there were perks to having an unexpected girl guest in an unheated lodge.

"Breakfast, Kate?"

She hadn't seen him, and she jolted in surprise, her brow creased with a frown. "I don't *do* breakfast," she snapped. "And you shouldn't go around sneaking up on people like that."

Jorey glanced down at his motionless legs, casually spread wide before him and planted on the floor in front of his decidedly unmoving chair. Obviously, the night had done nothing to improve her demeanor. But he caught the flicker of interest in her expression as she eyed his steaming coffee mug.

She nodded toward his beverage. "Is it halfway decent stuff?"

Jorey set down the mug and pushed himself to a stand. "Well, now, Miss Dreyfuss, you're at the foot of the Sangre de Cristo mountains about ten miles out of beautiful downtown Chimayo, New Mexico, perhaps the last inhabited place on earth untouched by a Starbucks. But sure, it's decent enough. Soy milk?"

Jorey heard her chuckle as she followed him into the kitchen. "Two sugars, two creams, but only if you have half and half. If you only have the powdered crap or if you aren't joking about the soy, then you can just skip it entirely and make it three sugars."

"Sugar will rot you from the inside out."

"So will caffeine, so don't give me any of that vegan granola garbage."

He poured her a big mug, shaking his head slowly, wondering why it was that this obnoxious woman made him smile, taking pleasure in the fact that he didn't plan to tell her it was decaf.

"Here you are, Princess. No cream. No sugar. I aim to please."

She laughed.

Jorey watched her cradle the big brown mug to her little pink lips. If it weren't for the dark circles and the off-kilter nose, she'd easily be one of the most beautiful women he'd ever shared air molecules with. Her hair was a rich, almost black brown, straight and glossy. Her eyes were ice blue. She was built like a dancer. Too bad the energy pouring off of her was that of frenetic distress.

Jorey saw her appraising the kitchen he'd made with his own hands. She glanced at the pine cabinets and let her fingertips graze across the chocolate marble countertop. "Cute place," she said. "Now get me out of here."

It was Jorey's turn to laugh, mostly at himself. After a fitful night of sleep on the floor in front of the fireplace, he'd already been up for three hours, watching it rain like it hadn't rained since last April. And after five years in the high desert, he knew exactly what that meant—raging arroyos, dirt roads turned to quicksand, and a washed-out bridge at the end of his isolated lane. It also meant that the Mistress of Morning Joy over there wasn't going anywhere for at least three days.

She scowled at him. "Don't tell me this is decaf."

"All right. I won't tell you. Did you sleep well?"

"No. I do not sleep well as a rule, and I certainly didn't last night. It was too quiet and I was freezing."

"I see."

"I need real coffee. We're about an hour out of Santa Fe, right? Can I borrow your car?"

Jorey tried not to laugh, but was unsuccessful. The last thing this woman needed was caffeine. "I don't have a car. I have a Land Rover."

Her eyes lit up. "So do I! Well I did, anyway, before I totaled it. So I'm experienced."

"Clearly."

"All right. Fine. I'll get my stuff and you can drive me back into town, then. My Blackberry isn't working up here, so I'll need to use your phone to call the airline."

Jorey didn't know which bit of good news to share with this woman first. She obviously wasn't the type who was cool with things not going according to plan. Monica had mentioned that Kate was one of those go-getter sales types. It figured. He'd certainly known enough of them in his previous life.

"Miss Dreyfuss?"

"I'll be packed in five minutes."

She'd already turned toward the kitchen doorway. Jorey allowed himself a few leisurely seconds to watch her tight little ass as she scurried her way across the room. Then, still enjoying the view, he recited the facts to her as he knew them. "The phone lines are down. The bridge is washed out. The roads are flooded. We're living on generator power at the moment."

She stopped. She spun around. Jorey observed a wave of emotions wash over Kate's face and flow out again, leaving in its wake an almost innocent stare.

"Pardon me?"

"Nobody's going anywhere for a few days, unless you're familiar with burros."

"Burros? What the hell?"

He hadn't been this amused in months. The way her mouth fell open and the way she blinked and the way she blindly reached for the counter to steady herself—it was entertaining.

She stared out the big kitchen window at the incessant rain and swallowed hard. "This shit *cannot* be happening," she whined.

Jorey shrugged and took a few steps toward her, momentarily brightened by the hope that she might be handy with a circular saw, though he wouldn't bet on it. "It'll be all right." He reached out to place a friendly hand on the bare skin of her elbow. The silky warmth he encountered reminded Jorey that Kate Dreyfuss was all woman—tense and angry and at least a decade younger than him, but all woman.

"Sweetheart, have you considered that this might be the divine spirit telling you to stop and smell the roses?"

Kate squinted at him, and Jorey could see the gears turning behind the creamy loveliness of her forehead.

"First of all, there are no roses up here." She put the coffee mug on the counter and her hands on her hips, shaking his hand free of her elbow. "And even if there were, it wouldn't matter because I can't smell jack with my broken nose. Plus, that right there—" She pointed a manicured nail at the mug. "That is decaffeinated coffee, so don't even try to lie to me. And the divine spirit can fuck off, and so can you."

She spun around so fast that her hair whipped out around her, momentarily chasing away the chaotic aura of oranges, violets, and magentas Jorey had watched dance around her pretty head all morning.

He grinned, thinking that there were only a select few ways to break through an aura that unruly, and one of them involved lots and lots of sex.

"Shall I expect you for lunch?" Jorey called after her retreating form. As she slammed his bedroom door with finality, he realized he'd never made it in there to get clean clothes. The dirty jeans he'd found on the laundry room floor would have to do until she came out again.

She woke up completely disoriented. Nothing felt right and nothing felt normal. It wasn't light but it wasn't dark, and she let her eyes roam around the room, trying to put the pieces together. For an eerie moment, Kate's mind floated, grasping for anything that would make sense, and when nothing came to her, she fancied herself the heroine in one of those Lifetime Television amnesia movies—What *day* was it? Where *was* she? What *time* was it? Oh God, what was her *name*?

Then the scent hit her nostrils—wood smoke and cold air and *that man*—that Jorey Matheny guy with the horrendous manners and even worse coffee. She squeezed her eyes tight and rolled over, pressing her face into the pillow, but all that served to do was force the scent of that man further into her brain.

Kate wanted to go home. She wanted her life back—the one where she juggled sixty million dollars in public relations accounts. The one where she spent weekends in Palm Springs with Brad. She wanted the life where Brad told her she was the most amazing woman in the world, the one where her nose and her car weren't smashed up, where her dad wasn't recovering from a triple bypass, and her brother wasn't asking for her recommendations on leg-waxing salons.

That life.

There was a tap at the door. "Miss Dreyfuss?"

"Leave me alone."

"I brought you some soup. You've been sleeping all day."

"No thanks."

"You have to eat. It's vegetable barley. I made it two months ago."

She rolled her eyes. "So you're trying to *kill* me?"

She heard his laugh from behind the door. It was a rumbling, happy sound. "The soup was in the deep freezer, Princess. I heated it up so it's nice and hot."

She raised her face from the pillow, feeling her exhaustion spread deeper into her bones. She wondered why she felt so tired—shouldn't so much sleep be rejuvenating? What was wrong with her? She tried to remember what she'd read about the symptoms for Chronic Fatigue Syndrome. Or fibromyalgia. "I'd rather have a double bacon cheese. Where's the nearest In-N-Out Burger?"

"Probably down the street from the Starbucks."

Kate snorted. With a sigh of effort, she pushed herself up in bed, rubbed her hands over her face, and raked her fingers through her hair. She was being a selfish, spoiled bitch and she knew it. Well, tough. Maybe that's all she was—an über-bitch—and she'd never be anything more, no matter how hard she tried. That's what Brad had said, just before he'd run off and married some bimbette just this side of puberty.

"Come on in, I guess."

She saw the scuffed toe of his cowboy boot first, easing the door open enough that he could step through, one hand carrying a tray and the other a stack of magazines. She was about to tell him to set everything down and get lost, when she noticed his jeans. As he walked over to a table by the window and pulled it toward the bedside, she observed how the worn and pale denim pulled softly against his narrow hips, rounded butt, and lean thighs. There was a slight tear in the left knee and a few drops of dark paint on the right leg just above the ankle. And the way they seemed to cradle what was hiding behind the zipper . . . Kate swallowed hard, trying not to stare.

Suddenly, he was standing right beside the bed, looking down at her. My God, the man was extraordinary. The clean, white smile and that single deep dimple on his right cheek made him look like a kid. The salt-and-pepper stubble and the self-assured set of his broad shoulders made him seem much older.

But it was the peaceful awareness in those dark eyes that suggested Jorey was far more than he was letting on. And all Kate could wonder was what was a man this fine doing hiding in the middle of Southwestern Bum-Fuck?

"How old are you, Jorey?"

"Old enough to know better. How about you?"

She supposed she should be offended, but she'd started the conversation. "The same. At least most of the time."

"Ah. Then we understand each other." Jorey's lips spread wide and his eyes lit up. He wasn't shy about letting his gaze stray from her face to her uncovered shoulders, upper arms, and . . .

Kate pulled the sheet up under her chin, suddenly aware that the combination of the cold air and the hot man was making a spectacle of her chest.

"Don't bother, Princess. I noticed those happy little girls first thing this morning." Jorey arranged the tray and magazines, smile still intact.

Kate remained calm, determined not to produce the shock he was clearly fishing for. In a pleasant voice, she said, "Not especially interested in the social niceties, are we?"

"I got expelled from charm school. That's why they sent me up here."

"Was this before or after you flunked out of the hospitality management program?"

"Enjoy your soup."

With that, he left her in the bedroom to mull it all over. Jorey Matheny was a strange man—about as far as she could get from the L.A. urban pretty boys she was accustomed to. He was too blunt. He was no-frills in his manner and his dress. But she didn't sense any bitterness in him, especially because no matter what he said, it was accented by that disarming, half-dimpled smile. Jorey seemed relaxed. Peaceful.

How strange.

The soup was good, full of flavor and texture, and Kate was surprised how much she enjoyed it, considering it wasn't even remotely related to the bacon double cheeseburger she craved. As she ate, she flipped through the back copies of *Vegetarian Times* and *Yoga Today,* finding some of the articles marginally interesting. Who knew that colonic irrigation could improve your love life?

She fell asleep again, not having a clue what time it was and not caring. She had a series of strange dreams. She dreamed her nose had swelled to the shape and size of her dearly departed Range Rover, that her brother wanted to borrow her favorite open-toed pumps, and that Jorey was riding naked on a burro, which, as she awoke the next morning, left her slightly disturbed. She chalked up the bizarre dreams to caffeine withdrawal combined with whatever disease she obviously had. Not to mention the excess sleep. She'd probably spent twenty of the last twenty-four hours unconscious.

Kate blinked a few times and stretched, then swung her legs over the side of the big bed. It was obvious that the sun was out. Bright light slashed through the louvered wooden blinds, and her heart skipped with the hope that now that the rain had stopped, she'd be back to Los Angeles and good coffee by nightfall.

While in the shower, she decided to take control of the situation. It was so obvious that Jorey was making more of this rainstorm than necessary. If he wouldn't take her into Santa Fe, she'd get there herself. When had she ever let a man define her limits, anyway? Moments later, Kate rummaged around in the front zipper pocket of her rolling suitcase and found the rain poncho she'd cleverly remembered to pack. A little rain wasn't going to kill her. The main road couldn't be more than a mile or so away. And once she got there it would be a cinch to find a ride to Santa Fe.

She'd be damned if some crazy, middle-aged vegetarian survivalist was going to keep her prisoner—no matter how cute his butt was.

2

Archie Apodaca had been kind enough to ride his roan mare through the muck to check on everything up at the lodge, so Jorey offered him a cup of tea and a seat in front of the fire. Jorey knew that as far as neighbors went, he'd lucked out with Archie and his wife, Joan. Their house was about a mile down Route 52 behind a wall of cottonwoods, far enough to keep their distance and close enough to offer a connection to the world beyond Windwalker Lodge. Since their kids left the nest, Archie and Joan had made a living raising chickens and selling woodcrafts to the busloads of tourists who wandered through nearby Sanctuario de Chimayo, seeking the legendary healing powers of the red dirt around the old Catholic church.

"Hope you hadn't planned on going into Santa Fe for anything." Archie handed Jorey a wire basket of brown eggs and eased himself into one of the two wooden rocking chairs by the lobby's large kiva fireplace. "The center support on your bridge has washed away again. Had to ride down the slope of the east escarpment to get here."

Jorey placed a cup of fragrant tea in his neighbor's work-worn hands and shook his head. The sandy arroyo that cut through his property—like thousands of natural gulches all over the region—was prone to flash flooding. In the five years he'd been up here, raging water had damaged or washed away his simple beam bridge at least eight times. The arroyos were deceptive—bone dry one second and a merciless torrent the next. He'd heard stories of children swept away out of their parents' arms. He'd seen everything from motorcycles to roosters rushed to their demise.

"I'll get to it tomorrow," he told Archie.

"Not likely. They say the rain will be back by noon today and it'll keep up 'til Thursday. But who knows? Nobody can forecast nothing up here. Never could, right?"

Jorey settled back in his rocking chair and clasped his hands behind his head, smiling. "That's one of the reasons I like it, Arch. It's a wild place. Keeps me on my toes."

The sun-browned skin of his neighbor's face crinkled when he grinned. "I don't see the beauty all the time, you know, unless I have to go into the city for something. Then I'm always glad to get back."

Jorey nodded, comfortable in the rhythm of this conversation, one of hundreds just like it he'd had with Archie over the years. The unpredictable weather. The evils of city life. The untamed magnificence all around them.

"Tell Joan I appreciate the eggs."

"Sure will."

Jorey remembered how mesmerized he was by the passing of time during the first full year at the lodge. Seattle had its own charms, of course, but after his heart attack and the divorce, he knew he had to change his path. Jorey came to New Mexico to find solitude, and ended up opening his home to people just like him—people who needed to reconnect with the sacred.

He'd started the pilgrimage business three years ago, and had found the work rewarding, fun, and good for his soul. He led people on hikes to ancient Anasazi ruins and took them to Native American ceremonies on the nearby Tewa Pueblo. He arranged for groups to study with tribal healers, led meditation hikes in the wilderness, taught visitors about the connection between Native American wisdom and the world's major spiritual traditions. He liked to think he gave people a place to open their minds and hearts to the power of the land and the culture tied to it. In the process, Jorey had been able to keep tofu on the table, keep his hands busy, and keep peace in his own spirit.

Archie moved closer to the fire and spread his fingers before the warmth. "So the burner you ordered for the furnace didn't show up before the rains? Nobody delivered it?"

"Unfortunately, no."

"When it does, I'll come up to help you install it."

"That would be much appreciated, Arch."

"In the meantime, it's too bad there ain't none of those beauty queens around to keep you warm." Archie laughed at his observation, and Jorey joined him. The fact that Jorey only occasionally had the pleasure of a woman's company was a running joke with them. When Archie had asked him why, Jorey had explained that he was "discriminating." Archie assumed that meant a woman would have to be Miss America to catch Jorey's eye, and had never let it drop.

Jorey grinned to himself, thinking that if the old guy knew what was sleeping the day away in his bed at that very moment, he'd probably flip backwards in his rocking chair. Jorey stared into the fire, imagining what she looked like in there. She was likely curled up under his covers, a slender, raven-haired, hard-nippled cutie with a real bad attitude, a woman who lived the kind of life he'd happily left behind, a woman he had no business lusting after. He sighed, knowing that Kate Dreyfuss may be trapped in his lodge, but that didn't give him the right to imagine how good she'd feel trapped between his body and damp, twisted sheets.

Jorey blinked hard. To hell with the bridge. He'd have to find another way to get that woman on her way to Santa Fe so he could reclaim his balance.

"Hey, Arch? Do you think I could borrow Joan's gelding to—"

"Madre de Dios."

Jorey looked up to see Archie staring right past him and out the lobby's big picture window. He turned to find what fascinated Archie so, and barely made out a small human figure trudging down the road. The figure wore some kind of yellow rain poncho and lugged what looked like a suitcase.

Archie's mug of tea landed with a thud on the rocking chair armrest. "You devil," he said to Jorey when he turned back around. "Here we were worried you weren't prepared for the rains!"

"Uh—"

"I hate to bring this up, but it looks like she's trying to get away from you."

Ignoring Archie's ribbing, Jorey rose from his chair and moved to the window where he could watch Miss America herself, making decent progress down the lane despite the inappropriate footwear, the muck, and her suitcase.

Jorey peered closely and grinned to himself, appreciating how she'd strapped her large shoulder bag to the suitcase handle. "Now that's a girl with some serious baggage," Jorey muttered to himself.

"At least it's on wheels," Archie noted, and they both laughed.

Jorey put his hand on his neighbor's shoulder and gave him a friendly pat. "She's the no-show from last month I was telling you about. Got the dates mixed up. She marched up on my porch two nights ago, demanding to check in, all uppity because I didn't put out the welcome mat."

Archie looked shocked. "Two nights ago? Are you sure?"

Archie was in rare nonsensical form today, it seemed. "I'm sure, my friend."

The old man laughed and shook his head, then returned his gaze to the retreating figure. "She looks kind of cute from here, but I can't see too much under that poncho."

"She is cute."

One of Archie's eyebrows shot high on his forehead. He bit his lip in thought. "You don't got no rooms right now."

"That's right."

Archie was about to continue with the inquisition when he suddenly squinted and cocked his head. "Here comes the rain again, like I said. You better go bring that lady in while I head home to Joan."

"I think she's trying to walk down to Route Fifty-two," Jorey said with a sigh, grabbing his cowboy hat off the peg near the door and tugging it down on his head.

"Might take her a couple days at that pace." Archie's chuckle faded away once they got out on the porch. The rain was coming hard. "She knows to stay clear of the arroyos though, right?"

A sharp jolt of fear sliced through Jorey's gut. His head snapped around and he stared at Archie. "No."

"No?" The old man's forehead crinkled up like an accordion. "Take the horse."

Heart pounding, Jorey raced down the steps and onto the dirt plaza, running through the rain to the horse. He unlooped the reins, jumped on, and galloped down into the gully. Briefly, it occurred to him that he was not the most qualified of men to be sent on this mission. Up until five years ago, he'd known close to nothing about horses.

That concern evaporated the instant he rode up over the rise and saw Kate Dreyfuss standing in the exact spot he'd prayed she wouldn't be. He'd be rescuing her, all right. There was no option.

"Kate!" His voice seemed to stop dead in the air, never making it the couple hundred feet to where she stood, heels dug into the dirt, smack in the middle of a wash. She had her back to the mountains, pulling on the handle of her suitcase. The woman had no idea that her little episode of stubbornness had put her in harm's way.

Something made Jorey glance to the east. Through the curtain of rain falling off the brim of his hat he could barely make it out: A fresh surge of angry brown water was churning down the path of least resistance and racing right toward Kate. In his estimation, he had ten seconds—tops.

He turned the horse and pressed his heels into the animal's sides. "Kate!" he screamed at the top of his lungs, but with the beat of the rain and the cover of her poncho she till didn't hear. "Kate! Get out of the ditch!"

Jorey urged the horse on, trying to figure exactly how he was going to do what needed to be done. There was no time for planning and no time for prayer. He was going to have to wing this. So he closed his eyes for an instant, summoned the power and spirit of this place—*his place*—and made it happen. The horse knew what they were attempting was just plain foolish, and balked, but Jorey forced him on.

"Kate! Grab my arm!"

Her head popped up, and her eyes went wide with shock at the sight of him racing toward her like a crazy man, his arm stretched down and out. Kate began to back away, but she must have felt a rumble. She looked to her left, up toward the mountains, and her eyes filled with terror. She let go of the suitcase handle, screamed, and snagged Jorey's forearm the exact second the horse thundered through the ditch, its hoofs splashing through the first kiss of water.

Kate leaped into the air just as Jorey pulled, and the saddle girth began to slip sideways from the tug of their combined body weight. With all his might, Jorey pressed his leg down into the opposite stirrup, and for a split second everything was happening at once—Kate was flying, the horse was carrying them up and out of the raging water, the saddle was sliding, and Jorey was once again thinking that he was thoroughly unqualified to be handling this situation.

But Kate helped tremendously by throwing her leg up and over the horse's back, causing the saddle to right, just as she landed with a thud tight against Jorey's back.

"Oh, my God!" Kate screeched, clutching onto his waist so tight the air whooshed out of his lungs.

Jorey tried to slow the now-panicking horse. The animal not only realized that water rushed behind them, but the ditch in front of them was swollen as well.

"Hold on tight!" Jorey screamed through the rain. "The horse is frightened!"

"No shit!" Kate yelled into his ear. "My suitcase! My suitcase! Everything's in there—my Blackberry! My Jimmy Choos! My . . . my . . . *everything!*"

Jorey was marveling at how she could still be attached to material things at a time like this, when he felt her body heave against him. She was sobbing. She continued to sob as the horse bucked and complained, and the rain began to beat down even harder.

They were alive. They were, at least temporarily, still in the saddle. And the rain would stop, of that he was sure. Jorey knew he needed to stay focused in the moment, the one in which he was living right then. He breathed deep, felt the blood return to his limbs, felt his lungs expand with wet air. He focused on sending his own calm into the animal and the woman connected to his body.

As the horse continued to buck and whinny, Jorey began to

whisper a stanza from one of his favorite Native American prayers, a Zuni night chant:

> *"Breathing in—I am alive*
> *Breathing out—I am alive*
> *In this precious moment*
> *In this sacred place*
> *In the Abundance of Love*
> *I dwell."*

He whispered the chant over and over and over, until he felt the horse's legs quiet and Kate's shaking sobs lessen and eventually stop. Within minutes, the rain ceased as abruptly as it had started. The sky began to clear. Jorey thought they must look odd—a man and a woman and a horse perched on a bit of dry land no bigger than a throw rug, nature swirling around them. He felt Kate's cheek press harder into his back, her breath steady. He felt her heat—even through the layers of wet clothing and the plastic rain poncho—he still felt the life force burst from that small female body.

"Are you all right, Kate?"

The poncho crinkled as she adjusted her position. "I think so." Her voice sounded small and far away. "Are you?"

Jorey needed to touch her, but found his fingers nearly paralyzed around the reins. He pried them free and cupped his palm over the back of Kate's small hand, still gripped tight around his middle. "I'm okay. We're all going to be just fine, Princess."

She was silent for a moment, then said, "Just because you saved my life doesn't mean you can call me Princess." Then she squeezed him tighter still.

Kate could not stop shaking and she could not stop crying. It didn't matter that six hours had passed since Jorey had saved her and they'd made it back to the lodge with body and soul intact. It didn't matter that she'd had a long, comforting chat with Jorey's neighbor, an older lady named Joan. It didn't matter that she'd taken a hot shower, eaten two servings of Joan's oven-baked rice pudding, and that she was safe and warm and dry.

Kate knew that something had thoroughly and finally broken apart inside her that day. It was a dramatic finish to the crumbling that began three months ago, with the Brad fiasco, and just kept going, one mishap after another. For a while now, Kate had sensed that something she'd carefully constructed was coming unglued, and there was no way she'd ever get the pieces to fit together the same way again. Maybe she didn't want it to. Maybe she was now forced to find another way to be in the world, a way that required less of a fight. But what that would look like—and how she'd get there—was a mystery.

She sighed, letting her head fall back against the rocker, staring out at the gloomy mountain range. She felt raw in her soul. She felt hollowed out. Strangely disconnected.

Probably because her Blackberry was somewhere in the Gulf of Mexico by now.

"You look better in that robe than I ever did." Jorey closed the sliding glass door to the back porch and walked up behind her. "Feel like some company?"

Kate nodded, gesturing to the empty rocking chair to her right, a little self-conscious that she was in nothing but Jorey's blue-and-white striped cotton bathrobe. She fiddled with the sash and made sure the lapels crossed high on her chest.

"Why, thank you ma'am," Jorey said, sinking back into the seat and stretching out his long legs, resting his sock-covered feet on the railing. Kate glanced in his direction and noticed immediately that he'd shaved, leaving his face looking serene and younger. He was once again wearing those forest-green lounge pants she loved so much. Thank God he'd been kind enough to wear a white T-shirt. She didn't think she was strong enough to resist him otherwise.

Because right that instant, nothing sounded better to Kate than a little skin-to-skin comfort, and there wasn't anyone in the world she'd rather have it with than Jorey.

He was quiet. He rocked back and forth with slight presses of his heels against the railing, looking out at the view. Jorey's entire demeanor seemed peaceful, like nothing out of the ordinary had happened that day.

Kate cleared her throat. "Is it pretty here when it's not overcast?"

Jorey grinned. "This is a fluke. You usually can't spend a whole day in New Mexico without seeing the blue sky we're so famous for. And the light here . . . it's amazing."

"Then why is it raining so much?"

"November and December make up the rainy season. Some years, that amounts to a quarter inch. Other years, it's like this—a real mess."

Kate said nothing for a while, just listened to the squeak of the rocking chairs and the rhythm of their breathing. "What was that poem you said out there today? It was beautiful."

"Yeah, it is." Jorey nodded. "It's part of a chant the Zuni people use to pray under the night sky. I've always loved it. It's so simple, but it says it all."

It took her several long moments, but eventually Kate said what she'd been leading up to this whole conversation. "I am a complete idiot. What I did was stupid, and I'm sorry!"

Jorey shrugged, never interrupting his steady rock. "Nothing is stupid if you learn something from it."

Kate laughed at the kindness in his voice. Jorey almost sounded like he didn't want to hurt her feelings.

"It was a stupid, stupid, *stupid* thing to do and you know it. Sometimes I amaze myself at how bullheaded I can be." She truly didn't want this, but the tears started again, and Kate used the baggy sleeve of the robe to wipe her cheeks. "I didn't even know where I was going, for God's sake! Where was I headed? What was I thinking? Now I don't even have a change of underwear!"

"Underwear is overrated," Jorey said, trying unsuccessfully to hide his amusement—she'd already gotten a glimpse of the skin crinkling around his eye and the arrival of that dimple. "Besides—" Jorey turned to her, then reached out to tuck a piece of hair behind Kate's ear. "My damsel-in-distress technique was getting a little rusty. I haven't had to snatch a babe from the jaws of death for weeks now."

She let go with a little snort of a laugh and continued to wipe her cheeks, trying not to feel too much of anything about the fact that Jorey hadn't stopped with that single touch of her hair. He was caressing her—his fingertips stroked her from the top of her head to where her hair fell on her shoulders. And she loved it. It felt wonderful—even though it was completely inappropriate. It felt too intimate. She hadn't given him permission to touch her like that. She cried some more, and the more she cried, the more Jorey's hand soothed her, permission or no.

Kate never cried. She couldn't stomach it in others and especially herself. The idea that she was crying in front of Jorey made her cringe. She'd spent her whole life proving to people that she wasn't a wimp, that for a woman her size she packed a wallop. She had brains, guts, beauty, savviness. She'd never needed anyone. Brad was a nice addition, but he hadn't been key to her satisfaction. She knew better than to give a man that much power over her happiness. It had always been her goal to be at the helm of her own ship.

So why did she suddenly feel like she was the captain of the *Titanic*? Why had she grieved so when Brad left her? Was she aching for what she'd never had instead of what she she'd lost? Was she crying because she was beginning to understand the depth of her emptiness—an emptiness she had with or without Brad?

"Maybe there was a reason you came here when you did, Kate." Jorey took his hand from her hair and placed it on her forearm, where she could feel the heat of his touch through the thin cotton fabric of the robe.

Kate sniffled. "The reason I'm here is that I never even looked at the dates on the brochure, and our office assistant—Monica's nephew—was in charge of my itinerary. Spencer is always sleep deprived from playing with his punk rock band in seedy L.A. bars, so details tend to slip through the cracks."

"Actually, Kate," Jorey said, the amusement clear in his voice. "What I was getting at was that it was destiny that you came when you did."

His words made her slightly uncomfortable. Was he hitting on her? Sure, the comments about her nipples and the flirty way he'd been teasing her—calling her Princess—that could possibly be considered hitting. But this? This was definitely hitting. Kate changed the subject. "Anyway, who is Monica to tell me I need to repair my spirituality? It's none of her business what's going on inside me."

"Unless it affects her bottom line. Then it's her business—literally."

Kate dragged her gaze from the dramatic landscape to Jorey's face. His eyes were kind, but the slight smile on his lips indicated he knew exactly what he was doing. He was prodding her, egging her on. It seemed to be a good-natured prodding, affectionate even, but he sure was enjoying himself.

"Maybe I was sent here to entertain Jorey Matheny, the lonely, vegetarian innkeeper."

Jorey's smile spread wide across his face. "I really like you, Kate," he said matter-of-factly.

Oh, what the hell, Kate thought to herself. *I can be just as direct as he can.* "I like you, too, Jorey."

"Then talk to me. Tell me about you."

"Uh . . ." Kate tucked her feet under her bottom and the rocker moved as she did. She fought the trembling she felt in her chin. She didn't want to cry anymore. She felt like such a wimp. "Things are kind of a mess for me right now."

"In what way?"

She took a big breath. "About three months ago, I completely spaced on a meeting and lost Monica's biggest client," she whispered.

"Ouch."

"Yeah. That was right after my boyfriend ran off with a woman so young that she decorated her bedroom in the SpongeBob SquarePants period."

Jorey's eyebrows arched high in surprise. "That's gotta hurt."

"Then my brother decided he was a woman trapped in a man's body."

"Sounds uncomfortable."

Seeing as how she was being spontaneous, Kate decided to move her arm from under Jorey's touch and just go straight for hand-holding. When she wrapped her fingers around Jorey's, he let go with an "Mmmm" of approval. "I totaled my Range Rover."

"So you said." He gently squeezed her fingers.

"I broke my nose. You should have seen it a few days after—I looked like road kill."

"It's healing great."

"I think I'm really starting to hate my job. Actually, I think I've always hated my job but figured everybody did, so why shouldn't I have to follow the same rules?"

Jorey chuckled softly. "We can make our own rules, Kate."

"And then—he's okay now—but my dad had a heart attack." Kate gulped back a sob and used her free hand to brush her cheek dry.

"*Ahhh.*" When Jorey cupped Kate's hand in both of his, warm sparks of awareness traveled through her body. "Now there's a topic I know a whole lot about, sweetheart."

Kate jerked back slightly to stare at him. Jorey had turned his body to face her and it was obvious he was not joking. "*You've* had a heart attack?" she asked, her voice high with surprise. "Mr. Barley Vegetable Soup?"

He chuckled and squeezed her hand tighter. "Seven years and three months ago. I was thirty-eight, working like a madman, sleeping five hours a night if I was lucky, paying no attention to what I ate or how negative my thoughts were. I didn't get out and move my body and I didn't have the guts to get out of a marriage that had never fed my soul—your basic textbook setup for blowing a gasket."

Kate felt her mouth fall open.

"It's really true what they say—something like that can be a wake-up call, a reminder that we are largely responsible for our own well-being, that some things in this life really are more important than others."

Her hand in his suddenly felt too intimate, and Kate pulled it away. She crossed her arms over her chest and allowed all the new information to sink in. Jorey was divorced. He was on the mend from a serious illness. He used to live the kind of life she still did. "So you're not from here?"

Jorey laughed. "Nope. I grew up in San Bernardino and went to UCLA for my degree in architecture. Lived in Palo Alto for several years, then settled in Seattle. I only bought this place five years ago, after my life went to hell. New Mexico has allowed me to heal. Windwalker Lodge was my medicine."

Kate nodded, not sure what to say. There was no such thing as small talk with Jorey, and she felt like she was using muscles she didn't even know she had.

"So you've been fixing it up?"

"A little bit each year during the off-season."

"The kitchen is beautiful. Did you do that yourself?"

"I did."

Kate was quiet for a long moment. She could hear Jorey's steady and slow breath next to her. "You're healthy now though, right? Your heart is good?"

"I'm better than good."

"So . . ." Kate tried to sound casual, though her heart was beating fast. She wanted to know everything about this man. She wasn't sure when she'd decided that. "How long were you married, Jorey?"

"Nine years. Have you ever been married?"

Kate snorted. "Oh God, no."

"Not the marrying kind?" Jorey produced a lopsided smile.

"Sure I am." Kate hugged herself tighter. "The snag has always been the fact that the right man has never wanted to marry *me*."

Jorey's grin expanded. "I'm sure it's time-consuming interviewing all those applicants."

"Ha." Kate shook her head. "Frankly, I think I scare men."

"It's your aura, sweetheart."

She stared at him and blinked, letting the disappointment thud inside her. She realized Jorey was a bit eccentric, but she'd never had patience for the outlandish. "Please don't tell me you're into that stuff."

Jorey leaned back into the chair and rocked for a few minutes, a faraway look in his eyes. "You were really angry when you got here the other night."

"I was tired. I had to use the bathroom like you wouldn't believe. And you left me standing on the porch in the cold."

He laughed. "I apologize for that. But it was more than just impatience—I could feel the negative energy pouring off of you. The next morning, in the daylight, I saw it in all its glory—anger and frustration and sadness in a rainbow of reds and purples and oranges. It was a physical manifestation. I could literally see it hovering around you."

Kate blinked. She had no idea what to say.

"It's very different today, Kate. It's calmer. I see some green and blue. I can see your beauty today." Jorey paused as if to consider whether he should continue. He did. "You are a beautiful woman, Kate."

"Thank you." She swallowed hard. She was turned on, touched by his sweetness, and very, very interested. "While I'm at it, I should probably thank you for saving my life, shouldn't I?"

Kate untucked her legs and leaned close to Jorey. Her strategy was to give him a sweet and chaste kiss of appreciation. Like everything else recently, it didn't quite happen according to plan.

Kate saw the look of surprise in Jorey's eyes as she brought her face to his. She gave him a friendly smile just before she pressed her lips to his.

All rightee, then.

Jorey's mouth was hot and sweet. His lips parted on contact, and she both heard and felt him moan his pleasure. In an instant, the kiss had gone from friendly to flaming. His hands were in her hair. She was half in his lap. He licked at the inside of her mouth and bit her lips. She groaned out her pleasure and sucked on his tongue. Then, as fast as it started, Kate stopped it.

"Yes. So . . ." Kate retreated back to her rocker, her whole body vibrating with desire. Her hands trembled as she adjusted the lapel of the bathrobe. "As I was saying, thank you for saving my life."

Jorey stared at her and blinked a few times. "Not a problem," he croaked out, beginning to rise from the rocker. He stopped, pressing his palms to his knees, still staring at her. "Would you like some tea?"

"Sure," she said.

Jorey rubbed a hand over his smooth chin, as if its hairless state fascinated him as much as it did her. He shook his head and smiled. "You should know that in many of the Pueblo Indian traditions, if you save someone's life they become part of you forever. The bond can never be broken, not by distance or even death."

Kate could barely breathe. She didn't know what to say, and was shocked to realize how much Jorey excited her. It was probably his voice. Or that dimple. Or those damn lounge pants.

No, it wasn't any of those things. It was because he was the most intriguing, complex, handsome man she'd ever met, and that kiss was better than most of the actual sex she'd had in last fifteen years of her life.

"Really?" Kate asked, quite breathless. "Is all that stuff true?"

Jorey rose to his feet and gave a sheepish shrug. "Hell if I know, but it sure sounds good, doesn't it?"

3

Alone in the kitchen, Jorey put the kettle on the stove, leaned his hands on the countertop, and took a few deep, steadying breaths. What the hell was he doing? If he kept this up, he was fairly certain he'd be in bed with Kate within the hour. Of course, she could always say no. He'd been shot down his share of times, and he'd just bet that Kate was well versed in the art. But there was something happening here with her. He felt it. Her brittle outer shell was cracking, and inside was real warmth, humor, and a whole lot of sexy. Though she might argue otherwise, he'd noticed that Kate's face was an open window to the complex spirit that lived within her. Her eyes revealed sharp intelligence, stubbornness, and a vulnerability he found irresistible. Despite the hard-ass exterior, Kate possessed a refined beauty that intoxicated him. Jorey groaned out loud and raked his fingers through his hair in frustration. The idea that his ratty old robe had been in direct contact with her nubile flesh all afternoon was making him crazy. It was also making his dick hard, and not for the first time since she'd come banging on his door. Jorey squeezed his eyes shut, remembering how he'd been so turned on by the sight of that angry, strikingly attractive nymph on his porch two nights ago that he had to delay opening the door.

As he gathered the mugs, honey, and spoons, he confirmed to himself that Kate's aura had indeed mellowed. It was now a manageable halo of purples and blues, outlined by the thinnest red overlay. The muscles of her face were beginning to relax and the dark circles under her eyes had faded. He'd seen her soft pink lips part in a genuine smile several times that afternoon. Even her voice had changed, and she'd been talking in a low, sleepy voice that made him think of secrets shared after sex—intimate and erotic. Oh yes, Kate was a babe, but for the first time, he was beginning to see the real beauty in her.

Jorey laughed at himself. He'd been just about to return to the porch when he realized Kate would have to wait for her tea, seeing as how he was once again afflicted with a case of hard-on related bad manners.

He sat down to wait it out, thinking this through. He'd never put much credence in coincidence. He'd seen enough to know that things usually happened for a reason. So there had to be a reason Kate Dreyfuss was delivered to his doorstep when she was, commanded to stay put by the forces of nature, and left stranded with only one pair of underwear to her name. Some things were just too perfect to be coincidence.

But the rain couldn't last forever, fluke or no. Jorey knew the sky would clear, bringing with it a sharp, blue world and dry roads. He and Archie would have the bridge repaired in a matter of hours. And there'd be no reason for Kate to linger at Windwalker Lodge—no reason for her to give herself time to rest, think, and just be. No reason for her to stay awhile longer with him.

Unless he gave her one.

With that goal in mind, Jorey found that he was presentable enough to return to the back porch. The sun was about to set behind the house, and the air had turned chilly. He placed the mugs on a table and turned to Kate with a smile. "Are you cold? I can get you a—"

Jorey stopped in midsentence, the oddest sensation of tenderness spreading through him as he looked at her. Kate was asleep, with her cheek pressed against the slats of the rocker. Her mouth was slightly open and—oh, boy—so was the neckline of the robe. Seeing her like this, so pure and quiet, made him want to rock her in his arms and protect her until his last breath.

His knees felt weak. Jorey collapsed into the rocker next to hers, put his chin in his hands, and simply observed.

It was fascinating how much activity took place in her stillness. The creamy peach flesh of her breasts rose and fell with her soft breath. A few strands of dark hair ruffled in the puff of breeze. Her thick eyelashes twitched as she dreamed. He could see her pulse beat just under the pale skin at her throat. Clearly, almost dying could take a lot out of a person.

Jorey chuckled to himself, stretched and yawned, and got up to open the sliding doors to the lodge. He quietly returned to Kate, bent down, and positioned his forearm under her knees. She stirred but didn't wake, so he slid his other arm around her back and lifted. As he adjusted Kate's weight, she grunted slightly and nuzzled her nose and mouth into his T-shirt. She was a solid little armful, and the feel of her thighs against the inside of his wrist just about did him in.

"Mmmmm." Kate snuggled closer and threw her arm around his neck, which struck him as a rather advanced move for a woman who was supposed to be asleep.

Jorey used his foot to shut the sliding door behind him and

carried his warm bundle of captive to his bedroom, where he carefully lowered her onto the sheets.

"Please stay."

Her whisper startled Jorey, and he pulled his arm out from under her back and straightened up enough to see her face. Those eyes were wide open, and the ice blue he'd once seen there had transformed into a color that was hot and alive and dancing with need.

"Do you always talk in your sleep, Princess?"

She laughed, and Jorey enjoyed seeing how easily her face blossomed in laughter. "It's handy when I'd prefer not to be accountable for what I'm saying."

"Really now?" Jorey brought his fingers up to brush the side of Kate's face. Her skin was smooth and warm to his touch, and at close range he could make out a million details of her, details he planned to memorize. Like the tiny nick of a scar below her left eye, the dainty crests of her upper lip, the fragile swirl of her ear. "Are you going to give me an example?"

Kate scrunched up her brow in a pretend moment of concentration. "Well, you know, I could say something nonsensical like, 'Don't forget to put plastic wrap on the potato salad.' "

"I can see why you'd not want to be held accountable for a statement like that."

She giggled. "Or maybe something like, 'Ooh, baby, baby, don't stop!' "

"Now we're getting somewhere," Jorey allowed his weight to settle against her small body. "Please go on."

Kate's amused expression softened and her voice lowered to a whisper. "I could say something like, 'That was the best freakin' kiss I've ever had in my life and I want more.' "

With a chuckle, Jorey pressed his hips into her, enjoying the way her thighs opened beneath him. He couldn't help himself—he lowered his lips to her throat and kissed and sucked, flicking his tongue on the delicate skin offered to him.

"Oh, God," Kate gasped.

After a few delicious moments of feeding on Kate's neck and shoulders, he raised his mouth to cover hers. He kissed her with purpose. He wanted her to know exactly what he intended—that he intended to be inside her, that he wanted to know her, body and soul. She opened her mouth to him, soft and wet and sweet, and he felt himself burn with passion for this woman. Her slim arms clutched at his back and pulled him tighter. As they kissed, Jorey let his hands explore the soft curves of her body, the slight swell of her hips, the inward curve of her waist, the plump handfuls that were her breasts. He allowed himself to fall into her, melt in the heat of her fire.

While drowning in this kiss, Jorey scooped Kate into his arms and rolled to his left, pulling her on top of him. In a single, seamless move, he brought his hands to the sash of the old bathrobe, yanked it open, and finally, blissfully, placed his palms on the bare skin of Kate's breasts.

Kate gasped again and raised her mouth from his. He took that opportunity to open the robe entirely, and the sight that blessed his eyes was almost too beautiful to be true.

"Anything else you'd like to say before you wake up?" As he teased her with his words, Jorey pressed his hands up the front of Kate's taut torso, bounced the weight of her breasts, then teased her luscious pink-brown nipples to hard points.

"Oh yes," Kate hissed, throwing back her head and arching her breasts into his hands. "I got a whole bunch of things I'd like to get out of my system."

As much as he adored the feel of her breasts in his hands, Jorey needed to explore all of her. When he grabbed the curve of her ass, the top of his head nearly blew off. She was perfect—solid with muscle and pliant with girl flesh. He smacked his hands down on her two buttocks. "I'm ready to hear it all, Princess."

"Okay." Her answer came out in a little whine that sounded almost like discomfort. That would work for Jorey. He wanted her uncomfortable—uncomfortable with need and desperate from the void she now recognized. Then he would sate that need and fill that void.

"Make love to me, Jorey," Kate said, her eyes half closed. She began to churn her hips against him. Jorey lowered his gaze, and as he helped move her bottom, he stared at the juncture of her perfect thighs—a small dark triangle of hair that couldn't hide her hunger. He caught a glimpse of pink inner flesh, swollen and wet with arousal. He wanted that wet flesh so damn bad. He wanted it more than he'd ever wanted anything in his life. How did it come this far this fast with Kate? He'd never acted like this in his life. What was it about her that made him lose his balance like this?

"I want you to fuck my aura into Texas," she said.

Jorey half moaned and half laughed as it all became clear to him—Kate was a woman he could love. She was funny and smart, and he had the feeling he was just about to discover that she was a hot little thing in bed, a world-class sexual experience.

"I want to rip off your shirt," she told him.

Not wanting to make the lady wait, Jorey obliged, holding his arms over his head and leaning forward enough for her to grab the bottom hem and pull the shirt over his head. She threw it across the room.

Without delay, Kate bent down and put her lips on his abdomen and kissed him, nipped him, then stroked her tongue from the tented waistband of his pants to his left nipple. Then she did it again, detouring to his right nipple.

"Anything else you need to say while you're asleep?" Jorey

croaked out. "You might want to get it all out while your mouth is still free."

Kate stopped licking and looked up at him with those blue eyes now clouded with lust. She smiled at him. "You're awfully rowdy for a reclusive innkeeper."

"When provoked, yes."

"I like rowdy."

"Good. We're going to get along just fine, then. Now tell me more."

"Would it be all right if I just show you?"

Jorey nodded, trying to keep his eyes focused but feeling faint. His dick was so hard he was afraid that if she touched it—merely breathed on it—he'd explode. Rowdy was fine, but he knew that a man of his seasoned age would be expected to have perfected some level of self-control.

Kate lowered her mouth to the front of his pajama pants. With the gentlest pressure, she bit on his cock through the fabric. Jorey throbbed under her ministrations, and he closed his eyes tight and fought off the urge to come. He thought of when the boiler would be delivered, and where in the barn he'd stashed the spare four-by-six he'd need to fix the bridge.

Kate released a hot breath, and Jorey felt it seep past the cotton and coat his cock with velvet agony. Then she put her soft, wet mouth over the head of his dick and began to suck on him through the material. Her pull was gentle and her rhythm was pure bliss, and he knew if he couldn't feel the direct heat of her bare lips on his flesh *right now* he would die.

She read his mind, and brought her little hands to his waistband, pulled it up and over his erection, and dragged the pants down his thighs, past his knees, and off the edge of his feet. She threw the pajamas across the room, and while she was standing, she let his old bathrobe slip away from her shoulders and fall to the floor. There she stood at the foot of the bed, naked, grinning, and clearly thrilled with what he had to offer her.

Her eyes got wide and she stared at his erection. "This wasn't in the brochure, was it?"

Jorey laughed. "This is the private tour."

"Right. I remember now." Kate bent forward and began to crawl up the bed, straddling Jorey's legs, her gorgeous breasts swaying with each bit of progress she made. *"Remove your clothes and take a pilgrimage into the landscape of your guide's bed . . ."* She was clearly enjoying herself.

"Fine. An invitation-only private tour."

She'd returned to her previous position, her mouth hovering over his jutting erection. She looked up at him with amusement. *"Experience the deep relaxation of the optional hot cock massage . . ."*

"You're killing me, Kate."

"I apologize. Let me make it up to you."

Pure ecstasy.

Complete sensation.

Torture and bliss and the power of all of nature built up in him as she sucked and licked and breathed on him. When she put a small, soft hand on his balls, he knew that the years of meditation training, yoga, visualization, and deep personal exploration didn't mean jack. He was going to blow.

"Baby, unless you want me coming in your mouth, you've got to stop."

Kate stopped. She dragged her lips off him, tilted her head inquisitively, and smiled. "I thought that was the whole point." Then she resumed sucking.

"Oh, shit," Jorey gasped. "I'll make up for this. You'll just have to give me about twenty minutes."

With that, Kate pushed down and took him into her throat. Jorey's entire being tensed and the colors of the rainbow raced through his mind and he began thrusting up into her. The entire universe had been reduced to the feel of his cock gripped tight in her mouth and throat, the wet silk of her tongue, and what felt like a lifetime of pent-up energy now ready to explode into her.

The force of his release obviously surprised Kate, and he felt her back away slightly to accommodate his offering.

Talk about near-death experiences—Jorey felt as though he'd lost his soul for a moment, felt that he'd been shot off into the black nothingness of the universe, only to be snatched back into joy. He heard his own howl of happiness ring in his ears.

He gasped for breath and pulled Kate up to him. He hugged her so hard he feared he'd crack her bones. Her soft giggle tickled the hair on his chest.

"I think you liked that," she whispered.

It took him a few seconds to get his lips to work. "God, Kate. That was . . . I can't . . ." He pulled her tighter. "That was such a gift. It was wonderful, and you are . . . wow . . ." Jorey used his fingertips to raise her chin and he kissed her, hoping that his kiss would convey all the things he was incapable of telling her with words. He kissed his thank-you into her. He kissed his amazement into her. He inhaled the genuine affection he felt pouring from Kate, and served it right back to her.

She was an equal partner in the communion of that kiss—completely present—and by the time the kiss ended, they both knew they'd reached an understanding. He and Kate had begun their own pilgrimage, and Jorey already knew it would be a trip of a lifetime.

"For a woman who doesn't *do* breakfast, you're doing a great impression of a teenage ranch hand."

Kate nodded in agreement, but she couldn't say anything, because her mouth was full. Jorey was right—she didn't remember the last time she'd eaten a real breakfast, let alone a three-egg omelet made with organic soy cheese and vegetarian sausage crumbles, a grapefruit, and three pieces of rich, hot cornbread smothered in strawberry jam.

"More cornbread?" he asked, grinning at her.

She shook her head and wiped her mouth with a napkin. While she was at it, she brushed away the cornbread crumbs that had fallen on the front of the old blue striped robe.

Kate sank into the kitchen chair and sighed deeply. This feeling was alien to Kate, and she was consciously trying to accept it and not fight it off. She was *relaxed*—that was the only word to describe it. Her bones felt like they'd been slow-roasted by the heat of multiple orgasms. The urgent chattering in her mind had been silenced by extremely good sex. Her lips were a little sore from all the kissing, but her soul was soothed.

"How are you, Princess?" Jorey smiled, leaning back and putting his hands behind his head.

"I'm full. Real full." Kate folded her hands in her lap.

"You were full all night."

She opened one eye to look at him. Rowdy? Oh, yes. Slightly warped? That too. Who'd have guessed that a man who lived alone in the wilderness, eschewed real coffee, and could recite Indian chants, would be the world's best lover?

"And you're quite full of yourself."

Jorey sighed and nodded, bringing his arms down in front of him on the table. "Bear with me, sweetheart. It's been a long time since I've done anything that gloat-worthy."

"Hah." Kate stood up and loosened the robe sash to accommodate breakfast. "I bet it was just another one of those flukes of nature. Are you done?" She'd reached for Jorey's plate, but he grabbed her wrist.

"Something that happens a bunch of times in a row is hardly a fluke. Like your orgasms—were all those flukes?"

Kate laughed, turned, and plopped down in his lap. She put her arms around his neck and gave him a kiss. "That was more like a crack in the space-time continuum."

"Hmm," he said, nuzzling her breast. "Have I told you how good you smell? How good you taste? Feel? Look? How good you sound when you're coming?"

"You have, Jorey." Kate kissed the top of his head and smiled big into his thick, dark curls. "Not that I'm complaining."

When she felt Jorey's mouth root around through the fabric of the robe looking for a nipple, a hot rush went through her belly. When he bit down gently she gasped with pleasure, then put a hand against his shoulder. "Hey, I thought you wanted to drywall today."

"It can wait." Jorey's hand traveled up inside the robe and squeezed her thigh.

"And I thought you wanted to go down and check on the bridge."

"I'd rather go down on you. Open your legs."

"Oh, God."

"Come on, open up, my sweet Kate. I'm still hungry."

"Oh my God!"

In a single motion, Jorey raised her off his lap and perched her on the edge of the breakfast table. He used his forearm to sweep away the remnants of his meal and make a spot for Kate to lie back. "Daddy needs another piece," he murmured, just as he placed his mouth on her pussy.

Kate didn't know whether to laugh or cry. Jorey was so free with himself, so free to be unusual or intense or just flat-out goofy. He was open and loose with his desire, and she didn't think she'd ever known a man with that kind of pure approach. There was no bullshit with Jorey Matheny—just passion and a need to connect.

His tongue was hot and smooth and insistent as he entered her, slid up and down her opening, and flicked at her. It was too much. She let her head fall back to the tabletop and she simply surrendered. What was there to hold on to?

Nothing.

Did her heart belong to someone else?

No, it had never belonged to anyone.

Had she already experienced all there was to life?

No.

Love?

She hadn't even started.

Was there room in her world for something good and powerful and important? Was there a place for something real? Would she finally let it happen in her life?

"Yes! Oh, Jorey, yes!"

The waves of pleasure and fire pounded her, spreading from her core to her fingers and toes. The joy was overwhelming, and it compounded as she felt her body lifted, her center pierced, her weight supported in this man's hands. Jorey's mouth covered hers with urgency. He sucked at her, nipped at her, flicked his tongue along hers. With each relentless kiss he breathed life into her. With each deep thrust of his cock, he blessed her with a rush of pleasure.

Over and over Jorey lifted her, brought her back down, and buried himself fully, his moans growing louder as his drives intensified. Jorey walked with Kate out the kitchen doorway and into the lobby, his mouth and his cock never letting up. Kate clasped her hands around his neck and held on—she was incapable of doing anything else.

Jorey made it all the way to the bedroom, and though he laughed at the unceremonious way they tumbled to the mattress together, he never broke his rhythm with Kate. He was relentless with her, driving into her hard, his eyes focused on hers.

Kate heard her own voice cry out his name as she gripped him tight against her. How could this be? How could she be so changed by this man, so fast? How could he have shown her something this wonderful this soon?

Another orgasm crashed into her, just as Jorey roared and tensed up, then exploded. Kate grabbed him tighter as the waves of hot release rolled over them both, and in that moment she felt her heart break away from its confines. She knew that a few days in a rambling adobe lodge without heat had lit a fire inside her. She knew that, courtesy of Jorey, the world had just opened up and the ice had melted away. They spent the whole day in a cycle of lovemaking and sleep, and after the sun had set they stumbled out to sit on cushions in front of the fireplace, where they ate apples and peanut butter—naked. When they were done, she took his hands in hers.

"I have a lot of vacation time coming to me. I just wanted you to know." Kate swallowed hard. She was taking a risk and she knew it. She'd never really been in love, but it occurred to her that this might be what it's all about—feeling more hope than fear, and acting on it.

Jorey's expression said it all. The flesh around his dark eyes wrinkled. His dimple appeared and his smile spread from one side of that handsome face to the other. "So how long can you stay with me, Kate?"

"I've worked it all out. Here." She reached for the piece of scrap paper she'd left on the table behind them and handed it to Jorey.

He squinted at her doodling and laughed. "Are you serious?"

"Oh yeah. I've had three weeks of vacation and two weeks of sick time each year I've worked for Monica, and I've never used a day of it. That's five weeks each year over a period of seven years, or thirty-five weeks. That's eight months, give or take a few days or however long I've been up here already."

One of Jorey's eyebrows arched high on his forehead. "You've only got one set of clothes," he reminded her, still laughing.

"In case you haven't noticed, that's turned out to be one more than I've needed." Kate glanced down at herself and shook her head in amazement that she'd actually felt comfortable eating *naked* with a man. She smiled when Jorey reached over and wiped a smidge of peanut butter from her cheek and licked his finger. "By the way, what day is it?" She sat up straighter. "I'm so out of it I don't even know what day it is!"

Jorey lunged for her, rolled with her on the floor, and landed on top of her. He pinned her wrists to the pile of cushions beneath them. "It's the best day of my life, Princess," was his answer.

The sky had been so clean and blue the last two days that if it weren't for Archie's continual teasing that she brought the rains with her, Kate would have completely forgotten the gloom. She stuck her shovel in the sandy dirt and looked up to see Jorey's neighbor smiling at her—again.

"Now, any woman who'll dig a hole for you is a real keeper," Archie said.

A lopsided grin appeared on Jorey's face as he tightened the last remaining bolt on the bridge support. He gave the post a hearty slap of approval. "The girl sure knows her tools," he replied, winking at her in case she didn't catch the inside joke.

Kate snorted. "Okay, guys. I'm done for. See you up at the lodge."

"We're driving the truck back in a few minutes," Archie said. "Wanna ride?"

Kate dismissed his offer with a friendly smile and a wave. "No, thanks. I'd like to walk. It's a beautiful day." She began to walk up the road.

"Then walk in beauty, dear."

Kate stopped. She turned around to study Archie. A big smile spread over his weatherbeaten face, and his dark eyes danced. He was an odd old man, and she remembered how calm he'd been in the moments after Jorey brought the horse back to dry ground. He soothed the animal in what was obviously a Native American language. Jorey later told her it was Navajo.

"Thank you," she said. "I will do that."

Walk in beauty. The words repeated in Kate's mind, proving the backdrop to the beat of her borrowed boots on the already dry earth. She produced a wistful smile and stared over the scrubby desert landscape, remembering the split second before her luggage was whisked away. There were some beautiful things in that La Tour Eiffel rolling suitcase—and every one of them were replaceable. Jorey had offered to drive down to the Chama River to see if anything had washed up, but suggested she not get her hopes too high.

Walk in beauty. Kate concentrated on the rhythm of her breathing, the way she and Jorey had practiced yesterday. As they sat cross-legged on the floor, he spoke of how to use breath to stay connected. "When we are alone, the shadows can creep in, bringing negativity and fear," he said. "Just remember to breathe, and know that we would not be able to appreciate the glow of the light, if it wasn't for the contrast provided by shadow."

She'd never been a real fan of yoga—it never seemed like she was *doing* anything—but then again, she'd never had an instructor as handsome, as sweet, and as patient as Jorey. She'd also never had an instructor who promised that if she mastered the basics, they could move right on to the tantric sex part.

Walk in beauty. The lodge appeared as she made progress up the slight hill. Its earth-tone adobe walls and fences were low-slung and rounded, and if it weren't for the bright blue shutters and trim the lodge would have been camouflaged by its surroundings. It used to be a convent, Jorey said. And it was quite run-down when he bought it. Kate smiled at how charming he'd made it, a reflection his own unassuming serenity.

Joan had mentioned that the phone lines were back up, and once she got to the lodge and made sure her help wasn't needed with dinner, Kate planned to call Monica and break the news. She wondered how exactly she'd put it . . . *Looks like I'm running a little late, Mon. Don't expect me until the Fourth of July, next year.*

"Is the bridge back in business?" The second she'd heard the heavy front door close, Joan had poked her head around the kitchen archway. Kate looked up at her as she tugged off the too-small cowboy boots.

"Yep!" She hopped around on one foot, then the other.

Joan laughed and wiped her hands on a kitchen towel as she made her way across the large lobby. "Sorry I have such darn tiny feet. It runs in my family."

Kate smiled at her, and thanked her again for the loan of the old jeans, boots, and wool work shirt. Kate's remaining wardrobe consisted only of what she'd worn the day she attempted to slog through the rain to the highway—a pair of Ralph Lauren pleated menswear slacks, a black cashmere turtleneck, and her Jimmy Choo ankle boots. And those weren't exactly things you could toss in the washer.

"I brought you another bag of stuff to last a bit. Nothing fancy, just a nicer pair of jeans and a couple more shirts. I put a pretty nightgown in there, too."

Kate cocked her head and nodded to Joan. She was a petite, white-haired woman with worn hands and a lovely smile. She'd ridden another one of their horses up to the lodge after the rains the other day, wanting to help Kate in whatever way she could. Since Joan had already seen her at her worst, it was like they were old friends. "That was very kind of you," Kate said, joining her on the oversized couch. "I'm lucky you and I are about the same size."

"I'd say we are."

By the look of anticipation in Joan's eyes, it was clear to Kate that Jorey's neighbor had about a million questions she'd rather be asking, but she was too polite to force the subject. Kate figured she'd give her something for her trouble.

"I think now that the bridge is up I'll get to do a little shopping in Santa Fe."

Joan's eyes got big. "You're going to stop on your way to the airport?"

Kate chuckled. "Actually, I've decided to stay on a little longer. I plan to help Jorey around the lodge, go on some hikes, and just enjoy myself."

Joan was trying very hard not to show her excitement, but wasn't succeeding. "A week longer?"

Kate shrugged. "Longer than a week. We'll see how it goes."

Joan slapped the kitchen towel over her shoulder and gave Kate a hard hug, then gripped her tight around her upper arms. "Does Archie know?"

All Kate could think was that these people needed cable TV in a bad way. "Uh, I'm not sure."

Joan let loose with a big laugh and started to get up from the couch. "I'm making Jorey's favorite—green chile stew. I made some fresh tortillas and I've got a little carne adovada going on the side for Archie. As far as he's concerned, if it don't have meat in it, it's not a meal."

The older woman headed back into the kitchen with a curious spring in her step. "Do you need some help?" Kate called after her.

"Oh no. There's a grand plan at work here." Joan waved an arm high in the air. "You just go on and clean up."

Joan's words bugged Kate the whole time she was in the shower. After selecting a pair of Levi's and a waffle-knit long-sleeve T-shirt from the bag, she decided to call Monica. If she remembered correctly, it was Friday, and back in Los Angeles it was about three in the afternoon.

"Kate! My God! I thought you were dead! I've been trying to reach you on your Blackberry for days and days—do you realize that Spencer sent you up there the wrong month?"

Kate snorted. "Yep. I figured that out pretty quick."

"Then where *are* you?" Monica sounded slightly perturbed. "Jorey didn't return any e-mails and didn't answer the phone up at the lodge. It's like you've fallen off the face of the earth."

"There was a storm and the bridge washed out, and we didn't have power or phones for most of the week. I couldn't get out and I couldn't get a message to you. I'm sorry."

Monica was quiet for a moment. "Okay, so where are you now?"

"I'm still here."

"Are you all right? You don't sound like yourself."

Kate chuckled. That about summed it up, all right. "Well, Mon, you know how you said I really needed to get away and make some changes?"

"Yes."

"I'm doing that."

"But—" Monica's breath hitched. "There's no pilgrimage, Kate. It was last month—in October. Spencer screwed up."

"That's correct."

"So what are you doing up there in the rain without the group? I don't under—"

For a moment, Kate thought the phone had gone dead. "Monica? Are you there?"

"Oh," she said, a new edge to her voice. "It's Jorey, isn't it?"

Kate's heart just about stopped. "What do you mean?"

"Oh, honey. He's a very spiritual guy, don't get me wrong, and I think he really does have the best intentions, but obviously, he's too gorgeous for his own good. Don't worry—we all fell in love with him. Why do you think most of the pilgrims are women? I mean, come on."

Kate's knees buckled and her butt hit the edge of Jorey's bed. She jumped right up again when it occurred to her that she couldn't be in that bed anymore. She'd never heard that most of his pilgrims were women. *What was Monica saying?*

"I hope I didn't burst your bubble or anything. And I'm really glad you're chilling out up there. I'm just bummed that you didn't get the whole pilgrimage experience—I just loved our day hike to the cliff dwellings in Bandelier. So are you coming home on Sunday like you'd planned?"

"Uh," Kate didn't know what to do or where to look in the room. Everything in there reminded her of the hours—days, really—they'd spent making love and talking. Jorey felt special. *She* felt special with him, in this place. She'd convinced herself that there was real magic at work here, not just hormones and loneliness.

Kate felt her heart snap shut. The heat of embarrassment spread through her.

How could she have been so stupid? How could she have allowed herself to fall in love with a stranger?

Kate brought a hand to cover her mouth. She was in love with Jorey. She'd given him the one thing she'd never given any man—her complete trust, her love. No, he'd not run off to Vegas with a community college student, but he'd hurt her just the same. He'd led her to believe she was the woman he'd been waiting for.

Stupid, stupid, stupid!

She had a lot to do—she needed to contact the airline about the lost ticket and lack of photo ID. She needed to arrange for transportation from LAX because her car keys were no more, and she really had to get to a boutique in Santa Fe because there was no way she'd be wearing this Green Acres getup back to Los Angeles.

She'd deal with the grief later. Not here. Not now.

"I'll see you at the office on Monday as planned," she said, then hung up.

Jorey had always had the ability to detect the slightest change in a person's mood and energy. He'd had the gift since he was a child. But after being ridiculed as "oversensitive" one too many times, he'd shoved it down, ashamed. It was only after his heart attack and the divorce that he felt hollowed out enough for the gift to reappear, and it did with a vengeance, welcome at last.

Such highly developed instinct wasn't needed that night at the dinner table. It was obvious that hell had broken loose in Kate, and if there was ever proof that all in the universe is interconnected, this little group of four was it.

He and Archie had come back from fixing the bridge victorious, tired, but pleased at a job well done. Joan had been singing in the kitchen when they disturbed her. She spun around and hugged her husband, whispering something in his ear that made him grin. Dinner smelled delicious. Jorey's heart was full.

His first indication that something was amiss was when his bedroom door was locked and Kate wasn't responding. His second indication was when she dragged herself out for the meal, her despair about as subtle as a nuclear bomb.

That aura was back—angry red and dark purple-black—and it vacuumed the joy right out of the air. Jorey had to hand it to Archie, that he had plowed right ahead and offered a prayer before they ate.

"Great Spirit, you designed the land and all of its creatures to have seasons." Kate let out a little sob, and Archie kept right on. "This land of yours is a powerful teacher, so help us to be open to its lessons. Oh, Spirit, we are all guests here. Help us to leave this place with eyes that see more compassionately, ears that hear more wisely, feet that step more gently, and a heart that loves more deeply. Let us walk in beauty."

Kate raised her head. Tears rolled from her big blue eyes and her chin trembled. Jorey wanted leap over the table and pull her into his arms, but he knew damn well that much of her anger was focused directly at him.

"That was . . . so . . ." Kate stood up from her chair. "I'm sorry. I'm not feeling well. Excuse me."

When she ran from the room the air went still.

"I really apologize," Jorey said, looking at the delicious and colorful meal spread out on the table before them. "I need to go see what's wrong."

"She's full of doubt," Archie said simply, looking to Joan before he continued. "That day I rode the gelding up here in the rain—it wasn't about no eggs."

Jorey let go with a surprised laugh. "Not about eggs?"

"No. See, Joan had a dream two nights before that. She told me she saw your life mate coming up the road with a sense of purpose. She bugged me all the next day to find out who'd come. She said—"

"I saw her coming in the dream, Jorey. I woke up the next morning and I knew it made no sense, because you're not doing retreats this month, but I knew she was coming. And what was so striking about the dream is that I kept thinking that you needed to save her, you needed to keep her from something dangerous and dark. And I told Archie—"

"She made me ride up here in the rain with them eggs! But I didn't see any life mate hanging around, and I was about to head home when I saw her out in the rain like that."

"Whoa." Jorey felt his body hum with awareness. No coincidences, indeed.

Archie continued, now thoroughly engrossed in the story. "And sure enough, you had to save her! She was standing right there and the water was coming right at her—"

"That's not what the dream meant, Archie." Joan gave him a little smack on his arm. "It was *my* dream, and I know what I saw; and I saw—" Joan pointed toward the alcove at the other end of the lobby, where Kate had just run. "I saw her struggling like that—so angry and sad. That's the saving you have to do."

Jorey stood up, knowing instantly that Joan was right. "I'm fortunate to have you two as friends," he said. He hurried around the table to give Joan a big kiss on her cheek, then he gave one to Archie.

Joan was on her feet. "I'll take the meat home with us and leave most of the stew here for you two."

"Thank you, Joan."

"My pleasure," she said. "Now go to her."

"Go away."

"Let me in, Kate. Right now."

"It doesn't matter, Jorey." He could barely hear her soft voice from behind the locked door. "If you get me to Santa Fe tomorrow, you can go on with whatever it is that you're going on to once I'm gone."

He screwed up his face in bewilderment. "Would you mind repeating that?"

"I'm going to sleep. Please drive me into town first thing tomorrow. If you don't want to take me all the way to Santa Fe, then get me to Chimayo and I'll hitch a ride on one of the tour buses."

Jorey took a moment to lean his forehead against the door and roll it from side to side, like that would give him a brilliant idea. No such luck.

"You need to talk to me, Kate. Tell me what happened when you came back here this afternoon. What happened to you?"

Her voice sounded tiny. "Reality happened."

Jorey pulled his head from the cool wooden surface and let her words sink in. It dawned on him—the phones were up. She'd called Monica. Archie had been so right.

"Don't doubt what you feel, Kate. You've got to trust yourself—trust your heart."

He waited a few moments until he heard the slightest movement behind the door. The knob turned ever so slightly.

"Kate, I'm terrified, too." He put his hand on the knob and willed her to feel his presence. "But sometimes we just have to go where the universe leads, and the universe led us to each other. I'm sure of it."

The door opened a crack. He could see one very bloodshot blue eye stare him down.

"I love you, Kate."

He heard a sharp intake of air. The door opened a bit more.

"Look, I realize this is insanely fast, but I've been working every day of the last five years to heal my heart enough so that when you came I would recognize you. And here you are, and I recognized you immediately. Now open this damn door."

The door opened a little further. He got a glimpse of a baggy, green pant leg. "Are you wearing my pajama bottoms?"

She sniffled. "I wanted to smell you."

Jorey laughed. "Princess, all you got to do is open this damn door and you can smell me to your heart's content."

"I think that's why they call it falling," she said with a big sigh, stretching out her leg so that he could see the fabric of his pants puddle on the floor around her dainty toes. It made him smile, even though he had no idea what she was talking about.

"See, Jorey, when you fall for someone, that automatically means you've let go of the rope, you have no control, and you're going to hit the ground hard."

"Hmm," he said. "Interesting philosophy." He wormed his hand through the door's narrow opening and touched her cheek. "Now open the door, Kate, before I kick it in."

She shook her head. "You know, it feels like a year ago that I was kicking at your front door in the middle of the night."

Jorey thought of Joan's dream. "Oh, yes—a woman with a purpose."

Kate snorted. "My purpose was to get to your bathroom."

"Your purpose was to get to me." Jorey was done cajoling and needed to go straight to the caressing. He pushed the door with his flat palm and shoved through. Kate went stumbling backward and he took advantage of her being off balance and guided her to the bed. A light tap sent her sprawling on her back. He fell on top of her.

"Tell me what happened, sweetie."

She turned her face away from his, and he could see pain. He already knew what had happened, but she needed to get it out—she needed to talk to him. She would always need to talk to him. That was the only way to do it.

She kept her face turned away as she spoke. "Monica said you were quite the ladies' man, that you were basically running an all-girl pilgrimage and stud service."

Jorey didn't think he'd ever laughed so hard in his life. When he finally opened his eyes, he saw that Kate didn't share his enthusiasm. "Ah, Kate. There's a story behind this. It's always best to have the facts before you make up your mind."

"Oh, really?" She shoved up against his chest and rolled away from him. Of course, the only reason she'd escaped was because he let her. Kate jumped from the bed and stood with her hands on her hips in defiance. Jorey was enjoying a flashback to that first morning in his kitchen, when she started to shout. "I thought I was special!"

Jorey looked up at her. "You are."

"But I'm not sure anymore what part is my wishful thinking and what part is real!"

"It's all real, Kate." He tried to make his voice as soothing as he could. On her face, he could see the forces of doubt and hope duke it out. "Please sit down and let me tell you about Monica."

Kate twisted up her pretty pink mouth and threw herself to the bed, where she sat against the headboard, arms crossed over her chest. "Let's hear it."

Jorey moved so that he sat cross-legged in front of her. "Monica's group was, in fact, all women. It was the only all-women group I'd ever had, and, if there's anything I have to say about it, the last."

"Oh? Wore you out, did they?" She bobbled her head back and forth for emphasis.

Jorey chuckled. "Yes they did, Princess. Wore my nerves to nubbins. I felt like a mouse invited to have dinner with a girl gang of cats." Kate wasn't impressed. "The sexual tension was so thick that week that you could barely breathe. Two of the women were sisters, two more were best friends, and there was a mother-daughter team thrown into the mix for extra drama. They were single, married, and divorced. All of them hit on me."

Kate wagged an eyebrow. "Monica, too?"

Jorey weighed his words carefully. "You've known Monica for how long?"

"We were best friends in high school."

"Then maybe I don't have to tell you the details."

He watched Kate relax some. She lowered her head and nodded. "I know she can be aggressive."

Jorey let out a quick laugh. "Yep. One night I finished getting the breakfast things together and answering e-mails, and I walk in here and she's right where you are—except you're wearing a whole lot more than she was."

Kate raised her head and her mouth hung open.

"Talk about something that wasn't in the brochure. I asked her to leave my room and respect my privacy. That was just two days into the pilgrimage—the rest of the week was pretty awkward. We made our peace by the end—at least I thought we had."

Kate's eyes narrowed. "So you're saying she's jealous."

Jorey looked at her calm and steady. "I have no reason to lie to you, Kate. Those are the facts. As a rule, I do not sleep with people I lead on pilgrimage."

"What about me?"

Jorey pulled one of her hands free and cradled it in both of his. Her skin was hot and sweaty. "There was no pilgrimage scheduled for this week."

"But I paid you."

"You can have your money back."

Kate's pretty little mouth pulled down at the corners. "I don't want the money. I just want—" She stopped and shook her head, as if to chase away her feelings.

"Tell me what you want, Kate."

She brought her soft blue eyes to his and sighed. "I just want to believe that this is what I think it is. I want to believe in this—in us."

"Then do it."

She fell into his arms, and Jorey finally got what he'd wanted all evening. Kate was tight in his arms. And that's where she stayed until the morning, except for when Jorey slipped out to the kitchen to heat up the tortillas and green chile stew, then make a quick phone call.

It was sure nice to have friends.

Kate was awestruck by Santa Fe and the rugged magnificence that surrounded it. They'd spent the night twisted up in each other's arms and legs, and left the lodge early. For the whole hour-long drive she'd bombarded Jorey with questions. What is the history here? What is that kind of valley called?

He patiently described the centuries-old clash and combination of cultures that made New Mexico what it was—the ancient Native American people, the Spanish conquerors, and the Anglos. He gave names to the wide variety of land formations—prehistoric fault lines, volcanic intrusions, mesas, canyons. He told her that he'd traveled here once as a teenager, and had never been able to shake the need to return.

"This is a sacred place, Kate. People have gravitated here for all of history for that reason. I've always believed it's one of those places on Earth where the division between body and soul narrows, and spirit is made known to us."

After a week in the wilderness, Kate felt giddy as she hit one boutique after the next. She chose a pair of dark blue jeans at one shop, several cotton sweaters and shirts at another, and a pair of her own cowboy boots—in a dusky purple leather. She still needed a jacket, because even in the bright sun it was cool. She and Jorey strolled through the plaza at the heart of the city, and wandered into the venerable old La Posada hotel. Jorey said he had a surprise for her.

Real coffee. She could smell it. And within ten minutes they were seated on a bench in the plaza and she was smelling and tasting wonderful, rich, dark caffeine with real cream, supremely comforted by the knowledge that the fancy little paper bag at Jorey's feet held three pounds of the treasure—just in case she decided to stay.

Jorey had tried several times to get her to talk about her decision to leave, but she didn't feel capable. She'd told him the truth—that she didn't know what to do. She didn't have to go home immediately, but she knew it had been foolish to dream of staying for months on end. She wanted to take it a day at a time, and see what developed. Jorey said he couldn't argue with that approach.

In search of a jacket for Kate, they strolled down Shelby Street and found themselves in an outdoor market. Kate's eyes were immediately drawn to a rack of wool ponchos. They stood apart from all the rest she'd seen in town that day. Their texture was fine and soft.

The patterns of the weave were intricate. The colors were the colors of the desert—browns and reds, muted purples, and sage greens.

Her eye fell on one in particular, and she was about to remove the hanger from the rack when a voice came behind her.

"I made this one for you, miss," he said. She turned around to see a small man with a very big smile, obviously using a practiced salesman line on her. "Come and see for yourself."

He led her to a full-length mirror propped against a tree and slipped it over her head. Sales pitch or no, the man was right. Kate looked at her reflection and laughed—jeans, cowboy boots, poncho, and a peaceful look on her face she was wholly unfamiliar with.

She watched in the mirror as Jorey walked up behind her, and something in her heart burst open. He was so tall and straight and handsome. The way he looked at her could not lie. Those dark and deep eyes could never lie. Those eyes were full of love.

He reached down into the nape of the poncho and set her hair free, then tenderly kissed her cheek.

It must have been the way the sunlight hit the mirror, but Kate was sure that for an instant, she and Jorey were surrounded by a cocoon of love. It shimmered gold and white and blue. She blinked and it was gone.

"Thanks. We'll take it," Jorey said, and within minutes, over Kate's protests, he'd happily shelled out several hundred dollars he probably didn't have.

After a delicious lunch at the New Mexican diner just off the plaza, Jorey told Kate that dessert was next, and he was taking her to the best place he knew.

"I can't eat anything else or I'll pop," she said.

"This is food for the soul, my dear," he said.

Another hour later, Jorey was driving down a two-lane road that ran parallel to a river lined with trees Jorey gave names to: Gambel Oak, Box Elder, and Cottonwood. They listened to a CD of Native

American flute music that floated around them, creating a cocoon of beauty inside the Range Rover. And they continued to drive. Kate knew that the last town they passed was a crossroads with the strange name of Abiquiu, and that was several miles back. She looked at the sky and could see the beginnings of a fiery red sunset.

"May I ask where we're going?"

"Nope."

She laughed. "You love teasing me."

"That's true, but this is about me wanting you to just be, to just look around you and see. I don't want you to have any preconceived notions. Just be open to what happens."

Kate folded her hands in her lap and took a breath. She felt the car begin to slow and heard the click of Jorey's turn signals. She had to squint and lean forward against her seat belt in order to read the small white wooden sign.

She snapped her head around and stared at Jorey. "You're taking me to a mosque? Out in the middle of nowhere?"

"Ah, well, it's a long story, but this community has always been kind to me. I bring groups here all the time and they never hesitate to give me permission. They own all the land around here."

"I'm trying to be open here, but a mosque?"

Jorey laughed. "There is a mosque, but it's way over the hill in that direction, and you can't even see it. We're not going there. We're going to a temple that wasn't built by human beings."

The Range Rover continued up a steep gravel road. Slowly, a shocking sight revealed itself. At first, Kate didn't know what to think—what she was seeing was so strange and so beautiful that it didn't register with her.

"What is this place?" she whispered.

"Plaza Blanca, the White Place," Jorey said, pulling into a small parking area and turning off the engine. "Are you up for a little walk?"

Kate got out of the car and stretched her legs, looking around with big eyes. After Jorey grabbed a blanket and a small backpack from the trunk, he took her hand in his.

"This is my favorite place on earth, Kate. I couldn't have you leave without seeing it."

They entered a narrow path that led into a huge, all-white canyon. It was startling because of the contrast—all around it was the more familiar reds and browns of the desert. But this place was pure white, and lined with the strangest rock formations.

"They look like people," she whispered, staring at one tall, thin rock after the next. Each was topped by what could be considered a head. Some had faces. Some had large noses. If she looked particularly hard, she could imagine that some wore hats or had long hair. "Holy shit," she said.

"Precisely." Jorey chuckled. "Locals have always considered this a home for the spirits of the holy ancient ones. It's believed that the ancestors really live here, and you can talk to them. You can seek their guidance."

"It's almost spooky."

Jorey put his arm around her shoulders. "Are you in the mood to expand your horizons a bit?"

Kate laughed slightly and shook her head. "Trust me, I'm expanding as we speak, Jorey."

"Good. Then come with me."

They walked in silence for a very long time, though all the while Kate knew it wasn't silence. There was a strange humming in her ears, and she could hear the wind move through the valley. At one section of the canyon wall, the rocks formed a huge natural amphitheater, and a grove of trees grew in its embrace. The wind moved through those trees, shaking millions of small, shiny leaves. The effect was a hissing, breathing symphony.

Jorey placed his hand at the small of her back and nudged her up a steep rise. Kate sighed, thinking that she was forever in the wrong shoes. But Jorey kept her steady and they eventually reached the peak of a flattened hill.

Kate gasped. Then she laughed. It was just too beautiful—the most beautiful thing she'd ever seen. It was nature at its most dramatic. The red sun spilled over the horizon and hit the white of the rocks so that they seemed to glow from an internal fire. It looked like there was warm blood running through those stone people. The whole canyon was awash in the light. Just then a hawk swooped low, cried out, and caught an updraft that lifted it high into the sky.

Jorey unzipped a compartment of his backpack, and the sound jerked Kate to attention.

"Sorry," he whispered.

Kate watched him reach into the pack and pull out a lighter, followed by a thick, silvery bundle of leaves and stems. She felt her eyes go wide.

"I was wondering when you'd pull out the peyote," she said, giggling.

Jorey giggled with her. "I'm trying to be spiritual here. Stop it."

"We're both going to be close to God in a big way if we smoke that."

Jorey shook his head, but his dimple appeared and his eyes crinkled, and Kate was overwhelmed with love for him. He stood up straight and flicked the lighter. "This is desert sage. I'm going to smudge you, then you'll return the favor. Now pay attention."

Jorey lit the bundle wrapped in twine, let the flame catch, then steadily exhaled over the burning end until it smoked. He asked Kate to face the sun, to breathe deep, and to close her eyes.

When she took the breath, a pungent blast of slightly bitter air filled her lungs. Jorey quietly told her that the smoke was purifying, that he would wave it over her whole body while saying a prayer, and the prayers would take wind.

Kate felt still at her core, aware of the presence of the stone people, of the wind's music, and able to feel the heat of Jorey's presence without him even touching her.

"May you be blessed with light. May your roads be fulfilled. May you grow old. May you be blessed in the chase."

Those words had come from low to the ground, and Kate had to peek. Jorey was squatting at her feet, slowly waving the sage over the tops of her new cowboy boots, her ankles, her shins. He looked up, catching her.

"Concentrate, sweetheart. Listen to the words and breathe."

She did. As he spoke, her shoulders relaxed and her back strengthened. Her feet felt bolted to the hard earth beneath her. Jorey's words moved up the front of her body, from her fingers up the length of each arm. The words paused over her heart.

"Breathing in, I am alive," he said. "Breathing out, I am alive."

He moved the smoke around her face and the back of her head. "In this precious moment, in this sacred place, in the abundance of love I dwell."

Kate stood still, her body and mind in deep calm. She had no idea how much time had passed, but she started at the soft touch of Jorey's hand on her shoulder.

"It's your turn, Kate. Please smudge me before the sun goes down."

She opened her eyes and was greeted with a changed world. The stone people were now deep red, and the entire canyon glowed with passion. She looked to Jorey and saw the same intensity in his face.

"I didn't expect this," she said, shaking her head. "I mean, I thought you were taking me for cheesecake."

He laughed. "I love you so much, Kate. I love you so much that I'd move back to Los Angeles to be near you."

She shook her head. "Never. We'll try, Jorey. I will stay here in your sacred place for as long as I can, and we'll see where this goes."

A very soft smile spread over his face, and Kate could see him blink back tears.

"I love you, too, Jorey. It's the damnedest thing. But I'm going where the universe has taken me, and it's taken me to you."

"Smudge me so we can go home and get back in bed."

"I don't know how to do this."

"You'll think of something. Just have faith."

Kate accepted the weightless bundle from Jorey and took a deep breath. "Face the sun and close your eyes, please," she said, squatting down at his feet. She took a moment to appreciate the broken-in brown leather of his hiking boots. He had walked all over this land, taking people where they needed to go. And it's exactly what he'd done with her.

"God, guide this man so he can walk in beauty always." She waved the sage, mesmerized by how the smoke danced and rose up the front of his body. She created a pattern around his feet, ankles, and legs. "Keep him strong and healthy." She paused at his chest and closed her eyes in concentration. "Guard his heart, because it is so pure, but keep it open to all of life's possibilities."

Jorey stood very still with his eyes closed, breathing evenly. She waved the sage around his beautiful eyes, ears, mouth, forehead. "Be with this man I love. Give him the strength and patience it will take to love me back."

She ground the tip of the sage in the sandy soil. And she waited for him to open his eyes.

"That was very nice, Kate."

She shrugged. "It was kind of weird, but I liked it a lot."

Jorey laughed. "Can't ask for more than that."

They gathered up their things and Jorey started down the hill in front of her, holding out his hand for her to steady herself. They walked to the car just before it became dark, and stood arm in arm to watch the last seconds of the sun's glory.

"I know this is a bad time to bring this up," Kate said, "but what in the hell am I supposed to do with myself up here, Jorey? Does Archie need a PR agent?"

He looked down at her and grinned. "I've been wondering that, too. Not about Archie, but about what you could do. What would you like to do? What would you do if you could do anything in the world?"

She thought for a moment. "I'd like to learn to ride horses. I'd like to read everything I've never had time to read. I'd like to discover things about myself and about you. Maybe write books someday. And I could grow brown eggs, like Archie and Joan."

"Technically, eggs aren't *grown*. They're laid."

"Right."

"But you could do that if you wanted."

She looked up at him with a wicked grin. "You want me to lay eggs?"

"Not necessarily, but that might happen." He put his hand on the back of her neck and pulled her face close to his. "I was thinking you'd just get laid—a lot."

"I didn't know there was any money in that."

"No money, just joy." He bent down closer and propped his forehead against hers. "And when I don't have you tied to the bed you can read and write and help me with the lodge."

"I could learn to make breakfasts."

"Cool."

"But we'd have to have real coffee."

"It's the least I could do."

"I saw our aura today, the one we make together." Kate had almost been afraid to say it out loud. She looked into Jorey's eyes and noticed that their fire burned, even in the twilight.

"I saw it, too. Gold and white and very, very real."

Jorey then pressed his mouth to hers with such finality that it drove the breath from Kate's lungs. She felt herself surrender—from the deepest core of her being she let go of the doubt. She would not allow this chance for something real to pass her by.

For Maggie's Sake

by

Lora Leigh

1

Maggie Samuels was pale. Too pale. The freckles across her creamy cheeks and along the bridge of her nose stood out clearly, emphasizing the frail, delicate look of her features. Her lush lips trembled, her wide green eyes were shocked and filled with unshed tears.

And he wanted to save her. Joe Merino stared through the two-way glass, his hands pushed into the pockets of his slacks as he watched Maggie wrap her arms across her chest and stare unseeing back at the detective questioning her. Detective Folker had been questioning her for hours.

Her husband had been dead less than a week, a husband who had supposedly adored her. Who lived for her. The same man who had supposedly been Joe's friend. And now, Maggie's life was being threatened as well. Because of that same man.

Joe knew he shouldn't give a damn. From all accounts, she had gotten herself into this; he should let her get herself out of it.

That's what his head was saying. His heart was saying something different. His heart was assuring him that there was no way Maggie was involved. He had slept with this woman at one time, held her in his arms, and watched her as she climaxed. The woman he had known couldn't be cold-blooded enough to be involved with this. But then again, he had never suspected for a second that Grant was part of Fuentes's organization. That he had helped rape and torture many of the young women that Fuentes had kidnapped.

And now, here he stood, days after Grant's death, trying to harden himself to the threat that someone else he cared for could be involved in the horror that operation had turned into. That his own life could have become such a mess.

He had let his bitterness, his distrust of women after his wife's deceit and death five years ago, stand between him and the woman he knew belonged to him. Hell, he had known it at the time. Each time he thought of forever with Maggie, the memory of Bettina's death hung over him like a haunting specter. She had died leaving him. She and her boyfriend, high on drugs, had run the car they were in over an embankment, killing them both. He hadn't been able to hold on to the woman he married, the woman who swore to love him. And two years later, there he had been, falling in love with Maggie.

Joe watched Maggie now, his jaw clenched, his back teeth grinding, as the past threatened to swallow him. Two and a half years before, Maggie had belonged to him for a few short months. But he hadn't taken what he knew could be his. Maggie had walked out of his arms, and months later had walked into Grant's.

The problem was, he hadn't stopped loving Maggie.

He stared into the interrogation room, fighting to ignore the tightening of his chest, the regret and the rage and the lust. He had been fighting the lust for two and a half years. A hunger that never slept, that never eased, for a woman he could never have again.

A woman who, it appeared, was involved in her husband's illegal activities.

He ignored the gut-clenching feeling that she couldn't be involved, that she was innocent. It was the same reaction he had when he began to suspect there was indeed a mole within his team. He had begun the investigation on all the team members, except Grant. He had shared his suspicions with his friend, discussed the best way to flush the traitor out. And Grant had sympathized, become angry on Joe's behalf, and pretended to help.

God, he had been a fool. Just as he was being a fool again, wanting to believe in Maggie when the evidence against her was mounting.

"Mrs. Samuels, your husband was working for Fuentes," Detective Matthew Folker told her, not for the first time, his plump face and hazel eyes appearing almost kind as he watched her. "Your neighbors have seen him." He pointed to Diego Fuentes's picture. "As well as his nephew Santiago Fuentes, and his brother Jose, at your home. Surely you overheard something?"

Maggie shook her head, the silken fall of her deep red hair caressing her shoulders as her lips trembled again. He knew how Maggie reacted when she was hiding something. Her lips didn't tremble. Her lips trembled when she couldn't understand the pain she felt or events unfolding. Her lips had trembled when she had seen another woman on his arm, and her face had gone that same pasty white.

"I saw them. They came to the house several times over the past months. . . ."

"You met with them," Folker accused, his voice benign, confident.

"I didn't meet with them." Her voice was thin, filled with fear. It sent a surge of fury racing through Joe. Was she lying? The evidence said she was. But the evidence had come from Grant. And they all now knew how reliable Grant had been. Even two and a half years ago Joe had known he knew Maggie better than he knew his best friend. He had acknowledged it, and it had scared the hell out of him.

"Agent Samuels left evidence that you were involved in his illegal activities," the detective repeated. The accusation had been voiced a half-dozen times in the two-hour-long interview.

"God. No," she whispered, as a tear slipped free and she shook her head again.

"There is proof you were involved. Pictures, Mrs. Samuels, as well as written notes. We're prepared to be lenient here. Give us the pictures and audio tapes Agent Samuels made of his meetings with the Fuentes family and we'll forget your part in this."

She shook her head again, her breathing jerky as she stared back at the detective.

"Mrs. Samuels," Folker sighed, pushing his hand over his balding head as he stared back at her, a glimmer of compassion in his eyes. "Would you like to call your lawyer? We do have evidence that you're involved. If you're frightened . . ."

"I don't know anything." Her hands tightened on her upper arms, her fingernails biting into her own flesh as a sob echoed in her voice. "I don't need a lawyer because I didn't know what Grant was doing. We've barely spoken for months."

"Mrs. Samuels, it's too late for this game." Folker slapped the table in frustration. "Look at the damned pictures." He pointed to the pictures of the young women murdered over the past two years; the morgue shots were horrendous. "Look at them, Maggie. He helped do this. You helped . . ."

"I didn't do this," she screamed back, tears washing over her cheeks as she stared back at the detective. "I didn't know. I don't have anything to do with it. I swear to God I don't. Please . . ."

Maggie lowered her head, her shoulders jerking from the sobs she was fighting to hold back, as Folker leaned back in his chair and looked over his shoulder to the mirror behind him. The disapproval in his gaze was heavy. He didn't like what he was doing to her, what he had been ordered to do. Detective Folker didn't believe Maggie could be involved. And, Joe admitted, he couldn't fully believe it himself.

Joe turned his head to the district attorney standing beside him, as well as the federal prosecutor observing the interrogation.

"I don't think she knows, Mark," he sighed wearily. "At least, not that she's aware of."

"Santiago and his uncle Jose will be out of jail before the day is out," Mark Johnson murmured. "We couldn't deny bail at this point because of the threats the judge has received. Our only chance is to trap them in this. If she walks out of this office without giving us the information, she's dead."

"We can't protect her, Agent Merino," Andrew Jordan, the federal prosecutor sent to oversee the interrogation spoke up. "She's our only hope at this point."

Joe breathed in, slow, deep. As he stared at Maggie he saw Grant, his face twisted with hatred as he prepared to kill Morganna Chavez when he couldn't get her to the exit of the club and to Fuentes. The attempted kidnapping, the drugging of the women before her, the rapes, the death of Agent Lyons. It all lay at Grant's feet, and now at his wife, Maggie's.

"Are we certain she could have had access to the information?" Joe asked as he crossed his arms over his chest, ignoring the instinctive demand that he go to her, hold her, take the fear out of her eyes.

"We're certain she lived with him for two years. She would have seen or heard something, even if she wasn't involved. We've found too many lies in those damned journals to take his word for it," Johnson grunted. "Word on the street is that the price is already on her head, though. And Grant would have tried to cover his ass. He had the evidence, I suspect; the question is where."

"And if she doesn't know anything, consciously or subconsciously?" Subconsciously, yeah, he was betting she knew something. Consciously? He couldn't make it work in his own mind. Maggie would have never been able to live with the rapes and deaths of those women. It wasn't possible.

"If she doesn't, she's dead anyway. We can't do anything to protect her if she doesn't cooperate," Jordan answered.

"She trusts you, Joe. She asked for you when we brought her in this morning."

There was a question in the district attorney's voice, one Joe heard clearly. The DA was well aware of the fact that Joe and Maggie had been involved in an affair. Grant's irrational journals had been filled with furious entries raging over the fact.

"What do you want me to do?" Joe steeled himself against the denial raging inside him. He couldn't interrogate Maggie. It would destroy them both.

"We need that proof, Joe. Without it, the nephew and the brother will walk and the Navy will never find the mole responsible for the death of that Navy SEAL and the young women that drug destroyed." Johnson sighed.

Joe wanted to trust her, he wanted to hold her, to take away her fear and promise her everything was going to be okay. She was his best friend's wife. . . . His jaw clenched. No, Grant hadn't been his friend—the illusion of friendship, of brotherhood, had been a game, nothing more.

In the days since Grant's death, the depth of his treachery had slowly been revealed. He had been on the take for years. More years than Joe could have imagined.

"You know me, Matthew." Joe heard Maggie's whisper clearly through the glass. "I wouldn't be involved in this."

Joe would have never thought she would be involved in this, but then again, he would have never believed Grant would betray him. The evidence supported her involvement. For now he had no choice but to go with the evidence, the tangible proof rather than his emotions. Because his emotions couldn't be trusted. Because Maggie's life depended on her knowing something, whether she realized it or not.

"Maggie, we have evidence." Matthew laid his arms on the table as he leaned forward. "Evidence that you were at the house during the meetings, that you know where the photos and recordings are hidden. Lying isn't going to help you."

"I'm not lying to you." She smacked the palm of her hand on the table, that Irish temper finally coming to the fore.

"I don't know what you're talking about, Matthew, and I'm not telling you that again. I didn't know what Grant was doing."

Despite the temper, she was trembling. He could see the fine tremors racing over her body, echoing in her lips.

"I'll take care of it." It was a promise Joe made not just to the DA, but to Maggie.

He was a fool. No greater fool had ever been born than he was at that moment, and he knew it.

Johnson watched him silently. Joe could feel the other man's gaze on him as he stared through the two-way mirror at Maggie.

"How?"

"Fuentes already put a price on her head. She's as good as dead without protection, until we can get the evidence she's hiding. I'll take her to a safe house, see if I can wear her down."

"If that doesn't work?" Andrew Jordan's eyes were narrowed as Joe stared over the district attorney's shoulder at the older man. Andrew Jordan was a sparse, tall man, with hawklike eyes and a jutting, pugnacious chin. He was the terror of the capital and a bulldog when it came to the cases he prosecuted.

"What do you want, Jordan?" He fought the anger welling inside him. "Arresting Maggie and terrifying her isn't going to help anyone at this point, and it won't get the evidence against the Fuentes gang. According to Grant's journal, his marriage to her was less than perfect. She wouldn't protect him."

"She wouldn't be the first woman to follow the money, Merino. You know that," Jordan pointed out, clearly referring to the rich bastard his first wife had died with.

It was well known that Joe refused to touch the money his parents made available to him. He used the inheritance his grandfather had left him, but his parents' money he had never touched. Not because of any anger or animosity toward it or his parents. There was none. He loved them, as interfering and broody as they could be. But he didn't want their money. With the inheritance he had, and his salary, he had more than he needed. More than Bettina would have needed if she hadn't gotten hooked on the drugs.

"If Maggie wanted money, she wouldn't help kill to get it," he snarled. "Give me a week, maybe two. Let me see what I can learn."

"She has to go voluntarily," Johnson warned him. "We can't make it official."

"She'll go."

Maggie had trusted him a long time ago. Once, she may have even loved him. He accepted the guilt from the past on his shoulders. That didn't mean he would allow more lives to be lost because of Grant's hatred and greed.

"I'll leave it in your hands then," Jordan murmured.

Mark Johnson nodded then. "Keep me up to date, Joe, and hurry. We need this information now."

Maggie had been telling herself for a week that she would wake up, that this was all a horrible dream, that any minute she was going to wake up and it was all going to be over. But, as she sat in the interrogation room and stared into Matthew Folker's suspicious gaze, she realized she wasn't going to wake up. It wasn't a nightmare, it was reality.

Where was Joe? The question kept racing through her mind, tearing through her emotions. She hadn't thought Joe would desert her, that he would allow Detective Folker to question her without his presence. They had been friends once, more than friends.

Then again, he had loved Grant like a brother, and had never realized how much Grant hated him. But Maggie had known. For two years she had listened to Grant rage about Joe. The petty jealousy and fury Grant felt toward the other man had begun frightening Maggie within months of their marriage.

"Maggie, let me help you." Matthew leaned closer, his hazel eyes compassionate as he watched her. "We're not interested in prosecuting you, not if we get that information. Otherwise . . ." Otherwise, they would hang her out to dry on whatever trumped-up evidence Grant had left.

"So, it wouldn't matter to you if I had been a part of this?" she accused, as she waved her hand toward the pictures before her, the morgue shots of the young women who had been killed because of the horrible drug Grant had helped to distribute. "As long as you get whatever Grant had hidden, then you would just wipe the slate clean?"

"I give you my promise, Maggie. The DA will put it in writing . . ."

"Then you're a fool," she screamed, jerking to her feet as she grabbed the nearest photo and slapped it beneath his face. "*You* look at her, Matthew. She was savaged. And you're willing to let go someone you suspect of being capable of helping in it?"

She was shaking so violently she could feel the very core of her threatening to shatter apart. She couldn't fight her tears any longer, or her rage. She wanted to leave here, she wanted to go home, and then she wanted to find whatever the hell it was she was supposed to have and throw it in Folker's face.

"Sit down, Maggie." He sat back in his chair, calm, remote.

She had known the detective for nearly ten years now, since she had come to the station with her father when he worked with the paper. It was as much her world as the newspaper office was.

"Don't tell me to sit down." She shook her head furiously. "I did not do this, Matthew. Not in any part." She pointed a shaky finger at the pictures between them. "And if you had the evidence you say you do, you and that son-of-a-bitch Jordan would have arrested me while he was spitting his accusations in my face earlier."

The door opened at that second. Maggie jerked around, her heart exploding in her chest at the sight of the man standing there, tall, remote, his brown eyes so cold and hard they were like chips of dark ice.

"No, Maggie, they wouldn't have arrested you," Joe told her softly. "Because I won't let them. Now get your stuff together and let's get the hell out of here."

Out of there? To where? She had thought he would be her salvation, that if anyone believed in her, Joe would. But as she stared into the cold hard depths of his eyes she was terribly afraid that Joe didn't believe in her any more than anyone else did.

2

One week later

Maggie stared into the misty morning of the South Carolina Mountains and contemplated mistakes. Past mistakes, present mistakes, and how they would lead into the future. She was twenty-eight years old, and she might not live to see twenty-nine. The choices she had made in the past two and a half years led her to this mountain, this cabin, and the man she couldn't forget.

She had been such a fool. Two and a half years before she had walked out of Joe Merino's life, believing she had left in time to save her heart, to go on and to find happiness with someone else.

He hadn't loved her. They were damned good in bed, but he had made it clear he didn't want or need her in his life. Real clear. Another woman on his arm type clear.

She curled her feet beneath her, tucking her body tighter in the rocking chair that sat on the weathered wood porch of the cabin Joe had brought her to a week before.

That had been the beginning of her downfall into hell. She had broken all ties to Joe Merino two years and six months before. Several months later, she had met Grant Samuels. Six months after meeting, they had married.

She should have known better. The moment she learned Grant was in law enforcement, she should have run. But Grant had been a detective with the Atlanta Police Department at the time, and Joe had been an agent in the DEA. They might know each other, but it had never occurred to her that they had been as close as they were. And Grant had kept the secret until only days before their wedding.

She should have broken off the engagement the day she learned Grant and Joe not only knew each other, but were supposedly best friends. And she would have, except Grant had pleaded with her, swore he loved her, and the wedding had been only days away.

Grant had claimed he had known about her and Joe, and hadn't told her who he was because he had been terrified of losing her. That much would have been the truth, considering how easily he had used her, how he had intended to use her.

She had loved Grant. Or she had thought she did. Within months she had learned that the man she loved didn't exist. Grant had married her because he believed Joe cared for her. She had been a trophy, something to torment Joe with, and nothing more.

She had tried to leave him. Three months after their marriage she had walked out, only to learn the true nature of the man she called her husband and the information he had gathered to ensure she never divorced him. Information that would destroy her father.

And now here she was, still fighting to escape the hell of a marriage that had been doomed from the start. Older, wiser, and more certain than ever that Joe Merino would end up breaking her heart, if Grant's deceptions didn't end up getting her killed first.

Where would he have hidden the information Joe needed so desperately? Information that would seal the government's case against the remaining Fuentes family? Hell, did he even have the proof his journal had stated he had? Everything else in that damned book had been a lie.

Oh, he had really managed to mess her life up completely. The journal claimed she knew the location of the proof he had taken against the Fuentes family. Pictures and video discs of Santiago and Jose Fuentes along with Roberto Manuelo, the cartel general that had been killed the night Grant had tried to kidnap a female DEA agent, coordinating the drugging and rapes of over a dozen women in the past two years. The location of the lab where the drug was created and even the identities of several influential political figures involved with Fuentes.

In the past week, Maggie had learned exactly why the police department was so eager to drop any charges they could bring against her in return for the information they were looking for.

So why couldn't the bastard Grant just write it in his journal with all the lies he had written against her? He could have included some truth in it, just for a change of pace.

She pushed her fingers through her hair, the circles in her mind exhausting her. There were no answers, and the cold suspicion in Joe's eyes was killing her. He had changed since Grant's death. Since he had been forced to kill Grant, rather. There was an edge of unrelenting ice in his expression, in his eyes, that hadn't been there before. Amusement had always lurked in the chocolate brown gaze, sensuality; playfulness had always curved his lips.

Even when they had argued, when she had walked out on the relationship they had, there had been regret, sadness, softness. There was none of that now. This wasn't the man she had given her heart to.

So why was he protecting her? Why did he give a damn? Those

were questions he had refused to answer since their arrival at the cabin, questions that garnered no more than a cold silence.

At this rate, she was going to have frostbite before the month was out.

"You're a sitting target out here."

Maggie flinched at the sound of his voice from the doorway. The dark sensuality of the tone couldn't be hidden, no matter how coldly furious he might be. It throbbed just beneath the ice and sent heat curling through her system.

She hated that. She hated the response to him, unwilling and unwanted, that she had learned she had no hope of controlling.

She stared into the forest, watching the mist rise like a veil of dreams above the treetops to meet the heat of the rising sun.

"If the Fuentes family knew where I was, then they would have already struck." She shrugged her shoulders, wishing she had worn a bra beneath the loose T-shirt she had slept in.

Her nipples were hardening, her breasts were swelling, and this was no time for it. She could feel the steadily rising sense of expectation building within her. She had spent a week with Joe, alone, and the tension was only growing worse by the day.

"You aren't showing much faith in my protective abilities," he grunted.

"Of course I am." She kept staring into the forest; she wasn't about to watch him. Watching him only aroused her further. "I'm sitting here watching the dew meet the sunrise, in plain view. See, I trust you to know I'm well hidden."

"You make about as much sense now as you ever did." His voice turned surly. "Come inside, I have coffee ready."

Yeah, she had smelled it for the past half hour, tempting, strong, teasing her senses. Rather like Joe did.

This was not going to work.

"You're sitting out here pouting," he accused, when she didn't move to follow him.

"I don't pout, Joe," she reminded him. "I think."

"You think too much then," he growled. "Now get your butt in the house. Maybe the coffee will even out your temper."

She clenched her teeth. She was not going to argue with him. Arguing with him was a pointless exercise. It was like beating her head against a wall. She only ended up hurting herself.

"I don't have a temper." She was restrained. Hell, he was still alive, wasn't he?

"Uh-huh." Was that amusement she heard in his voice?

After a week?

She couldn't help herself, she turned and looked at him and her senses went into overload. He wasn't wearing a shirt. The leanly muscled contours of his hair-matted chest brought back memories better forgotten. Memories she had never forgotten.

The warmth of him as he came over her, his thighs parting hers, the feel of his cock nudging against her sex, filling her slowly, riding her fiercely.

Maggie shivered as her vagina clenched with a sudden spasm of hungry need, a clenching of lust as the heated dampness began to prepare her for a touch that certainly wasn't coming. She jerked her eyes from his chest and lifted them to his face. Beard-roughened, the darker growth contrasted with the dark blond, rakishly cut hair that framed his face. The two days' growth was nearly black, and gave him a piratical appearance that was too mouthwatering for words. It just made his lips appear sexier, more lickable. And she really wanted to lick them.

"Come on, Maggie. Coffee and breakfast. Then we can talk." He held his hand out to her, the ice that had filled his eyes for the past week thawing, warming.

Maggie licked her lips nervously, feeling her heart racing in her chest, her nerve endings sensitizing. She rose from the chair, though she ignored his outstretched hand as she watched him warily. He was like a damned chameleon, and the abrupt changes were throwing her off balance.

"So where's the prick I've spent the last seven days with?" she asked as she moved around him to enter the cabin, feeling the walls closing in on her as he stepped in behind her.

He had a habit of that, sucking all the space out of a room until nothing remained except him. At least, that was all she was aware of. The warm, cheery tones of burnt reds and soft desert browns of the living room were lost on her. The couch was wide, comfortable. Joe liked making love on couches. Floors. Coffee tables. Kitchen counters.

She stepped back quickly, giving him plenty of room as the corner of his lips kicked up in a grin.

"Same cautious Maggie," he said, as he moved past her and headed to the kitchen. "How long did it take me to get you into bed the first time?"

"Not long enough," she stated. "And I am not having sex with you again, Joe." Yeah. Right. Her body was all in agreement on that one. In another second, the dampness building on the folds of her sex was going to start dampening the fleece of her pajama bottoms. If it wasn't already.

"We're sleeping in the same bed . . ."

"That's not my choice," she argued, as he glanced over his shoulder, casting her a wicked look. "You wouldn't let me sleep on the couch."

"Sure you can." He shrugged his tanned shoulders negligently. "But it's going to be an awful tight fit with both of us there."

That was pretty much his stand on it seven days ago. She followed him slowly into the kitchen, admiring the tight contours of his rear beneath the snug jeans he had only zipped, not buttoned. Yeah, she had caught that little detail out on the porch.

"How much longer are we staying here?" She finally asked the question that had been hovering on her lips for days. "When are you going to give up, Joe?"

"When the Fuentes family is dead." He padded to the coffeepot, lifted the carafe, and poured the liquid into waiting cups.

His answer shocked her. Before, his answer would have been once a culprit was behind bars, not dead.

"I just want to know how they managed bail," she sighed, moving to the kitchen table as he turned back, the coffee cups firmly in hand.

"One of Fuentes's lieutenants paid off the judge. We have the money and evidence in hand. Judge Gilmore was none too pleased with the offer. He could take the money and let them out, or his grandchildren could suffer the consequences. We opted to go with the bribe, taped it, and now have the money impounded in a safe location until it's needed. All with Jose's and Santiago's fingerprints."

She couldn't have been more surprised if he had said he was Santa Claus.

"And that's not enough to lock them up for a while?" she asked, amazed.

"We need it all, Maggie. We want them locked away forever, if they're smart enough to live until the trial. I don't want them out on a technicality. And I don't want families murdered to get them there."

Maggie stared back at him suspiciously. She had been questioning him for a week now, and he was finally giving her the answers she wanted: Why?

"If I'm suspected of being part of this, then didn't you just put several people in danger by telling me?"

His gaze was hooded as he glanced back at her before shrugging. "I don't believe you're part of this."

Oh yeah, she really believed that one at this late date.

"So I'm here why?" she questioned him as he sat the coffee in front of her. "And they are still out on bail for what reason?"

"We need that proof Grant hid and the Fuentes family still believes you have that." Joe took his seat across from her, watching her steadily. "You don't know where it's at; that means your life is still in danger. And the Navy needs that mole. There's too much at stake here to risk a trial on what little evidence we have of the two aiding and abetting Diego. If we want to shut down this cartel and that drug, then we have to do it here."

Ahh, so the truth was emerging, perhaps.

"You're using me . . ."

"Hell no!" Anger flashed across his expression. "You are not bait, Maggie. No matter what you think. I told you I'd protect you, and I meant it."

And she didn't trust him, not even for a second. Fear raced down her spine as she stared back at him, suddenly wondering to what lengths he would go in capturing the Fuentes men. But she knew the lengths he would go to, she reminded herself. He blamed the Fuentes family for what happened to Grant, rather than blaming Grant himself.

"And this information the federal prosecutor thinks I'm hiding?" she asked, not bothering to hide the mockery in her voice. "Have you just given up on it, Joe?"

He tilted his head as he regarded her for several seconds. "You don't know where it's at. That's a dead end."

"Oh, you are so good." She would have cried if it didn't hurt so damned bad. The truth was there in his eyes, the suspicion, the calculation. Others might not have recognized it, but Maggie saw it and knew it for what it was. "Do you really expect me to swallow that line of crap, Joe? Do you think I'm that stupid?"

"On the contrary, you're not stupid at all. Suspicious," he chided her with a quirk of amusement. "But not stupid."

Maggie ignored the coffee sitting before her, the smell of it suddenly as unappetizing as the lies passing his lips. Standing slowly to her feet, she stared back at him impassively, fighting to hide the pain exploding inside her.

"You've changed, Joe," she whispered. "I never pegged you for a liar. An asshole and a prick maybe, but not an out-and-out liar. Congratulations, you did the impossible. You made my opinion of you sink lower than it was two and a half years ago."

Turning on her heels, she moved to stalk from the kitchen, to put distance between herself and his games, his lies. She hated lies. She hated herself. Because she wanted to believe him, she wanted to trust in the arousal and the warmth that had heated his eyes, just as she wanted to believe that he could trust in her, just once. She was a fool.

"No, you don't." She came to an abrupt stop as he jumped from his chair, his hand reaching out to catch her upper arm as she moved to pass him.

The shock of his flesh touching hers, the heat and strength in it nearly drove the breath from her body.

"Let me go." She jerked against his hold, feeling the anger growing inside her, the hurt burning through her heart.

"I won't let you go, Maggie." He suddenly snarled, jerking her around, as his free hand buried in her hair, his fingers locking into the strands. He jerked her head back and stared into her eyes fiercely. "I won't let you go and I won't let you die. Lie to me all you need to. Fuck it. I'll get Fuentes in the end, if I have to kill him to do it. But I won't let you go."

"You don't have a choice." She pushed against his chest, desperate to escape him, to break free of the hard temptation of his body. "I don't belong to you, Joe, not anymore . . ."

"By God, you always belonged to me. Always."

Before she could stop him his head lowered, his lips covered hers, and time came to a stop. There was only Joe's kiss. His lips moving against hers, his tongue licking, piercing her lips, moving between them in a fierce, dominant kiss.

Her fingers curled against his chest, then spread out, nerve endings soaking in the feel of him, remembering, relishing the rasp of the short, crisp hairs on her palms, the fiery warmth beneath his flesh.

Against her lower stomach she felt his erection pressing intently through the material of his jeans. His arms enfolded her, his kiss intoxicated her.

"Joe," she whimpered as his lips slid to her cheek, to her jaw. "Don't do this."

Don't make her feel again. Don't make her ache for all the things she knew she couldn't have. Don't make her love him more than she already did.

"I dreamed of you." The arousal and the anger pulsed in his voice as he nipped at her ear. "For more than two years, I remembered what it was like to feel you beneath me, to hear the soft little catch in your voice when you came beneath me, the feel of your body tightening around me. I remembered, Maggie, and it drove me insane."

She whimpered at the pain that enveloped her, the raking fingers of need, regret, and sorrow that filled her.

"This won't fix the past." She tightened her fingers on his biceps, feeling the power and the tension that vibrated in his body. "It won't solve anything, Joe."

He wanted to punish her. She could feel it pulsing in the air around them, feel it in the rake of his teeth along her neck, the nipping little kisses, and the press of his erection against her.

Even as her head screamed out a warning against his touch and the probability of heartbreak down the road, she felt herself relaxing, leaning into him, the response he had always commanded from her leaping through her system.

"I know one thing it will definitely solve." One hand slid down her back, gripped the swell of a buttock, and lifted her to him.

Maggie moaned at the feel of his cock notching between her thighs, his lips at her neck, his tongue licking erotically at her skin. Blood pulsed hot and fast through her veins, heating her flesh, sensitizing her nerve endings, as lust began to spike the air around them.

Hunger surged through her. More than two years of aching, of needing, of suffering the restless, shadowed dissatisfaction that edged at her mind, culminated here. In Joe's arms. His touch. His kiss. It was the drug she had never recovered from, the one very likely to destroy her.

3

The feel of her lips beneath his, her body pulled against his, was heaven and hell. Memories swamped him, and following close on its heels was a lust that tightened in his balls and sent hunger slamming through his system. This was Maggie. Redheaded, fiery, a need he had never exorcised, from his heart. A hunger he couldn't forget. No matter how hard he tried—and he had tried, for two and a half years he had tried. He was tired of denying himself.

His lips moved over her jaw, back to her lips, and he stole the words he could feel rushing past them. A denial, the cautious, intuitive part of her that had always driven him crazy. There was only one way to silence it, one way to steal beneath her defenses and make her melt in his arms.

"Maggie," he whispered, lifting his lips until they ghosted over hers. "Let me love you . . ."

"You son of a bitch!"

He was unprepared for the raging fury let loose on him. A red-headed mini tornado that kicked, slapped, and threw herself at him like a force of nature intent on destruction.

"Dammit, Maggie . . ." He grabbed her wrists, only to let go as she kicked at his shin.

Jumping back, he stared at the aberration confronting him. Her red hair was wild, waves of fiery splendor cascading to her shoulders, her cheeks flushed, her green eyes brilliant with tears.

"I can't believe you!" Her fists were clenched at her sides as her breasts rose and fell with the quick pace of her breathing. " 'Let me love you'," she mimicked him. "You know about as much about that emotion as Grant did. Zero, Joe. Nada. And you can kiss my ass."

"Give me the chance." He narrowed his eyes on her, letting a mocking smile curl his lips. "If you had put the bitch on hold for a minute, I might have gotten around to it. And the next time you compare me to Grant, you might find that sweet ass spanked rather than kissed."

"Lay a hand on me and I'll charge you with assault," she yelled back. "You had your chance to love me, Joe, and you blew it."

"Like hell," he snarled, sexual tension and raging anger rising inside him. "I loved you every damned chance you gave me, Maggie. Completely. Neither of us could move after we were finished."

"You fucked me," she corrected him brutally.

Joe flinched at the explicit wording, something dark and inexplicable rising inside him to deny it.

"And what did you do, Maggie? I hardly think it was love; you married the man you believed was my best friend six months later."

"I didn't know until he brought you to the wedding rehearsal." Her gaze was filled with disgust as it raked over him. "I nearly broke the engagement then, and I would have if he hadn't begged me not to. I knew." Her laughter was tinged with bitterness. "God, I knew better. I should have never listened to him when he swore to me that my relationship with you didn't matter. That he hadn't known about it."

The pain in her eyes made him pause. Maggie had never been much of liar, at least not before her marriage to Grant. She wore her heart on her sleeve, loved or hated with equal intensity. A person didn't have to guess where he stood with her.

"He knew about our relationship," he informed her, watching her closely. "He knew the night you walked out on me, and he knew why."

Her lips parted for a second before closing firmly, tightening into a bitter line. There was no surprise there, though, only remembered pain. Grant's lies couldn't surprise her anymore, only her own stupidity at the time still had the power to hurt her.

"Yes," she finally admitted. "He did. He knew about our relationship and he used it the entire time we were married. Too bad I didn't know any better before the vows were spoken."

"Why did you marry him?" That question had haunted him, had driven him to drink more nights than he could count.

"Because I thought he loved me," she threw back at him fiercely. "And I thought I loved him. I thought he was honest, that he wanted more than the quick fuck his buddy had decided was all I was good for."

"Say that word again and you're going to regret it, Maggie," he snapped.

"What? Fuck?" she sneered. "What's wrong, Joe, does it offend you to know what a complete bastard you were?"

"I know well how damned stupid I was." God knew it had been driven home night after lonely night for two and a half years. "But you were never just a fuck."

"Oh, you loved me?" she asked mockingly. "Yeah, sure you did, Joe. Even while you were parading Miss Big Boobs around on your tuxedoed arm for a night out? Did you think I had forgotten that one?"

Miss Big Boobs. Fake boobs maybe, not that he had checked. The woman in question, Carolyn Delorents, had been the daughter of a suspected drug kingpin. He had been on assignment. Nothing more. An assignment he hadn't told Maggie about.

"I haven't forgotten," he growled. "And you would never listen to explanations."

"Explanations come before you spend the night with another woman hanging off you, not after," she pointed out sarcastically. "And I didn't want explanations. The fact that you did it, without telling me, was enough."

"We weren't married . . ."

"I was falling in love with you," she cried out. "You knew it. You knew it, and rather than telling me I was wasting my time you let me find it out at an event I was covering for the paper. You didn't tell me anything."

"I didn't know you would be there."

"Which only makes it worse." She swiped her fingers beneath her eyes before blinking back her tears. "I've paid enough for our affair, Joe."

She turned, stalking from the room before he could stop her. Following her, he caught the bedroom door before she could slam it closed and moved slowly into the room.

"Explain that comment." Suspicion uncurled in his stomach. He had tried to convince himself that Grant had been good to her, that he had loved her. Through the past two years he had never imagined she had been anything but worshipped.

"He married me because he was convinced you cared about me." Her eyes flashed with pain and anger. "Three months after our marriage I left him, Joe." Mockery twisted her features. "Only to be forced back. He blackmailed me with a mistake my father made when first starting the newspaper. He wasn't about to let me leave, to lose the one thing he had to torment you with."

"Why didn't you tell me?" He forced back his anger, his disbelief.

"Blackmail, Joe. You understand the concept, right?"

"I understand the concept." He held on to his control by a thread.

She wasn't lying. He knew Maggie. In that moment he realized that he knew her better than he had ever known anyone in his life. And he couldn't make himself believe that she was lying.

"He left me alone for the most part, as long as I played the role." She sniffed back her tears as she sat slowly on the edge of the bed. "We had separate bedrooms. He never tried to touch me. He got off on hurting you. He hated you." She shook her head, confusion filling her voice. "I never understood that."

Joe met her gaze as she lifted her eyes to his, watching him with such perplexed anger that it caused his chest to clench.

"Did he ever say why?" He had never really known Grant—Joe realized that now—but a lifetime of believing in the friendship he thought they had was hard to put behind him. He had trusted Grant above anyone else in the world, even his family. Grant had been the brother Joe had never had. At least, he had thought he was. Separating himself from those memories sometimes felt as though he were separating a part of his soul from his body.

"Oh, he had plenty of reasons." Weariness washed over her expression. "The promotion you got and he didn't. Something about bullies in school. But I think most of it came down to the fact that your family was stinking rich, according to him. That bothered him most of all."

And Joe had never known. That was the hardest part for him. He had never suspected that Grant had hated him so thoroughly.

"I loved him like a brother." And he had, since they were boys. "That's why I didn't stand between you when I learned who he was dating, then marrying. It's the reason I left it alone, Maggie. I thought you deserved someone to love you, and I thought he loved you."

She stared back at him for long moments, remnants of anger glittering in her dark green eyes.

"Such sacrifice," she snorted, the sound causing him to clench his teeth against the frustration eating at him. "You should apply for sainthood, Joe."

She rose to her feet once again, moving slowly around the bedroom before stopping on the far side and turning back to face him.

"What did you think I was going to do now? Fall back into your arms as though the past two and a half years never happened?"

"I could have handled it." He shrugged tensely. "I never forgot, Maggie—"

"Then forget now."

Joe read the wariness in her eyes.

"Have *you* forgotten, Maggie?" He moved toward her slowly, dying to touch her, to taste her one more time. "Did you forget how hot I could make you? How hot and wet you got for me, baby?"

He didn't touch her as he moved to her; he stared into her eyes, feeling the needs rising inside him as fiercely as they reflected in her eyes.

"This isn't going to get us anywhere," she whispered, her hands clenching the material at the front of her shirt. "I won't let you do this to me again."

"That's what I swore about you a week ago," he admitted. "That I wouldn't get so hard for you that the only thing that mattered was getting you beneath me, burying my cock so deep inside you I didn't know where you ended and where I began. That I wouldn't ache for you, that I wouldn't need to hear that soft little cry you make when you come for me."

"That you wouldn't use what I felt for you to try to trap me?" she suggested mockingly, causing him to grit his teeth in frustration.

"I wouldn't use the sex against you, Maggie." Would he? He was telling himself he wouldn't, but he knew he would push her. She had to know where that information was, if only subconsciously.

"You would use any weapon against me that you could find," she threw back at him as she edged away.

Joe followed.

"You were married to him for two years," he said softly. "You may have hated every minute of it, but you were there, in that house with him. There had to have been something he said, something he did . . ."

"And you think I haven't thought of that?" she spat out. "That's all I've thought of, Joe. Because if I could give you that damned information you want so bad, then I'd be free. Of you, of Fuentes, *and* of Grant. Trust me, no one wants you to have that information more than I do."

"You want to leave me that bad, Maggie?" He moved behind her, leaning in close, careful not to touch. "I remember a time when you found excuses to stay in my bed, to remain at my place."

"And I remember a time when you found excuses to escape," she reminded him, stepping away again, but not before he saw the little tremor of response that washed over her. "You didn't want what I had to offer before, Joe, and now, whatever you're offering, I'm passing on."

He watched her move across the bedroom and enter the bathroom. Unhurried, her slender body shifting beneath the loose clothes she had worn to sleep in. Her head was lifted, her shoulders straight, and the pride that reflected in her stance caused a grin to edge at his lips.

He wondered if she knew she moved against him in that big bed each night. More often than not, her head ended up on his shoulder, a shapely leg thrown over his, and her hand lying directly over his heart. Just as she had lain when she had shared his bed so long ago.

And each night his control withered further away as his cock became more demanding. She could argue until she was blue in the face, and sometimes she could, but he knew what he felt each night. Hard nipples pressing against his side through her T-shirt. Her hands touching him tentatively, as though he were a dream.

He was a fool to let her go the first time, and he could be playing a bigger fool now. Only time would tell. And that was why he'd brought her here, he reminded himself. If she were lying, he would find out. If she were telling the truth . . . then he would protect her with everything he had. If she were telling the truth, then he would never let her out of his life again. She would be his. One way or the other.

4

Men sucked. They were the root of every problem any woman could ever have. They were the reason for bras, the need for makeup, hair stylists, shaving legs, and high heels that made the arch feel like it had a steel rod slammed up it. They were picky, arrogant, argumentative, and so damned certain of themselves it made her grind her teeth in fury.

And Joe was the worst. He always had been. He didn't argue, debate, or consider anything; it was his way, however he had to make certain it came about. And once again he was working her. She could feel it.

He watched her now in a way he hadn't all week, eyelids lowered, his expression brooding, thoughtful, calculating. His dark eyes rarely left her, and she could feel the sexual hunger thickening in the air around him. He had a look when he was aroused to the point that the sex would be hard and brutally satisfying. And he was getting that look.

"Stay away from me," she ordered, as he moved close to her that evening, brushing against her as she stacked the dishwasher with dinner dishes.

His male grunt did little to calm her nerves. Nothing he could do, though, could calm her nerves. He wasn't the only one aroused after a week of enforced confinement, of nights spent in the same bed with him, feeling the heat of his body.

Dressed in jeans and T-shirt, and a bra, the layers of clothing did absolutely nothing to stem the needs that only grew. She remembered nights, hours on end that he would take her, throwing her into one orgasm after another, leaving her breathless, exhausted as the sun rose beyond the windows of his apartment. He was inexhaustible. And the memory of it was killing her.

"You've changed," he remarked as he stood back from her, propping himself against the counter as he watched her. "You were never so confrontational before, Maggie."

"I was never in danger for my life before," she reminded him, flashing him a short glare. "It does change a girl's perspective, Joe."

"You're going to be fine." A quick frown edged at his dark blond brows as he watched her. "We'll figure out where the information is and we'll take Fuentes down."

"One thing you never lacked was confidence." Maggie closed the door to the dishwasher before setting the power and flipping it on. "There has to be someplace Grant hid things. What about his other journals?" he asked her. "We only found the current one, it began six months before. Where did he keep the others?"

"I have no idea." She shook her head as she breathed out roughly. "I spent as little time around Grant as I had to. I didn't question him, I just wanted him to leave me alone, so I left *him* alone."

"Did he mention a safe deposit box?"

"Joe, these are all questions the detective asked me at the station," she reminded him abruptly. "If he had one, I didn't know. I never cared about his journals, his friends, or his comings and goings. If I had suspected for a moment what he was up to, I would have paid more attention. But I didn't."

"Men like Grant like to brag."

"Grant bitched, accused, and went into paranoid delusions." She shook her head at his perception that Grant would tell her anything. "Everyone was to blame for everything that had gone wrong in his life, except him. I assumed his journals were filled with the same crap, so I never gave them a thought."

He was silent then, but she could feel his eyes on her as she wiped down the counter and the table before pulling out the Swiffer to go over the floor.

She could feel the little tremors of response building beneath her flesh as he watched her, she could almost feel his eyes raking over her snug jeans, the press of her breasts beneath the T-shirt.

Minutes later she propped the Swiffer back in its place before turning and heading for the living room. She was aware of Joe following her, stalking her like a damned animal. As though he could sense her arousal and was debating the best way to act on it.

Let me love you, he had whispered earlier. He had no idea how those words had ripped through her heart. She had dreamed of him loving her, had believed he was beginning to until she covered that damned party she had no idea he had been invited to. Because he hadn't told her. Hadn't invited her. Oh no, he'd had one of his society women on his arm, decked out in silk and diamonds and platinum blonde hair.

Had he slept with her?

She couldn't let herself think of that. Even now, two and a half years later, the thought that he would take another woman so quickly after having shared a bed with her had the power to rip her defenses to shreds.

"You can't ignore me forever, Maggie."

She stopped in the middle of the living room, breathing in deeply before turning to face him.

"I'm not trying to ignore you, Joe."

His eyes were brilliant with lust, the same look that had the power to bring her to her knees during their relationship. Literally.

He tucked his hands into the pockets of his slacks and stared back at her silently, as her gaze flickered to the action. The heavy bulge between his thighs sent heat burning through her body. Her vagina ached, echoed with emptiness, as her nipples pressed hard against the material of her bra.

She swallowed tightly as she felt the need for oxygen increase.

"Did he please you in bed?"

The question took her by surprise.

"Excuse me?"

"Grant." He frowned back at her. "Did he please you in bed? Did he make you scream and beg for more, even when you were too exhausted to take more?"

Her eyes widened at the flicker of anger in his eyes.

"That's none of your business—"

"The hell it's not," he snapped. "I went crazy for two and a half years wondering if he pleased you, knowing he shared your bed . . ."

"Stop it, Joe. This isn't going to get us anywhere."

"I'll know." He kept his voice low, even, a sure indication that he wasn't going to let the subject go.

"No, you won't." She lifted her chin as she stared back at him, her fists clenched at her side as she fought to maintain her control. "Because I'm not answering you."

Shame filled her at the thought of revealing the truth. She had known on her wedding night that the mistake she had made in her marriage was more severe than she had expected. Grant's lust had sickened her, his spoken perversions filling her with disgust and fear.

"His journal was pretty in-depth concerning your sex life," he informed her then. "He was quite descriptive."

Maggie felt herself pale. "We weren't having sex then. I hadn't shared his bed since the first months of our marriage, I told you that."

"Why?" He moved closer, stalking her like a predator.

"That's none of your business, Joe. Let it go." She watched him closely, wary, uncertain as to how he would react.

"You're a very passionate woman, Maggie. I can't imagine you denying yourself, or cheating on your husband to attain satisfaction."

"I like sex, so automatically I had to be fucking someone?" she snapped out furiously. God save her from hardheaded men.

"That wasn't what I said."

"Yes, Joe, that was what you were saying." She waved her hand back at him in a gesture of frustration. "What did you do for the last two and a half years? We both know you weren't a virgin when you came to my bed. How many women have you had since me?"

"No one."

The answer had her flailing for a response; instead, she could only stare back at him in shock.

She stared back at him silently as he came closer, his expression dark, intent as he watched her.

"You tormented me, Maggie."

She shook her head desperately. "Don't play with me like this, Joe. Please." She was willing to beg. She had left him, believing he didn't hold her heart. Now, two and a half years later, she admitted the truth she hadn't wanted to face then. She had loved him then, and that love had never died.

"I'm not playing with you, Maggie." His hand covered her cheek as she lost her breath. The sound of her tremulous gasp would have been humiliating if his touch weren't so warm, so needed. "I'm trying to save us both this time."

She was panting for air, certain her shaky knees would give out before she found the strength to move away from him.

"Do you remember what it was like?" he asked her gently.

Maggie stared back at him, dazed, uncertain, as his lips lowered to breathe a kiss against hers.

"All night long," he whispered over her lips. "I would fall asleep, still buried in your body, still hungry for you. Do you remember that?"

"I remember seeing you with another woman." She forced the words past her lips. "I remember you staring at me across the room, your expression as cold as ice. That's what I remember, Joe."

His jaw clenched. "You can forget that."

"No, I can't forget that." She pushed away from him slowly, fighting back the regret as she did so.

"I didn't sleep with her, Maggie."

The tension tightening his body had her stepping back further. She could feel the certainty that he was at the edge of his control. Once he slipped past the veneer of civility, denying him wouldn't be an option. The hunger in him called to her too fiercely, pulled at her too desperately. When Joe began coming after her in earnest, she would be lost, and she knew it.

"It doesn't matter that you didn't sleep with her," she told him softly as she moved to the couch. There was no way in hell she was heading to the bedroom. "It's not about the woman, Joe, it's the fact that you did it. You weren't as invested in me as I was in you, otherwise, you would have told me about the party. You would have told me about your date."

She curled into the corner of the overstuffed couch, drawing her legs up until they bent to her side and gave her a measure of protection against the throbbing heat between her thighs.

He hadn't moved from where he stood, other than to turn and follow her progress across the room with his eyes. She knew what he was doing, what he had been doing all day. Trying to push her buttons. From the first words out of his mouth that morning, when he accused her of pouting, to now, he was trying to work her, to get what he wanted without giving any of himself in return.

That wasn't enough for her now. She wanted as much in return as she had to give, or she wanted nothing at all. And giving all of himself wasn't something she thought Joe would do easily. He faced her, his jaw flexing with tension, his brown eyes raging with frustration and arousal.

"Why didn't you tell me, Joe?" She tilted her head when he said nothing. "What would you have done if you'd seen me on another man's arm that night?"

"I would have torn him apart," he snapped.

"Your date left with all her hair and teeth intact," she pointed out gently.

"And you never came back," he growled. "You wouldn't answer my calls. By God, you didn't want to hear explanations."

"No, I didn't," she admitted sadly. "The explanation should have come before the reality of it kicked me in the gut, Joe. I watched you that night, pretending you didn't know me, that I was nothing, as you danced with another woman. . . ."

"I never took my eyes off you."

"Or your hand off her," she reminded him.

"It was a fucking case, Maggie," he snapped, a grimace contorting his face. "Do you think I wouldn't have told you if I thought you would be there? After I saw you it was too late; I couldn't jeopardize the case."

"I cover the society page, Joe," she yelled back, infuriated with his logic. "You should have known I would be there. You should have warned me."

"How?" He pushed his fingers restlessly through his long hair. "What the hell was I supposed to do, Maggie? I was in the middle of an operation, I couldn't just tell you what the hell was going on."

"You could have warned me you had a job to do. That's all I needed." She jumped to her feet, anger surging through her. "I knew you worked for the DEA, Joe. I wasn't stupid or incompetent. I wouldn't have asked questions, but I would have been warned. Why the hell do you think you walked out of that party with all appendages intact that night? I didn't strike out just in case you were working, rather than trying to fuck Miss Big Boobs hanging on your arm."

"Then why are you still so pissed?" He was genuinely confused. "Why did you avoid me, Maggie? We could have worked this out."

"Because you didn't warn me, Joe," she reminded him with false patience. "Because you expected more from me than you were willing to give, and every damned message you left on my phone proved it."

"What?" He frowned back at her in confusion. "I asked you to call me."

"You demanded I call you. You informed me, more than once, that I was being silly, childish, petulant," she sneered. "No, Joe, I wasn't. I expected no more from you than you would have from me, and you weren't willing to give it. You would never have tolerated seeing me with another man; why did I have to endure seeing you with another woman? No warning. No explanation. No nothing."

He was silent, staring back at her with narrowed eyes and stubborn features. His arrogance was one of the things she used to admire, that complete male self-confidence that drove her crazy and turned her on all at the same time.

"I didn't expect that from you," he ground out. "I would have explained."

"The explanation was too late." She tossed her hair back before smiling tightly into the growing anger in his dark eyes. "I'm not arguing this with you any longer, Joe. My relationship or lack thereof with Grant is none of your business. Just as your job and what it requires of you is none of mine. You're here to do a job. To protect me, and to find out if I know where Grant hid your precious proof. Stick to the job. You're good at that."

With that, she stalked from the living room into the bedroom and slammed the door behind her. She really prayed he took the hint and left her alone. The hurt and anger she had buried when she had left Joe was rising inside her now. The lack of outlet over the years, and her determination to hide from her feelings for him, had kept her safe from the repercussions. Now the pain was flowing through her, the remembered shock and heartache when she realized how little she had meant to him, slammed into her now with a force she hadn't expected.

She deserved the same love she was willing to give, and her marriage to Grant had taught her that she wasn't willing to settle for less. Especially not from Joe.

5

The bedside clock read two in the morning before Joe heard the deep, even breathing that indicated Maggie had slipped off into sleep. Within minutes, as she had every other night, she rolled from the edge of the bed to the middle, and her slender body tucked in against his.

He gritted his teeth against the arousal pounding between his thighs, and knew Craig wasn't going to be happy to be pulling the extra hours of watch that he would be stuck with in the morning.

Maggie was unaware that Craig was watching the outside of the cabin. The other man slept through the day, then took up watch at midnight until Joe moved onto the porch each morning to indicate he was awake and on the job. Joe was getting up later every morning, though. Sleep was becoming harder with each successive night.

As Maggie shifted against him demandingly, he lifted his arm, allowing her to settle against his chest before he let himself hold her close. She felt right in his arms, but hell, she always had.

How many times had she slept against him like this? How many times had he awakened in the middle of the night, just to listen to her breathe, to feel the softness of her hair as he held her close?

He stared up at the ceiling, his lips compressing as he remembered the accusations she had thrown at him earlier that evening. Had he really expected more from her than he was willing to give?

Maybe he had. He had been so busy assuring himself that what they had was just an affair, that the volatile little redhead wasn't getting beneath his skin, that he had missed the fact that she was firmly entrenched in his heart.

That was why he had jerked her out of the interrogation room when she had been brought in for questioning. That was why he couldn't accept that she had been part of Grant's criminal activities, despite the proof—pictures of Maggie handing Diego and Santiago Fuentes several envelopes at an upper-class restaurant, pictures of her greeting them at the door of their home, and exchanging small talk at several parties she had attended for the paper.

She had told Detective Folker she was unaware of what the envelopes contained. That she had run the errand for Grant simply because it was easier than fighting over it, and she had been going into that part of the city anyway.

The journal Grant kept had held pages and pages of accusations against Maggie. Implying that he had begun betraying the agency and his friends because of her spending habits, because of her determination to always have more.

But Maggie hadn't dressed any differently than she had before her marriage to Grant. There were no expensive clothes, no fancy jewels, and she had never driven the new car Grant had bought her. So where was the money Fuentes had given him?

He buried his fingers in Maggie's hair as he tried to work

through the questions. After a week with her, his suspicion that she might have been involved was dissolving beneath his hunger for her and the knowledge that if money had been what Maggie was after, then she would have never cut him out of her life as she had.

He had money. A DEA agent's pay sucked, but his family was one of the most influential in Georgia, and his trust fund would see any children he had into old age if they were careful. Not to mention what his parents would one day leave him. If Maggie had been after money, then she had missed a much easier opportunity than marrying Grant and becoming involved with the Fuentes family.

Instead of trying to snag him for marriage or money, Maggie had left him. Not that Joe claimed anything as his own. Money was accessible if he needed it. But his parents' money wasn't his own, and he refused to touch it. Still, that wasn't the reason she had been so furious. She hadn't forgiven him for not warning her before she saw the daughter of the man they were investigating on his arm.

He had been there to get information. He had gotten the information, but he had lost the girl. His girl. Was he willing to lose her again?

A soft moan slipped past her lips as she moved against him again, her lips pressing the bare flesh of his chest. Joe clenched his teeth against the heated pleasure of her soft little tongue stroking over the flat, hard disk of his male nipple.

Could he survive another night of her in his arms without touching her? God, it was getting hard. She was like a little kitten, pressing to get closer, her fingers curling against his abdomen, her nails raking his flesh and sending a flash of clenching sensation to seize his balls. Sweat popped out on his forehead, along his chest and thighs, and his cock tightened further.

His erection was so damned hard, so sensitive he bit back a tortured groan as the crest flexed against the material of his sweatpants. And there was no relief. He sure as hell wasn't going to try jacking off with her in the bed with him, and doing it any other time was out of the question. Besides, the hollow release gained from the act wasn't what he needed. He needed Maggie, her sweet, tight pussy enveloping him, burning him as he possessed her.

"Joe." His name whispered past her lips, that sleepy little plea he remembered from the past, the throb of hunger in her voice that had once had him turning to her, slipping easily inside her as he awakened her fully to his touch.

Instead, he now lay still, tortured, tormented as her silken hand moved over his stomach, caressing, raking her short nails over his flesh and sending agonizing bursts of pleasure through his cock.

He breathed in slow and deep as her teeth raked over his nipple, a murmur of feminine pleasure vibrating from her throat as her hand moved lower.

Joe lifted his arm, his free hand gripping a slat in the headboard behind his head as he fought for control as anticipation began to spiral inside him. He knew her like this. Drowsy, when she would awaken in the middle night, hungry for him, all kittenish and relaxed. And he wasn't about to fuck this up. No way in hell. In those brief minutes between sleep and awake, Maggie had the most amazing habit of forgetting if she was pissed off with him. If she didn't remember it right now, he wasn't reminding her. Uh-uh. Was not going to happen.

"Maggie." He couldn't stem the hoarse groan that left his throat as her fingers played with the elastic band of the sweats.

He could feel his mouth drying out as anticipation began to build, his erection flexing in need as her fingers began to move beneath the band.

"Hmm," she murmured against his chest, her teeth sinking against his flesh in a sensual, warning little bite, as he parted his thighs and let her have her way.

Hell no, he wasn't reminding her of nothin'. If he did, then she was likely to turn away, to be embarrassed, angry. Whichever, it meant she would stop touching him, that the blazing heat of her hand wouldn't . . .

Son of a bitch!

His hips jerked violently as she moved again. Slender fingers tried to encircle the raging shaft as she shifted against him again, her lips moving lower on his chest.

Oh hell, he knew what was coming. He remembered this well, and if she came to her senses while his dick was in her mouth then she was likely to get violent.

But it wasn't like he was encouraging her, he assured himself as he lifted his other hand to the headboard, determined not to guide her head lower. Hell no. He wasn't going to stop her. She was a grown woman. If she wasn't going to remember she was pissed, then he was not reminding her. Wasn't going to happen.

He fought to breathe as he stared in dazed pleasure at the ceiling above the bed, nearly panting in lust as her fingers pushed his sweatpants down, struggling to guide the material over the erection.

"Good," she mumbled with a soft smile against his flesh, as the cloth finally slid beneath the thick, iron-hard flesh rising eagerly to her touch.

Her fingers wrapped around him again, stroking slowly from his balls to his crest, as his hips arched involuntarily to her caress. Her fingers were like living silk as they rasped over the sensitive flesh. Her lips and tongue were hungry, heated as they moved below his chest, kissing, licking, taking sensual little nips from his flesh.

It always amazed him in the past when she would do this. That her need could so overtake her in those moments when she awoke that nothing mattered to her but being with him. Touching him. Tasting him. Destroying him with her hunger.

She was destroying him now. He ground his head into the pillow, bit back a violent growl that she hurry, and fought to enjoy as much as possible before she remembered she was supposed to be mad at him.

Two and a half years. He hadn't had a woman since the last night Maggie had spent in his bed. And God, he had missed her. This was why no other woman had shared his passion, because he knew no other could compare to what he was finding at this moment.

Knowing he was making an even bigger mistake, he moved his gaze from the ceiling, looking down the line of his body, as the dim light that burned past the partially closed bathroom door fell on Maggie's head as he watched her move lower. Lower.

"Sweet heaven. Maggie, baby," he panted.

He couldn't take much more. He was shaking; sweat pouring from his body as she moved to his abdomen, her tongue painting a path of fiery need across his flesh.

Closer. Ah, God, her tongue was so close. It was torture, the worst sort of agonizing pleasure, to have her silken tongue so close and yet so far away from his engorged erection.

Her fingers stroked his burning cock as her tongue came within inches, inches. He was shaking with anticipation, sweat building on his body and running in small rivulets down his chest as he fought to hold on to his control.

"Maggie. God, baby. Tell me you're awake." His hands clenched on the slats and he blinked back the sweat dripping to his eyes as he told himself to stop her. To put an end to the sweet torment before she took a bite out of him that he might not recover from. Maggie could be amazingly fiery, both in passion and in her fury.

He could move his hands. He could grip her head and force her to stop. But he was terrified that if he let go of the death grip he had on the bed, that rather than waking her as he pulled her from him, he would awaken her as he filled her mouth instead.

"God. Damn, Maggie." His ragged cry filled the darkness as her tongue swiped over the head of his cock. The hardened flesh flexed then spurted a hard stream of pre-come to her waiting lips.

Shit. That wasn't supposed to happen.

But her murmur of appreciation was followed by burning ecstasy. Her mouth enveloped the thick head, her tongue swirling around it, probing at the small eye as she greedily consumed him. Arching to her as another curse tore past his lips, he thrust deeper, feeling her lips tighten on him, her tongue lashing at him.

Ah God. He had to stop this. Didn't he?

How? How the hell was he supposed to find the strength to make her stop?

"Maggie, baby . . . please . . . ," he groaned harshly as she began to suck him with slow, tight strokes of her mouth.

Nearly to her throat, only to retreat, her tongue laving with quick little licks before sinking down again, her lips meeting her fingers as she stroked the lower portion of his shaft.

She was going to destroy him. Tonight, she would steal his soul and there wasn't a damn thing he could do about it. Once he spilled into her mouth there would be no returning to sanity. There never had been. Like an animal, reality receded and nothing mattered but spreading her thighs and fucking them both into exhaustion.

"God yes." He blinked again against the moisture stinging his eyes as his hips moved to her suckling mouth. Thrusting in and out, his scrotum tightening until pleasure was near pain and the need to come was torture.

"There you go, sweetheart," he panted. "Hell yes. Suck it, baby. Suck it so deep and good. Your mouth is heaven, Maggie. Paradise."

He strained in her grip, desperate to reach deeper, to thrust harder. He fought the need to climax, his head thrashing on the pillow as he fought it with every ounce of control he could hang on to.

She was unaware of what she was doing. Surely she was. She had gone to bed furious with him, hadn't she?

Then she moved again, sliding between his thighs, one hand cupping the tight sack beneath his cock as she took him deeper, moaned, and her eyes opened in drowsy sensuality.

There was no shock. Green eyes stared back at him with drugged lust as her entire mouth caressed him, flexed around him, and he was lost. She knew what the hell she was doing. Just as she always had.

A hard growl tore from his lips as he drove hard against her grip and lost the last threads of control. He felt his semen exploding into her mouth, her lips moving as she consumed him, accepting his release as her hands stroked, caressed. Her tongue milked at the underside of his cock, urging more of the creamy release to her mouth as she moaned in rising hunger.

"I tried." His hands tore from the slats of the headboard. "God help us both, Maggie, I tried . . ."

6

She was so weak. Maggie cursed her weakness even as she let Joe bear her to her back on the bed. He was her weakness. His lips on hers, the sharp, fierce kisses that left her drugged as his hands pulled at her shirt. He lifted only enough to drag the material over her head and toss it aside before he was back.

Cool air rippled over the tender, aching tips of her breasts only a second before Joe's heat enveloped her once again. He had that power, the power to warm her, to fuel a fire inside her so hot, so desperate that nothing mattered but his touch.

Maggie opened to him, her hands clutching at his back as the rasp of his chest hair stimulated her sensitive nipples and stole her breath with the pleasure. So good. It had been so long. Too long without him, without his touch. She had sworn she wouldn't let this happen, but her own dreams and hunger had stolen her will.

She had dreamed of him every night that they had been apart.

Aching dreams. Dreams of anger or of lust. Dreams of reunion or of parting. It didn't matter which, she looked forward to each one, to touching him, to seeing him, if only in those dreams.

But this hadn't been a dream. When she slowly awake, forgetting for a few brief moments where they were, and the trouble she was in, Maggie had touched him. Her hand sliding over his abdomen. Her body heating with need. Just as quickly reality had tried to intrude. But Joe was there, tense but quiet beneath her touch, letting her lead.

He had never done that before. Never had he lain back and allowed her to set the pace of any part of their lovemaking.

Having that control had broken her resolve. That and her own hunger. God, such hunger for him. She couldn't bear the longing whipping through her, the emotions tearing into her heart, filling her soul.

As she moved between his thighs she had expected him to dominate the act, to move her head as he wanted it, to hold her to him as he took over the pace. Instead, his ragged voice had encouraged her as he arched to her. His hands had gripped the headboard, his body tight, tortured with need.

And now she arched to him. As his lips moved from hers, to her neck, then her breasts, his hands pushed at the pajama bottoms she wore.

Heat built around them until Maggie felt perspiration coat her flesh. Reaching for him, a whimper left her lips as he caught her hands and stretched her arms above her head.

"Hold on," he growled. "It's my turn now."

Her fingers latched onto the slats behind her as she watched him with dazed fascination. The expression on his face was one she had never seen, not at any time before. Savagery tightened it as hunger lent a dark cast that sent a shiver racing down her spine. He wanted her, wanted her with a depth and a strength she had never seen in him before.

His head lowered over a breast again, his lips poised just above the hard point rising eagerly toward him. His gaze lifted, meeting hers in the dim light of the room as his tongue extended to lick over the stiff peak, demanding that she watch. That she see the naked lust and pleasure tearing through him, as it tore through her. Sensation whipped through her, jerking her body violently upwards as a cry left her lips.

"Joe. Don't tease me. It's been too long."

Years too long. An aching, sorrow-filled lifetime since she had known his touch.

"I know how long it's been." His voice was raspy, deep. "Every day, every hour, I counted with my need for you, Maggie. I'm a very hungry man now. Let me relish what little time my control will allow me here."

He turned his head, rubbing his rough cheek against the sensitive flesh of her swollen breast. Maggie bit her lip as she panted for air and shuddered beneath the caress.

"I love your breasts." His hands framed the hardened mounds, his thumbs raking over her nipples as the hard bursts of pleasure had her whimpering in rising anticipation. "Such pretty, flushed nipples." He lowered his head, his lips covering the hard tips, his tongue flickering over them with rapid, hot strokes. "So sensitive and easy to please. I love pleasing your nipples, Maggie."

Maggie's hands tightened on the headboard, as her gaze dimmed and pleasure rocked through her. It was so good, the slow worshipping of her breasts. She remembered that well, how he loved making her nipples hard, then driving her crazy as he made them more sensitive by the second.

Which was pretty much what he was doing now. Laving each

with his tongue, raking them with his teeth, only to come back to suck at them firmly, one by one, until she swore she was going to climax from the intense pleasure of that alone.

"Beautiful." He breathed the word from one nipple to the other before giving each a parting kiss and moving lower.

As he touched her, Maggie could feel her heart melting, her soul reaching out to him. There was a difference in his touch, it was gentler, almost reverent. As though the time spent apart had hurt him as much as it had hurt her. Was she being fanciful? Probably. But God, she loved him. She always had. And for just this one night she would let her heart have its way and convince her that he loved her as well. Just a little bit. Just enough to sustain the dreams she had kept hidden, even from herself.

"Joe . . ." The pleasure grew, wrapping around her until she knew she wasn't going to be able to bear much more. The agonizing arousal tearing through her clenched her womb, throbbed in her vagina. She was desperate for release, for his possession.

"I have to taste you again, Maggie," he whispered, his voice whisky-rough as his hands moved to push the pajama bottoms further down her thighs and over her knees.

With an impatient kick, Maggie discarded the bottoms. Arching her back, she lifted closer to the tormenting lips moving along her torso, then her abdomen. With hot licks and slow kisses, Joe had her stretched on a rack of lust nearly too intense to bear. The pleasure was burning through her nervous system, creating a vortex of need, hunger, and intense blinding arousal so deep it became the very center of her existence.

She needed more.

As he lifted himself between her thighs, his hands parting her legs and lifting them until her knees bent, Maggie could only watch in rising anticipation. Breathing was nearly impossible as she waited for that first touch, that first blinding, intimate kiss.

"I dreamed of this, Maggie." He moved his hand until the backs of his fingers were feathering over the short curls that shielded her sex. "Touching you, tasting you again. Did you dream of me, baby?"

His thumb rasped over her clit and she jerked in pleasured response.

"You know I did." The dreams had kept her going, had kept her hoping through two years of a marriage that had turned into hell.

She wasn't in the mood for games now, though. She needed to orgasm, needed that sharp brutal edge of lust to dissipate as it only did after Joe brought her to climax.

"Hmm, were your dreams this good?"

His head bent, his tongue swiping quickly through the drenched slit of her sex, as her hips arched violently and a cry tore from her lips. Electrical impulses of lava-hot sensation tore through her body, leaving her hovering on the edge of climax as Joe retreated.

"Don't stop." Her head thrashed on the pillow. "Joe, don't stop."

"I don't want to rush it." His voice was strained, his breath hot against the damp flesh between her thighs as he blew against the sodden curls.

His tongue licked over her, teasing the swollen bud of her clit before going lower. With wicked, knowing licks, he outlined the sensitive entrance to her vagina, his tongue flickering over it as she lifted to him, only to retreat teasingly.

She would never survive his teasing. She knew how he teased, knew how long he could hold off as he made her hotter by the second. She was more desperate now than she had ever been for his touch. The teasing wasn't going to happen, because she would never survive it.

"Rush it. You can go slow later."

She released the slats of the headboard, and before he could catch her hands, her fingers were tangling in his hair and pulling him to her desperate flesh.

She heard a growl a second before his lips covered the aching, burning nub between the sensitive folds of her pussy. Sucking it into his mouth, his tongue licked with a driving rhythm, as a thick male finger worked deep inside the pulsing depths of her vagina.

Oh yeah, that was what she needed.

Pleasure exploded inside her, brilliant shards of white-hot lightning sizzled over her nerve endings, burned through her flesh. Her clitoris swelled beneath the assault, her body tightened, and seconds later the orgasm that tore through her flung her into ecstasy.

She was unaware of the tight grip she had on his hair, or his grip as he forced her fingers free. All she knew was the rapture flying through her, and the feel of him kneeling between her thighs seconds later.

Opening her eyes, she arched her hips to him as he rolled a condom quickly over the straining cock rising between his thighs.

He was powerful, all sleek flesh and rippling muscles. His chest was heaving with the effort to breathe as he secured the protection, then moved into position between her thighs.

"How do you want it?" His voice was strained. "Fast and hard, or hard and fast?"

The limited choice would have amused her, if she weren't so damned desperate for the coming penetration.

"How about hard and fast?" she moaned. "God, I don't care, just do it, Joe. Now . . ."

She screamed at the penetration. It was hard. Fast. In three strokes he had buried himself to the depths of her needy pussy. Coming over her, his arms tucked beneath her shoulders, his elbows holding the majority of his weight from her as he began to move.

"Hell, yes. Take me, baby. Take all of me." The harsh demand, voiced in a tone desperate with pleasure, had her breath lodging in her chest.

All of him. She needed all of him. His body, his heart.

"Joe. Oh God. Joe." Her fingers clenched on his shoulders as her legs lifted, wrapping around his pounding hips and locking in the small of his back as he drove her to insanity with the pleasure burning through her.

"There, baby," he crooned, as his head lowered to her neck. "So sweet and tight." His voice was guttural, throbbing with lust. "I could fuck you forever, Maggie. Never stop. I never want to stop."

The fierce rhythm was too much to contain. Nerve endings untouched in more than two years rioted with the intensity of the sensations stroking over them. Explosions of nearing orgasm began to ripple through the tender tissue, as Joe groaned roughly at the further tightening around his plunging erection.

He liked that, she remembered. The way she tightened around him before climax, the feel of her racing toward completion.

"Come for me, Maggie." He nipped her ear erotically. "Come for me, baby, let me feel you milk me. Now, baby. Now."

He moved faster, impossibly deeper. Maggie felt the sensations splinter inside her as a stronger, harder orgasm gripped her. She couldn't scream, there was no breath to scream, no strength to fight the rolling explosions tearing through her as Joe's male cry filtered through her mind.

He tensed above her, driving deep in one last plunging thrust before she felt the convulsive throb of his cock inside her, felt him spilling himself into the condom he wore.

"Maggie. God, Maggie. I missed you . . ."

Her heart clenched at the words, at the emotion she fooled herself into believing she heard. She loved him. She had always loved him. In that moment, Maggie knew that nothing and no one would ever replace Joe in her heart.

7

"Did you really love him?"

Joe's question wasn't unexpected. Hours after the lust and hunger had burned itself down to a dull glow, sleep had stolen their strength. Now, awake, he held her, her back against his chest as she watched the day lighten beyond the bedroom window.

He wasn't confrontational this time, not as he had been when he questioned her about Grant before. He was quiet, reflective. Unfortunately, it was also when he was at his most dangerous. And she was very aware of the fact that right now he had no intentions of allowing her to brush the subject away. And maybe it was time to face it, to face the truth of the mistakes she had made.

"I thought I did," she finally answered. "I wanted to, until a few weeks after the wedding. Had he been the man I thought I married . . ." She paused. She didn't want to break the fragile peace between them.

"You would have," he answered for her.

He sounded accepting. There was no anger in his tone, he wasn't tense. She hadn't expected that. In the past two and a half years she had seen Joe only once, at her wedding, where he had been best man. It had been hell. The moment she whispered her vows to Grant something had shattered inside her soul.

She should have walked out then; she admitted that to herself long ago. When the vows had stuck in her throat, and the tears had flowed, not from happiness, but from sadness, sorrow, she should have turned and walked out.

But she hadn't wanted to hurt Grant. She had cared for him deeply.

"I could have," she amended. "If I had let myself."

"Would you have let yourself?"

That question no longer haunted her. At first it had, in those first weeks when she had questioned herself so deeply, before Grant had shown himself for the bastard he was.

"If he had been the man I thought he was." Admitting it to herself was the hardest part. "Then I would have loved him." She would have lived her life loving two men, rather than just one.

"You wouldn't have." His answer had her jerking in his arms, turning until she could face him.

"I married him," she pointed out, ignoring the dark look he flashed her. "I cared for him then, Joe. Deeply."

"You cared for him, you didn't love him." His broad hand cupped her face, his thumb caressing over her swollen lips gently. "You would never have loved him, Maggie. Because you loved me."

She breathed in roughly as she stared back at him, remembering the nights she had ached for him, dreamed of him. The nights she had cried for him.

"I cared for him," she repeated. "He wasn't the man I thought he was, so I wasn't given the chance to love him."

She felt him behind her, hard, erect. There was no demand in him though, at least not yet. He smoothed her hair back from her face as he watched her patiently, his gaze velvet-soft, flickering with emotion.

"Wouldn't have mattered." The arrogance that suddenly stamped his features moments later had anger simmering inside her. "You loved me, Maggie. You still love me. You married Grant loving another man and you know it."

She gritted her teeth. She was not going to argue with him. Arguing with him got her nowhere.

"Stop it, Joe."

His smile was patronizing. "You knew when you married him that you didn't love him. You loved me. Admit it."

"Why? So you can gloat? So you know you've won?"

"Oh baby, I already know I've won," he growled. "I just want to make certain you know it."

"I know you have got to be the most infuriating man I have ever met in my life," she snapped, jerking out of his embrace as she moved from the bed. "You just can't help yourself, can you, Joe? Being an asshole is so deeply ingrained inside you . . ."

"I loved you, Maggie."

His calm, quiet announcement shut her up. She stared back at him in surprise, her eyes wide, the elation she would have once felt overshadowed by more than two years of pain.

"You loved me?"

Maggie watched as Joe flicked the blankets back and moved to the opposite side of the bed. The muscles in his back and lean buttocks flexed as he rose to his feet before turning back to her.

He was aroused. The hard length of his erection jutted forward demandingly. Muscular, hard, and proud, the sheer power in his body had always commanded her attention.

"You seem surprised," he grunted. "I haven't had a woman since you left my bed. Do you think it was from choice?"

Of course it wouldn't be. Joe was highly sexed, a creature of lust when it came to his pleasure. That didn't mean it was love. Did it? Or could it?

"I think I'm very much afraid you're playing one hell of a game with me," she admitted the possibility to herself. "You terrify me, Joe, simply because you hold the power to destroy me in the palms of your hands. And if you've already judged me guilty, you wouldn't hesitate to use whatever weapons you could come by. Even lying."

His eyes narrowed on her; the distance of the bed between them suddenly seemed much farther and much more difficult to cross than it had been even days before.

"You're right," he finally answered. "If I thought you were lying, if I thought you were involved, nothing would save you, Maggie. But I haven't lied to you. I don't believe you were involved."

"You've just suddenly found all this love for me that wasn't there two and a half years ago?" She jerked her long shirt from the floor and pulled it on with shaking hands.

"It was always there, Maggie." He didn't bother to pull his sweatpants on, he just stood facing her, aroused and proud and so damned confident she wanted to throw something at him.

Her smile was mocking as she shook her head slowly. "I don't believe you, Joe."

A frown jerked between his brows. "Oh, really?"

The dangerous undertone of his voice wasn't exactly a comfortable sound.

"Really." Maggie ignored the nerves building in the pit of her stomach as she faced him.

She had never truly challenged Joe, not in anything he said or the parameters of their relationship. Confrontations weren't her first choice in solving anything, but as she stared back at him she realized that this particular confrontation had been coming since he had taken her from the police station.

"You don't want to do this right now, Maggie," he warned her quietly. The velvet softness of his voice was a sure sign that his temper was rousing.

"I don't want to push you, period, Joe." She turned from him, bending to pick up her pajama bottoms before putting them on. "It's not worth the heartache you can deliver. But I stopped believing in fairy tales two and a half years ago." She turned back to him, fighting the need to believe him even as she doubted him. "Especially yours."

She didn't expect his sudden response. Joe always handled himself calmly. Coolly. He never lost control. Until that moment.

The change came over his expression so suddenly that Maggie had no chance to react. From one second to the next the easygoing facade was stripped. His dark eyes narrowed, the flesh along his cheekbones tightened, and he had vaulted onto the bed, crossing it in one step before he was in front of her.

Turning to run wasn't really an option, but she tried anyway. With a squeak of alarm she turned and tried to jump for the safety of the bathroom, only to feel the manacle of his heavily muscled arm wrap around her waist as he pushed her against the wall.

"You stopped believing in my fucking fairy tales?" His voice was a hoarse snarl at her ear as she felt her heart rate increase, the blood suddenly thundering erratically through her veins. Not from fear. There was no fear as his hands literally ripped the T-shirt from her body and flung the scraps aside, all the while holding her in place as she struggled against him.

"Are you crazy?" she yelled out, more from shock than any other emotion. Where the hell had *this* Joe come from? She could feel the anger, the lust, and more. Some added edge to his touch that had her heart leaping in hope.

His hands were gentle despite their commanding strength, his body controlling her, even as it stroked against her. This was no act. She could feel it in his hands, in the sudden, dominant hunger blazing in the air around them.

"Believe in this fairy tale then, damn you," he snarled at her ear as the straining length of his cock pressed into the crevice of her buttocks. "You want reality, by God? This is reality, Maggie. I can't bear another woman's touch, and knowing you slept in that bastard's bed ate into my guts like fucking acid. My best goddamned friend, and all I wanted to do was slip into his bed and fuck his wife until she screamed my name and begged me for more. Is that enough reality for you?"

She was panting for him, in the space of seconds just as aroused, just as hungry for him as he obviously was for her. She could feel the pulsing, driving lust in the engorged length of his throbbing erection as he moved back, then spread her thighs further apart.

"You make me fucking crazy."

One hard, desperate thrust filled her with his flesh, took her to her tiptoes and had her crying out his name.

"Joe, please . . ."

"Yes," he snapped, his voice thick with lust. "Joe. It's Joe, Maggie. It's Joe fucking you and it's Joe that's going to make you come. Come for me, baby. Oh God . . . Maggie."

He stilled as she felt him inside her, bare, the latex barrier he normally wore no longer there.

"Shit. Oh hell, Maggie, you feel so fucking good."

He was lost. Joe knew he was lost and there wasn't a damned thing he could do about it. The bitterness and pain in her voice and her expression as she doubted the emotions that had tortured him for so long, had broken his control. Control he had built for his own sanity, control he had sworn he would never lose with Maggie.

But there he was, his dick buried full length inside her, as bare as hell, throbbing with the need to spurt his semen inside her. No condom. Some primal instinct inside him screamed out the denial as he clenched his teeth and fought to pull back, only to return in a thrust that ripped the breath from his body.

"Oh fuck, it's so good," he whispered at her ear as he held her hands to the wall, shifted his hips, and stroked the brutally tight tissue clasping him. "Maggie, baby. You're so sweet and soft. So hot . . ."

He didn't know how to let her go. He knew he should, he needed to. This was a risk he shouldn't be taking, a risk he should have never allowed. But he couldn't release her. God, he couldn't let her go.

"Joe . . ." There was a sense of wonderment in her voice. The cynicism was stripped away, the doubt gone. Innocence filled her tone, the same innocence he heard the night he took her virginity.

Hell, he had been just as shocked then as he was now by the sound of it. A woman nearly twenty-six years old should not be a virgin in this day and age. But Maggie had been. She had laughingly told him she was just waiting on a man who could do more than make her tingle. One who could make her desperate. And he made her desperate.

She made him desperate.

"It's okay, baby." He was panting with the effort not to come, not to fill her with the raging release drawing his balls tight. "Oh God, Maggie. Tell me it's okay. Tell me it's okay."

He had to move. She was so silky soft, slick, tight, gripping him and moving with him as he moved in short, hard strokes that sent radiant pleasure racing down the shaft to clench in his scrotum. He was shaking, literally, with the pleasure tightening along his cock. It was agonizing, blistering, the most sensation he had ever known in his life.

"Joe, please . . . harder. Please."

Her hips were twisting against him, her internal muscles milking him. Hell, it wasn't as though she were the first woman he had taken without a condom. There had been others. A few. But it had never been like this. She was so slick, so tight that the soft sucking sounds of their movements were killing him.

The effort not to come had him drawn on a rack of torturous pleasure. He was going to pull out, he assured himself. He was.

"Are you on . . . the Pill? The Pill, Maggie." *Please, God, let her be on the Pill. Let her be protected.*

She shook her head, even as her pussy tightened on him. His hips slammed against her, driving him in deep, hard before he forced himself to stillness.

He couldn't breathe for the need to come.

"Move." He was at the point of begging. "Get away from me, Maggie. God, do it now. I can't do it."

He loosened his grip on her hands, but he couldn't pull free of her. Hell, where had his control gone? Where was his good sense? If he spilled inside her, she was going to get pregnant. He knew she would. Some instinctive knowledge tightened his gut, flared in his chest.

She didn't move away from him, she moved closer. Her hips shifted as her fingers splayed against the wall.

"Baby . . ." He stared at the side of her face, her cheek was pressed into the wall, her eyes opening with drowsy, sensual pleasure. "I'll come inside you, Maggie."

Her breath caught. He saw it, saw the flush that mounted her cheeks, felt the further tightening of her pussy as her excitement mounted.

"I'll give you my child, Maggie. My baby. Is that what you

want?" He wanted it. Oh God, he wanted it so bad. His baby growing beneath Maggie's heart, sheltered by the woman who owned his soul.

Her doubt didn't matter. He loved her, and he was man enough to admit he had been a fool to ever believe Maggie would have aided Grant in any way. This was his woman. She had always been his woman.

He had dreamed of her for over two years. Dreamed of her back in his life, in his arms, her body growing heavy with his baby. God, he wanted that. Wanted to tie her to him in the most elemental way, in a bond that could never be broken.

"I love you, Maggie," he whispered again as he lowered his lips to her cheek and a fierce involuntary motion of his hips had him thrusting against her again.

It was heaven. Ecstasy. The feel of her surrounding him, clasping him so tight he could barely breathe for the pleasure.

"Joe . . ." Emotion thickened her voice as her fingers tightened around his. "God, please don't hurt me again. Please, Joe . . ."

He saw the tear that tracked down her cheek, glimpsed the ragged fear and emotion that filled her eyes. And he knew the pain she feared, that he would let her go, that he would hide the need, the hunger, the desperation he felt for her again.

There was no hiding now. Not now, not ever. He was instinct, a male claiming his female; more animal than man, as he fought to hold to him the one person he knew he could no longer survive without.

"I'll not let you go again, Maggie." He was on autopilot and he knew it. Hated it. Only Maggie could do this to him, and that was why she had terrified him two and a half years before. This was why he had let her run when she had believed there was no hope for the emotion she needed from him.

"Oh God, Joe. I can't live without you again." She was moving against him, gripping him, writhing against him. "I've always loved you, Joe . . ."

Sanity disintegrated beneath her words. His head lowered, his lips covering the sensitive point between neck and shoulder as he began to move. Hard. Fast. Deep. He was fighting to breathe, feeling her tighten around him, hearing her cries in his ears, and finally feeling her dissolve around him.

Sweet and tight, the hot clasp of her cunt began to milk at his erection, long contractions of pleasure that had him slamming inside her, his back arching, his neck tipping back as he felt his semen pouring from him. Thick, hard jets of ecstasy spurted inside the flexing depths of her pussy as he cried out her name. He heard his own voice, guttural, unnaturally hoarse, as he tried to drive deeper inside her, to fill her womb, to tie her to him in the most fundamental, primal way possible.

She was his. Only his. And for Maggie's sake, not to mention his own, he hoped she realized that.

8

Maggie was stepping out of the shower hours later, her body pleasantly sore and aching, a delightful reminder of Joe's loss of control and the feel of his semen spurting inside her.

As she dried, she rubbed the towel over her belly slowly, thoughtfully. She had always wanted children, had dreamed of having Joe's children. The knowledge that life could be growing inside her now sent an exciting shiver up her spine.

She had never allowed herself to hope, or to dream, that this could actually happen. But in the hours since that first shocking display of primal domination, Joe had done nothing to regain that control. No sooner than he had spent himself inside her, he had her back in the bed, moving over her, and claiming her again. And he hadn't stopped until morning was well on its way and a hunger for food had driven them to the kitchen.

They had showered together, though Joe had finished quickly

and rushed to leave the small shower stall, swearing that if he didn't get away from her, he was going to kill both of them taking her.

Maggie smiled at the thought as she dressed, pulling a pair of silken panties up her sore thighs before easing into her bra, and then jeans and a T-shirt.

She had a feeling that anything requiring much exertion was going off her to-do list for the day. Which meant the hike she had been thinking of talking Joe into was definitely out.

Sitting on the small stool in the corner of the bathroom, she pulled on her socks before rising and padding into the bedroom. She slid her feet into laceless sneakers before moving for the closed bedroom door and pulling it open.

Stepping through the doorway she came to a stop as first Joe, then Craig, moved from the kitchen. Both men were carrying coffee cups and had their weapons hanging on their belts. Joe had been armed for the past week she knew, but never so blatantly.

"Maggie." He paused just inside the living room, his brown eyes watching her worriedly. "Come on in, honey. Get some coffee."

Craig shot him a startled glance at the endearment.

"Is everything okay?" she asked.

Craig Allen was part of the DEA unit Joe commanded before Grant's death. He had been unaware of her involvement with Joe before her marriage, just as everyone else had been.

"We have some information." His expression wasn't comforting, but at least he wasn't pretending they were strangers.

Unconsciously, her hand dropped to her stomach as she fought the nervousness rising inside her. Joe's eyes followed the movement, his nostrils flaring as his cheekbones flushed with lust. Response trembled up her spine, sending a small tremor through her body as he watched.

Maggie swallowed tightly, drawing her gaze from Joe to Craig, who watched them both suspiciously.

"I can do without the coffee for now, then." She breathed in deeply, feeling an insidious sense of disaster building in her chest.

"Come here, baby." He obviously didn't care what Craig saw or thought.

He crossed to her, drew her into his arms, and kissed her cheek comfortingly.

"It's going to be okay," he promised.

Maggie glimpsed Craig's expression. Surprise definitely, and suspicion. But the cold calculation that lurked behind both made her nervous.

"What's going on?" She let Joe lead her to the couch, sitting down nervously as Craig took the chair across from them.

"Your house was trashed yesterday." Craig wasn't one to beat around the bush, either.

As he sat down, his hazel eyes watched her closely, looking, she knew, for a guilty, frightened response.

"It was Grant's house." She shrugged. "If they just got around to trashing it . . ."

"It wasn't trashed in the typical fashion," Craig broke in. "The carpet was ripped through most of the rooms and pulled back. We've had a team going through it, but we've found nothing beneath any of it. We got there before every room was hit, but we've found nothing, and we know whoever went through it didn't find anything."

"The carpet?" She shook her head in confusion. "Why rip away the carpet?"

"They were looking for hidden pockets in the floor," Joe said as he curved his arm around her shoulders, his fingers rubbing at her arm in comfort.

She glanced at him with a frown, shaking her head. "That doesn't make sense."

"The carpet could have been carefully cut to blend in with the nap of the material, but could be pulled away to access a hidden safe or loose boards in the floor where objects can be hidden," Joe explained.

Maggie glanced back at Craig. He was watching her closely, doubtfully. He thought she knew where the information they were looking for was hidden. God, she wished she did.

"Did you check all the rooms after you saw where they were looking?"

Craig nodded shortly. "We had a team stripping carpet all night last night. We found nothing."

Maggie rubbed at her forehead. Where would Grant have hidden that information?

"It could have been a lie," she finally whispered, turning to stare at Joe dismally. "The journal was a lie, Joe. He could have lied about the information."

"He had it, Maggie." Craig informed her coldly.

She couldn't sit still. She had fought to calm the fear rising inside her for the past week, to take one day at a time and pray the information would be found. Rising to her feet, she paced across the living room, listening distantly to Joe and Craig discussing the search the night before.

The house Grant had been so proud of would be a mess. The two-story brick colonial design had been a major buy for him. He had bragged about that house incessantly. Because it was better than Joe's. Because as much money as Joe's family obviously had, they weren't real fond of sharing, because Joe's house was so much smaller, so much less classy. She remembered how he would laugh about that. How Joe's house, right down to the dank, unkempt basement, was so much less superior than the one Grant had managed to buy.

She paced to the edge of the room, turning back to stare at the two men as they continued to talk. Joe was frowning thoughtfully, his eyes narrowed as Craig explained the areas searched and how in-depth it had gone.

Grant wouldn't have hidden anything in his own house. He would have known that was the first place they would look. He was smarter than that. He was demonic. He would have found a way to hurt Joe, even in this. She was actually surprised he hadn't tried to frame Joe instead of her.

"We found several hidden caches of cash. Some drugs." Craig was shaking his head. "And some more journals. Man, he was sick, Joe."

Maggie watched Joe's expression even out, become distant. Grant had nearly destroyed a part of Joe. The two men had been friends for most of their lives. Joe claimed him as a brother, a confidant. He hadn't known the cruel, bitter side to Grant that she had.

"Any clues in the journals?" Joe leaned forward, balancing his elbows on his knees as he watched the other man.

"Pretty much what we found in the others." Craig shrugged. "Different topics, same shit." He shook his head wearily. "We really didn't know him, did we?"

Grant had often laughed over that. How the others didn't really know him, had no idea how much smarter he was, how he could always stay one step ahead of them. Especially Joe. Poor dumb Joe, he would snicker, who would never know how easy he was to fool, how easy it was to use him. Right down to the car Joe had treasured. The '69 Mustang Joe cherished . . .

The Mustang. Grant had hated that car. He always sneered when he spoke of it, with an edge of smug satisfaction.

That taunting, self-satisfied gloat had always entered his voice.

She turned from the two men slowly, praying she appeared casual as she moved into the kitchen, toward the coffeepot. She didn't know Craig well enough, and she could be wrong. And, oh God, if she managed to lead Joe to the information after all, he was never going to believe she had nothing to do with Grant's illegal activities.

She pressed her hand to her stomach, breathing in deeply when she paused by the counter. If he didn't believe in her, he would never have dared to risk a pregnancy with her, she thought with a surge of hope. Joe was very family-oriented. Even though he had many disagreements with his family, she knew he loved them and she knew he was fiercely protective of them.

She hated this. Hated the position Grant had placed her in. He was so lucky he was dead; if he weren't, Maggie believed she would have been tempted to kill him herself at this moment.

As she reached for a coffee cup she heard the two men in the living room moving for the front door.

"Let me know what Johnson says," Joe was saying as the front door opened. Maggie knew the "Johnson" in question had to be the DA she had met at the police station.

"Will do, and you watch your ass," Craig grunted. "Hopefully this will be over soon."

"Hopefully," Joe answered just before Maggie heard the door close.

She left the cup sitting on the counter in front of the coffeepot as she waited. Within seconds, she felt him. First, it was just an impression of strength, of warmth, then his arms were coming around her waist and his lips were pressing into her hair.

"What's wrong, Maggie?" His voice was husky, the dark undertone of arousal threading through it.

She breathed in roughly.

"Grant wouldn't have hidden that information at the house." Her heart was racing in fear. "It would have been too easily found. He didn't work that way."

"I figured as much." He kissed the top of her head again before pulling away and allowing her to turn and face him.

Meeting his gaze wasn't easy, but she did. She found the dark chocolate depths of his eyes filled with warmth and a question. The suspicion she had feared wasn't there, but that did little to temper her fears.

"What did you remember, Maggie?" He tipped his head to the side, watching her closely as she clenched her fingers together in front of her.

"You're so sure I remembered it? Not that I already knew it?" She was slicing her own throat, and she felt the breath strangling in her throat from it.

A small smile quirked his lips.

"I deserved that," he admitted with a small nod of his head. "I'm not stupid, baby. You lived with him for two years. It's only logical that you may have heard of something that you'll eventually remember."

"Not that I was working with him?"

"Maggie." He reached up to push back the strands of hair that had fallen over her face back behind her ear. "I don't believe you were involved with this, so let's stop tiptoeing around each other and finish this up. If you've remembered something, then let me know. We'll get this taken care of, get the danger off your back and start our lives together."

She inhaled with a trembling breath, tears filling her eyes at the gentleness in his voice.

"Your car," she whispered. "Grant was always going on and on about that Mustang. While you were talking to Craig, I remember how smug he acted the last time. The expression on his face. I think he might have hidden the information in that car someplace."

His eyes narrowed as he rubbed at his jaw.

"He helped me put that car back together," he finally sighed. "We worked on that for months."

The painful knowledge that the man he believed was his friend had betrayed him still lingered in his eyes, in the tight grimace in his expression as he turned away from her.

"He would have hidden it where you would never think to look," she pointed out. "He didn't expect to get killed. This was insurance in case he needed to buy his way free of a conviction," she said slowly. "The last few months, before he was killed, he was so certain he was suddenly better than you were. I never thought he would go this far."

She had thought he was insane, not criminal. She should have known better, she admitted. Grant had dropped enough hints, she just hadn't wanted to hear them.

"We'll head back to Atlanta tonight." He nodded abruptly. "The Fuentes family will know by now that I'm the one watching you. They'll be watching my house. I doubt very seriously Grant was the only spy they had in either the Atlanta Police Department or the DEA. So we'll go in quiet, check out the car, and if it's there, we'll head straight to the department from there."

"What about Craig?" she asked nervously.

Joe's broad shoulders tightened before he turned back to her.

"Craig's my backup," he sighed. "But at this point, I'm not trusting anyone else with your life." His expression hardened as he faced her. "We'll go in alone. I'm not taking any chances."

"And if the information is there?" she asked him. She could see the doubt in his eyes that it could be.

"If it's there, then we'll do just as I said." There was a fighting tension in his body now, a readiness that assured her he was planning, plotting out each move from here on out.

"And where will that leave us? Your DA, Craig, and everyone else involved will believe I knew where it was all along, Joe."

"We'll cross that bridge if we come to it," he growled. "And we won't. The DA doesn't give a shit one way or the other as long as he gets what he wants, and neither do the Feds. And I'll make certain they don't want you."

Which didn't reassure her on the fears rising inside her. But did it really matter? The main objective was to see if the information was there. If it was, then she would deal with whatever came later the best way possible. The way she had always dealt with unpleasantness. Straight ahead. She was going into this with her eyes open. Joe was here to get the information. If he believed in her, then he would trust in her. If he didn't . . . Well, if he didn't, then she would face it, and she would survive, just as she always had. The main thing was to get the proof needed and get Fuentes and his men off her back.

She nodded slowly. It was only a matter of hours before dark, and the trip to Atlanta wouldn't take long.

"Do I need to pack?"

He shook his head. "No need. If the information is there then your part in this will be over. The DA won't need your testimony or much of a statement. I'll bring you back here until we're certain it's safe."

But where would he be? Suddenly, she felt as distant from him as she had the first day they had come here. On the periphery of his life, a job, and nothing more. And the thought of that truly terrified her.

9

Joe could feel Maggie's fear. Not her guilt, just her fear. It was amazing how easily he could read her. The way her green eyes would darken to the color of shadowed moss, the frown that puckered her brow. The way she caught the corner of her lower lip between her teeth and worried it absently. That was worry, concern, not guilt.

He remembered guilt. During the months they had spent together, Joe realized he had learned quite a bit about Maggie. Things he hadn't known he had learned until this past week.

Guilt was a careful absence of expression. She had used it several times during their earlier relationship when she tried to deny that she was pushing for more—more commitment, more emotion from him. It was the way she would look down as she played with the hem of a shirt or she picked at her nails. It was the shadowed tone of her voice that deepened her accent. That was guilt.

What he saw now was fear, and it wasn't fear for herself. It was the same fear she showed just before he took her virginity, staring up at him, her eyes dark, her teeth worrying that lower lip, that little frown between her brows. The fear of a broken heart, of putting herself in a place where she truly wasn't wanted.

Maggie was easy to read, unlike Grant. Grant had been trained to lie—being with the DEA demanded a certain talent in subterfuge—and Grant had always done amazingly well at it. So well, in fact, that when it blended into the friendship Joe thought they had, he had never suspected.

Or maybe he had.

He remembered the uneasy feeling he had just before meeting Grant's "fiancée." The feeling that the other man was playing a carefully calculated game. Joe had pushed it behind him, especially after meeting Maggie. Little things, Joe admitted, that he should have taken into consideration long ago. Grant had shown brief spurts of mocking jealousy. It had made Joe uncomfortable at the time, though he had fought to ignore it. He should have never ignored it.

As he watched Maggie turn back to the coffee, he saw the sorrow in her eyes and knew he should do something, anything, to alleviate it.

She had no idea, even now, how much he did love her. Hell, he hadn't known himself until early this morning, until the need to tie her to him for all time had overtaken him.

Primal. He had been like an animal taking his mate, and damn if he didn't want to do it again.

He watched her, the defensive hunching of her shoulders as though expecting a blow, the careful movements as she poured her coffee. She kept her face lowered, but he swore he could feel the fear and pain radiating from her. As fiery as she could be, he knew Maggie had a core of sensitivity that was often her downfall. A sensitivity that would be breaking her heart right now. He bet dollars to donuts that her thoughts weren't on herself, but rather on him, and how it would look to him that she had thought of a possible place Grant could have hidden the information.

Trusting might be the biggest mistake he had made in his life, as Craig obviously believed. Joe had fought trusting her, just as he had fought loving her once before. A battle he had lost, and he hadn't even had the sense to realize it.

She lifted the coffee cup and sipped before sitting it back on the counter. She knew he was behind her, and in most people that avoidance would apply to guilt. Thankfully, Maggie wasn't most people.

"Craig wasn't pleased by what he saw when I came in the room," she whispered.

Joe heard the uncertainty in her voice, the fear that Craig's misgivings could drive a wedge between them. His track record with her wasn't the best, and he admitted that getting past her fears wasn't going to be easy.

"Craig is still dealing with what happened with Grant." Hell, so was he. Out of a four-man team, only he and Craig were left. They were both still aching with the grief over Lyons's loss, as well as Grant's betrayal.

"Aren't we all?" Her painful comment had him grimacing in regret.

"It's a lesson learned," he sighed. "I trusted Grant to the point that I never ran the required security checks on him, and I pushed back doubt when I should have followed through with it. It's a mistake I won't make again."

She still didn't face him. God, he hoped she wasn't crying. He didn't think he could handle Maggie's tears; they would break his heart.

"I should have protected you better," he finally said, his voice rough with his guilt. "I was so damned jealous of what I thought he had with you that I couldn't bear coming around. If I had, I would have known something was wrong."

"So you're just going to take the blame for my marriage as well?" Her vibrant red hair rippled over her shoulders as she shook her head. "You're a glutton for punishment, Joe. And you're wrong. I would have never let you see the nightmare that marriage had turned into. I couldn't have borne it."

She sat her cup down then turned to him slowly, crossing her arms over her breasts as she stared back at him, sorrow shimmering in her eyes.

A weary smile edged his lips. "I would have known, Maggie." He would have seen it in her eyes. She wasn't a liar. Her emotions were always so clear in her eyes, so easy to read, that he had always been able to stay one step ahead of her in their previous relationship. "I would have known and I would have gone crazy with it."

"Because you loved me?" The doubt in her voice was clear.

"Because I loved you, because I've always loved you," he amended. "Because no matter how hard I've tried, you were a part of me. I knew, without seeing you, that something was wrong. For two years I avoided that house and I avoided you, and that's not like me. And I couldn't understand why I avoided it. I think a part of me always knew."

Admitting that was like cutting out his own heart. He had let her down in a way so fundamental that it ached through ever portion of his being. It was bad enough that he had let her go, but he hadn't made certain she was safe.

"Grant was very good at his lies," she whispered, rubbing her hands over her arms as though to ward off a chill. "He fooled us both."

Yes, he had, and Joe would never forget that lesson. It didn't mean he was going to let Maggie pay any more than she already had.

"Maggie, have I ever taken you on a kitchen table?" The need to have her was growing by the second.

Her eyes widened in shock, as though the change in subject had come too quickly for her to process. "Do what?"

He moved closer, his hands going to the snap of her jeans, as her fingers curled over his wrists in surprised reflex.

"Have I ever fucked you on a kitchen table?" He lowered his voice, watching the small shiver that raced over her body at the sound of it.

Maggie was a sensualist. Taste, touch, the sounds of arousal, turned her on as much as the act itself.

As he slid the metal button of her jeans free, her eyes darkened further and a flush filled her face. Her lashes swept over her eyes as her gaze became drowsy, hungry, and suspicious.

"Sex doesn't solve everything." Her breathing was rough, causing her breasts to rise and fall in quick little movements.

Hard little nipples pressed beneath the cloth, and Joe's mouth watered to taste them. She had the softest, sweetest flesh, and the hardest nipples he had ever taken into his mouth.

"Sex doesn't solve everything, but it can sure as hell make life sweeter." He laid his forehead against hers as he slid the zipper to her jeans down. "I trusted Grant with your life once," he whispered, staring into her eyes, giving her the truth of himself, as she had always given him the truth of who and what she was. "I'll never trust another man to protect what belongs to me, or to hold what is mine to hold, Maggie. You taught me to trust you in a way Grant never did. With your heart and your soul, long before I ever learned of his betrayal."

It was the most basic truth that he knew how to give her. Two and a half years ago she had walked away from him rather than staying in half a relationship and hiding what she felt, as he had been content to do. She had broken away and tried to go on, tried to live without him. Any woman greedy enough to involve herself with Grant's schemes would have never done such a thing, especially considering the cushy little life he offered her as his mistress. And he had made the offer, exactly four hours before he arrived at that party with another woman on his arm.

She had shown him then what she was. Who she was. A woman willing to walk away from what she wanted most, rather than to lower herself to meet the selfish needs of someone else.

"You didn't believe me at the station," she reminded him, though her voice broke as his hands pushed beneath her T-shirt. "I could see it in your eyes, Joe. And after we came here . . ."

"I didn't believe in me, Maggie." He lifted the shirt along her smooth stomach, over her breasts and finally leaned back to pull it from her. "It was never you I doubted. Every instinct inside me pushed me to get you the hell out of there. It was me I doubted. For a little while."

She wore a lacy white bra that did nothing to hide the swollen mounds of her breasts, or the spiked tips of her nipples.

"Have I mentioned I love your nipples?" He released the catch between her breasts before peeling the cups back from the rapidly rising and falling mounds.

"Not in a while." She was panting now. He loved it when she panted for him. "We need to discuss things, Joe. Not have sex."

"Hmm, I'll have to remember to mention that. And nothing else matters Maggie, not right now. The rest we'll deal with as we have to."

He lowered his head, licking over one straining tip with a slow, wet glide of his tongue, as he heard the tremulous gasp that left her lips.

That was how he liked her, soft and melting in his arms, those strangled little gasps falling from her lips as pleasure began to overwhelm her. Words would never convince her at this point that he trusted her. That trust would have to come in time, and he understood that. He expected it. But that didn't mean he couldn't edge the odds in his own favor. Her body knew what her mind hadn't yet accepted. She belonged to him just as surely as he belonged to her.

"Joe, are you sure?" Her short nails were digging into his wrists, her gaze worried, but growing hotter by the second.

"More certain than I've been of anything, baby." He laid his hand on her lower stomach, watching her closely. "Certain enough to want more with you than I have ever wanted with anyone else."

He didn't give her time to answer, or time to protest. He had never known anything as sweet or as erotic as loving Maggie. She was like a drug in his system; one he had no hope of breaking his addiction to. And God knew he had tried.

He had fought the arousal, the need and his belief in her for nearly a week. And even as he fought it, he had known it was a losing battle. Just as he had known as he watched her interrogation through that two-way mirror.

His lips covered hers as he drew in the sobbing response to his declaration, his tongue tasting the sweetness of her passion as he pushed the bra from her shoulders before moving to her jeans.

He wanted her naked. Naked and open for him, welcoming him with all the sweet, generous fire that was so much a part of her.

Clothes were ripped, torn, pushed at, and pulled off until only bare flesh met eager hands and muted moans met open-mouthed kisses that filled the senses with an aroused, imperative demand.

Hunger arced through Joe's mind as Maggie's hand attempted to wrap around the base of his cock. Her fingers didn't quite meet, but that didn't detract from the sheer pleasure of her touch.

As always, nothing mattered except pushing inside her, taking her, feeling her orgasm pulsing around him. He didn't bother with the bed or the floor. His hands moved to her buttocks and he lifted her and bore her to the table.

Maggie was fighting to breathe as the overwhelming pleasure rushed through her with a force that swept through her senses like wildfire. All she felt was the heat and demand, a need pulsing through every cell of her body as she clutched Joe to her.

She felt the cool wood of the table meet her back as Joe came over her. He didn't bother with keeping his feet on the floor, instead, he clambered to the tabletop after her, knees bent, his hips thrusting against her, driving the hard wedge of his cock deep into the fiery heat between her thighs.

There was little grace to the act, even less finesse. The clawing hunger, fear, and desperation that spurred their passion allowed for only the most primitive response. She felt the fierce width of his erection sear the tender tissue of her vagina, and arched closer. The fiery pleasure/pain whipped through her nerve endings, ricocheting through tissue and muscle until every cell of her body was focused on one point only. The penetration of her body, the hard, fierce thrusts of his cock inside her, and the fiery sensation tightening her womb with every thrust.

Orgasm was imperative. With each stroke he threw her higher, seemed to go deeper, until every sense she possessed became focused on the steady impalement.

Perspiration gathered between their bodies, creating an exciting friction as they slid against one another. The building heat between their bodies had them both panting for air, forced to break off the kiss that had consumed them as they fought for breath.

Maggie struggled to open her eyes, staring up at Joe as his hands gripped her hips to hold her in place and the strokes pistoning his cock into her vagina increased. The cords in his neck stood out in sharp relief as the tendons of his arms and chest rippled with power.

He was as out of control now, as he had been earlier that morning. As though once lost, the power to hold himself distant, in this area at least, was gone forever.

The ability to think receded as he whispered her name, his eyes opening, his gaze spearing hers.

"I love you, Maggie." The words were torn from him, ripped from his chest in a growling, harsh sound that spiked through her womb and sent her release crashing through her.

Maggie felt the involuntary arching of her back as the wave of sensation tore through her with pleasure that bordered on violent. It exploded through every nerve ending in her body and sent convulsions crashing through her womb, as her pussy began to milk desperately at his cock. Nothing mattered but the pinnacle of pleasure, the sweeping completion she had only found in this man's arms, and a love she knew she could never survive without. Not intact. Not completely. She would live, but without Joe, Maggie knew her soul would never breathe.

In that moment, as she felt him surge inside her one last time before his own release began to spurt heatedly inside her to join her own, Maggie knew that never again could she hope for love outside of Joe's arms. Because to her heart, her soul, Joe *was* love. He was life.

10

The drive from the cabin to Atlanta was made after dark, and to Maggie it seemed as though it had taken a lifetime to accomplish. Each mile crept by despite Joe's steady speed and his attempts at a conversation. Maggie wanted nothing more than to get to his house, to check the car, and to get the hell out of there.

As Joe pulled slowly into the alley behind the two-story older home, Maggie glanced over at him nervously. She had seen the house before, though Joe rarely stayed at it, preferring the apartment he kept farther in town. The house had belonged to his father's parents, and had been their home before his grandfather struck it rich in various business enterprises.

The siding was rough wood, though in perfect condition, and sheltered by a wide front porch that gave it a charm and elegance that had always attracted Maggie. The garage that housed Joe's prized Mustang was attached to the back of the house rather than the side, and led into a large, homey kitchen.

Joe pulled the SUV into the back driveway and sat for several moments, the engine idling as he stared at the garage doors.

"Grant had a key to the garage." He ran his hand wearily over his face.

They had napped for several hours before leaving, and though he didn't look tired, he did appear weary. Much as she felt, Maggie thought. After two years of a hellish marriage to Grant, and then the past week of knowing the danger her life was in, she felt exhausted inside.

"Did he have a key to the house?" She turned back to the garage, staring at the darkened windows as her heart raced in her chest.

"No. Just the garage." He turned off the ignition but made no move to leave the vehicle.

They had driven around the block several times over the past hour. Joe had parked across from the house for what seemed like forever, before driving around again and heading for the back drive.

"Do you think someone is watching the house?" she asked, as he continued to watch the shadows.

"I have no doubt," he sighed. "If they tracked who I am, and I'm going to assume they have. As often as Grant railed about me in his journals, I'm certain he would have carried the bitch over to his new friends." The bitterness in his voice had her heart clenching in pain.

"What do we do then? How do we get in there without being seen?"

"*We* don't do anything . . ."

"I'm not staying in the vehicle, Joe." She shook her head fiercely at the thought. "It would be too easy for someone to get the jump on me."

"Leave the doors locked."

"If they had a gun to your head I'd unlock them." Her nerves were about to choke her.

He breathed in roughly. "Okay, we'll go in together, but stay on my ass and be ready to move. You jump when I say jump, don't bother asking how high."

Her lips twitched at the follow-up order.

"Don't ask how high. Got it." She nodded firmly.

"And carry this." He opened the glove box, reached in, and pulled out a small revolver. "I know you know how to use it."

Of course, she did—he had made certain she took firearms lessons the minute they had begun seeing each other years before.

"A woman's best friend." She gripped the weapon firmly.

"I thought that was diamonds?" he quipped as he scanned the area again.

"What do you think protects the diamonds?" she shot back, fighting to steady her nerves, to find at least a small measure of the calm he was displaying.

"The area is pretty sheltered here with the trees." He pointed out the large trunks of the oaks growing between his property and the houses on each side. "We should be secure as we move to the garage. Keep your ears open and stay ready, Maggie."

He reached beneath the dash, disabled the interior lights, then opened the door slowly and eased out of the vehicle. As he stood to the side, Maggie scrambled out after him, easing behind him as he pushed the door closed silently.

They moved quickly to the garage, where Joe unlocked the side door and opened it carefully before pulling her along with him.

The air in the garage was stale, rife with the scents of motor oil, a hint of paint and old grease. Maggie wrinkled her nose at the smell as her eyes struggled to adjust to the near pitch-black darkness.

A second later a small beam of light pierced the black

surroundings, directing low, and angling toward the cherry red '69 Mustang Joe pampered like a baby.

"Hello, baby," he murmured as he walked to the car, patting the hood affectionately.

Maggie rolled her eyes.

"It's not a baby, Joe," she reminded him as she restrained her grin. It was an old argument, and one of the few she often instigated herself.

" 'Course she is," he sighed, as his hand slid over the hood before releasing the lock and raising it slowly.

The penlight beam moved slowly over the engine, as Joe leaned in, checking around it and inside the fender walls.

"Finding parts for her was a bitch," he said softly. "There are very few original parts left for this model. She's a true classic."

Yeah, yeah yeah, Maggie smirked. Joe was doing more than just checking for whatever Grant may have hidden, he was petting and caressing that damned engine like it could actually feel his touch.

"Do I need to leave the two of you alone?" she asked, keeping her voice at a whisper as he ran his fingers in and out of the maze of parts that made up the engine.

"You might want to look the other way," he murmured. "She gets embarrassed if others see her naked like this."

Maggie rolled her eyes.

Finally, he straightened from the motor with a sigh before lowering the hood back into place.

"Nothing in there." There was an edge of relief in his voice as he moved along the side of the car.

His hand smoothed over the top before trailing down the door and gripping the handle. "Do you know how hard it was to find completely original parts? How many years I spent putting her together perfectly?"

"Your dream woman, huh?"

"She doesn't back-talk me."

"She can't get on the kitchen table with you, either. I'd remember that one if I were you."

He turned back to look at her, and even in the dim glow of the penlight, his gaze was frankly sexual.

"Oh baby, that one is just set in stone," he murmured. "You have nothing to fear."

She rolled her eyes at him again as he turned back to the car, moving into it to begin searching the interior. Maggie drew in a deep breath, rubbing her hands against her arms as a nervous chill raced over her flesh.

The garage was damned creepy. There were too many shadows, too many places where someone could hide. She stared around the dark interior, her eyes struggling to pierce the darkness of the corners, the long shadows cast by the multitude of boxes, appliances, and only God knew what that had been stacked against the walls. If she wasn't mistaken, she had even glimpsed the hull of an old motorcycle hanging high on the far wall.

"You're a pack rat, Joe," she muttered.

He grunted from inside the car, the shadow of his large body moving in the interior as he searched each nook and cranny. He was thorough, and though her freedom depended on finding the information, she was beginning to pray it wasn't here. If it wasn't here, then she couldn't be implicated, and there would be no reason to fear Joe's distrust.

Tucking the small handgun he gave her into the back pocket of her jeans, Maggie bit her lip and waited in nervous fear as Joe took his good ole, easy time searching. He worked his way from the passenger side, back to the driver's side, searching under seats, along the sides, the carpet, the walls, anywhere that Grant could have hidden whatever it was he hid.

As he knelt at the driver's side door again, he ran his hands along the sides of the seat, pushing beneath it, then paused. She heard his muttered curse, heavy with bitterness, a second before he pulled a small package from beneath the seat.

"He cut my seat," Joe muttered. "Bastard. It took me two years to find that seat."

He sat back on his haunches, staring down at the dark package in his hands.

"Is that it?" She moved closer.

"Yeah." His voice was heavy with distaste. "I pretty much bet this is it. Feels like a few discs, a video, pictures." He felt around the wrapping. "I think we have it."

The garage door opened abruptly.

"And here Santiago was certain our friend Grant was such a liar."

The heavily accented voice was followed by four large bodies stepping into the garage, weapons raised, and their guns sure as hell looked bigger than hers and Joe's.

"Down."

A hard hand locked around Maggie's wrist, jerking her down, as Joe pulled her around the side of the car and toward the long shadows cast from the junk piled along the walls.

She expected gunfire. Pain. Blood.

"Get them," the order was harsh, commanding, but the sound of bodies moving behind them was the only indication that the Fuentes gang was in pursuit. The fact that they weren't firing guns yet made her even more nervous.

"I'm going to assume you are going to be difficult about this," the voice sighed as a bright light suddenly flared and began sweeping through the garage. "Don't risk your lady's life, Agent Merino. Give us the package and we will leave as quietly as we came in."

Maggie felt the tenseness of Joe's body, just as she heard the lie in the stranger's voice. They would never make it out of there alive, no matter what they did.

"Jose, kill them now. You are making Roberto's mistake in attempting to play with them," a younger voice hissed. "Finish them off and we leave."

"Shut up, Santiago. Roberto was less than the piss running down his father's leg. He had no concept of the lessons Carmelita tried to teach us, whereas I paid careful attention. I will defeat this American dog on my own terms. Is this not so, Agent Merino?" He laughed slyly. "There is no triumph in a quick death. A humiliating life is another matter."

Maggie had a feeling Jose had no intentions of allowing them either choice. She could hear it in his voice, feel it in the tension whipping through the room. She stayed down, pressed against the side of an old washer, with Joe in front of her, completely hiding her. She bit her lip, fighting back her harsh breathing, forcing herself to stay utterly silent as the flashlight swept through the garage.

Crouched low, with decades worth of junk heaped around them, Maggie bit her lip as the sound of footsteps neared. They were searching around the stacks of accumulated boxes, appliances, and miscellaneous junk heaped six to eight feet from the sides of the large garage. It was a mess. Thank God.

She held her breath as the footsteps passed and moved away, the bright flare of the light skirting inches in front of where Joe crouched.

"Agent Merino, we can do this the easy way, or we may do it the hard way. If you make me exert effort, then I will take your woman and play with her a bit before I allow her to die. I will let you live long enough to watch. Or you can hand over the package easily, and you may just walk away."

Maggie shuddered at the offer as Joe reached back, gripped her wrist again, and they began moving slowly through the shadows, hunkered low, working around along the side of the garage toward the far wall. The direction they were going would have them coming up behind the men standing at the doorway. If they moved further into the garage, then there was a slim chance for escape.

"How disappointing," Jose finally sighed. "But, I'll enjoy punishing you for the effort I must make."

Joe moved quickly along a row of boxes before pushing her between a higher stack and an old dresser. There was a maze built through the stacks of junk, haphazard and less than safe, but with a few hidden passageways that seemed more by accident than by design.

They moved into the narrow tunnel, easing slowly behind the dresser as the sound of footsteps began to near their hiding place.

Joe paused behind the dresser, crouched, and waited as the footsteps passed before moving slowly out of the impromptu tunnel and into a mess of old clothes hanging from a long rack. Maybe being a pack rat wasn't such a bad thing after all.

"Americans are so interesting." Amusement filled the voice that spoke from just in front of the rack of clothing a second before the glare of a flashlight illuminated the floor. "Come out my friends, let us talk for a bit."

As the rack of clothing began to move, Joe kicked into action. Before Maggie could do more than gasp he pushed her back behind the heavy dresser and opened fire.

Maggie scrambled through the unnatural tunnel, her hand fumbling behind her as she attempted to reach the revolver tucked into her back pocket.

She had just moved to the other side of the dresser when the boxes that lined the tunnel crashed around her, and cruel fingers reached in, latching into her hair.

"No!" Her fingers formed claws as she tore at the fingers holding her, fighting the grip as she was jerked from the safety of the boxes.

"Redheaded whore!" A heavily accented voice hissed at her ear as one arm was jerked behind her back, her hand pressed against her shoulder blades as she cried out in pain.

"Do you hear her cries, Merino?" the voice called out as the gunfire was silenced. "I have your whore now."

She was shaken like a rag doll as she fought against the pain ripping through her shoulders and her scalp. She was dragged through the dimly lit garage and brought to a stop next to the man she had met in her home, introduced as Juan Martinez. This was Jose Fuentes, not Martinez, and he was just as frightening now as he had been the year before, when he met with Grant.

"She's very pretty, my friend." Jose gripped her jaw in his hand, twisting her face around until she was forced to stare up at him. "I warned Grant when he married her that he had chosen one he could not tame. I was correct in this assessment, was I not?"

She fought his hold, tears filling her eyes from the burning pain tearing through her shoulders as her captor twisted her arm more forcibly behind her back.

"Let her go, Fuentes," Joe snapped. "She doesn't have what you want."

Jose Fuentes held her head in place, refusing to allow her to look over to Joe as he glanced to his side.

"Ah, there you are, Agent Merino." His smile was sickly evil, a twisted parody of humor. "It is very kind of you to join us."

"Jose, get the package from him and we will leave," Santiago snapped. "We have no time for these games."

"We have time for whatever I wish, boy. Diego is not here to listen to your sniveling. You follow my orders."

Jose tightened his grip on Maggie's face as she finally whimpered with the pain.

His teeth flashed within the expanse of scarred, dark flesh as he chuckled at the sound.

"She's a strong woman. Women such as this, they fight the drug Diego created. They are the enjoyable little tramps once they succumb, both fighting and pleading for the agony to come."

Maggie shuddered at the threat as Jose released her face and stared back at her sneeringly.

"I think I will let our Agent Merino live," he sighed. "After I relieve him of the package it would appear he has dropped."

Breathing harshly, Maggie turned her head to the side, seeing the shadowed form of Joe standing tall, his hands raised behind his head as one of Jose's men stood behind him. The package was no place to be found.

"Let her go." He nodded to Maggie. "She has nothing to do with this."

"She has much to do with this." Jose ran the backs of his fingers over her cheek as she jerked back in response. He chuckled a second before backhanding her. "Grant made certain he teased us often with tales of what a cold little wife he had. I do so enjoy breaking in such women. Frigid little bitches who think their bodies are too good for a little rough, sweaty sex."

The pain ripped through her mind as the blow blinded her, nearly tearing her neck from her shoulders with the force of it. Sagging against the man holding her, Maggie fought to catch her breath as she heard the rough laughter that echoed around her.

"I will take Señora Samuels with me," Jose stated then. "The videos make us much money. She will bring quite a price from those viewers who enjoy watching the battle between the needs of the flesh and the denials of the mind. I will take her in payment for my trouble."

"Then you can forget the package."

Maggie's eyes widened as Jose's gun came up to her head.

"I can kill her now."

"Same deal. I know where the package is, you don't."

"I will find it once you are both dead," Jose snarled furiously. "I do not need you to find the package."

Joe glanced around the shadowed garage before turning back to Jose, his lips kicking into a grin. "Good luck."

A tense silence filled the garage as Jose's and Joe's eyes met in a battle of wills. Moments later, Jose bent, the hiss of a knife sliding from an ankle sheath sliding over Maggie's nerve endings like a serpent's warning.

As he rose he turned to Maggie once again, his hand lifting until the blade touched her skin. "How long would you last, my friend, as I begin slicing her open, inch by inch. Her beautiful face." The knife slid down her jaw. "Or these pretty breasts." It moved to her breasts as Maggie fought to shrink back. "It would be a shame to destroy such beauty, Agent Merino."

Maggie fought to make out Joe's expression, to see through the dim light provided by the flashlight Jose had aimed more at the floor rather than Joe. It left Joe's expression in shadow to her, though she was certain Jose had the required light to watch it closely.

She shook her head slowly as Joe watched her. It wasn't worth it. The Fuentes gang would continue to kill, to rape, and to maim if they were allowed to go free. But could she bear the pain Jose could deal her? She was horribly afraid she couldn't.

"Decide now, Merino." The blade pressed into the upper portion of her breasts, pricking the flesh. "There is no time left."

In more ways than one.

As Maggie's gasp tore from her throat, light flared in the garage, brilliant and intense as sirens began to blast through the interior. Maggie felt someone's rough hands jerking her away to the side as the feel of the blade biting into her flesh had her crying out in shock.

"Stay down."

She heard Joe's fierce order at her ear as she was dragged to the other side of his precious car, the sound of bullets pinging around it sending a flash of dread through her chest.

"Sons of bitches," Joe yelled. "Be careful of my fucking car!"

The garage doors flew open as Maggie's eyes adjusted to the light, the sight of black-clad figures pouring into the interior, sending jubilation rushing through her.

Within seconds it was over. Maggie rolled to her back, staring up at Joe as he leaned over her, his lips curving into a smile as she watched him in surprise.

"Looks like Craig knew me better than I thought he did," he grunted with a short laugh. "I'd have pulled that one over easy on Grant, Maggie. He would have never known I was gone until I didn't return."

"Craig did this?" Joe helped her to her feet, his arm curving around her waist as they watched the SWAT team gather up Jose, Roberto, and their henchmen, under the close supervision of Craig Allen, the district attorney, Mark Johnson, and the federal prosecutor, Andrew Johnson.

Craig turned to them slowly, his eyes watching them for long assessing moments before he lifted his hand, touched his fingers to his forehead, and nodded slowly.

"My car is ruined," Joe sighed.

Maggie jerked her gaze to the car. It was scarred with bullet holes from one end to the other.

"You can fix it." She was still breathing harshly, hardly daring to believe that it was all over. The information they needed was found, the Fuentes group was back in custody, and she was free.

"How about 'we' fix it?" He turned to her, staring down at her with sudden sobriety, his brown eyes almost black with emotion. "We could redecorate the house while we're at it."

"We?" she whispered.

"We." He nodded slowly, his fingers lifting to the bloody

scratch on her chest before his gaze came back to hers. "I won't let you go again, Maggie. Ever. So for your sake, I hope you love me as much I love you, because if not, we're in for a hell of a battle."

"We're in for a hell of a battle anyway." She couldn't stop smiling. Couldn't stop crying as she threw her arms around his neck, felt his surround her and knew, in that moment, that her dreams had come true.

She was in Joe's arms, and he was talking forever. And forever was a good thing.

Epilogue

Three weeks later

Joe found the little plastic stick with the line running through the result window when he dragged himself out of the bed and stumbled into the bathroom.

Sleep wasn't something he had gotten a lot of the night before. Maggie, on the other hand—he had gotten a lot of her. He had taken her until he was certain sex would be the furthest thing from his mind for days. Only to reach for her again, impossibly hard, desperate to feel her coming around him.

He stared down at the home pregnancy test, hardly daring to believe what it meant. That in the weeks since he had her back in his bed, that a child had developed. The child he had dreamed of having with her every fucking night she had been married to Grant.

He had lived in fear of the other man announcing pending

fatherhood. Certain that the moment he heard the news, life would crumble around him. Two years he had spent in hell, aching, tormented by memories of Maggie and a hunger that never slept. A hunger that still didn't sleep.

How had one tiny woman buried herself so deeply within his heart without his knowledge of it? Yet Maggie had. He loved her in ways he had never loved his first wife. In ways that still defied his own understanding. He would die for her. Without thought. Without regret. He would die for Maggie. And now for their child.

He reached out and picked up the stick, feeling his chest clench as emotion threatened to overwhelm him. And amazingly, he felt the erection between his thighs, his cock thickening, straining as arousal began to tear through him.

Maggie was pregnant.

Joe blinked back the moisture that filled his eyes as the knowledge overwhelmed him, weakened his knees, and made him feel like whimpering in excitement and fear. Damn, he felt like a fucking teenager with his first woman now. His flesh prickled with awareness of the bond he was suddenly aware of, and his chest felt too tight as his heart seemed to swell with the overabundance of emotion flooding through him.

He backed slowly from the bathroom, his eyes on that small line of color in the result box of the test stick.

"There's still time to escape."

He swung around, meeting the brilliance of Maggie's uncertain gaze. Her gaze moved from his face to his cock, her expression flickering with surprise before her eyes returned to his.

"Escape?" He winced at the sound of his own voice, hoarse, ragged. "Maggie . . ." He shook his head.

Son of a bitch, there were words he should be saying right now. Something poetic or romantic, something that would alleviate the uncertainty in her gaze. But his throat was locked with emotion, his chest heaving from it as he fought to breathe.

But he could still move, and he did so without conscious effort. He dropped the result stick, strode to her, and within seconds he had her in his arms. She wore nothing but his shirt and he could feel the heat of her body searing him through it. Emotion threatened to overwhelm him as he stared into her eyes, saw the hope, the fears and the love. Maggie had always stared at him with such love. Then slowly, desperate to feel her, to feel the life within her, Joe went to his knees as his arms wrapped around her hips, pulling her to him. He jerked her shirt over her abdomen, his face pressing against the soft flesh as he felt the moisture that refused to evaporate from his eyes.

Fuck, he was a grown man. Grown men didn't cry.

"Joe?" Her voice was low, a sweet little cry filled with hope and love, joy and innocence.

He pressed his lips to her stomach, his hands moving around to grip her hips and hold her close as he imagined he felt the life growing beneath his lips, inside her precious body.

"I love you." He couldn't say the words enough as he felt a tremor rushing through him, through her. "I love you, Maggie."

Then he was pulling her to him, dragging her down to face him, staring into those beautiful green eyes and the tears that washed over her cheeks.

"I love you, Joe." Her hands touched his cheeks as his smoothed back the fiery strands of hair that had fallen across her cheeks. "I guess this means you're happy about the baby?"

Her tremulous smile had his lips quirking as he fought the shudders racing through his body.

"I want you again," he whispered, dragging the material of her shirt to her neck as he fought to remove the hated clothing she had donned.

She didn't need to wear clothes. He wanted to see her body, wanted to watch it change, to become heavy with their child. He wanted to see the pearly sheen of her skin and feel every inch of the warm satin flesh against him.

"We're going to kill each other like this." Her laughter was thick with arousal, with the same hungers that drove him as he laid her back on the carpet and came slowly over her.

Her thighs parted for him, knees bending as he settled between them, his cock lodging at the entrance to the fiery, sweetly aroused flesh awaiting him. Soft nether lips enfolded the head of his cock as he pressed against the entrance of her pussy, they caressed his sensitive flesh, the damp friction causing his teeth to grit at the subtle, torturous pleasure as he began to take her.

Maggie stared up at Joe, seeing the track of the tears he had shed on his lean cheeks, the intensity of emotion that darkened his eyes. Dark blond hair fell over his forehead, softening the savage cast of his features, and his lips appeared softer, hungry, as he stared at her.

He filled her slowly, tenderly, as though aware of the sensitivity her inner flesh held after the hunger that had raged through them the night before.

As he pressed inside her, filling her, stretching her, his fingers brushed over her cheeks, her lips, feathering over her skin as though memorizing her by touch, even as his eyes traced each feature.

"I died when I lost you." The sound of his voice shocked her. It was guttural, thick with remembered pain.

"Joe." She tried to shake her head, to halt the flow of pain she could see in his eyes.

"No. Hear me out. Now." He pressed deeper inside her and suddenly the joining of their bodies was more than just pleasure, or bonding. As though the embrace had become elemental, a fusion of body and soul. "I don't want to ever be that stupid again, Maggie. I don't want to ever forget the agony I felt every day that you lived under his roof, that I thought he lived in your heart. Because I don't want to ever be that stupid again, Maggie. Ever."

"As though I would let you, ever again," she whispered, a smile trembling over her lips as tears fell from her eyes. "I love you, too, Joe. And walking away isn't something I'll do again. I'm here. For always."

He moved then, as though he couldn't help himself, his hips shifting, moving against her as his erection began to thrust slow and deep inside her.

Her back arched with pleasure as a whimpering cry escaped her chest. God, she loved this, feeling him inside her, touching her, loving her in a way she knew she would never know with another man. Only Joe.

"Ah, Maggie," he groaned as his hands lowered from her face, his fingers sinking into her hair as he bent to her.

Gentle lips nipped at hers as he gazed into her eyes. She could see her reflection in the dark gaze, as well as the emotion that poured from him.

"Sweetheart, you fill my soul," he groaned as he began to thrust harder, his cock spearing into her, stroking tender nerve endings, sensitive flesh, and creating a blaze of lust as the friction increased.

Her legs lifted, wrapping around his hips as she fought to deepen the kiss, to hold him tighter to her as she felt a part of her soul lifting, lightening, melding with his as he took her with a gentleness she wouldn't have believed possible.

It seemed never-ending. He kissed her with devouring hunger, though his thrusts were tender, stretching her vagina with easy strokes as his fingers caressed her scalp. She could feel him from her lips to her ankles, his harder, stronger body moving, flexing against hers as the building pleasure began to tighten through her body.

"Joe. Oh God, it feels so good . . ." Her head thrashed against the carpet as his lips moved to her neck, his tongue licking over her flesh as he moved lower.

"Hmm. Damned good, baby. But only with you. Sweet heaven, Maggie, only with you."

Maggie fought to breathe as his lips moved to her breast, his tongue painting her tight nipple with liquid fire a second before the heat of his mouth enveloped it. The firm suckling of his mouth heralded a harsh groan from his lips before he began thrusting inside her harder, faster, fucking into her with a depth and intensity that sent her spiraling into an orgasm that swept through her soul.

Maggie was barely aware of her own cries as release raced through her, but she clearly heard Joe's. Harsh, a guttural male cry, almost animalistic, that preceded the harsh shudders that tore through his body and the feel of his release pulsing inside her.

Exhausted. Ravished. Maggie lay bonelessly on the floor as Joe collapsed to her side, breathing harshly.

"Well, that's the first time we did it on the bedroom floor." It was all she could do to form coherent words, but that thought struck her as funny.

"It was 'bout time then," he panted beside her.

His hand moved lazily to her stomach, his fingers splaying across her flesh as he turned to her then.

"I love you, Joe." There was no containing that love, or the happiness blooming inside her.

"I worship you, Maggie," he whispered. "For your sake, I hope you can live with it."

"Always, Joe." She smiled back at him tearfully. "Always."

Siren's Call

by

Lori Wilde

1

Duncan Stewart sauntered into Annie Graves's dive shop trailing groupies like chum.

Annie dug her fingernails into her palms and resisted the urge to duck under the counter and hide out until he went away. It had been five years since she'd seen Duncan face-to-face, and she'd convinced herself she was over him. But the double punch of jubilance and jealousy kicking her stomach took her completely by surprise.

Oh, God, he's the last person on earth I want to see.

But that was a big, fat lie, and Annie's heart knew it.

Secretly, she'd been wishing and hoping and praying that she and Duncan might run into each other while they were both back in St. Augustine. She just hadn't expected him to show up at the shop. Truth was, she missed him and mourned the loss of the friendship they'd once shared.

A friendship destroyed by one passionate, regrettable night.

Once upon a time, the ruggedly handsome Scot had been not only her closest confidant and surrogate big brother, but also the object of her unrequited teenaged affections. That was what had ruined it all. Annie's desperate need for something more than Duncan could give.

An insouciant smile graced his lips, and the closer he came, the tighter her chest constricted. Suppressing the instinct to flee, she did the mature thing and simply refused to make eye contact with him. Instead, she glowered at the bimbos in itsy-bitsy bikinis giggling and touching Duncan's sun-bronzed, rock-slab biceps, and begging him to autograph their ample cleavages with felt-tip markers.

Possessiveness gripped her like a fist, but she shrugged it off with a determined roll of her shoulders. Some things never changed. Duncan's charm with women was legendary. She ought to know. Annie had been singed firsthand.

I don't care with whom he chooses to fritter his time. It's none of my business.

She had enough problems. Like how she was going to care for her ailing grandfather and keep his dive shop open after she ran out of vacation time and had to return to her job as a Wall Street stockbroker. Not to mention what she planned to do about the very important question her boyfriend, Eric Hammond, had told her he wanted to ask her when she got back home.

A question she didn't want to answer.

She and Eric had dated for three years and he was exactly what she needed—calm, steady, reliable, unemotional. So why did the thought that he was going to pop *the* question unsettle her?

The reason, Annie was forced to acknowledge, was standing right in front of her. Here was the man who had stolen her good-girl heart with his bad-boy ways and had never given it back. There'd been no closure between them, and that, she assured herself, was why she couldn't forget him. Not because she was still in love with him.

Oh yeah? demanded her aching heart. *If you're not in love with him, how come it still hurts so damned much?*

"Sorry ladies, no more autographs," Duncan told his bevy of lovelies. "I've business to transact."

With disappointed sighs, his fan club dispersed throughout the store. The women pretended to be interested in pressure valve regulators and wet suits and weight belts, but all the while they sneaked adoring glances at Duncan before angling suspicious glares at Annie. She censored a childish urge to stick out her tongue at them.

"Hello, Harvard. I didn't know you'd come home." Duncan's voice was deeper than she remembered, but the faint hint of Scottish brogue was still there. The sound of it curled her toes and cemented her tongue to the roof of her mouth. He leaned across the counter, encroaching upon her personal space and leaving her little choice except to meet his insistent gaze.

"I'm not home," she replied, more tartly than necessary. "My home is in Manhattan, and don't call me Harvard."

His calling her Harvard irritated Annie. Like he thought, that she thought, she was better than he was because of where she'd attended university.

"Manhattan may be the place where you sleep, but your heart will forever belong in St. Augustine."

"Where I choose to sleep, or for that matter with whom I choose to sleep, is none of your business."

Duncan's eyes crinkled. He threw back his head and let loose a hearty laugh. The sound, so wickedly familiar it hurt, unraveled something inside her.

"Ah, Annie. I've missed your feistiness. You're a fine sight for sore eyes and more beautiful than ever."

Not wanting to draw attention to her physical imperfection, Annie resisted the urge to reach up and finger the deep scar at her chin, courtesy of a childhood accident. She had a tendency to touch the scar whenever she was feeling fragile, and the fact that he'd called her beautiful made her feel very fragile indeed.

Duncan was so full of shit. The ego of the man. He was boldly flirting with her when a half-dozen gorgeous, unscarred women were lurking in the back of her store just waiting to pounce on him. In comparison, with her short stature, well-rounded body, and damaged chin, she felt like a chubby little field mouse who'd suffered a near-death experience at the paws of an evil tabby.

"I see you didn't get lost in the Bermuda Triangle."

"Nay." With a impish gleam in his eyes, he patted his chest with both palms. "It's all me. Safe and sound."

"Damn the luck. I had a fiver riding on your disappearance," she quipped, denying what she was really feeling—supreme relief that he'd made it home uninjured.

Duncan had just returned from guiding a team of *National Geographic* photojournalists on a rigorous dive through the mysterious section of the Atlantic. They had recovered the remains of a two-hundred-year-old pirate clipper ship in the Triangle, and Duncan was the talk of St. Augustine. That explained the groupies waiting to have their boobs autographed.

He pinned her to the spot with his hot gaze. "Would you have cried if I'd died?"

"Not for a second," she lied.

They breathed in tandem. Their eyes were locked. Stances identical. Hands on hips, chests outthrust.

She could hear the wall clock behind her ticking loudly. *Tock. Tock. Tock.* Annie did not flinch or squirm. She dealt with multimillion dollar trust funds on a daily basis. She knew real pressure. She could handle one rugged, slightly arrogant seafaring man.

Ha! Who you trying to kid?

Annie struggled not to notice how good he looked. His dark brown, wind-tousled hair was streaked with lighter shades of sun-bleached strands. He had a heavy five-o'clock shadow that enhanced his natural rakishness. His shoulders were so broad they strained the seams of his white T-shirt, emblazoned with WHATEVER GETS YOU THROUGH THE NIGHT, the slogan for a company that manufactured diving lanterns. He was so overtly masculine, so dominantly sexual that she couldn't really blame the bimbos for falling all over him.

He was big. He was strong. He was sexy. And he was not a man you could ignore.

"Harvard hardened you," he murmured. "Or maybe it's living in New York City."

Don't blame Harvard or Manhattan. You're the one who hardened me.

Unbidden, her thought tumbled back to the past. To the first reckless, headlong moment when she'd thrown caution to the wind and dared him to kiss her. In lucid detail she recalled the shock of his lips the first time they'd claimed hers. How the power of it entered her like a bolt of electricity. How her body tingled when his rough, calloused palms had pushed up underneath her yellow cotton blouse to rub against the hard buds of her straining nipples.

The urgency in his kiss had stunned and excited her. She'd dared to act on her long-restrained impulses, never guessing that he'd been lusting after her just as much as she'd been lusting after him.

Annie hadn't believed it possible, but Duncan was even more attractive now than he'd been the one and only night they'd slept together. Unfortunately, that one and only time had become the yardstick to which she measured every encounter with all other men, and no one else had ever seemed to measure up.

Either literally or figuratively.

She resented him for being so good in bed that even five years later she could still vividly recall their lovemaking.

"What do you and your harem want, Stewart?" She laced her voice with sarcasm. She was in no mood for his highlander charm.

Or her weak-kneed reaction to it.

His laugh was genuine, his dark eyes dancing in amusement. No one on earth could irritate her quicker or cause her heart to beat harder. What was this unshakeable hold he held over her emotions?

"Jealous, Annie?" His eyes latched onto hers as she tried her best not to become spellbound.

"Of you?" She snorted. "Not damned likely."

"Liar. But don't worry. You have nothing to be jealous over. I'm not seeing anyone at present."

"Honestly, I couldn't care less."

"Liar."

"Stop calling me that."

"Then stop lying."

"What do you want?" she repeated, crossing her arms over her chest. He was staring so intently at her mouth, it was all she could do to keep from licking her lips.

Duncan's heated gaze drifted to her breasts at the same time she realized her posture was enhancing her cleavage. She straightened, dropping her arms to her side, and glared at him.

Annie noticed one of his groupies monkeying with a top-of-the-line aluminum diving tank. She snapped her fingers at the blonde woman. "You there, put that down, unless you're going to buy it."

"Shiny." The blonde smiled vacantly and settled the tank back in its slot.

Annie shot Duncan a pointed look.

"I'll get rid of them," he said conspiratorially. "So we can be alone."

So we can be alone.

She hated the way that made her feel, all excited and hot and edgy. No matter how much she told herself she disliked the man, just one look from him, one turn of phrase, and she was pudding.

Damn him. Damn her. Damn them both.

Diplomatically Duncan sent the women away. The bell over the door tinkled as he ushered them out. Then he turned around and ambled back toward her, all manly swagger and burgeoning testosterone.

Annie's pulse kicked.

"Sorry about that. I'm giving them diving lessons this afternoon."

She glowered. "I just bet you are."

"Prickly as always, eh, Harvard? Nice to see some things never change."

"Go away, Stewart." She waved a dismissive hand. "You bother me."

"I'm here to see your grandfather. Is Jock about?"

"Do you see him?"

Duncan craned his neck, glanced around the shop. "Nay."

"There you go."

"Annie, why are you so mean to me?"

"Because you deserve someone in your life who doesn't fall at your feet. Cruel to be kind, so the saying goes."

"You have a point. So are you saying that you're back in my life?"

"Over my dead corpse."

"Playing hard to get. Do you have any idea how much of a turn-on that is?" He started around the side of the counter, eyes glittering darkly.

Annie grabbed the harpoon off the wall behind her and swished it through the air between them. "Stay back, Stewart. I'm warning you."

"As if you would poke me with that thing." Undeterred he moved closer.

"Don't tempt me."

"Tempting you was always my favorite activity. Remember when I dared you to go skinny-dipping off the pier and we got caught by a pack of Japanese tourists with flash photography?"

Annie blushed. She remembered.

Mischievously, he lowered his eyelids, assessing her with frank appraisal. She wore a cobalt blue spaghetti-strap tank top and low-rise blue jean shorts. There was a gap between the bottom of her shirt and the top of her blue jeans, revealing her bare belly and the pearl navel ring nestled there. One corner of his lip curled up in amusement when he spied the pearl.

Trust him to admire the navel ring. She'd gotten it on an impulse, on an uncharacteristic whim, when she was feeling stuck in a rut. She thought it might help jazz up her sex life with Eric, but he hadn't approved. He'd said it wasn't dignified or appropriate for a woman of her distinguished accomplishments. But Annie liked the piercing. It reminded her of the beach, of the life she'd left behind.

Annie could tell by the expression in Duncan's eyes that he admired the navel ring. His look was as powerful as a caress. She could almost feel his lips against her skin, his fingertips grazing her bare belly.

She dropped her gaze, then wished she hadn't as she noticed the erection bulging against the zipper of his cargo shorts. Tried not to wish that he was poking *her* with *his* spear.

"You never know. I might jab you." She scowled against the warmth rolling stickily through her body. "I could mortally wound you. I'm unpredictable."

He burst out laughing. "Oh, right. You're unpredictable as heat in summer."

"Shows how little you know me."

"Annie Marie Graves, I know you better than you know yourself." He placed a hand on top of the harpoon and took another step closer until the razor-sharp tip of it was almost touching his flat, taut abdomen.

Annie's hands trembled. She had to clench them around the harpoon to keep him from discovering just how aroused she was.

Her skin tingled. Her nipples drew up hard and tight under her lace bra. A hot slickness filled her aching pussy. In her head she heard the strains of Marvin Gaye's "Sexual Healing."

"You're wearing white cotton panties," he said. "Bikini style, not a thong. You had cereal for breakfast, some sort of muesli. You took a three-mile jog on the beach at six A.M. You brown-bagged your lunch, either tuna fish on rye or all-natural peanut butter on whole wheat. But, in spite of all that healthy stuff, you've got a stash of Ding Dongs and Ho Hos and chocolate chip cookies under the counter for when you get nervous or bored and need a dose of comfort food. How am I doing so far?"

He was right on every count. At that very moment she was seriously jonesing for a Twinkie, and it certainly wasn't from boredom. God, she *was* predictable. She loosened her grip on the harpoon.

Duncan took it from her and settled the spear back on the wall mount.

"There now. That's better." His voice was low and even, his black scoundrel eyes shimmering with blatant sexuality. He reached over to toy with a curl that had fallen over her shoulder. His touch sent blood rushing through her veins, hotly suffusing her pelvis. "Where were we?"

"You were leaving."

"I meant to ask," he said, ignoring her comment—he was good at ignoring the things he did not want to hear—"are you still dating that lawyer? What's his name?"

"Eric. And we're getting married."

Duncan's face dropped with shock. Suddenly, all his brashness was gone, and instead there was a stark, naked expression in his eyes she'd rarely seen, and his vulnerability rattled her to the core. If he was going to look at her like that she was in deep trouble.

"You're engaged?" he whispered, his gaze snapping to her bare ring finger.

"Yes." She raised her chin.

"Where's the rock?" The haunted expression disappeared and the old, cocky tilt was back on his lips. It was the same practiced grin that once upon a time could bring her to her knees.

But no more.

Annie jerked her left hand behind her back. "Well, it's not official. Not yet. We're going to be, we're almost engaged."

"But you're not engaged."

"Yes. No. Stop looking at me that way."

"What way?"

"You know."

As if you've got another shot with me. Not after what you pulled.

She scowled, but her heart was reeling. She was not going to let this man get under her skin again. It had taken her months to get over him.

Ha! You're still not over him.

Which was precisely why she wanted him out of her shop, out of her life for good.

His gaze met hers and the rueful expression in his eyes was so intense she had to look away. He opened his mouth, but no words came out.

"Jock's in a rehab hospital," she blurted, anxious to get out of this conversation and shake off these feelings. "He fell at the pier two weeks ago, broke his hip, and had to have hip replacement surgery. That's why I'm home."

"Jock's bedridden?" Duncan sounded stunned.

Annie understood. The news had stunned her, too. She shrugged, trying her best not to let her emotions show. The thought of losing Jock, the last family she had left, terrified her. "He *is* seventy-four."

"He's one of the toughest men I've ever known. Jock's a fighter. He'll come through this thing."

The vulnerability was back, tingeing his voice with anxiety. He and her grandfather had once been very close, and she was the cause of the rift between them. Jock had loved Duncan like a grandson, but he couldn't condone the way he'd treated Annie and they'd quarreled bitterly. For the first time Annie realized exactly how much their ill-fated fling had cost Duncan.

"What did you want to see him about?" she asked.

He paused for the longest moment, studying her with eyes the color of a turbulent midnight sea. There was something different about him. His face seemed wiser, more grounded, as if at twenty-eight he'd finally grown into the man he was supposed to be. Had his trip to Bermuda changed him? Or was it something else?

His mouth seemed different, too. Less carefree, more prudent. As if it no longer kissed impulsively. She wondered if he tasted differently and if the texture of his lips had changed. Rougher now, perhaps, than they'd been, but gentler, less cavalier.

Knock it off. You're imagining things. He's the same self-absorbed flirt he's always been. You're susceptible, lonely, and no one's ever tripped your sexual trigger the way he did. You're ripe for the picking. Don't you dare let him pluck you.

Duncan shifted his weight, scrutinizing her for a moment that stretched long and fiery, the sultry look in his eyes deepening, kindling the flammable tension. He stood so near, if she reached out a hand she could brush her fingertips along his tanned cheek.

The heat of awareness intensified, spreading throughout her entire body, lodging deep within her belly, growing heavy with longing. The very core of her burned for him, churned her juices, aroused her most feminine instincts.

Forget the Twinkies. He made her so nervous she craved mainlining double-fudge brownies.

"I discovered something on that clipper ship we found in Bermuda," he murmured at last. "The *Lorelei*."

"Oh?" She wanted to tell him she couldn't care less, but some small, twisted part of her couldn't help imagining he was going to say he'd discovered what a big jerk he'd been five years ago, beg her forgiveness, and vow his undying love. In which case, she'd laugh in his face and walk away.

"A very special treasure map."

His words filled her with hope and dismay. Thrill, trepidation, euphoria, and fear tangled into a hard knot inside her. Annie's heart careened against her chest. She sucked in her breath.

"What?"

The look on his face told her his find was monumental and that he'd kept it a secret from everyone else. And then she knew what he was going to say before the words tumbled from his mouth. She felt the past pressing in on her, heavy and dark. A flood, a swamp, a mire of regret and pain.

"The Siren's Call," he said, confirming at once both her worst nightmare and her most heartfelt desire. "I know where she is."

Giddy goosebumps glided up her arm. Could it be true? The Siren's Call? After all these years?

Her body flushed. Her head swam. Her vision blurred. Then Annie's knees just crumpled.

2

Duncan expected his news to come as a shock, but he hadn't imagined his tough-minded Annie would faint. One second she was damning him to eternal hell with her gorgeous green eyes, and the next second her legs buckled and she was pitching forward face-first. He grabbed her around the waist, stopping her inches short of cracking her head on the concrete floor. Corkscrew tendrils of her honey brown hair fell softly against his knee and her pearl navel ring pressed hard on the inside of his wrist.

He smiled. She might have gone to Harvard and she might be living in Manhattan far from home, but that small pearl nestled in the alcove of her rounded belly told him she was still a beach bunny at heart.

She smelled of coconut and summertime and the complexity of their past. Five years later and nothing had altered. Even unconscious, Annie Graves welded a mysterious influence over him. She'd held him in her sway since the moment he realized she morphed from a pigtailed, tomboyish teen who'd followed him around like a puppy, to a full-grown woman with adult needs. Still, he'd held back, knowing she was too young, knowing their relationship was too complicated.

He thought of the first time he'd seen her. Nate Graves, Annie's father, had hired him to work in the dive shop, renting out diving equipment to tourists. When Nate learned Duncan was a runaway with no place to stay, he'd offered him the small garage apartment behind the family house that fronted the beach. Duncan had been in heaven. He'd never lived in a place that nice. He'd been four months on his own—after his alcoholic father had beaten him one time too many—living on the streets, rummaging through garbage cans for food, doing he what he must in order to survive.

Duncan had been sweeping out the storeroom that first afternoon, when Annie walked through the door, all tomboy in her cutoff blue jean shorts and red halter top. She was wearing pink rubber flip-flops with rhinestones, and her cute little toes were painted a fetching color of purple. She'd been working over a wad of bubble gum with her smooth glossy lips. He could smell the watermelony scent when she blew a bubble and it exploded in a soft pop as she stared at him wide-eyed.

She was only thirteen, but she already possessed the fully rounded curves of a grown woman. He'd been sixteen and filled with all the hormones and impulses indigenous to that age group. She'd looked at him like he was one of the Backstreet Boys, and he'd felt something deep in his chest just explode.

He'd wanted her, and in that wanting was his damnation. He knew he could never betray Nate Graves's kindness by taking advantage of his young daughter's crush on him. Duncan had fought his desires the only way he knew how. By teasing Annie and acting as if she was an annoying kid sister.

And by finding himself a girlfriend, fast.

Annie had no idea that the string of women who'd come in and out of Duncan's life had been nothing more than a desperate effort to keep his mind and his hands off her. The older they grew, the harder it became to fight his feelings whenever he was around her, so he'd moved out of the garage apartment and into a houseboat when he was eighteen. He became such an accomplished diver, Nate let him take over giving diving lessons to the tourists while he and Annie's mother went trekking around the world in search of the Siren's Call.

And then Annie's parents had been killed.

Their relationship could have shifted then. Become what Duncan had always dreamed of. But Annie was still underage and she was vulnerable and hurting. She needed friendship and understanding, not groping and hot breathing. Plus, he had nothing to offer her. He worked for Jock now, who'd taken over the dive shop, but he needed to prove to himself that he could provide for her before he dared to tell her how he felt.

Things went on like that for a few more years. Duncan perfecting his diving skills, dreaming of the day he could dive for and find the Siren's Call himself. Showing Annie exactly how much he loved her. He dated plenty, yes, but never seriously. He never lied to other women. He was always honest. Told them that his heart would forever belong to someone else.

Until the eve of her twentieth birthday, when she'd kissed him and Duncan could no longer hold his passion at bay. He wasn't ready. He hadn't proven himself worthy of her, but she'd pushed him to the limits of his endurance, and he'd made love to her prematurely.

And that fateful night had wrecked everything between them.

Now swinging the unconscious Annie into his arms, he carried her into the storeroom. The dive shop had changed since the last time he'd been there. Supplies had been inventoried, boxes stacked neatly and color coded. The floor had been swept, windows cleaned, files sorted. Annie was home again.

But not for good. Not unless he did something drastic. She'd hardened her heart against him and while he understood why, he also knew he was on the verge of losing her forever. He had only a small window of time to change her mind about him. That's what he was doing back in St. Augustine.

Gently, he laid her on the scarred wooden table where, in the past, he and Jock and her grandfather's cronies had played many a hand of Texas Hold 'Em. He gazed at her face, his eyes lingering on the scar at her chin. His breath caught in his lungs. She looked so fragile, so small and delicate. Next to her he felt like some great oversized beast, lumbering and clumsy.

Memory transported him back five years. Images of the night they'd finally made love after years of flirting, indelibly etched into his brain. Duncan could see his fingers stroking the curve of the small of her back. He could hear her purrs of pleasure. Could feel her body arching into his as they swayed together on the dance floor at a summer solstice beach party. His cock was throbbing and she had boldly ground her pelvis against him, letting him know she wanted him, too.

He should have put a stop to it then, but her mouth had been so pink and ripe. It made Duncan think of all the raunchy things she could do to him with those lips.

Somehow, he couldn't recall exactly—his brain had been so frosted with lust—they made it back to the houseboat where he'd been living at the time. All he could recollect was his desperate, hungry need for her. How they'd ripped off each other's clothes and ignited in each other's arms.

And that's when he'd discovered she was a virgin.

Emotion overcame him then. Ambivalence. Joy. He'd felt

honored and overwhelmed by the gift she was offering him, but also frightened by it. This encounter meant something. To her, to him, to both of them.

Not wanting to do anything they both might regret later, he'd tried to call it off.

But Annie had been the one who'd taken the lead at that point. Pleading with him to make love to her and to put an end to her sexual torture. He lost his last shred of control. He'd been as gentle and thoughtful as he could, treasuring the gift she'd given him.

He'd coiled his body around hers, tracing his quivering hands over her skin, memorizing every precious detail of her—the freckles dotting her cheeks, the little valley between her nose and her lips, the faint dusky network of veins beneath her pale softness.

Her exuberance had surprised and delighted him. Incandescent, they lit up the bedroom. It had been and still was to this day, the most perfect sex Duncan had ever had.

Then he remembered that awful morning after, when he'd realized what a mistake he'd made. He knew he could never hope to hold on to her. She was much too smart for a guy like him. He was nothing more than a scruffy salvage diver with more bravado than brains. He had nothing to offer. He simply wasn't man enough for her. Duncan had panicked and done the only thing he knew to do. He'd pretended their blissful night of pleasure had meant nothing more than great sex.

Many times over the years he'd regretted that decision. Not just because he'd lost Annie's friendship and Jock's, but because he'd hurt them both so deeply. He yearned to reach into the past, grab tight hold of his mistake, and erase what he'd done. To take it all back. To make a different choice. But if he could do that Annie wouldn't have an MBA from Harvard. She wouldn't be a Wall Street stockbroker.

Nor would she be almost engaged to Eric Hammond.

He growled, perturbed and jealous at the thought of another man touching her.

Three weeks ago, Jock had called him in Bermuda. Duncan had rarely spoken to the older man since he and Annie had broken up. He was surprised to hear from him until Jock related that Eric Hammond had phoned, seeking his permission to ask for Annie's hand in marriage.

"You're going to go to your grave regretting letting her slip through your fingers, Stewart," Jock had warned. "Get home as soon as you can. I've stayed out of your affair because I hoped you two would eventually realize you were meant to be together and work this out on your own, but since you're both stubborn as donkeys, I've got to put in my two cents worth before Annie ends up marrying that jackass lawyer. I bought you some time. I told Hammond I needed Annie to come down and help me get my business affairs in order. I convinced him to hold off until then."

Coincidentally, Jock's call had come on the very same day Duncan had discovered the Siren's Call. When he told his old friend about his find, they came up with an elaborate plan. Question was, would the underhanded ploy they'd cooked up work? Or would it drive an even bigger wedge between Duncan and Annie when she discovered what he was up to?

Annie moaned softly.

"Sweetheart," he murmured, stunned by the tenderness sweeping through him.

Her eyelids flew open. She jerked to a sitting position. "What happened? Why are you staring at me like that?"

Duncan swallowed hard, struggling to hold on to some semblance of self-control. He couldn't reveal too much too quickly or he'd chase her off. He'd hurt her once, and he knew she'd be nervous about letting him get close to her again. "You passed out."

She raised a hand to her head, smoothing her riotous curls. "I did?" Her face paled as she remembered. "It's true, then? You've really found the Siren's Call?"

"I found a treasure map on the *Lorelei* leading to the Siren's Call," he lied, feeling like an utter shit, but knowing this was the only thing that could convince her to give him a second chance.

She sucked in her breath. He wanted so badly to take her in his arms and kiss her, but it was too soon. If he touched her now, she would resist.

"I can't believe I fainted." She pressed her palm against her forehead. "How silly was that?"

He wanted to tell her that it wasn't silly at all. It was perfectly understandable to faint when you learned the artifact your parents had died trying to find not only existed, but was actually within reach. But he couldn't say it. Her father had been Duncan's boss, but he'd also been his mentor and even something of a father figure. He understood the depth of emotions running through Annie—nervousness, suspicion, anticipation, confusion—but he didn't know how to address it.

Instead, he said, "You probably had your knees locked. You shouldn't lock your knees."

"You're probably right," she echoed. "Locking my knees was a bad idea."

"I remember when you used to lock your keys in your car. Trying to be safe, but ending up shutting yourself out of your own vehicle? Remember how many times you called me and my trusty Slim Jim to the rescue?" He wondered who came to her rescue now. Was it Hammond? He hated thinking about it. "Do you still lock your keys in your car?"

"I live in Manhattan. I don't own a car."

It disturbed him to realize how little he knew about the life she led. It was an unpleasant sensation. Once upon a time he'd known every detail of her daily routine, but no more.

Their eyes met.

The look was hot. Electric. Full of expectation and regret and yearning and hunger. It was a look that sent his balls feverishly drawing up tight against his hardening shaft. He watched her eyes spark, the verdant green turning mossy as she struggled to control her own arousal. Duncan spied the flare of wide-eyed panic she tried to camouflage.

She canted her head and studied him, pulling her bottom lip up between her teeth in a gesture that never failed to drive him to distraction. He wanted those full, rich lips between *his* teeth. She swung her legs. Back and forth. The rhythm matching the desperate pounding in his dick.

Duncan fisted his hands to keep from touching her. "How much do you remember about your parents' search for the Siren's Call?"

She made a funny little noise, half sigh, half chuckle. "You were there. You know how they were."

"Yeah, obsessed. But I came late on the scene. How did it all start? Or were you too young to recall?"

"I was probably six or seven at the time. My mother was studying myths and legends for some class she was taking. Mom was always taking classes." A faint smile flitted across her face. "In fact, I ran across her textbook when I was straightening up the storeroom."

Annie hopped off the table and went to the shelf beside the file cabinets stacked with books. She studied the titles, pulled out the one she was searching for, flipped it open, and tapped the illustration. "Here."

Duncan gazed over her shoulder at the fabled Siren's Call. It was a cylindrical piece of glass with the face of a beautiful woman etched into the surface and a fish tail curling up at the end of the figurine. The inset where the mermaid's heart should be was a star-shaped magnetic lodestone. According to legend, the Siren's

Call had potent aphrodisiac qualities. Purportedly, whoever possessed the idol became sexually irresistible to the object of their affections.

"She was a sharp woman, your mother, and very brave," Duncan said. "You're a lot like her."

"Oh no. Mom was way more adventuresome than I'll ever be. I think that's why she was so attracted to my father. They had a rare passion for life. You have it, Duncan. The kind of fearless courage it takes to make a living as a deep-sea salvage diver."

"You have it too, Annie."

"No." She shook her head. "I don't, and furthermore, I don't want it. Passion that intense is destructive."

"Not always," he disagreed, feeling as if her argument mired him in quicksand. If she didn't believe in passion, how could he convince her the passion they shared was worth fighting for?

"Always," she said. "I remember this one time, Mom was pushing me in a swing at the park and chattering about the Siren's Call. She was so caught up in her own story that she didn't even realize how high she was pushing me on the swing, or that I had gotten scared and was begging her to stop. A stranger had to come over and grab her by the shoulders to make her snap out of it. It's that kind of obsession that drove my parents to keep diving wrecks in search of the Siren's Call. It's why they died. Because they couldn't let go. It was like an addiction."

"I know. That's what was so inspiring about your parents. They never, ever gave up."

"And because of their stubborn obsession they left me orphaned at sixteen."

"You weren't alone. You had Jock and you had me."

"I had my grandfather. I never had you."

Her words sliced deep. Did she really believe that? It hurt. Five years ago, he'd crossed a line he shouldn't have crossed. She'd looked up to him and he'd taken advantage of her vulnerability. But hell, he'd been vulnerable, too. Years of fantasies, of desperate need, had worn down his resolve. He hadn't been able to resist her kiss. He'd stumbled and fallen. But here he was, ready, willing and able to make amends, if only she would give him a chance.

"You taught me a lot, Duncan. You reiterated the painful lesson I should have learned from my folks, and I have to thank you for that."

"I don't understand. What lesson are you talking about?"

"Never let your heart rule your head." The weary note in her voice tore at him.

"Take a look at this." Duncan drew a plastic bag from the side pocket of his cargo shorts. He eased out the tanned animal hide etched with the treasure map. Carefully he unfolded it, passed the map to Annie, and held his breath.

She examined it, tracing her fingers over the etchings. "You found this in the wreck of the *Lorelei*?"

"It leads to where Captain Remy stashed the Siren's Call in an underwater cave off Dead Man's Island, a deserted atoll, just below the Keys."

"I still can't believe it's real." She raised her head and looked at him again. "The Siren's Call. After all these years."

Annie was one helluva a siren herself, even if she didn't seem to know it. She possessed the face of a madonna, but the body of a red-hot vamp. To Duncan, she was far more potent than the purported aphrodisiac qualities of that overrated mermaid idol. His hands burned with the urge to grab her full rounded hips and squeeze them tight as he pushed himself into her. He yearned to hear her scream his name with reverential fierceness. He raked his gaze over her.

"What?" she asked.

"What do you mean 'what'?"

"You're staring at me funny."

Twin pink flushes rose to color her creamy white cheeks gone too long without Florida sun. Her lips parted, giving him a peek at her straight pearly teeth. It took all he had inside him not to throw her across his shoulder and carry her off to his boat like some lust-crazed pirate.

Patience, he told himself. But patience was hard won, especially since he'd already waited five long years for this. Changing her mind about him was going to take time. He had to accept it. That's why he was counting so hard on help from the Siren's Call. Sexual magic was precisely what they both needed.

"Who else knows about the map?" she asked.

"Only you."

"No one else on the Triangle dive was with you?"

He had to be careful. He was treading deep water, and he had to tell her what she needed to hear or this wasn't going to work. "I found it when I went diving alone."

"Duncan Stewart!" A scandalized breath escaped her lungs. "You know better than that. My father taught you better."

He shrugged. "What can I say?"

"Still the maverick, aren't you? Still have to be the hotshot. If Jock knew about this he would bawl you out but good." She sounded like the girl he remembered. No controlled, businesslike Harvard in her voice now. She was upset.

"Jock would want us to go after her." Duncan thumped the map.

"Well, it's a moot point because we're not telling him."

"Why not?"

"I won't have you turning his world upside down. He's sick. He might not pull through this. I won't get his hopes up and risk dashing them."

Duncan looked into her eyes and knew it wasn't her grandfather's life she feared getting turned upside down, but her own. Annie was scared. And if Annie was scared, that meant she cared, and if she still cared, that meant he had to keep pushing.

"But what if we find it? It'd be the best medicine Jock could have."

"And if this map is a hoax?" Frowning, Annie held it closer to her face.

Terror gripped him. Duncan froze. *She knows*!

He'd weathered the leather for two weeks in salt water, but was it long enough to fool her? His gut knotted and he held his breath, waiting for her accusations.

But it never came. Finally, she put the map aside. "My family has suffered enough over that cursed figurine. Let's keep the past buried."

"What are you saying?"

"Destroy the map. We're not going after the Siren's Call."

"Wah?" The noise strangled from his throat. He couldn't believe she wasn't taking the bait. Everything he'd plotted and planned was falling apart. Then again, he should have known Annie wouldn't make it easy.

"You heard me."

"But we have to go after it." He did his best to sound cool. He couldn't let her know exactly how much power she held over him. "To honor your parents."

"I'll honor them more by staying far away from that damn idol."

"How do you figure?"

Annie didn't answer his question and marched for the door. "I've got to get back to work. This store won't run itself."

Duncan went after her. Just the sight of her swaying ass lit up his circuit boards in a hundred different ways. No matter how hard he'd tried, no matter how many adventures he'd lived or women he'd bedded, he could not stop craving her. This time he did not deny the demanding urge rampaging through him. In two long-legged strides, he caught up with her, grabbed her by the arm, and whirled her around to face him.

Annie's eyes widened. "What do you think you're doing?"

"If you have to ask, then it's been too long since you've had a proper kiss." He yanked her into his arms, forcefully crushed her lips underneath his.

Her lush breasts were smashed against his chest, her firm thighs nudging his. She gasped, but he swallowed her protest. Initially, she struggled, squirming in his arms to get free, but seconds later, she relaxed and started kissing him back. Just like he knew she would.

Delight detonated in his mouth. A wildfire burned through his nerve endings. She was more essential to him than oxygen. God, he'd forgotten just how good she tasted. How plush and warm she felt in his arms. How she smelled so hot and sassy. He wanted to fuck her so badly his cock hurt.

Something dark and dodgy fisted inside him.

If he had the slightest doubt that what he was doing was wrong it vanished. He tightened his arms around her. Her teeth parted and he speared his tongue deep inside her.

Moaning softly, she slid her arms around his neck.

She tasted so delicious. Like heat and those cinnamon breath mints she adored. More, he had to have more. Craving her, he tipped her back. He inhaled her, merged with her. She dizzied his head like champagne bubbles. She was amazing. Smooth as honey and twice as sweet.

Her breasts were soft against his chest, her hair tickled his shoulder. He traced her spine to the small of her back, then gently kneaded her shapely ass. Her body, which seconds before was tense and resistant, turned fluid, supple at this touch.

"Annie," he whispered into her mouth. "Annie."

She twisted away from him, breathing heavily, her eyes glazed with the sheen of lust and surprise. She splayed her palms against his chest and pushed him away. "You don't get to do that. You gave up your right to do that five years ago. Now please, just go."

She stared at him hard with those dazzling green eyes, but he could not read her thoughts.

This was different. This new ability she'd developed to hide her feelings from him. He didn't like it. Once upon a time he could read her like a book. But no longer. Had he lost her for good?

"Annie," he beseeched.

Fiercely, she frowned and pointed toward the door. "Just leave, Duncan. We both know it's what you do best."

3

The Siren's Call was luring Annie to her ruin, just as surely it had lured her parents ten years earlier. The legendary mermaid idol lay in an underground cave off the coast of the Florida Keys. Not so far from the very bed she was lying in.

She couldn't stop thinking about it. She was already under the spell of the passionate Scot who'd brought the treasure map to her. Annie groaned, overwhelmed by fear, trepidation, embarrassment, and a healthy dose of excitement. Dammit, she shouldn't be excited, but she was. This couldn't be happening at a worse time.

Forget about the Siren's Call. Forget about Duncan Stewart. Go to sleep.

But she could not.

Obsessively, her mind replayed the afternoon, from the moment Duncan had swaggered into the dive shop until he'd kissed her. She didn't know which disturbed her more, her intense sexual feelings for Duncan, or her compelling desire to find the enchanted mermaid idol that had eluded her parents.

This was ridiculous. Hadn't she vowed to break the cycle? Hadn't she sworn that she would never let irrational passion dominate her life the way it had dominated her parents'? Most of all, hadn't she learned her lesson where Duncan Stewart was concerned? The man could not be trusted. He'd hurt her once; was she willing to give him the opportunity to do it again?

She couldn't think of a more deadly combination than the two of them together in possession of the Siren's Call. It would be like fueling a cigarette lighter with high-octane gasoline.

Believing in the power of the talisman wasn't something that a Harvard-educated MBA should believe in, but Annie couldn't help herself. Believe she did. A deep-seated family indoctrination in superstition and fables and lost treasures trumped years at the country's finest institute of higher education.

Sorry, Harvard.

She flipped and flopped. Punched her pillows and tried to calm her mind. Nothing worked.

The room was too hot. That's why she couldn't sleep. She threw back the covers, hopped out of bed, and opened the window. Fresh sea air filled the room, billowing the curtains. She'd forgotten how good home smelt.

Home. The word conjured feelings inside of her she'd been denying. Nostalgia, wistfulness, and a lonely longing for everything she'd left behind. Was St. Augustine still her home? If she married Eric she knew she'd be stuck in New York City for the rest of her life.

Stuck? Where had that thought come from? She liked her job, liked living in Manhattan, yet she could not imagine spending the rest of her life far from St. Augustine's seafaring history.

The seafaring life and one seafaring man in particular is the very reason you left St. Augustine in the first place. Don't ever forget that.

The sound of the surf soothed her, and finally she fell into a fitful sleep.

Duncan swaggered into her dreams as if he had every right to be there. He had one of those grins that could turn a woman's insides to instant pudding, and a way of cocking his head and leveling her with a look that made her feel both breathless and brain dead.

He smelled sensuously luscious, like the thick amber taste of butterscotch on the back of her tongue. The flavor made her crave him and filled her with a tight, hot longing that promised serious trouble. His dark eyes danced with inherent mischief and he crooked an index finger at her.

"Come 'ere," he said in his husky Scottish accent, as if he could see right down inside her soul. He held out his hand.

And God help her, she took it.

That's when things had gotten really interesting.

The dream transported them to a lush tropical island. They lay on a white sand beach beneath a brilliant yellow moon. All around them cactuses, heavy with expectant pods, glowed in the moonlight. Under his deft fingers, her body ached into full bloom as rich and ripe as the flowering plants.

As their bodies joined and hotly fused, thousands of sphinx moths shuttled from one blossoming bud to another. The ruffling rush of their fluttering wings was as primal as the heavy breathing Annie shared with her midnight lover. The air was thick with the steeping drench of vanilla-scented nectar and the smell of their mingling sex. They were part of an ancient dance, a classic ritual, a timeless mating.

Annie jerked awake, sopping with sweat, her body blazing hot all over, in spite of the cool ocean breeze blowing across her skin. Her breasts were swollen and achy. Her mouth bone dry.

"Duncan," she whispered and ran her fingers along the inside of her damp thigh. She imagined that it was his fingers touching her in that tender spot. Imagined it and moaned softly. Annie put her fingers to her mouth and wet them, then trailed them down her hot skin, pretending it was Duncan's fingers instead of her own.

Casting her mind back, she remembered how it had felt to be touched by him. Rapture. It had been pure rapture. A bliss beyond anything she'd ever known before or since. She shivered as she stroked herself the way he'd once stroked her.

Slowly, she slid her wet ring finger into the slick moistness of her engorged pussy, pretending Duncan was finger-fucking her. It felt good. Hot and wet. But how much better if it were Duncan's manly hands?

Annie pictured him moving over her, as her fingers quickened the pace. One finger inside her, the other rubbed juices against her aching clit.

She wanted him so badly it was a burning fire in the pit of her belly, and the intensity of her desire told her exactly how wrong it was for her to want him. Too much passion was never a good thing. Too much longing could destroy a person. She forced herself to remember how devastated she'd been when he'd left. How she'd spent days sobbing into her pillow before, hardening her heart, she pulled herself up by her bootstraps and headed off to Harvard. She shouldn't want him. Not ever again. But damn her, she did.

Duncan. The man she'd been in love with since he'd come to work for her father when they were both teenagers. She was thirteen, he sixteen. She with a bad case of hero worship, he a streetwise boy with a dark past. He was her first lover. He'd taken her virginity and her heart. Duncan was the one her body would forever crave, no matter whom she ended up with.

She touched herself by proxy, seeing him, feeling his touch stroke the sensitive bud of her arousal, stoking herself into a frenzy. Thrashing her head she rode the wave of pleasure, felt it building to a shattering release.

"Duncan, Duncan," she cried and arched her hips upward, pushing against her own hand.

Her climax came, quick and hard, but it left her feeling sad and empty. Wretchedly, she buried her face in the pillow, blinking back tears. Oh God, what was she doing, letting herself get sucked into the past?

She remembered everything about him that she missed. His smile, his strength, the wonderful way he smelled. All she could think about was the one and only time he'd fucked her on his houseboat, the swell of the sea rocking them as they rocked each other. She recalled how gentle he'd been with her and the reverential look on his face when she'd told him she was a virgin.

The memory of how he'd slowly peeled her clothes off and kissed her and licked her until she was so hot and wet she'd ripped the clothes off his body was permanently branded in her brain. How he'd kept licking her, trailing his tongue lower and lower until he'd found her sweet-aching innocent clit. He'd teased her mercilessly with his tongue, sliding it in and out of her as wave after wave after wave rocked the boat, rocked her world.

Then she remembered something else. Lying together, breathing hard, gazing into each other's eyes, and how he'd told her what a good friend she was and how much he treasured their friendship. Emphasis on the word *friend*.

She'd known then he was going to leave her.

And she experienced anew what it had felt like when he

walked her off the boat and left her standing on the pier, while he went straight over to Ginger Jones's boat without a backward look, and she could still feel the imprint of his body inside hers. Could still feel the kiss he'd planted on her lips before he'd turned away.

Duncan had broken her heart once and Annie wasn't about to let him have a second crack at it.

The next morning, achy and embarrassed over her midnight indiscretion with her imaginary lover, Annie phoned Eric. She desperately needed to hear his voice. Because, try as she might, she could not remember what her soon-to-be fiancé looked like. Whenever she attempted to call up Eric's appealing but unobtrusive features, she saw instead Duncan's roguish face.

"Hello, Anne," Eric answered.

Annie cleared her throat. Hearing his voice wasn't bolstering her mood the way she'd expected. "You know that thing you said you wanted to ask me when I got back home?"

"Yes."

"Ask me now."

"It's not something you ask over the phone. The time and place must be perfect."

Perfect. Right. Everything with Eric had to go by some predetermined plan, by his timetable. Why did his refusal feel like a rejection? Why did she suddenly want to tell him it was all right with her if he never asked her the question?

"Listen, Anne, could we make this quick? I have an early meeting."

"Sure, sure." Disappointment bunched in her stomach. "I was feeling lonesome and wanted to touch base. See how you were doing."

He launched into a long spiel about the case he was working. Some conglomerate suing their competition.

"I miss you," she said, when he'd finished talking, although at this point she wasn't sure that she did.

"Miss you, too."

His response was automatic. She could hear him doing things. Putting his cereal bowl in the dishwasher. Snapping his briefcase closed. Jangling his keys. Normally she lauded his work ethic, but today it irritated her. Couldn't he, for once, give her his undivided attention?

"When do you foresee that you'll be able to come home? I'm ready for our lives to get back to normal."

"I don't know. Jock will be in the rehab hospital for another week at least."

"You'll be out of vacation time by then."

"I'm thinking about asking for unpaid leave."

Eric made a noise of disapproval. "You're putting your career in jeopardy. You do know that. People who have too many family distractions don't get promoted as quickly as those of us who devote our full attention to our jobs."

Feeling chastised, Annie sighed. "Yes, I know."

"Have you hired anyone to run the dive shop yet?"

"No." She'd been dragging her feet on the issue and she couldn't say why.

"You ought to just sell the thing."

"What would Jock do with himself if he didn't have the shop?"

"Be realistic, Anne. More than likely your grandfather is going to end up in a nursing home, if he pulls through this at all."

Eric was right, but that didn't stop her from fisting her hand in her lap as anger and despair washed over her. Odds were against Jock making a full recovery at his age, but she didn't want to hear what was practical or common sense. She wanted to believe her grandfather was going to live for a long, long time. Couldn't Eric offer her a little hope?

"I've got to go now. Call me tonight and we'll discuss this further."

"Okay," she said, feeling bereft and very alone.

"Love you."

But when Annie tried to say it back, her tongue stuck to the roof of her mouth. "Have a nice day," she mumbled instead and hung up, feeling as if the safe, ordered life she'd carefully constructed was rapidly unraveling.

Down in the dumps after her conversation with Eric, Annie went to see her grandfather in the rehab hospital. She tapped on the door of his room and stepped inside with a smile on her lips, only to have it vanish the minute she spied Duncan sitting in a chair at the foot of Jock's bed.

She caught her breath, disturbed by the effect he had on her. She wore a pink sundress with a short flirty hem and matching flip-flops. She caught him unabashedly ogling her legs. The way he stared sent a hot jolt of erotic sensation shooting through her. How dare he seduce her with his eyes right here in her grandfather's sickroom.

"What are you doing here?" She glared.

"I dropped by to offer my sympathy to your grandfather," Duncan said, looking far more handsome than he had any right to look, in a light blue T-shirt and tight-fitting jeans.

"Liar," she countered. "You came to tell him about the Siren's Call."

"Not me. I made a promise to keep my lips zipped."

"The Siren's Call?" Jock perked up. "What about the Siren's Call?"

Inwardly, she groaned. She'd stuck her foot in it by assuming Duncan had already spilled the beans.

"Well?" Jock looked from Duncan to Annie and back again.

"Nothing," they said in unison.

"Don't lie to an old man with a bum hip. What's going on?"

Annie shunted a glance at Duncan. His eyes burned into hers.

Might as well tell him the whole thing, Duncan telegraphed her with his gaze. She had a sneaking suspicion he'd orchestrated this whole thing. She didn't know how, but she felt as if he'd guessed she would show up and stick her foot in her mouth by accusing him of telling Jock about the Siren's Call.

Was she really that predictable?

"Somebody talk," Jock demanded.

Annie blew out her breath. "Duncan found a map on his Bermuda Triangle dive that appears to lead to where the captain of the pirate ship *Lorelei* stashed the Siren's Call."

"I'll be damned. She really does exist." The look of joy on her grandfather's wrinkled face ate at Annie's heart. How could she deny Jock access to the Siren's Call? He'd lost a son and daughter-in-law over the damned thing. He deserved it.

"That she does," Duncan confirmed.

"You got the map with you?" her grandfather asked.

Duncan pulled the map from his pocket and handed it to him.

Jock studied it, tears glistening in his eyes. "You're going after her."

"I really don't think that it's such a good idea."

"Annie, girl, you've got to go after her." Jock struggled to sit up higher in bed, wincing against the effort it cost him.

She rushed over to help him, touched his arm. He felt so fragile. Jock looked into her eyes. "You know it's what your folks would have wanted."

Guilt, that nasty monster, chewed her up. Anxiety lay like an iron fist in the pit of her stomach. She sneaked a glance over her shoulder at Duncan, and damn if he wasn't smirking. He had her and he knew it. She made a face at him and turned back to Jock.

"I haven't been diving in ten years. Since Mom and Dad died."

" 'Tis a shame, too," Duncan said. "You were a damn fine diver, Annie."

Jock nodded. "He's got a point. You used to love diving."

"I'm out of practice."

"But you're in good physical shape. It's like riding a bicycle. You never forget how to dive and Duncan will look after you."

That's exactly what she was afraid of.

"Just think of it, Annie. How proud your folks would be if you found her. Just imagine. The Siren's Call. At long last."

"But look at the map again. See where the underground cave is located?"

Jock took a second look. "Dead Man's Island."

"Right. You know how the locals believe it's haunted by the ghost of men forced to walk the planks of pirate ships." She sounded ridiculously superstitious, and Eric would be angered by such an argument, but she was grasping at straws, trying to do anything to stay out of the water with Duncan. "We'll have a hell of a time trying to find anyone to ferry us out to the dive site."

"I'll find someone," Duncan assured her.

"What if you can't?" she challenged.

"Duncan will take care of it," Jock reiterated.

"I'll have to close the dive shop," Annie warned, knowing how much Jock hated to shut down the store. "Maybe for two or three days."

"But it's for the Siren's Call. What better cause?"

Sighing, Annie remembered how passionate her parents had been about the artifact. She recalled the late nights they'd stayed up with their friends, speculating where the fabled mermaid idol might be hidden. Plotting their dives. Doing the research. She would often stand in the door in her pajamas, watching them, feeling left out. They'd been obsessed to the point of neglecting their only child. It was her first lesson in the power of obsession.

Nervously, she fingered her chin. Her second lesson in the danger of obsession came from her own passion for gymnastics and the obsessive need to push herself to the limit—a passionate obsession that had ended in an accident on the balance beam.

And her third bitter lesson about obsessive desire, the lesson that had finally sunk in, had come from the man sitting at the foot of the bed.

She thought of the pain Duncan could wield like a sword because she still cared about him. Annie thought of the Siren's Call and its seductive promise of sexual potency. She thought of her parents, who'd made finding the idol their life's work and how they'd died in the pursuit of it. Damn. She wanted that idol, but not the complications that went along with possessing it.

Then she looked into the eyes of the man who'd raised her after her parents had died. The man who himself might not be long for this world, and she knew there was no way around it. She had to team up with Duncan Stewart and go after the damned thing.

"What do you say, Annie?" Duncan winked in that irritatingly charming way of his. "Is it a go?"

Sucking in her breath, Annie wrenched out the words she did not want to say. "All right, I'll go."

Duncan watched Annie flounce away in a whirl, her pink skirt giving him a provocative peek at her upper thighs. He knew this was not a dress she wore in Wall Street boardrooms. She'd bought that sexy little number right here in Florida. Her heart was longing to come home, no matter how much her head might deny it.

"We got her, Dunc." Jock laughed and rubbed his palms together. "Our girl's back for good."

"I'm having trouble lying to her, Jock. It's a cheap shot."

"Cheap shot it may be, but you know how stubborn she is. Nothing else was going to work. When you told me about finding the real Siren's Call on the *Lorelei,* I knew it was the ace in the hole you needed to win her back from Hammond. Unfortunately, my dancing a jig on the dock was what landed me here." He swept a hand at his hip. "But you know what? It was worth it."

"You really love your granddaughter."

"No more than you do."

They stared at each other.

"Damn, Jock," Duncan said. "I've missed you."

"I've missed you, too."

Duncan's throat clogged. "We wasted a lot of time."

"I'm sorry, boy, for how I treated you," Jock said. It was a magnanimous statement, coming from the old sailor. He was a bold, salty man who rarely admitted to weakness or mistakes.

"Me, too."

"I should have given you the benefit of the doubt with Annie. It's clear as the nose on your face you love her deeply. I don't know what happened between you five years ago, but she needs you now, Dunc. If we don't do this she's going to end up married to that peckerhead corporate lawyer and spend the rest of her life denying who she really is. And you'll go to your grave regretting letting her get away."

"You're dead right and I know it, but what happens if she can't forgive me when she learns we've tricked her?"

"It's up to you to convince her. Dig down inside your heart. You'll find a way. Bring our girl home for good. Do what you should have done five years ago, you scoundrel." Jock grinned. "Marry her."

4

Annie and Duncan slipped into the ocean together, leaving the man he had hired to ferry them out to the dive site just off Dead Man's Island waiting for them in the boat.

The waves rose and fell in a sleepy, heavy way, and beyond her tightly fitting dive mask all she could see was a vast swell of plankton green sea. The water encompassed her. It was around her, in her, swallowing her like a lover's embrace. Annie felt fluid and free and flawless in a way she never felt on dry land. She glanced over at Duncan and he was smiling at her. He loved the water, too, delighting in the way it rolled over him.

God, how she'd missed diving. How she'd missed Duncan. She hadn't realized until now how empty her life had become without both.

He caught her by the elbow and spun her through the water. He was frowning, and she realized she'd been diving too far, too fast. More commanding than Neptune himself, he shook his head and signaled for her to slow down. Behind his mask, black eyes simmered with strength and sexuality.

He took her deeper. The coldness at this new depth startled her face and hands. The tension in the water was sharp. He felt it, too, she knew. The swells waved through her. Up and down.

Duncan tugged on her elbow. She followed the direction he was pointing and then she saw it, what she had forgotten. The reason they were here. The entrance to the underground cave. The mystery of the legend drew her like a magnet. For the first time she understood her parents' fascination. She was compelled to enter the cave, no matter what the risk.

He motioned for her to stay back while he went in first. A contrary part of her wanted to argue, but she realized he was the expert and to contest his authority was foolhardy. He unclipped his flashlight from his weight belt and switched it on.

Treading water, she watched as Duncan slipped between the rocky crevice and disappeared into the murk. She felt a momentary tug of panic when she could no longer see him, but assured herself he was a highly trained salvage diver. He knew what he was doing.

Yes, and your parents had known what they were doing, too, and they'd still been killed by decompression sickness. But they'd been diving much deeper than this fifty-foot depth.

It was easy to get disoriented to time and place underneath the water. It seemed a half hour had passed but she checked her watch and saw it had been less than a minute. Just when she was about to go into the cave looking for him, he reappeared, waving for her to join him.

The beam of his flashlight barely illuminated the blackness. She stayed behind Duncan, mindful of the jutting rocks. One wrong move and a jagged shard could pierce her oxygen tank.

Fear and danger accelerated her sense of adventure, and at the same time bumped up her awareness of how dependent she and Duncan were upon each other. She could feel history pressing in on them, could easily imagine ghosts of men forced to walk pirates' planks prowling the ocean depths, protecting their treasure.

The hush was deafening.

She heard nothing except the sound of blood whooshing through her ears. She checked the time again. They had another twenty minutes of air, including ascent time.

She tugged on Duncan's arm and when he turned to look at her over his shoulder, she tapped the face of her watch. He nodded, but gestured for her to follow him. Curiosity seized her as he guided her deeper into the cave. It was total black except for the thin beam of light from his diving lantern.

Eerie. Annie's pulse leapt.

The underground cave expanded into a narrow room. He directed the light over the walls and stopped when it lighted an alcove in the rocks.

They swam closer.

Duncan handed Annie the light and reached into the alcove. When he hauled out a locked trunk coated in alga and gunk, she stared at it, incredulous. She was about to hold the Siren's Call in her hands. She thought of her parents and her heart swelled with sadness and anticipation. It was an odd sensation.

Duncan took out his utility knife and went to work on the hasp. She had to remind herself to inhale. It was surprisingly easy to forget to breathe in the dark wetness, in the excitement.

A couple of hard hits with the utility knife and the rusted hasp fell apart. Duncan raised his head and met her gaze. Even in the shrouded gloom, with only the flashlight for illumination, there was no mistaking the triumph on his face.

You do the honors, his eyes spoke. They'd shared glances weighed with meaning before, but nothing to match this. They were making history.

To tell the truth, she was scared. What would happen once she finally held the Siren's Call? Would she learn that the idol possessed magnetic qualities more powerful than any aphrodisiac? Or would she discover that it was all make-believe? Did she really want to debunk the myth?

Bracing herself, she grabbed hold of the corner of the lid and raised it up. Duncan played the flashlight beam over the contents and it hit the carved face of a beautiful woman. Awestruck, Annie sucked in oxygen. She reached inside, picked up the idol, and then let the box tumble to the floor of the cave.

The mermaid idol was a foot long, made of glass and shaped in a phallic design. It weighed much less than she expected. A star-shaped lodestone was embedded in the mermaid's breast—her attracting, magnetic force. The damned thing looked like some kind of exotic dildo.

Annie cradled the Siren's Call in her palms. Felt the energy of it vibrating up her arms, through her shoulders, and into her chest. Rippling, tingling, moving through her. The sensation was so strong she thrust the Siren's Call away from her and let go.

Duncan caught it before it fell away in the dark water and held it out to her.

Nervously, she touched it.

They were both touching it.

From behind their diving masks, their gazes met, fused over the idol. The cold heaviness of the water surrounded them, but Annie had never felt so hot and light. Longing, regret, shame, sadness welled into a potent cocktail of emotions. They'd shared so much, lost so much, and now they were back together again. But it wasn't a fresh start. This was the ending she'd needed for a long time.

Closure. Both for her parents' death and her ill-fated relationship with Duncan.

I want, she thought. *I want, I want, I want.*

God, how miserable this feeling. She'd trained herself not to want. To instead go after what she needed. To ignore her passions, sublimate her desires with practical, sensible things. Instead of the degree in anthropology she'd wanted, she'd chosen an MBA in business. Instead of the exciting man who made her blood sing, she'd settled for a staid corporate lawyer who never did anything unexpected. She'd chosen safety over adventure.

Her breathing was raspy as everything she'd sacrificed for a dependable life grabbed her heart and squeezed. This idol was truly wicked. Making her want so fiercely all the things she'd forsaken.

She let go of the Siren's Call again, but Duncan held on to it. Annie glanced away. She felt confused, upset, and anxious. Her goal was accomplished. She'd found what she'd come for. And if she wasn't careful, it would destroy everything she'd built.

Duncan slipped the mermaid idol into the mesh bag clipped to his weight belt. Annie didn't wait for him. She had to get out of this place. She slipped out the way they came, Duncan shining the light from behind her.

In the darkness she banged into the rocks, heard her tank scrape ominously against the wall. Out, out, she had to get out.

Don't panic. The worst thing you can do on a deep-sea dive is panic. Diving lesson 101.

She kicked harder, found the cave opening, and popped out into open water. She turned her head, searching for the boat's anchor line, but she couldn't find it.

Where was the anchor?

Was there a second opening in the cave and she'd come out in the wrong place? Puzzled, she looked behind her and signaled to Duncan with a pulling motion.

He shook his head.

The water was murky, thick with plankton. Visibility was less than a foot in front of their masks. Duncan motioned her to the right and he swam left. They made a circle and came back to meet in the middle, unable to find the anchor line.

Had the driver of the boat pulled up anchor?

But why would he do that? She tried not to worry, drew strength from Duncan's calm demeanor. He pointed. *Let's go up to the surface and have a look.*

He went first and she followed, ascending slowly, even though she wanted to rip off her weight belt and let herself bob to the top like a fishing cork. It seemed to take hours, but in reality was little more than five minutes. Her head was achy from not breathing enough. She inhaled more oxygen, trying to shake off the feelings that had gripped her inside the cave.

At last they broke through the water, and Annie wasted no time in ripping her mask off. Her eyes burned from the rush of salt water. She blinked, looking for the boat. She spied dark storm clouds collecting on the northern horizon, but nothing else.

"Where is he?" she asked Duncan, who'd also peeled off his mask. "Where's the driver? Where's our boat?"

But he didn't have to answer. She understood.

The boat was gone and they were stranded in the middle of the deep blue sea. Just the two of them.

All alone with the potent aphrodisiac of the Siren's Call.

They swam for Dead Man's Island.

The impending storm whipped the waters. Annie felt a bizarre exhilaration. She should have been upset that their boat pilot had taken off and left them bobbing in the middle of the ocean. Instead, all she could think about was how sexy the water made her feel as it splashed across her body. And how happy she was to be here with Duncan.

Her skin heated, her nerve endings tingled. Just looking at the hunky man beside her made her pussy ache with need. The Siren's Call was doing its dastardly deed. Making her throb for a man who was no good for her.

Additional clouds hunched on the horizon, darkening the sky. Lightning flashed. Annie shivered as her desire became a living thing, burning like a torch inside her. They stumbled onto the sandy beach in their swim fins. Annie thought of the sexy movies she'd seen with people making hot frantic love on the beach. Her mouth watered.

Duncan seemed to be feeling the effects of the mermaid idol, too. He was looking at her with the sultriest eyes she'd ever seen, heavy-lidded and dark with sexual need.

Annie gulped. She could tell it took everything inside Duncan not to jerk her into his arms and kiss her mouth raw. *Do it,* she mentally dared him. *Do it, do it, do it.*

"We have to get to shelter." He nodded at the sky. He looked like Neptune in the wetsuit. Big and strong and bronze. Water dripping from his hair.

"Where?" She scanned the beach.

"Inland. There're cliffs and overhanging rocks."

"You've been here before?"

"I studied a map of the island."

Prudence. She hadn't expected that of him. Maybe Duncan had changed. She cocked her head and studied him. He looked different. Solid, more peaceful than before. Hope sprouted inside, took root, and grew. Maybe they could turn back time and start fresh. Maybe they could revive their lost friendship.

Be careful, she warned herself. Those are dangerous thoughts.

They stripped off their swim fins, oxygen tanks, and diving mask, and found a safe spot to leave them on the beach along with Duncan's harpoon, out of reach of the rising tide. They headed inland, their feet sinking into the damp sand. The cooling air was rife with electrically charged ions, and goose bumps danced along Annie's arms.

The storm was rolling in fast. Lightning flared again, hot and brilliant in the dark blue sky.

Duncan led the way, the Siren's Call inside his diving bag banging against his thick, muscular thigh clad in the sleek black material of his dive suit. His shaggy, damp hair curled against his head. Here walked the King of the Sea.

Her stomach tightened, sending sexy messages shooting straight to her pussy. She tried to ignore them, but she knew she was in trouble. Stranded. Alone. With an incredibly hot-bodied man and a magical mermaid idol with the potency of an aphrodisiac.

Duncan pushed back the overgrowth, clearing the way for her. By the time they'd walked half a mile into the tropical forest, the storm was swirling overhead and fat drops of rain were splattering against the palm fronds.

"Look there." He pointed to an outcropping rising out of a stony bluff. It overhung a nice alcove, providing shelter from the storm. "Crawl under."

She ducked her head and slipped beneath the cliff. Duncan didn't follow. Instead, he slipped the utility knife from his pocket and began slashing at palm fronds.

"What are you doing?" she called, the wind whipping so loudly she had to shout to be heard.

Duncan didn't answer, just kept slashing at the fronds until he had collected a large pile. He gathered them up and strolled toward her. He looked down at her, and she looked up at him as the ache inside her grew to fever pitch.

She saw the pulse pounding in his neck and she felt a corresponding throb between her legs. There was too much rubber between them. She wanted him naked. Now. Biting into her lip to suppress that crazy thought, she dropped her gaze.

"Scoot over," he commanded.

When she did, he laid the palm fronds out across the rock slab, cushioning it.

"Strip."

"I beg your pardon." She bristled.

"Take off your wetsuit."

"I will not."

"You can't sit around in it. Besides, we can use the wetsuits to pad the palm fronds."

He had a point. What was comfortable in the water was miserably clingy and hot on shore. She had to leave the protective overhang in order to stand up. Duncan loomed over her, breathing hard and heavy, watching her shimmy out of her wetsuit as rain pelted their skin and lightning danced through the clouds.

"Turn your head," she said, feeling vulnerable and exposed.

"What for, Annie? I've seen you naked before."

"I'm not naked. I have on a swimsuit."

His eyes blazed with overt sexual desire.

"I mean it." She tapped her foot.

"Afraid the Siren's Call will send me into a lust-filled frenzy at the sight of your bare skin?"

"Something like that."

He laughed.

"You're such a tease," she groused.

"Admit it, you like that about me." He wriggled his eyebrows.

She did indeed, but she wasn't about to admit it. She snapped her fingers and pointed in the opposite direction. "Avert your gaze."

He pretended to look away, but the minute she went to work

on the zipper of her wetsuit she could feel his eyes on her again. She chose to ignore him, peeling the wetsuit off her body like it was a banana skin.

Duncan audibly sucked in his breath, and belatedly Annie realized the top of her bikini had shifted underneath the wetsuit and one of her breasts was hanging out.

She snapped her head around and met Duncan's gaze.

The look in his eye was so feral, so wild and hungry, she could scarcely breathe. He was the only man who'd ever looked at her with that much raw desire. It was a scary thing to acknowledge. Did she really hold that much sexual power over him? Before she had time to explore this new realization, a fresh clap of thunder brought a downpour. She tucked her breast back inside her bikini top and tossed him her wetsuit.

He had taken off his wetsuit, too. God, he looked so good with those washboard abs. He laid their wetsuits atop the palm fronds, sat down, and held out his hand to her.

In spite of her doubts about what was happening between them, she took his hand and crawled up under the overhang beside him.

He wrapped one big strong arm around her waist and stretched them both out across the length of their makeshift bed. He nestled her into the curve of his body, her bottom pressed against his pelvis. She felt the determined poke of his cock through his swimsuit, but he made no move to take things further. They lay together, watching the rain tumble.

Annie tried to deny the desire pushing up through her, closed her eyes and forced herself to concentrate on something other than the need knotting her entire body.

They breathed in tandem. Close. Snug. Pressed together. But Duncan did not make a move on her.

Why wasn't he making a move on her? What in the hell was

wrong with the man? How was he staying so controlled? He'd never been this controlled before.

He *had* changed.

And the more restraint he showed, the more desperate she became to have him. Oh, fuck this.

She wanted him and she was going to have him. She wasn't so young and naïve anymore, expecting happily-ever-after from a man who could never promise it. She was going to enjoy the sex for good sex's sake and not read any more into the encounter. The Siren's Call might be responsible for her uncontrollable horniness, but this time she knew what she was getting into. It was just sex and she was in control. This time, she'd keep her heart safe.

"Let me see the Siren's Call. I want to see her up close."

He sat up. She felt him rummaging around in his diving bag and a second later he was leaning over her, dangling the idol in front of her. She claimed it.

Here was the enemy.

The Siren's Call stared at her through sultry, somnolent eyes, stirring her hormones, daring her to forget her pride, urging her to block out the chatter in her brain for one minute and listen to the throb of her hot, wet pussy.

Do it. Fuck this man. You know you want to. It doesn't have to mean happily-ever-after, just happily-ever-now.

Her body responded in a gush, chemicals colliding, expanding. She felt a racy sense of exuberance, of a glorious feminine power. When she'd made love to Duncan the first time she'd been a shy virgin. But no more.

She was a woman indulging her sexuality. Like froth on the ocean's tide, captured by the pull of the moon, carried by the swell of pheromones, mesmerized by the lure of the Siren's Call, she let herself be swept away. Setting the idol aside, she rolled onto her back on the bed of palm fronds and wetsuits.

Duncan was propped up on one elbow, his head just inches below the top of the overhang. "I know exactly what you need," he murmured.

Normally she wouldn't have let him get away with sounding so cocky, but she wanted him so much, and her aching clit was just throbbing for his caress. "Oh, yeah?"

He winked wickedly.

She swallowed great thick gulps of air. "What's that?"

"You need to be cherished by a man who knows how to take care of you."

She wasn't going to let him turn this into something romantic. "Wrong, I need your hard, hot cock, and I need it now."

He looked taken aback, but just for a moment. A smug smile curled his lips. "Well, when you put it like that, how can I refuse?"

"Hurry, hurry, I can't stand waiting."

"That starved are you, Harvard?"

"You have no idea."

"The Siren's Call strikes again. Unfortunately she's played a cruel trick on us."

"What are you talking about?"

"No condoms."

Dammit! The Siren's Call had made her so irrational she hadn't even thought of protection. Annie bit her bottom lip and then smiled provocatively. "Um . . . there are other things we could do."

"Why, Annie Graves, what are you suggesting?" He pretended to be shocked.

Her pussy was already slicked up and juicy for him. The look in his eyes, the tone of his voice was driving her to distraction.

The overhanging rock cast his face in shadows. He looked savage, primitive. His high cheekbones appeared razor-sharp, his lips full and foreboding, his chin a cleft darkened by beard stubble. For a moment, the man she had known since she was thirteen looked like a total stranger.

The sensation skyrocketed her arousal. Her erogenous triggers went off, nipples pebbling, womb contracting, every nerve ending taking note of this strong, determined male.

"You look like you're about to go on a salvage dive, Duncan. That's the only other time I've seen such focus on your face."

"I am on a salvage dive, babe," he teased, and she caught his meaning. He slipped a hand between her thighs, which she had pressed tightly together, just above her knees. "Going after the treasure I lost."

Every muscle in her body clamped down hard, and she had to bite the inside of her cheek to keep from moaning.

"Go ahead." His voice lowered, went huskier, just like in her dream. "Moan all you want. There's no one around to hear you but me. Ah, the things I'm going to do to you."

Things? What things? A dozen stimulating images tumbled through her head.

Keeping his hand wedged between her thighs, Duncan twisted his body around until his head was resting at her feet and his own bare toes were rubbing against her hair. He dusted off her feet, dispersing the fine grains of sand clinging to her skin, and then slowly took her big toe into his hot mouth.

"Oh, Duncan," she breathed. The sensation was so erotic. "You've acquired a toe fetish, you big perv."

He suckled her toe while his hand tickled the inside of her thigh. She let her knees drop outward, giving him easier access. He made a noise of satisfaction, took his fingers and massaged the sole of her foot as he continued to lap at her toes.

What a feeling!

He must have hit some kind of reflexology trigger point because a glorious sensation shot through the bottom of her foot, straight up into her clenching womb. Automatically, her hips arched up off the ground. A desperate keening cry slipped past her lips. She fisted her hands, swept away like a boat in a storm, as his mouth left her toes and trailed up her right leg, his fingers gliding over her left.

His tongue was her master, commanding her to moan and squirm and beg as he inched from her ankles to her shin to her kneecap. This was the sexiest thing that had ever happened to her. She had no idea her toes and feet and legs were so sensitive, so desperate for attention. Who would have thought that Duncan's mouth against her inner thigh would feel so fucking erotic?

He reached up with one hand to touch her bare midriff. His fingers brushed against the pearl at her navel, enlivening things even more. His mouth moved higher and higher up her thigh. One hand was strumming her navel. The other hand was rubbing the back of her kneecap.

Annie was in tumult. She shouldn't want this. She should resist. Should fight the lure of the Siren's Call. But she was hamstrung by her desire. Overcome by the passion she tried so hard to deny. All her long-held values and beliefs about life and passion and safety just crumbled. Helplessly, she quivered in his arms.

"You're more beautiful than ever," he breathed, pulling his lips from her skin, raising his head, and gazing into her eyes.

Nervously, she reached up to finger her chin.

"Stop doing that," he said.

"Doing what?"

"Touching your chin. The scar doesn't detract from your beauty one bit."

"I'm not beautiful," she denied. "I'm well-rounded, not leggy. I'm short and I have freckles and, of course, there's this." She touched the scar again.

"Who says well-rounded and petite and freckled isn't beautiful?"

"You."

"When did I ever say that?"

"Not in words, but in action. You go for tall, leggy blondes with flawless features. Think about those women who followed you into the dive shop."

"You're kidding me, right?"

"Face it, Duncan, I'm not your type."

"I'll show you my type," he growled, shifting positions again, straddling her, his hard throbbing cock pressing against her belly as he leaned down to kiss her.

His tongue drifted over her teeth. His fingers teased her nipples beneath the material of her bikini top. The sensation was out of this world. Blood pumped through her body, echoed in her ears, the strum of life singing inside her.

Annie's nipples were rock hard, her breasts swollen and achy. A strange, wondrous surge of heat blazed from her tense nipples straight into her womb. She was dripping for him. Juicy and ready.

"You like?" He pulled his mouth from hers, his voice rough as a caveman's, and peered deeply into her eyes.

She nodded. His fingers were busy slipping the strap of her bikini slowly off her shoulders. Annie whimpered.

Where had this come from? She was a strong woman who didn't let her desires reduce her to a quivering mass. Why was she so willingly capitulating to him? Especially when she knew exactly how much he could hurt her.

It's the Siren's Call.

This was miserable. This was joy. This boomerang of emotions. How could she want him so much yet be so afraid of her desire? Her brain told her to fight it, to push him away, to jump up and run out into the pouring rain. To drown herself in the ocean, if that's what it took not to make the same mistake. But her body wasn't having any of it.

Her hands were on his face, caressing his cheek, peering into his eyes, begging him for more. Passion—the thing she feared most—crowded out prudence. All she could think about was his masculine fingers stroking her super-sensitive flesh to a five-alarm blaze.

"Oh, God, Annie," he said once her bikini top was off. "You're fucking fabulous."

She blushed, never believing but always secretly hoping she'd be back here again. Duncan's fiery gaze roved over her, his hands sending ribbons of pleasure unfurling throughout her body.

A sneaky, double-crossing part of her wanted to cry out with joy that she was in Duncan's arms. That they had a second chance. The euphoria of that idea was sweet, but dangerous. She refused to explore the possibility. This was strictly sex, nothing more.

"Duncan," she breathed, tossed by her tumultuous thoughts. Longing overwhelmed her. She couldn't resist. He was so damned handsome with that shock of brown hair plastered against his thick, tanned skin.

A smile tilted his lips when she reached up, threaded her arms around his neck, and brought his head down for another kiss. The length of his hard body was pressed against hers. His tongue dipped languidly into her mouth.

She strummed her tongue against his, making herself an active participant. If she was going to go through with this, then she was going to take full responsibility for what happened. Afterward, she could tell herself she'd known exactly what she was doing. This time, there would be no regrets. Annie didn't stop him when his hand drifted to her bikini bottoms.

"Lift up your hips," he commanded.

She obeyed, levering her lower back off the bed of palm fronds as his big hand made short work of the slight material.

He made a guttural sound low in his throat. This was it. No begging off now. He rolled to one side and stripped off his swim trunks in a motion so practiced she had to wonder how many bedrooms he'd performed it in. How many other women he'd slept with. His erection burgeoned, thick and heavily veined, the velvety head purpled and pulsating.

"My, my," she cooed. "You're bigger than I remembered."

It was his turn to blush, and that blush did a strange thing to her heart. He was shy with her. This big, commanding man.

Stop it! Don't let his vulnerability get to you.

She sat up and reached for him, but he grabbed her around the wrist to stop her. "Touch me now, Annie Graves," he said, his accent heavier than usual, "and I'll blow."

Lowering his head, he pressed his lips to her bare belly and kissed his way back up to her straining nipples. She quivered.

"Does that feel good, Annie? Tell me what you like."

"Good." It was all she could manage.

He flicked his tongue over one straining bud and then oh-so-lightly bit down. Razor-thin shards of pleasure spread throughout her breast. She moaned.

"Good?" he asked.

"No."

"No?"

"Fabulous."

He grinned and kept at it. His mouth sucking, his tongue teasing, fingers tickling. Brilliant. He'd learned a lot in five years. He'd honed his technique.

He left her nipples and traveled downward. He spent a little time at her navel, pulling the pearl ring in and out of his mouth. The maneuver produced crazy, erotic ripples in her belly that undulated all the way down into her pussy. When his lips reached her straining, hungry clit, he stopped just short of touching her with his tongue. His breath was hot against her tender flesh, igniting her beyond comprehension.

She arched her hips again, trying to bring his mouth and her clit into contact, but he read her like a GPS tracking device and moved with her, keeping his mouth just out of her reach,

"Beast," she hissed.

He laughed.

"Bastard."

"Hang on, babe. Well get there."

She didn't want to hang on. She wanted him to fuck her with his mouth right this second. Her brain was glazed with lust, her body worked to a fevered pitch.

Gently he spread her thighs wider and moved his body around so that he knelt between her legs. "Gorgeous."

The head of his massive cock throbbed against her knee as he leaned forward. Annie's excitement escalated. Unbearable. She couldn't stand it. She'd never felt such desperate pressure.

His big fingers caressed her clit as his tongue probed the folds of her labia. Her eyes slid closed so she could savor what he was doing to her.

"Yes," she whispered. "Yes."

His tongue captured her clit.

"Oh, God." Never, in all her life, had she been pleasured this way. It was ecstasy. He seemed to know exactly what she wanted, what she needed from him. Knew it even better than she did. He reveled in her and she had never felt so cherished. It was dangerous territory, these tender feelings. But she couldn't stop them. They were part and parcel of what was going on.

While he suckled her clit with his mouth, he slipped a finger into her slick, wet pussy. The walls of her vagina sucked at his finger, gripping and kneading him in rhythmic waves, pulling him deeper and deeper into her.

Sound was altered and she existed in the delicious void. Floating, without a body, it seemed. She was total sensation. Aware of everything. Her entire being a giant throbbing clit of energy.

"You are so damn hot."

She rode the sensation of his tongue, got lost in it. She hovered on the brink of orgasm, but he would not let her fall over. A steady strumming vibration began deep in her throat and it emerged as a wild moan.

"Please," she begged. "Please."

"Please what, babe? You have to ask for what you need."

"Please make me come."

"That's all I wanted to hear."

He let loose then. Gave her his all. His tongue danced, his fingers manipulated. She let go of all control. Let go and just allowed him to take over. It seemed he was everywhere. Over her, around her, in her, outside of her. He was magic. He was amazing. He played her with accomplished precision. She was his instrument, tuned and ready.

"More." She thrashed her head. "Harder."

He gave it to her just the way she asked for it. Pumping his hand into her, while his thumb pressed her clit, the secret button of her release.

"Come, babe, come," he coaxed.

She came. Exploded into great, writhing pleasure. She screamed. Her voice echoing across Dead Man's Island. Slapping against the rain. Bouncing off the confines of the overhang. Sating her soul for the first time in five years.

5

Annie was limp in his arms, drained, sated. Duncan gathered her close, nuzzled her neck, nibbled her earlobe. Her delicious feminine aroma surrounding him. She smelled of the sea he loved, salty and rich and verdant. Hungrily, he inhaled her. Stunned at how intensely she stirred him.

So personal was her smell, so tuned in was he to her fragrance, that if he were blindfolded in a room with a hundred women he could pick her out by scent alone. Yearning clutched his throat, squeezed his heart. Whether she knew it or not, she had him on the ropes. One frown from her and he was jumping to turn it into a smile. One smile and his day was made.

Duncan stared at her sleeping form and his heart was stone in his throat. What was going to happen, he wondered, when they got back to civilization and she learned the Siren's Call was a fake?

That he'd orchestrated this whole expedition because he'd known it was the only way she would allow him to make love to her again.

Guilt had him snared tight in its teeth. He should tell her the truth, tell her now, face her anger, and beg for her forgiveness.

But she was sleeping soundly and he could not bring himself to disturb her. He wished he could sleep. He needed to sleep if he expected to keep up with his insatiable woman.

His woman.

Duncan cradled the back of his head in his palms and smiled up at the rocky overhang above them. If he had to use sex and the Siren's Call to hang on to her, then that's what he would do. She was his woman, and he was determined that this time he was never going to let her go.

When Annie awoke sometime later, the rain had stopped and Duncan was gone.

For a minute, she felt the same treacherous flash of panic she'd experienced five years earlier, on the morning after they'd first made love and he'd blithely announced he had signed up as a salvage diver on a ship run by the most beautiful and sexually aggressive woman in St. Augustine. The betrayal of that long-ago morning was so fresh in her mind she could feel the sting of it, could smell orange blossoms blooming on the trees from the field near Duncan's houseboat.

That was then and this is now, she told herself. Totally different circumstances. Then, she'd been a shattered kid. Now, she was fully in control of her own destiny.

She sat up. Should she go search for him? Or simply wait for him to return?

Waiting idly by for him to return was too passive. Too much like she'd given up and just let him have his way. Besides, it was his turn, and she was in the driver's seat.

She put on her bikini. Her body was sore and achy from his lovemaking. Grinning, she wandered down to the beach.

When she reached the clearing, she saw he'd made a fire on the beach. How had he managed that?

He came strolling from the sea, naked as the day he was born. His harpoon in one hand, a large fish in the other. Annie had never seen a more compelling sight.

Duncan stalked toward her, his cock, jutting proudly in the air, already hard for her.

She was so excited her pulse banged through her veins. "You caught a fish."

He shrugged as if providing for her was expected, not exceptional.

"And built a fire." Annie gestured.

"I had matches in my waterproof emergency diving kit," he explained. "You hungry?"

"Starving." She followed, watching him as he fashioned a makeshift barbecue spit, cleaned the fish, skewered it with a stick, and stuck it over the fire to grill. He did it all while he was still hard as a rock.

Poor baby. He'd given her a rousing orgasm without ever coming himself. How selfish of her. How thoughtless. She should even the score.

"Duncan."

The expression on his face was so intense she could feel it deep down in her soul. He looked so good. So manly. Muscles bulging, he stepped closer, encroaching on her personal space.

"Annie, we need to talk."

"Shh," she hushed him. "Not now."

Then without another word, she dropped to her knees in the sand, took his big, thick, beautiful cock into her hand, touched her lips to him.

"That's it, babe," he gasped and a shudder went through him. He cupped the top of her head in his palms, channeling her in his preferred rhythm. "That's right," he cried, his voice gravelly as ground rocks. "Suck me."

As she took him in her mouth, she realized she'd never felt more powerful in her life.

Annie's lips were on his cock, her fingers digging into his buttocks. Duncan had never felt anything so damned wonderful. He couldn't believe what she was doing for him.

He thought he'd had her figured out. Thought he knew her through and through. But this was not what he'd been expecting. A blow job. On the beach.

She took his breath.

He looked down at her dark brown curls and his heart contracted. This wasn't right. He didn't want her on her knees subservient to him. He was the one who revered and treasured her. He was the one who was guilty and wrong. He was the one who'd made all the mistakes.

But it felt so incredible, and he understood that she was trying to give to him what he'd given to her earlier that afternoon. He stood beneath the sky as the sun went down, and the woman he loved made him feel more like a man than he'd ever felt in his life.

Her mouth was so hot!

And she was doing things with her tongue, twirling it up and down along his shaft at the same time she sucked him. He had to reached down and grip her shoulders to keep himself from toppling over.

She held all the power. She was in control. He was putty. He was liquid. He was both nothing and everything in her willing hands. God, he'd missed out on so much! He'd missed out on five years of Annie.

Stupid fucker.

But he couldn't keep berating himself. Not when the things she was doing made him forget his own name.

Back and forth, she went. Sliding her mouth up and down his shaft. Duncan's knees tensed and when she reached up to cup his balls in one of her hot little hands dusted lightly with sand, he let out an explosive groan.

Annie made a noise of pure feminine satisfaction. She loved what she was doing to him. The minx. Duncan could not even think. He was swept away by sensation. Pressure, tension, and Annie's amazing tongue. His head swirled. He was a piece of debris caught in a water spout, tossed across the sea.

The tension built and built and built. Just when he thought he was going over the edge, she stopped moving.

"Wah . . . wah?" he gasped.

"Just thought you should see what it feels like to be tortured," she chuckled.

He let out a strangled cry.

And then her mouth was on him again, slick and velvety hot. Building him up only to let him down a second time.

He was crazy at this point. Lost to everything. He reached for his cock, but she slapped his hand away.

"No, no," she scolded. "This is my job."

Then back she was again. Rocking forward in the sand, sucking, licking, gobbling him up.

"Stop, stop, I'm about to come," he said.

But she ignored him, kept sucking him until he was within an inch of crazy.

Duncan shot his load into her mouth. Hot and quick.

He let out a sound of complete destruction. Dammit. He hadn't meant to do that.

"Annie," he cried.

He looked down at her and she was looking up at him, a wicked grin on her face, cheeks puffy, a drop of his semen on her bottom lip, gleaming wetly in the waning sunlight.

She winked at him.

And then she swallowed.

They dined on the roasted fish Duncan had caught and shared a small bottle of water from his emergency dive kit.

He had carried the bed of palm fronds and wetsuits down to the campfire. They'd decided to spend the night on the beach instead of at the overhang in case their boat driver decided to return to the island for them.

"Why do you suppose the driver left us?" Annie asked.

Duncan shrugged guiltily. No doubt he felt responsible for choosing such an unreliable boat captain. "You were right. The locals are afraid of Dead Man's Island. Our driver must have gotten spooked while we were diving and took off."

"But to leave us out here alone." She shook her head. "That's pretty cowardly."

He met her eyes. "People often have reasons for things we can't always understand."

"Do you have any plans for how we're going to get home?"

"Someone will come for us soon," he reassured her.

"How can you be so sure?"

"Your grandfather knows where we are. Plus, I filed a dive plan with the dive shop in Key West."

"You've thought of everything," she said, impressed by his thoroughness. Annie realized there was absolutely no one else in the world she'd rather be stranded on a desert island with than this man.

Duncan added a fresh log to the fire. It was still damp and it smoldered for a while before it dried out and began to snap and crack. Sparks shot skyward. They sat there for a long time in companionable silence, leaning against each other, gazing into the fire.

"What about this guy you're unofficially engaged to?" Duncan asked her. "This corporate lawyer. Tell me about him."

"Nothing much to tell," she said uneasily.

She did not want to talk about Eric. She'd already come to the conclusion, before she'd ever set on foot in the ocean with Duncan, that she was going to break up with Eric. Being back home, seeing Duncan again, had her examining the path she was on, and she'd realized it was taking her farther and farther away from the things she loved.

"So you're really going to marry him."

"I had planned on it," she said. Even if she was breaking up with Eric, she had no idea where she stood with Duncan. She wasn't giving away any more than she had to. Not until she'd gotten away from this island and the pull of the Siren's Call and sorted out her true feelings.

Duncan growled low in his throat. "Are you still planning on it? After what we just did together today?"

"The Siren's Call was responsible for what happened today. It was just sex."

"But how can you have sex with me and still love this other guy?" Duncan's voice was tight.

Annie didn't answer. She realized she'd never really loved Eric. She thought she loved him, but now she knew she'd only loved what he represented. Stability, safety, security.

"Are you still going to marry him?" His eyes drilled into her.

Annie hesitated, anxious about revealing too much to him.

He closed his big hand over hers and prompted, "Annie?"

"No."

Relief slacked his features. "Really?" he asked hopefully. "Why not?"

She shrugged, stared into the fire, unable to meet his gaze.

"Is it because of me? Because of us?"

"There is no 'us,' Duncan," she said, terrified to acknowledge the truth.

"Don't lie to yourself. There's never been anything but 'us,' and you know it."

"Great oral sex does not a permanent bond make."

"What's that supposed to mean?"

"You know." She picked up a stick and poked the fire.

He clamped his fingers around her wrist, forced her to stop stirring the coals. "No. No I don't."

"We can't go back in time, Duncan. We're not the same people anymore."

"I don't want to go back. I want to go forward."

"I can't make you any promises."

"Why'd you take up with a guy like Hammond? What's the appeal?"

She drew her knees to her chest and hugged them. *Because he isn't you.* "I needed someone stable that I could depend on to be there. Especially after the way you screwed with my head. Leaving town the morning after you'd bedded me and stole my virginity like it meant nothing."

"I'm sorry for that." His voice cracked painfully. It sounded as if the words had been savagely ripped from his throat.

"Yeah, well, so am I." She looked at him then and it hurt her to see that his eyes were haunted, and in that moment she realized he had suffered as much as she.

"I think you're kidding yourself," he said after a long time had passed, with no sounds breaking the silence except for the whoosh of the surf and the crackling fire.

Annie was thinking about the past, the way they used to be, about all the things they'd shared. All the things they could share again, if she were brave enough to take a chance. "What about?"

"I don't think you wanted someone stable and secure. I think you wanted someone you knew you wouldn't fall in love with. You can't fool me, Annie Marie. You make out like you want an intimate relationship, but the truth is you're terrified of commitment. Scared as hell that if you let yourself feel true passion you'll end up like your parents."

"I'm not afraid of commitment. You're projecting your fears onto me. You're the one who jumps from woman to woman, like Tarzan swinging from vine to vine."

"You want to know why I went from woman to woman?"

"Yes, please, enlighten me."

"Because I couldn't have you."

"What in the hell are you talking about? I threw myself at you. Time and again."

"First, you were too young. And then I didn't want to ruin our friendship and after your parents died, I was your shoulder to lean on. I couldn't take advantage of that. You were so vulnerable. I wanted you more than you can possibly know."

"Why didn't you ever tell me this?" Annie held her breath, wanting to believe him, but afraid.

"I had nothing to offer you. I came from nothing. I had nothing except for what your parents had given me. I had to make something of myself before I could tell you how I felt. But then you kissed me on your twentieth birthday, and all those years of holding myself in check just fell in on me, and I couldn't stop myself from making love to you even though I knew the timing was bad, that neither of us were ready for it."

"You hurt me bad, Duncan," she said, finally telling him what she'd longed to say for years. Emotion clogged her throat. She looked at him and saw tears glistening in his eyes. That rattled her clean to her soul.

"I know and I'm so sorry." He raised a hand to his mouth. "I was stupid and immature, and I didn't feel worthy of the precious gift you'd given. I thought there had to be a catch. That if I let you love me before I deserved it, I was bound to lose you."

"Oh, Duncan." She swallowed hard. "I thought you left me because I wasn't pretty enough for you.

"Dammit, Annie, no. Are you bloody insane?"

"Then why? Why did you wait until you took my virginity before you told me that you'd signed up to crew with Ginger Jones and were off to dive the seven seas? Why did you leave me?"

His eyes met hers. "I saw the letter."

"What letter?"

"Your acceptance letter from Harvard. The morning after we made love I got up to cook breakfast for you. Your purse was on the kitchen counter and I accidentally knocked it off. The letter fell out. I shouldn't have read it. Damn, I wish I hadn't read it, but read it I did." He stared at her hard. She squirmed under his scrutiny. "You lied to me, Annie. You told me you didn't get into Harvard."

"Because I didn't want to go," she said. "Because I wanted to stay in St. Augustine with you and Jock."

"I knew that," he said. "I also knew you were too smart to waste your opportunities running your grandfather's dive shop and being the wife of a salvage diver. You've got book smarts, Annie, and I never even finished high school. You deserved the best life had to offer, and I couldn't give it to you. So I did what I had to do to make you go to Harvard. I lied and told you I'd already hired on with Ginger Jones. I promised myself that I would become the best salvage diver in the world. That I would find the Siren's Call for you. And then I could come back when you were finished with Harvard and ask you to marry me." He laughed harshly. "I sure fucked that up."

Annie sucked in her breath. Could it be true? All this time she'd thought she was just another notch on Duncan's bedpost, and now to find out that he'd loved her so much he'd let her go for her greatest good? They stared as if seeing each other for the first time.

The fire anchored them on the island, while every fiber of their souls were reaching into the past, touching the pain they'd caused each other. The tide whispered up onto the beach, then sank back in a breathless hush.

"Duncan . . ."

"Annie . . ."

They sat without speaking for what seemed like a very long time. Then Duncan leaned forward to study her face in the firelight. Gently, he hooked two fingers under her jaw and tilted her head back, his eyes zeroing on her chin.

He sketched his fingertips over the scar and then dipped his lips to kiss it, tracing the jagged edges with his tongue. His touch grew firmer, grazing her old wound with his teeth, sucking and nibbling at her chin, mouthing her skin with the appetite of a lover, evoking a powerful sensation Annie instantly identified as rapture.

The sheer intimacy of his tenderness sprang tears to her eyes. Tenderness and concern, followed by anxiousness, profound sadness, and an odd fear. He whispered her name, "Annie," and pulled her into his lap. She kissed his mouth, wanting to breathe his breath, wanting him to breathe hers.

And for the first time in her life, Annie Graves truly felt beautiful.

6

"Ahoy there!"

A cheery voice woke Annie. Startled, she sat up, rubbing her eyes, and saw Duncan walking out to meet a tour boat anchored just off the beach. It took her a moment to realize they were being rescued.

Thank God! Much more time alone with Duncan and Annie didn't know what she might have done. After his confession last night, something inside of her had slipped. The hard resolve, the resentment she'd bottled up melted away like snow on sauna stones. He'd done what he'd done, not because he didn't care as she'd supposed, but because he cared so much. So where did that leave them now?

She got to her feet, wiped the sand from the seat of her bikini, and followed him to greet their visitors.

It turned out the people in the tour boat were a group of newlyweds heading for a week at a private resort on a nearby island.

Apparently, the driver of the boat who'd abandoned Annie and Duncan had met the tour boat captain in Key West, told him how he'd been spooked by Dead Man's Island and confessed to have stranded them. The tour boat captain had promised to stop by and pick them up on his way to the resort. From there, they could catch a returning boat to Key West the following day.

It was a bit unsettling to be cruising along with couples who were constantly kissing and touching each other. Annie had never considered herself a voyeur, but she couldn't seem to stop watching a particularly bold and handsome couple making out in the back of the boat.

Their tongues flicked languidly over each other's mouths, their hands touching, caressing, stroking. The woman was dressed in a skimpy thong bikini that showcased her ample breasts, tanned skin, and taut butt. The man's chest was chiseled, but he wasn't, she noticed, as intricately ripped as Duncan.

She kept thinking about yesterday. About what she'd done with Duncan. How they'd licked and sucked and fucked each other with their mouths. She pressed her knees together and stared out at the water. It was all she could do not to beg Duncan to touch her inappropriately right there in front of everyone. Just like the other couple was doing.

The man was trailing his tongue along the woman's throat now and she was moaning softly.

Annie's body flared like a match head struck against sandpaper. She suppressed a shudder of arousal. God, but she was turned on.

Duncan circled her waist with his arm and put his mouth against her ear. She felt his chin brush her cheek, all raspy from a day's growth of beard stubble, and this time she did shudder.

"Don't you wish that was us?" he whispered.

She clenched her hands, closed her eyes, bit down on her bottom lip.

He chuckled. "Hold on, babe, we'll be at the resort soon."

When they arrived, Duncan left her waiting in the luxurious lobby while he went to speak to the resort manager. Annie didn't know what magic he'd wrought without ID or credit cards, but he came back with a room assignment. Damn, but the man was magic. Fishing for their dinner, starting a fire with wet wood, and now procuring them a honeymoon suite in a five-star resort solely on the strength of his charm.

It's the Siren's Call, she thought. *Paving the way for romance.*

Carrying their meager gear, Duncan led the way to their room. Annie took the key card they'd given him at the front desk and slashed it through the card reader.

They stepped over the threshold into the spacious room furnished for newlyweds. There was an oversized hot tub situated near French doors leading out onto a balcony overlooking the ocean. The king-sized bed was plush and mounded high with lots of pillows. Mirrors lined not only the ceiling, but also ran along the wall behind the hot tub as well. Annie shivered, imagining what was to come.

There was a bucket of iced champagne and a goodie basket resting on the bureau. Annie stepped closer and peered at the basket. Fruit and chocolate and massage oils and, oh, my goodness, were those condoms?

She looked up to see Duncan looking. He grinned. "Seems they've anticipated our every need. Food, champagne, and condoms. Who could ask for anything more?"

Unnerved, Annie turned to set the Siren's Call down on the bedside table. The lodestone in the mermaid's breast caught the light, and damn if it didn't appear as if she was winking at her.

"I think it's time for a hot shower." Duncan tossed their diving equipment in the closet and turned for the bathroom. He stopped at the door, held out a hand. "Care to join me?"

"Shower?" she said without knowing the words were going to spill from her lips. "How about a dip in the hot tub?"

"Ah," he replied. "I like the way you think."

Two seconds later their swimsuits were off and they were in the churning bubbly water of the hot tub.

Duncan was looking at her as if she was the most delicious feast he'd ever seen. She licked her lips. A sinful smile played across his lips. One look, one smile from him, and her womb did cartwheels.

He reached out a hand and drew her to him. This felt right, and it shouldn't. But it did. He was so familiar to her. They fit. She and Duncan. Never mind that he was a big and she was a petite. Or that she was brainy and he was brawny. They balanced each other out. All this time she thought she'd needed someone just like her. That she needed stability and security when all along what she really needed was heartfelt passion to balance her seriousness.

His fingers curled around her waist and he lifted her up in the water and settled her in his lap, her legs straddling his. She felt the thick ridge of his hard cock against the back of her bare ass and it shoved her into crazy territory.

Heat engulfed her. From inside and out. She was in hot water and loving it. Her hands gripped his shoulder as she stared into his eyes. He looked so powerful, so dominant, so totally male. She just melted. She needed him so much it scared the living hell out of her. Needed, wanted, yearned, and ached for him.

"God, Annie, you've no idea how much I've missed you. Missed getting to do things like this with you." The expression in his eyes was not quite like anything she'd ever seen there. A combination of remorse and desire, tenderness and male pride, and overt sexual appreciation of her. He kissed her and she kissed him back, both trying to see how deep they could take it. "We wasted so much time."

"Duncan," she whispered. The water churned and pulsed

around them, the powerful jets caressing every sensitive area of her body.

"Come here," he commanded, in his husky Scottish brogue.

Her body trembled. It felt as if her internal temperature was as hot as the water around her, sizzling at a hundred and six. Her pussy throbbed for him.

He reached underneath the swirling bubbles, found her foot, and trolled her to him until she was riding the water just above his waist. His big fingers kneaded the flesh of her ass until tingles of delight shot through her body.

His lips brushed against her neck, then found her earlobe. His breathing was rapid and hard as his tongue moistened the curve of her ear. She turned her head to meet his lips. They were rough and warm.

Her fingers reached down to touch his erect cock, bobbing provocatively in the water. He was so thick and he felt so good between her hands.

"The water isn't going to cut it." Duncan wrapped his hands around her waist and without another word, he climbed from the hot tub with Annie clasped snuggly in his arms.

He sat her down on the tile floor. The difference between the hot tub and the cool floor shocked her feet. Electric. He whipped a fluffy bath towel off the rack and rubbed her down with it, drying first her body and then his.

She stared at him as he tenderly toweled her off. His dick was so hard, she couldn't stand not touching him. She reached for him, but he blocked her hand with his elbow.

"Not yet," he said.

She groaned.

When he was finished, he flung the towel aside and reached for her again. His lips were on hers, his inquisitive fingers drawn to the curve of her butt.

Her excitement grew. She loved how his fingers felt on her ass, and when he kissed her cheeks, she almost came unglued.

"You've got the most gorgeous ass," he breathed heavily. "Totally fuckable." The stroke of his palms, calloused and broad, sent Annie's stomach springing into her throat with anticipation.

"So fuck it," she whispered.

She had just thought her body was on fire before, but nothing prepared her for this inferno. Or the thick richness of the juice flowing from her pussy, readying her body to accept his big throbbing cock.

His mouth took hers hostage. His tongue thrusting boldly past her lips, invading, demanding.

She made not a single protest. In fact, she kissed him back with a hunger so fierce he made a startled noise of extreme pleasure.

He pulled her down with him and they collapsed together onto the bed. Duncan was pressed against the length of her, the heat of his body warming her from head to toe.

Their legs were entangled. She dug her fingers into his firm chest muscles, admiring his taut skin. Down her hands went, to rub the velvety purplish head of him. Hot clear juice oozed from his tip. She licked her finger. He tasted virile, sweet.

She felt him getting harder and harder. Was it possible for a man to be so hard and not explode?

He positioned her on her back and rose above her, cradling the back of her head in the palm of his hands, his body poised just over hers, his cock jutting against her inner thigh. He looked deeply into her eyes, his hair glistening dark in the sunlight slanting through the open French doors.

Passion was a tidal wave, washing over her, scaring her with its intensity. This was what she'd fought for so long to avoid. This maniacal madness. This typhoon that sent her spinning heedlessly, helplessly into the abyss.

His mouth was on hers, his fingers at her breasts, pinching her nipples into marbles.

Biting need gushed like blood through ventricles. Swift. Pulsating

"I'm going to fuck you now, babe," he whispered. "The way you need to be fucked.

Holding her locked in place with his elbows on either side of her, his hands interlaced at the top of her head and his dark eyes lasered into hers. He felt so real, so alive. She could feel his heart beating throughout his body. Her heartbeat joined his until they pulsed with identical energy.

Home, she thought. *I've come home.* It was a dangerous, reckless thought, but she couldn't stop thinking it. Her body lit up, tingling from her scalp to her toes.

"You are so beautiful." He stared into her eyes. "I've missed you so damned much." And then she realized he was trembling, her big strong Scotsman shaking with emotion. His vulnerability touched her so deeply that tears welled in her eyes and slid hotly down her cheeks. He was laying everything on the line for her.

"What's wrong?" he sounded alarmed.

"Nothing's wrong." She smiled and swiped the tears away with the back of her hand.

"Are you having second thoughts? Do you want to stop?"

"No! Yes! I don't know. I'm confused. Please."

"Please what?"

She glanced away, unable to deal with the look in his eyes and the strange twisting sensation in her heart. Her gaze landed on the Siren's Call resting on the bedside table. How much of this was that stupid idol's doing? How much was her own long-buried passion she'd tried so hard to deny? How could she trust what she was feeling was real?

Annie could feel the energy of the Siren's Call, radiating

through her like a microwave, pulling her to the edge of reason. Making her believe in things she had no business believing in.

"Talk to me, babe. Tell me what you need."

"Just fuck me, Duncan. Fuck me like you promised. Give me your big, hard cock. It's all I want."

He made a noise low in his throat, like a wounded lion. "That's all you want?" he echoed, anger flicking in his eyes.

She nodded, even though it wasn't true. She was afraid to say what she really wanted from him. Afraid to claim the truth. Afraid that in the long run he was going to break her heart again.

The past was not just a link between them, but a chain, roping them to each other, whether they liked it or not. She had given Duncan her virginity when she was twenty. Had loved him since she was thirteen. There was no escaping. She could marry Eric. She could marry someone else entirely, but she would never escape the feelings she had for Duncan. She knew this and it scared her.

He's your destiny. Why fight it? a voice in the back of her head whispered.

She stared up at the mirrored ceiling, saw their bodies entwined, and she caught her breath. His nakedness was so glorious. She bit down on her bottom lip as she gazed at his image. Big, masculine, dominant, rugged. A man who feared nothing.

Except commitment? How could she ever trust that he wouldn't run away on her again?

He fumbled for a condom from the bedside table and savagely tore open the package with his teeth. "If you just want to be fucked, if my dick is all you want, then we'll do it animal style," he rasped.

She shuddered and almost came at the rough sound of his voice, at his provocatively crude words. Her womb contracted, eager for the fucking he promised.

Duncan's hands went around her waist and he flipped her over onto all fours. His grip was firm and she tensed, waiting, her body tight with anticipation.

She felt his cock teasing the entrance to her pussy. He pushed in, but ever so slightly.

The hard tip of him was barely inside her. He pulled back and then pushed again, sliding in just a little bit deeper this time.

Back and forth.

Out and then in again, controlled, smooth, driving her insane. She whimpered, begging him to enter her completely, fully. She'd waited so long to have him again, and now he was making her wait even longer. It wasn't fair and she wasn't going to stand for it. She thrashed her head.

"Give me all you've got. Give it to me now, dammit."

"Yes, yes, Annie, this is how I like to see you. Wild, passionate, out of control. Don't hold back. Let go. Tell me everything you want."

Tossing her hair over her shoulder, she looked up and saw their reflection in the mirror. The sight of his tanned hands splayed over her creamy white ass sent her blood pumping fast and furious.

She tried to push back against his cock, to make him plunge deeper inside her, but he pulled out completely.

"Bastard," she cried.

He laughed and reached his hand around to slip two fingers inside her aching cunt while he caressed her hot clit with a third finger. She writhed, impaled on his fingers.

Then his other hand slid over the curve of her butt.

Shocked but delighted, her gaze transfixed on the mirror, she watched him. Her muscles tensed in anticipation.

"Relax," he coaxed and gently massaged her.

Slowly, her muscles relaxed.

"That's it."

He reached for something. Her eyes tracked his movements. He was going for the Siren's Call.

What was he doing with that?

She quivered, speculating.

He brought the smooth glass tip of the idol to the entrance of her cunt and moistened it with her pussy juices. Was he going to fuck her with the Siren's Call?

"Pervert," she gasped excitedly.

"You ain't seen nothing yet," he murmured.

And she couldn't stop watching, anxious for what would happen next. With one broad hand, he separated the folds of her labia. She panted.

He paused, driving her insane. Then suddenly, he grasped her around the waist with one hand to hold her in place and plunged his cock deeply into her. He was so huge! He stretched her to capacity.

She gasped at the insurgence of pleasure. He was still holding the Siren's Call. Through the mirror, she could see it glistening wetly with the sheen of her honeyed essence.

What was he going to do with it?

Moaning, Annie grasped the bedcovers in both fists.

His cock pounded against her clit, taking her higher and higher. Her ears rang. Flashes of heat rolled over her like lava down a mountainside. The sight of his big body behind her, his tanned fingers fanned out over her pale white ass was highly erotic and jettisoned her excitement into the stratosphere.

Duncan rocked against her, fucking her and fucking her and fucking her. She screamed her pleasure, not caring if anyone heard. He grabbed her ass again, separating her cheeks with his hand. A lightning bolt of blue-white heat shot through the nerve endings in her anus.

She felt something cold and smooth against her ass. Her eyes flashed to the mirror and she watched him draw the Siren's Call down the small of her back to the crease that separated her cheeks. She bucked against him, nervous but eager.

"What are you doing?" she gasped.

"Do you trust me?"

She nodded.

"Then just let yourself go. Relax and enjoy what's happening."

He'd pulled out of her, his cock laden with her cream. He smeared the crevice of her ass with her own slick moisture, getting her wet all over.

Annie held her breath.

"Do you want to lose control?" he whispered.

She nodded.

"Say it."

"I want to lose control."

"What else?"

"Passion. I want mad passion."

"Good girl." He leaned forward to kiss the back of her neck. "What do you want me to do?"

"Anything, everything. Make me crazy, Duncan. Make me lose it. I want to be taken under, swept away."

"Rest your chest on the pillows, but keep your butt up."

Wriggling, she did as he commanded. Her ass was high in the air, her juices rolling down her thighs.

Then at the same moment Duncan plunged his cock back into her pussy, he gently eased the tip of Siren's Call into her ass.

Annie went wild. She'd never felt anything so exquisite. She cried out and her spine arched at the piercing intensity of the pleasurable ache blasting through her.

Duncan was wild, too. He slammed relentlessly into her, his cock was a blade. It felt as if she were coming apart. He moved his hips and his hand in unison, fucking her pussy with his cock, fucking her ass with the Siren's Call.

She gasped, sobbing with rapture.

The dual invasion was more than she could comprehend. The

sensations were completely out of the realm of anything she had ever experienced. Annie was transported. The pleasure was that intense. Her passion that great. He pounded into her. His cock finding her G-spot and working it over.

She was gasping and crying and begging for more. She was tumbling, soaring, shuddering.

Who knew, who knew, who knew it could feel like this?

Duncan. That was who.

"Annie," he cried. "I'm coming."

The muscles of her womb spasmed, squeezing his cock tight as her anus puckered around the cool smoothness of the Siren's Call.

Their gazes met in the mirror.

Annie experienced a release that transcended any orgasm she'd ever felt. It sent her soaring, past time and place. Through galaxies and universes. In great writhing echoes of pleasure, she came and came and came.

In a haze, Annie heard Duncan's moans mingling with hers, felt him shudder against her as he pulled the idol out of her, saw his face contort into a mask of ecstasy. Inside her she felt him swell, and then she felt the hotness of his release as it filled the condom.

His hands went around her waist and he fell to one side of the mattress, bringing her down off all fours, dragging her to the covers beside him. They lay together panting and spent. Touching, murmuring, kissing softly until they both fell into the deepest sleep either one of them had ever slept.

7

Annie woke before dawn feeling happier than she'd ever felt. She lay staring up at the mirrored ceiling, watching Duncan sleeping beside her. How many times over the last five years had she dreamed of this moment? She could hardly believe it. Giddiness stole over and she pinched herself just to make sure she wasn't dreaming.

The thing she had never dared hope for because she'd wanted it so badly, had happened. She was reunited with the love of her life. For Annie, there had never really ever been anyone else.

Silently, so as not to awaken him, she slipped out of bed. She almost tripped over the Siren's Call lying on the floor. She picked it up and took the idol to the bathroom with her.

Imagine: she had not only recovered the Siren's Call her parents had spent their life searching for, but she'd also recovered the love she'd thought she'd lost forever. As she carefully washed the idol in the bathroom sink, she thought about the reason Duncan had dumped her all those years ago. It wasn't because he'd had another woman, or because she wasn't pretty enough for him as she'd always feared, but because he loved her too much to keep her from achieving her potential. Her heart clutched. She couldn't wait for Duncan to wake up so she could tell him exactly how much she loved him.

She rinsed off the Siren's Call, turned it upside down to shake off the water. There was lettering on the bottom.

What was this? Annie stared, struggling to absorb what she read.

Made in Taiwan.

What? She blinked. The Siren's Call was made in Taiwan?

No. It couldn't be. The Siren's Call was over two hundred years old.

Reality slapped her hard as she scrutinized the figurine. This wasn't the Siren's Call at all, but some modern day replica churned out in a factory that made sex toys.

A con job.

A sick feeling curled in her stomach. Suddenly it all made sense. The map that Duncan had supposedly found in the *Lorelei* while diving all alone. The strangeness of the idol being hidden in the underground sea cave. The boat driver sailing away to leave them alone on the island. The tour boat showing up unexpectedly to bring them to the resort.

Lies. All lies.

It was a setup to get her into his bed.

She'd been had.

Ice cold water in his face zapped Duncan from delicious dreams about Annie. Shocked, he bolted upright, wiping water from his eyes.

"Annie . . . wh . . . what the hell?" he sputtered.

She was standing in front of him, totally naked, hair wild, eyes flashing pure fire. She threw the Siren's Call onto the bed beside him. "Made in Taiwan, huh? Just how big an idiot do you think I am?"

"Annie, let me explain." He reached out to her, but she slapped his hand away.

"You tricked me." She picked her bikini bottoms up off the floor and wriggled into them.

"Yeah," he admitted, throwing back the covers and leaping to his feet. "I did, but only because . . ."

"I don't want to hear it." She found the top to her bikini and put it on. "I thought you'd changed. I thought you were different. But you lied about the Siren's Call. You did it just to get me in bed. You knew it was the one thing that would make me go diving with you. The one thing you could use against me to convince me to explore my passion."

"That's not the reason why."

"I get that you wanted to screw me, what I don't get is that you would make up a story about finding the real Siren's Call. I can't believe you would disappoint Jock like this."

"Annie, will you please just listen?"

"I've had enough of your cock-and-bull blarney. What else was a lie, Duncan? The malarkey about giving me up so I would go to Harvard? The bullshit about needing to prove yourself man enough for me." Her laugh was harsh and humorless.

"I'm going to make you listen." He stalked across the room, determined to grab her and make her listen, but before he could get to her, she picked up his swim trunks and their wetsuits and ran out the door leaving him alone and naked with nothing to wear.

"Dammit," he swore.

Annie Graves was the most stubborn, contentious woman he'd ever met. When it came to expressing her passion, she had the most repressed ideas. She was so scared to let go, so afraid to trust that something good had happened, she'd rather jump to conclusions and assume the worst.

Dammit all, he loved her for it. Because along with her flaws, she possessed the sweetest lips he'd ever kissed, the kindest eyes, and the most tender heart. She was different from any woman he'd ever known. Everything about her was unique. Her taste, her smell, the feel of her silky skin beneath his calloused fingertips. He was addicted to her. Fully, completely, couldn't live with her, didn't want to live without her. She made his senses whirl and his head spin and his heart pound like a jackhammer.

And one way or the other, he was determined that this time, he was going to hold on to her forever.

Back in St. Augustine, Annie was packing Jock's things on a wheeled cart, getting ready to take him home. "Once I get your stuff loaded up and the car parked at the patient pick-up area, I'll come back and get a nurse to escort you out in a wheelchair," she told him.

Two days had passed since the ill-fated diving trip. She'd told her grandfather that Duncan's map had been wrong. That there had been no underground cave, no Siren's Call. He'd taken the news much better than she expected, and to her surprise he hadn't asked questions.

She'd mentally put her heart in deep freeze so she wouldn't feel the pain, but she knew it was there, lurking, waiting, ready to pounce the minute she let down her guard. Why oh why had she let Duncan Stewart back into her life? She felt utterly broken, and only the tasks of hiring a live-in nurse to stay with her grandfather and finding someone to run the dive shop kept her from dwelling on her dark situation.

"That looks like everything. I'll be back in a bit." Pasting on a perky smile for her grandfather's sake, Annie kissed him on the forehead. She wheeled the cart down the corridor, headed for the elevator.

The elevator doors opened.

She started to walk inside, just as Duncan stepped out, carrying a gift-wrapped box. They both stopped in midstride, their gazes snagged on each other.

"Duncan." She sucked in her breath at the crazy erratic beating of her heart.

"Annie."

They stood there looking at each other, the elevator doors trying to close, then popping when the sensors detected the cart. In his eyes she saw all the same sorrow knotting her chest. Why was it always like this between them?

Because you love him.

Annie's lungs constricted so tightly, she couldn't inhale. "What are you doing here?" she asked breathlessly.

"Looking for you."

"I don't have anything to say to you," she retorted coldly, desperate to keep from bursting into tears in front of him.

"Too bad. I've got a lot of things to say to you and you're going to hear me out."

"This isn't the time or the place." She hissed in her breath, struggling to keep from throwing her arms around his neck and begging him never to let her go.

"There is no better time or place," he disagreed and eyed the cart. "What's this?"

"Jock's things. He's being dismissed and I'm going back to Manhattan."

"The hell you are."

Then before she knew what he was doing, he pulled the wheel cart off to one side, grabbed her by the elbow, and tugged her through a door marked LINEN CLOSET.

Once they were in the linen closet amidst the blankets and sheets, he pushed her back against the wall and positioned his big body between her and the door. "You were going to leave town without saying good-bye?"

"There wouldn't have been a point."

"You want to leave things unfinished between us again?"

"Oh, we're finished all right. I can't forgive you for lying about the Siren's Call."

"I didn't lie." He thrust the gift-wrapped package at her.

"What's this?" She looked at him warily, not sure what to do next.

"Open it."

"You're not going to win me back with a present."

"Open it," he ground out the words, his eyes flashing a warning. He was serious.

Tentatively, she reached for the box and undid the pink ribbon. She lifted the lid and there, nestled in pink tissue paper, was a mermaid figurine fragile with age.

"It's the real Siren's Call." Lightly, she traced a finger over the idol. It bore little resemblance to the Made-in-Taiwan replica.

"Yeah."

"You had it all along."

He nodded. "I found it on the *Lorelei,* just like I said."

She stared into his eyes. In spite of her fears, hope bloomed.

"I found her on the same day that Jock called to tell me Eric Hammond was going to ask for your hand in marriage. I knew I couldn't let you marry him without giving us one more shot. Without explaining to you why I'd let you go. To show to you that I'd become a man you could be proud of."

"Duncan." She breathed, feeling suddenly light-headed with giddiness. "Why lie? Why the replica Siren's Call?"

"I had to prove to you that the passion you felt for me was real. It wasn't the Siren's Call's doing. I didn't want you using the idol as an excuse."

He stepped closer and she could feel his heat radiating over the length of her. The manly, ocean smell of him invaded her nostrils. The masculine sound of his voice made her mouth water. He reached up to run his fingertips along her chin. It seemed like years, not days, since she'd felt his touch.

"Don't go back to Manhattan. Don't marry that corporate lawyer. Please."

His vulnerable plea tugged at her heart. "Duncan . . ."

"Forgive me. For being a damned fool. For not having the courage to tell you the truth about how I felt."

She reached up and touched his dear, sweet face. "I'll forgive you if you forgive me."

"Annie, there's nothing to forgive." He pulled her close, his manly sea smell filling her nose. "I love you." His eyes glistened with tears. "And I think you love me, too. Do you love me, Annie?"

The lump in her throat was so huge she couldn't speak. All she could do was nod. Duncan lowered his head and kissed her, and Annie felt his growing erection tighten against her leg.

"Say it," he whispered. "I need to hear it. I've waited so long to hear it."

"I love you, Duncan Stewart." Her eyes misted with tears. "I've loved you since I was thirteen years old. I loved you when I gave you my virginity, and I've never stopped loving you."

He took her left hand in his and sank down on one knee.

"What are you doing? What's going on?"

And then she saw the glitter of diamonds and her heart just sang.

"Will you marry me, Annie Marie?" He looked up into her face, his eyes vulnerable, his heart on his sleeve, waiting for her answer, a diamond ring the size of an ice cube poised above her third finger. "Please forgive me. Don't let me be too late. Marry me, Annie. I want you now and forever."

"Oh, Duncan, I've never wanted anything more. Yes, yes, I'll marry you." Tears of joy tracked down both their cheeks as Duncan slipped his ring on her finger.

He got to his feet, hugging and kissing her. "I'm never leaving you again."

"Never?"

"Ever. You're my woman, and I've been your man ever since that day you walked into the back room of the dive shop where I was sweeping up, wearing pink, rhinestone-studded flip-flops and chewing watermelon bubble gum."

"You remember that day?"

"I've never forgotten it. I wanted you so badly I couldn't think straight. But here's the deal, Annie, I want you even more now."

She wrapped her arms around his neck. "So take me."

With a low growl, Duncan hiked up her skirt.

Instantly, her panties were wet for him. He stripped them off of her and dropped his trousers. She spread her legs for him.

He slid straight into her, harpooning her against the wall of the hospital linen closet. He filled her fully, completely. Annie wrapped her legs around his muscular waist as he thrust slowly, deeply. They stared into each other's eyes.

This was different than before. Different than her virginal coupling on his houseboat, different than oral sex on the beach, different than their savage mating at the resort. This time they were making sweet love. Engaged. United as they were always meant to be. The past was gone, forgotten. The future lay ahead of them, full of promise and hope.

Quietly, softly, gently, they came together and as they reached a simultaneous climax, both Annie and Duncan knew they'd finally found their way home.

FOR REFUND OR EXCHANGE, MERCHANDISE MUST BE RETURNED
WITHIN 14 DAYS OF PURCHASE, ACCOMPANIED BY THE BILL OF
SALE.
CREDIT NOTE ISSUED IF MERCHANDISE IS RETURNED WITHIN 14 -
30 DAYS OF PURCHASE, ACCOMPANIED BY THE BILL OF SALE.
NO EXCHANGE OR REFUND ON HOSIERY OR
SWIMWEAR.

POUR LE REMBOURSEMENT OU L'ÉCHANGE, LA MARCHANDISE
DOIT ÊTRE RETOURNÉE, ACCOMPAGNÉE DE LA FACTURE DE VENTE,
DANS LES 14 JOURS QUI SUIVENT LA DATE D'ACHAT.
UNE NOTE DE CRÉDIT SERA ÉMISE SI LA MARCHANDISE EST
RETOURNÉE, ACCOMPAGNÉE DE LA FACTURE DE VENTE, DANS LES
[14 - 30 JOURS QUI SUIV]ENT LA DATE D'ACHAT.
[AUCUN ÉCHANGE NI RE]MBOURSEMENT DANS
[LE CAS DE BAS OU DE COS]TUMES DE BAIN.